ANN ARBOR DISTRICT LIBRARY
W9-AKE-728
WITHDRAWN

RED STAR BURNING

ALSO BY BRIAN FREEMANTLE

Red Star Rising

Triple Cross

Kings of Many Castles

Watchmen

Dead Men Living

Bomb Grade

Charlie's Apprentice

Comrade Charlie

The Run Around

See Charlie Run

The Blind Run

Madrigal for Charlie Muffin

Charlie Muffin's Uncle Sam

The Inscrutable Charlie Muffin

Here Comes Charlie M

Charlie M

BRIAN FREEMANTLE

RED STAR BURNING

A THRILLER

THOMAS DUNNE BOOKS
ST. MARTIN'S PRESS NEW YORK

This is a work of fiction. All of the characters, organizations, and events portrayed in this novel are either products of the author's imagination or are used fictitiously.

THOMAS DUNNE BOOKS.
An imprint of St. Martin's Press.

RED STAR BURNING. Copyright © 2012 by Brian Freemantle. All rights reserved. Printed in the United States of America. For information, address St. Martin's Press, 175 Fifth Avenue, New York, N.Y. 10010.

www.thomasdunnebooks.com
www.stmartins.com

ISBN 978-1-250-00636-3 (hardcover)
ISBN 978-1-250-01306-4 (e-book)

First Edition: June 2012

10 9 8 7 6 5 4 3 2 1

To Eliza Bunny and Montgomery Flaxman

With much much love

RED STAR BURNING

Prologue

"IT'S COMING DOWN TO ME," DECLARED MAXIM RADTSIC.

Elana stopped with her knife and fork suspended before her, gazing at her husband across the dinner table. "You weren't responsible for it going wrong, Maxim Mickailovich: not for any of it."

"I'm directly below the Director, held the position the longest: even before Gorbachev or Yeltsin came to power."

"What about Andrei?"

"Andrei has to come too."

"There must be some other way."

"There isn't."

"I don't want to. Andrei won't want to, either. You can't do this to him."

"It'll save us. Andrei, too."

"How?"

"Trust me."

"I'm frightened."

"Just trust me," said Radtsic, hating the words as he uttered them.

"KILL MYSELF?" ECHOED CHARLIE, DERISION AND ASTONISHment combined.

"That's what I think you'll end up doing."

"Bollocks," rejected Charlie. At the back—too often in the forefront—of his mind had always hovered the expectation of dying. But violently: from a breath-sucking assassin's bullet or the burn of a back-alley knife or a shattering explosion. But never of killing himself, not even while confronting his now fossilized existence.

"It would be understandable," sympathized the small, hunched psychiatrist, George Cowley. "You've spent almost thirty years at the front end of British intelligence, always on the edge. Now you're blown, in a Protection Program with a new identity, a retirement salary, a safe house, and a protection regime. All of which you're refusing to acknowledge or observe. From which the only conclusion is that you're either inviting Russian assassination or intending to kill yourself."

"Bollocks," repeated Charlie. He had to do better than this: convince this asshole of an MI5 psychiatrist that he'd got it all wrong. As he, in turn, had got it all wrong, staging an intentionally deceiving performance for the too easily detected minders during his limited excursions from the safe house. The internal cameras and listening devices would be recording everything of this performance, too, he accepted.

"It would have been easier for you, if maybe not for them, if you'd had a family: a wife, children, to fill the emptiness within you,"

Cowley pressed on. "But you haven't, have you, Charlie? All you've ever had is the job and now you don't have that anymore."

Wrong again! agonized Charlie. He did have a wife. And a daughter. A family still in Russia that no one knew about. Nor could they ever know, because Natalia Fedova was a senior officer in the Federal'naya Sluzhba Bezopasnosti, the intelligence agency of the Russian Federation that his own MI5 service believed was determined to assassinate him.

"You expect me to adjust in five minutes to all that's happened!" demanded Charlie, discomfited at his inadequate reply.

Cowley, who had the highest security clearance, tapped Charlie's file on the table between them. "I've read every word that's in here: know everything you've done. And having read it I'd expect you to understand the very real danger you're in and accept all the protection that's being offered."

What danger was Natalia facing after his most recent Moscow assignment? Charlie asked himself, as he had repeatedly over the past three months. If he was blown, as MI5 believed him to be, the search might stretch back to his phoney Moscow defection, when Natalia Fedova had been his interrogator. Charlie had never been totally satisfied then she'd sanitized their subsequent relationship from what then would have been KGB records. "I'm not convinced the risk is as great as everyone believes it to be."

"That's for the Director-General to decide, not you. And that decision's been made."

"As yours has been made," Charlie fought back. "And it's wrong."

"You ever kill anyone, Charlie?" demanded the psychiatrist, unexpectedly.

"Never intentionally." That was debatable, thought Charlie, uneasy at the prescience of the other man. Charlie hoped there was nothing in the bulky personnel dossier with which Cowley could catch him out.

"Didn't it ever worry you, people getting killed? Assassinated?" persisted the other man.

"It didn't happen often and when it did—or had to—it was part of the job: I never pulled a trigger." That reply was a cop-out, Charlie acknowledged, but they'd been talking of death and dying for the past thirty minutes and he was fed up at the verbal ping-pong.

"Could you have pulled a trigger, if you'd had to?"

"I'd been trained to that level, as a last resort: I never got to that resort." Charlie was surprised at the sudden although easily suppressed anger, an emotion he hadn't experienced for a long time because it indicated lack of control, which was always dangerous professionally.

"Do you still think you could pull the trigger, if you had to?"

"Not with the barrel against my own head, no," refused Charlie, guessing the direction in which Cowley was leading.

"You sure about that?" demanded the psychiatrist. "Or are you pissed off that the rest of your life is going to be spent incarcerated in security-covered, audio-and-CCTV-equipped safe houses, forever buried deep within a protection program, never ever able again to meet or speak to anyone you once knew?"

"I'll get there," responded Charlie, dismissively.

"You're not even trying," accused Cowley, dismissive in return. "You're supposed to have adopted the new name—the entirely new identity—you've been allocated and you haven't. You're supposed never to establish patterns—never the same restaurants, never the same pub, never the same cinema, never the same route or transport to the same supermarket—and you haven't. You're supposed to alter the way you dress, alter as much of your appearance as possible, and you haven't: you're even still wearing those spread-apart Hush Puppies about to fall off your awkward feet. As part of that appearance change—in your particular case, all the more essential because of the target you now are—you're supposed seriously to consider surgical facial reconstruction and you haven't bothered to attend three specialist appointments to discuss it."

"I told you I'd get round to it!" Lame again, Charlie recognized.

"How often, since you've been in the program, have you seriously considered suicide?"

"Since entering the protection program I have never, ever, considered suicide," replied Charlie, enunciating each word for emphasis.

"I don't believe you," declared Cowley. "It's a fucking awful existence. I've never had a protected patient who hasn't thought of taking his or her own life."

"How many actually did?"

"Six," Cowley came back at once.

"I'm not going to become your seventh!" assured Charlie.

"I know you're not," agreed the psychiatrist. "I'm going to put you on suicide watch to ensure you don't."

Fuck it, thought Charlie. He had to hurry to reach Natalia in time.

"Defect to the British!" exclaimed Elana, her voice breaking. "You can't . . . we can't . . ." She tried to continue but couldn't, her mind seized by the enormity of what Radtsic had told her, her eyes fixed farther ahead of the embankment road along which they were walking, the river-bordered British embassy in the distance. "We can't . . . you're the virtual head of Russian intelligence . . . it's unthinkable. . . ." She tried again: "What about Andrei?"

"It'll be easy with Andrei at the Sorbonne," insisted Radtsic, whose heavy mustache, gray like his thick hair, and heavy, indulged body had in the past made him the butt of jokes about his physical resemblance to Stalin. "Paris is closer to London than we are here in Moscow. The moment we run he'll be picked up and brought to us there. We'll be together and we'll be safe."

"It's too much for me to understand," protested the woman. In contrast to her husband, who was fifteen years her senior, Elana was a slim, even elegant woman committed to her career as professor of physics at Moscow University. "My work . . . what about my work . . . I mean . . . I don't know."

"I can't go without you. You'd be arrested: dismissed from the university." Radtsic was agonized by the conversation, his whole body clammy with perspiration.

"I didn't mean I wouldn't come with you. I was thinking of everything I would be abandoning . . . leaving behind. Are you sure, really sure, that you're being targeted?"

"I found two listening devices in my office today, one actually in the telephone handset, the other in the base of the desk light: that's why we're walking—so we can talk—out in the open like this," disclosed Radtsic. "And today I was told there's no reason for my attending the quarterly operational review, which I've done ever since I was appointed deputy chairman: actually headed more sessions than the chairman himself."

"Oh my God!" said Elana, who was a devoted churchgoer. "It's true, isn't it? You're going to be purged."

"No, I'm not," insisted Radtsic, defiantly. "I'm going to get out."

HE'D SCREWED UP BIG TIME, CHARLIE ACKNOWLEDGED. HOW big he didn't yet know, nor how to find out: whether, even, if he would. Feigning inferiority to encourage the underestimation of those against whom he was pitted was one of several chameleonlike survival cloaks in which Charlie Muffin so often professionally wrapped himself. But it hadn't worked with George Cowley. On film and on sound, Charlie knew, he'd looked a lost, vacant-eyed idiot who, in the specialized environment in which, until now, he'd existed, had lost not just the will but the professional ability to live. And become a potential liability.

How, in his eagerness to reassure Natalia that he was still alive—and financially to provide for her and Sasha—could he have failed properly to consider the possible misunderstandings! The core concern of MI5 heirarchy had to be that pissing about as he'd intentionally, stupidly, done—neither properly in nor improperly out of the protection regime—risked his detection by those murderously hunting him. And that however they chose to destroy him would publicly expose how close Russian intelligence had come to insinuating itself into the very heart of the Oval Office in Washington D.C., with an equally gullible, puppy dog Britain led unsuspectingly by the nose to the same disaster.

Charlie stirred from the chair into which he'd slumped after Cowley's departure fifteen minutes earlier. It would appear on the all-seeing cameras as bad as the confrontation itself, as if exhausted by it he'd collapsed into continuing depression, not what he'd objectively been doing, taking time for self-critical self-examination. Resulting in what? Irritation, predominantly, Charlie answered himself: irritated at having been so obviously beaten in a verbal who-can-shout-loudest contest and at that humiliation being filmed and recorded and at being so completely cut off from everything and everyone and because of that isolation not able to gauge the full extent of his self-created situation.

Charlie started up, determined to identify all the cameras upon which his every waking—and sleeping, through infrared technology—moment was monitored. By the time he reached the kitchen and the cupboard containing the Islay single malt, he was reasonably sure he'd located four before abandoning the pointless exercise. Miniaturized as the lenses were, he'd never pick them all out. And what if he did? He wasn't on an operational assignment, where he had to protect himself against every eventuality. He was in a permanently recorded goldfish bowl. And there was no recovery advantage from his being able to pose or perform to mislead his constant watchers. Whatever he did would be further misconstrued as proof of his mentally eroding hold on reality.

Which it most certainly wasn't, Charlie assured himself, as he splashed whiskey into his glass intentionally to be visible to a camera in the window-blind coping. The whiskey and how much of it he drank would scarcely be a revelation to his observers. They actually provided it because of its rarity: known as it inevitably would be to his pursuers, it could have led to his whereabouts if he'd placed a regular order with an outside supplier.

How many pursuers would there be? wondered Charlie, carrying his tumbler back to his accustomed lounge chair overlooking the small, sensor-seeded garden. This soon, only three months after he'd wrecked an espionage operation the Russians had nurtured over practically eighteen years, there'd be a lot: a code-name-designated operation, in fact. Would it be only Russian? Almost certainly not. The Russian target had been the CIA, convincing them—which it had, completely—that a former KGB-cum-FSB officer about to be elected president of the Russian Federation would, once in absolute power, remain their deeply embedded agent through whom America could virtually manipulate the Moscow government, never suspecting that it would have been the misguided occupant of the White House on Pennsylvania Avenue, Washington, D.C., who would have been the puppet on the Kremlin's strings. There would doubtless have been a lot of head rolling at the CIA's Langley headquarters. Enough, certainly, for the Agency to consider matching, murderous retribution. Was he safe even from his own people? Charlie knew the mass clear-out of those who'd swallowed the Russian bait at MI5's Thames House headquarters had been only slightly less sweeping at the MI6 building on the other side of the river at Vauxhall Cross, both sufficient to gain him far more enemies than admirers.

He wasn't simply caught between a rock and a hard place, Charlie accepted. He was trapped beneath a collapsing mountain range: if one avalanche didn't sweep him away, another one would. Most of which, to some extent, he'd already worked out. Today's humiliating psychoanalysis had simply concentrated it in its entirety. As much as it had concentrated his mind, which was no longer fogged by the indignation with which he'd rejected the psychiatrist's accusation. He definitely hadn't contemplated suicide. But subconsciously he'd allowed himself to sink into an acceptance of his eventually being detected: of his being killed by one or other of the groups committed to his destruction.

Which was preposterous and unthinkable: he'd never capitulated to anything or anyone and he didn't intend rolling onto his back and spreading his legs in submission now, no matter how different or stultified that life might now be.

Charlie smiled and looked up in the direction of another suspected camera. It was, he determined, a decision that deserved another drink, in celebration this time.

"What the hell does he think he's got to smile about?" demanded Aubrey Smith, turning away from the safe-house recording that directly followed Charlie Muffin's psychoanalysis.

"Normally I'd try an answer that would help," apologized George Cowley. "This time I don't think I can."

"You've put him on suicide watch, for Christ's sake!" exploded Jane Ambersom, the androgynously featured, newly appointed deputy director. "You actually think he's going to top himself!"

"I also find that difficult to accept," said the mild-mannered, mild-voiced Smith, whose confidence remained undermined by his knowing how dangerously close his overthrow, orchestrated by Ambersom's predecessor, had been. As it fortunately turned out, Jeffrey Smale had been the highest-profile casualty from Charlie Muffin's success.

"I think he's a potential danger to himself and because of that a danger to the service," insisted Cowley, repeating the warning with which he'd begun the assessment meeting.

"There's no way, no set of circumstances, in which Charlie Muffin could be suicidal," persisted the Director-General.

"I've just spelt out the circumstances to you. And to him," reminded Cowley. "He knows just how much of a target he is. And always will be. Just as he knows, simply to survive, what every day of every week of every month is going to be for that survival. I can't imagine—no one can truthfully imagine—what the constant awareness of that is like. It's worse than being imprisoned for life, in solitary confinement. In those circumstances a man quite quickly becomes dehumanized, robotlike, because there is no human contact apart from his guards, which isn't enough. Charlie Muffin doesn't have anyone with whom to adjust, to make a new life. But he's not incarcerated. He can go out, to pubs and restaurants and cinemas and theaters, and see other people all around him. But never risk getting involved, never knowing whom he can trust. It's permanent, unremitting torture."

"Charlie Muffin's always been a loner and never trusted anyone," disputed Ambersom, gesturing to her own copy of Charlie's personnel file. "What's new now?"

"How he lived before was by his own choice," the psychiatrist pointed out. "And before, he had the job. Which I acknowledge from everything I've read he did by his own rules and upset a lot of people in the process. But he was doing *something:* he had a reason to live. He doesn't have that reason now: any reason whatsoever to go on living now."

"What are you suggesting?" asked Smith, whose deceptive, quietly spoken demeanor hinted to his post-Oxford career as professor of Middle East studies, one of the core credos of which was that once-suffered harm had always to be avenged, a philosophy he'd quickly recognized in Charlie Muffin.

"I'm not employed here to suggest," refused Cowley. "I'm here to assess his mental health and that's what I've done."

"Are you saying he's mentally ill?" demanded the sharply suited, precisely spoken Ambersom, who'd bitterly opposed and still resented her manipulated transfer to MI5 from the external Secret Intelligence Service, MI6.

"Not yet," qualified Cowley, forcefully. "I think in time, a comparatively short period of time, he could begin to develop a psychosis. I also think that he would be intelligent enough to realize himself what was happening to him and that with the emptiness of his existence, an emptiness that's never going to be filled, he'd prefer to kill himself than gradually, knowingly, degenerate into mental decline." The psychiatrist shifted his own copy of Charlie's personnel file. "It might be difficult for most people to decipher from all that's in here, but from what I've read and from the sessions I've had with him, I've got Charlie Muffin marked as an extremely proud, even arrogant man. He'd rather kill himself than end up mentally confused, wearing an incontinence pad."

"Charlie Muffin has been an active intelligence officer for twenty years," reminded Ambersom. "Quite irrespective of his most recent operation, we cannot risk the slightest mental uncertainty in someone who knows as much as he does about British intelligence activities over such a period. A lame workhorse that can no longer serve its purpose is put out of its misery, as an act of kindness."

"I don't want this conversation taken in that direction," said Smith, who resented the woman's appointment even more than she did, believing it the most positive indication that his attempted overthrow by Jeffrey Smale had only been postponed.

"If we accept the opinion of Dr. Cowley, which I certainly do, I don't believe there is any alternative for us to consider," argued the deputy director, eager to establish herself.

"There will be no discussion or consideration of physically disposing of anyone while I am Director-General," declared Smith.

"The Americans have formally asked to debrief Charlie themselves," disclosed Ambersom, one of whose new responsibilities was to liaise with U.S intelligence.

"Are you proposing they do your dirty work for us?" demanded Smith.

"I am bringing to your attention a formal request from Washington," qualified Ambersom. "Their request comes with a number of questions not answered in our official debriefing of Charlie Muffin, an abbreviated version of which was made available to them."

"Tell both the FBI and CIA to provide a full list of what more they want from the debriefing, with the understanding that we'll answer what we can," ordered Smith. "And in doing so remind them how many of their executive staff, including the CIA's deputy director of operations, were present here in England, with every opportunity to debrief him, at the moment he exposed their naïveté in believing that Stepan Lvov was their double-agent coup of the century when he was elected president of the Russian Federation."

"The request was specifically for personal access to Charlie."

"Which I'm not allowing."

"They won't consider that the sort of cooperation that's supposed to exist between our services."

"I don't give a damn how they'll consider it," rejected the Director-General. "The last time Charlie Muffin was in a room with CIA and

FBI people—which was the occasion he saved them all from making the biggest mistake in their combined histories—there was a U.S. plane at Northolt air base fueled and ready to take him God knows where on a rendition flight from which he would not have returned after whatever interrogation techniques they'd perfected at Guantanamo. You have any problem with CIA or FBI, pass it on to me to resolve."

"Which leaves unanswered the question of what to do with a mentally declining Charlie Muffin," Ambersom said, trying to fight back, flushed at the man's rejection.

"Not quite. We've decided against letting him be put down like a workhorse for which there's no further use, haven't we?" said Aubrey Smith, very aware that there was no answering agreement from the woman.

"It could too easily be a trap, after the way we so recently humiliated them." Gerald Monsford knew he'd come perilously close to being the highest-ranking victim of the Lvov debacle, surviving only by switching onto Jane Ambersom the responsibility for his own ill-timed and insufficiently considered attempts at self-promoting involvement, which he'd further concealed by decimating MI6's Moscow embassy staffing. He was terrified now of another near disaster so soon afterward.

"Maxim Radtsic, whose identity has been confirmed by photographs in our own files, is the specifically designated executive deputy to the FSB," replied Harry Jacobson, MI6's newly replaced station chief. "He personally approached me at a diplomatic reception at the French embassy. Unless he was as desperate as he certainly appeared, he would not have identified his son as a potential kidnap victim by volunteering that Andrei was studying at the Sorbonne, would he?"

"You talked to Straughan about this?" Monsford protectively demanded. James Straughan was the service's operational field director.

"It was Straughan who provided the photographic confirmation from the files, as well as establishing through our Paris *rezidentura* that Andrei definitely is a student at the Sorbonne."

"Why didn't Radtsic approach the French?"

Jacobson sighed in frustration at the Director's unanswerable questions, despite the warning from Straughan before the Moscow call had been transferred that Monsford was a worryingly unpredictable, frequently erratic man. "I don't know why he didn't! It didn't occur to me to ask. What occurred to me was that it was the opportunity of a lifetime."

"It could be a trap," repeated the other man, nervously.

"Radtsic couldn't have acted out the nervousness. He was practically breaking apart. No attempted entrapment would be personally baited by the FSB's deputy director!"

"What's he offering to prove it's genuine?"

"Himself! What more could we expect? Or hope for?"

"Something to prove himself, first."

"Isn't the fact that he isn't, which could be fabricated any way the FSB chose, further and better proof that this is kosher?"

"He'll give us everything we want when we get him and his wife—and the boy—here?"

"He told me that once he was here, safe, he'd cooperate in whatever way we asked."

After the near disaster with Lvov, this coup could secure his MI6 directorship for life and conceivably secure him the directorship-in-chief of MI5, calculated Monsford. "Be very, very careful. Tell him yes. We'll set everything up, get them all out, new identity, house, pension, everything. And keep it tight. Don't tell anyone in the *rezidentura*: certainly not anyone attached to MI5. Put nothing on the general traffic channels. Everything under Eyes Only, limited to you, me, and Straughan."

"Radtsic wants to get out right away."

"Tell him we'll get him out as soon as we can set it all up. And stress he's not to tell his son until we tell him it's okay to do so. A nineteen-year-old might not like the idea of being born again, which is what's going to happen when we give them their new life."

3

THE SELF-ADMISSION WASN'T EASY FOR CHARLIE MUFFIN BUT he acknowledged that his mistake had been reverting to tradecraft. Establishing a predictable daily routine and unexpectedly breaking it was an operational ploy Charlie had frequently used to lose lulled-into-complacency observers. And precisely what he'd set out to achieve to continue his financial support for Natalia and Sasha.

Now there wouldn't be any lulled complacency. Now, because of a Middle Earth hobbit psychiatrist's belief that he was suicidal, his observers would be on a higher than normal alert. With their number increased, which was a compounding setback because Charlie was sure he'd identified his five regular walkabout watchers. Which was scarcely surprising. Under strict supervision—and budgetary restraints—it was standard practice to train surveillance teams in protection situations like this, where those within a program were expected to cooperate by protecting themselves in the first place. But George Cowley's ridiculous diagnosis would change all standard practice.

If the concern were as great as Cowley intimated, the improved surveillance would be fully qualified professionals, conceivably some who guarded defectors and at-risk foreign royalty and dignitaries.

But not yet, not today. Today the changeover wouldn't be complete.

The one ever-present weakness in Charlie's determination to conceal his relationship with Natalia was their unavoidable link to the money he provided. It hadn't been a problem when he was operational, with unfettered freedom of movement between assignments. But even then he'd been ultracareful, personally carrying the money—in cash, practically all amassed from expense-account banditry—to a lawyer-nominee-controlled Credit Suisse fiduciary holding in the bank secrecy haven of Jersey, in the Channel Islands off the coast of northern France. From where it was electronically transferred to Natalia in Moscow in tranches kept below any legally enforced Russian reporting requirement.

There was nine thousand pounds in expense-account profits still in the Harrods safe deposit box that Charlie, who distrusted his own service almost as much as those of his supposed enemies, had rented under an assumed name years before ever meeting Natalia. That now had to be moved to Jersey, as much to reassure Natalia of his survival as to continue her financial support, alone as she was with Sasha, and for which, after three too-closely-watched months, there remained insufficient funds in the Credit Suisse account. And if her allowance stopped she might believe he'd been killed, like the others about whom there'd been so much publicity.

Charlie was eager to gain as much advantage as possible from the morning rush-hour crush but at the same time was concerned at alerting his CCTV monitors that today's outing was different from those previously. He was ready an hour earlier than usual, although he maintained the cultivated aimlessness as he meandered from room to room up to the moment when he made as if to return to his upstairs bedroom but instead snatched his jacket from the closet in which he'd stored it in readiness the night before.

The Chelsea safe house was expertly chosen, a solitary building lost among a coppice of one- and two-story utility blocks and garages, additionally dwarfed by anonymous high-rise mansion apartments—in one if not more of which his observers would be housed—on all four sides. The layout created a choice of four escape runs intersected by a spider's web of walkways connecting each of the four overshadowing buildings. Charlie followed the regular route his watchers would expect to the traffic-clogged King's Road and used its gridlocked congestion to pick his way through the unmoving traffic to the far side to isolate his followers. Which, worryingly, he didn't. He let people board the bus ahead of him until he was sure he could recognize the few who followed. The most immediate was a harassed woman with an uncontrollably screaming child in a buggy from which it was desperate to escape and a scarlet-coated, medal-decorated Chelsea Hospital pensioner.

Neither disembarked after him at Sloane Square, and all those who did hurried away while he lingered at reflecting store windows. Charlie bought a newspaper from the underground station seller, grateful that this early the pavement café on the corner with the Eaton Square approach was already open. It was from this spot, over the preceding three months, that he'd identified two of his regular watchers. Neither was evident today. As his coffee and croissants were served, Charlie was aware of a raincoated man seating himself on a bench on the pedestrianized central square behind a half-raised newspaper. Charlie felt a blip of relief at the identification, curious where the backup team was. It was ten minutes before three vacant-lighted taxis emerged in convoy from Sloane Street, the first two turning for their cab stand, the last continuing toward Eaton Square. Charlie hailed it at the controlled crossing, aware of the newspaper-reading follower in Sloane Square jerking up from his bench.

No hurriedly mobilized vehicle joined those directly behind before Charlie's taxi turned into Pimlico's grid system, by which time Charlie was talking to the driver of his, being late for a cross channel ferry, introducing the Belgian town of Bruges as his destination as he urged the man to hurry for his Victoria Station train. Charlie had his fare ready when the taxi pulled up, threading his way through the last of the rush-hour commuters not to the overland-departure gates serving Channel ports but down into the underground system. He went one stop to Green Park and took another cab as far as Trafalgar Square, reluctantly walking on already protesting feet to Covent Garden to ensure he'd cleared his trail, despite which he still boarded another underground train to Oxford Circus. From there he took a third taxi to the huge Park Lane subterranean parking lot, scuffing his burning feet its full length to Marble Arch and ground level.

Charlie got to the Harrods bank by one thirty, hesitating after removing the nine thousand pounds from his safe deposit and the long-held and always meticulously renewed passport, international driving license, and American Express card in the assumed name of David Merryweather, in which the facility was rented. After fifteen undecided minutes, Charlie firmly closed and relocked the box. Knowing from already having established the train-connecting times of trains to and from Poole, in Dorset, to Jersey, he allowed himself a leisurely lunch in the store's premier restaurant, complete with a bottle of celebratory Aloxe Corton.

The small conference room adjoining the Director-General's office suite was totally silent, everyone waiting for someone else to risk the first contribution.

Relentlessly, Aubrey Smith demanded: "How was it allowed to happen?"

Simon Harding, the head of the surveillance bureau, managed, "Things weren't fully in place."

"Why weren't things fully in place?" echoed Smith.

"The upgrading designation wasn't issued until the evening of the psychiatric interview," said Harding, an exercise-toned, Lycra-wearing health fitness exponent whose discomfort at wearing a suit was heightened by his being the focus of the inquest.

"Between which and the time Charlie Muffin disappeared there was a period of more than twenty-four hours," said the ever aggressive Jane Ambersom.

"Personnel had to be reassigned from other duties," tried Harding.

"Tell me from the beginning," demanded Smith.

"The watch personnel were doubled, to be in place today," said Harding, defensively. "But it wasn't *in* place, not that early: the rota hadn't been finalized and we're stretched pretty thin. The only thing different from how he's acted over the preceding three months was his leaving early, which was instantly picked up. We had people with him all the way up the King's Road and again at his usual café. I was moving a pursuit car into Sedding Street, which would have kept him fully in sight at all times—"

"But it wasn't in place either," anticipated Ambersom, too eagerly.

"No," admitted the surveillance supervisor. "We found Muffin's taxi at Victoria Station, his most obvious destination. He'd talked to the driver of cross-channel ferries, actually mentioned Bruges. I got people on all but one Channel port trains leaving Victoria. He wasn't on any of them."

"He didn't go across the Channel," dismissed the exasperated Director-General. "He just left you a stinking red herring."

"So your guess is that he's still somewhere in England?" said Harding.

"I don't have any idea where the hell he is or what the hell he's going to do," complained Smith. "He could by now have flown from a dozen airports into Europe, where he wouldn't have had to show his passport, and from any airport in Europe flown on to anywhere in the world."

"You still determined against bringing in America's help?" asked Ambersom, hopefully.

"I won't even acknowledge that stupidity with an answer," snapped Aubrey Smith.

"From what I've heard of Charlie Muffin's background, I wouldn't think he's on a suicide mission," offered Harding.

"Neither do I and I know him far better than you," agreed Smith, holding the attention of the discomforted surveillance chief. "I think he'd done this to frighten the shit out of us at the same time as proving how good he still is."

"We can't afford to assume that," cautioned the deputy director.

"We can't afford to assume anything," accepted Smith. "Or do anything."

"What, proactively, can we do?" asked Harding.

"I've already told you," said the Director-General, testily. "Nothing but sit and wait." He paused. "And hope."

Which was what Charlie Muffin was doing—although lying, not sitting—on a sun lounger by the pool at Longueville House Hotel, conveniently close to the Jersey capital of St. Helier, his hammertoed feet freed from the captivity of socks and Hush Puppies, trousers rolled up to just below his knees, the nine thousand pounds set up in undiscoverable transfers to Moscow.

He was glad he'd stayed an extra day and was tempted to extend further, enjoying the almost light-headed feeling of no longer being under goldfish-bowl observation: fantasizing, even, of continuing to run, sure he'd escaped and that he could always keep ahead. He didn't have any doubts—or fears—of keeping himself alive: that's what he'd been doing for virtually the whole of his operational career. Assessed against the current success of those supposed to be protecting him, he'd probably be safer on his own.

But practicality—the practicality of no longer officially existing—was against him. The only income he now had was the more-than-generous allowance deposited into the bank account of the officially christened—complete with birth certificate—new name of Malcolm Stoat, the identity in which was registered the credit cards automatically paid from that account, his ownership of the Chelsea safe house and its utility services, local council and national election voting eligibility, along with a driving license and National Insurance number, National Health card and hospital registration card, and Christ knows what else he'd forgotten and couldn't, lying there in the sunshine, be bothered to remember. More red-taped than goldfish-bowled, reflected Charlie, reluctantly pulling himself up from the lounger.

They were going to be very pissed off when he reappeared, Charlie accepted. But that was scarcely going to be a new or different experience: certainly not as new or as difficult as adjusting to the totally regimented future he'd spent the past two and a half days fully considering in all its stultifying detail. Before concluding, as he just had concluded, that he never would be able to adjust. Which was, as always, a subjective, not a suicidal, decision, although he could well imagine anyone stuck with a name like Malcolm Stoat would seriously contemplate suicide.

"He's back," announced Simon Harding. "Three o'clock this morning. He was clean. He was so quick disabling the entry alarm we didn't actually know he was in there until the house lights went on and we saw him up on CCTV."

"I'm not going to have him make fools of us like this," declared Aubrey Smith. "And he's going to hear it from me!"

"There's something else," said the protection-service controller.

The two men spent fifteen minutes unspeaking, huddled together over the disk that Harding had produced before summoning Jane Ambersom to replay it several more times.

The deputy director finally said: "What the hell is it?"

"I don't know," admitted Smith. "But we've got to find out."

Maxim Mikhailovich Radtsic's insistence had been that he choose their rendezvous, and Jacobson was moderately impressed. The riverboat-tour pier was close to the long distance steamer terminal on Klenovy Boulevard, which ensured a perpetual throng of people in which to disappear, although by the same token providing virtually undetectable surveillance cover. Apparently to guard against which the Russian had imposed a trail-clearing ritual requiring Jacobson to board the vessel thirty minutes ahead of Radtsic and to remain at the rail overlooking the gangway to guarantee the deputy FSB director did not have followers. Additionally, Jacobson was forbidden to make any approach for thirty minutes after departure for Radtsic to complete the same check on the British MI6 officer. Radtsic's satisfaction signal was to drop his empty cigarette packet into the Moskva River.

"It's good to see you again," greeted Jacobson, coming up alongside the other man.

"What does London say?" instantly demanded Radtsic.

"They welcome you and your wife. And Andrei, too, of course."

"It must be soon. Very soon."

"Arrangements have to be made. We have to coordinate you and your wife leaving here with moving Andrei from Paris. We have to find a suitable house and equip it with all its necessary security. As well as arranging new identities and setting up financial arrangements that'll be acceptable to you."

"Most of it can be done when we're there."

"There will need to be cooperation, once you are completely safe," warned Jacobson, guardedly.

Radtsic covered his hesitation by lighting a fresh cigarette from the stub of the old. "I told you I would cooperate."

"Very full cooperation."

"We can decide all that when I get there."

"No, sir," refused Jacobson. "There must be complete understanding between us now."

"You are recording this conversation!" demanded the Russian, looking sideways for the first time.

"Yes. I could, of course, have lied and said no, but I want everything to be honest and clear between us."

"I respect and appreciate that."

"And I would appreciate an answer."

Radtsic hesitated further. Then he said: "Of course I will cooperate. That's the deal, isn't it?"

"Yes, sir," confirmed Jacobson. "That's the deal."

THE WARNING OF AN OFFICIAL VISIT WAS ALWAYS MADE BY A recorded voice quoting Charlie's four-digit protection designation, 1716. He had to acknowledge it with a binary response, the first sequence by using his telephone keypad to provide a separate five-digit identification, 10063. That had to be verified by his verbally reciting, for voiceprint recognition, a different number—1316—to separate recording equipment. His failure to provide both in sequential order or wrongly numbering either was his alarm signal that he believed himself to be compromised.

Charlie's telephone rang at eight thirty on the morning of his return, slightly earlier than he'd expected although he was already shaved and showered, waiting. By the time he completed the answering ritual he had the impression of the walls closing claustrophobically around him, coupled with a flicker of nostalgia for the brief freedom of his Jersey escape. He sloughed off the memory by looking at continuous TV news programs, particularly for any coverage of the impending Russian presidential elections, about which there had been intense international speculation in the assassination's aftermath, of which his incarceration was a living-death outcome. There was nothing, as it had been for weeks now.

There were security CCTV monitors relaying into three rooms of the safe house. Charlie watched the arrival of his case officer from the one in the kitchen. Brian Cooper was a balding, rotund testimony to the more flamboyant style of Savile Row tailoring, to which

Charlie took as much attention-attracting exception as Cooper did of his shambling, trouser-shone charity-shop preference.

Charlie opened the door at the first ring, matching the other man's critical head-to-toe appraisal. Standing aside for Cooper to enter, Charlie said: "I wasn't sure if it would be you who'd come."

"You ready?" Cooper demanded, not moving. The voice was brittle-toned public school.

"Ready for what?"

"It's not going to be here." The suit was a muted gray and Charlie guessed he could have achieved a closer shave from the sharpness of the trouser crease than he'd got earlier from his razor.

"What isn't?"

"What do you think? I asked if you were ready."

"We going far?" asked Charlie, stumbling awkwardly into step behind the other man, vaguely disconcerted that he hadn't anticipated the inevitable inquest being elsewhere. It indicated greater irritation than he'd imagined.

Cooper didn't reply, jerking his head toward the back of the anonymous, unwashed Ford. All the glass was smoked, even the fully raised screen between the driver and his rear-seat passengers.

"I asked if we were going far," Charlie repeated.

"I don't know," said the man, not bothering to look across the car.

It was possible Cooper didn't, Charlie accepted. The Ford made a full, pursuit-testing circle around Sloane Square and two sharp, unsignaled diversions before resuming a gradually emerging northern route.

"Maybe I should have packed an overnight bag?" Charlie tried again.

"I'm not interested in small-talk shit," announced Cooper, abruptly. "You're one great big pain in the ass. You want to go on being stupid enough to do what you're doing, whatever the fuck that is, that's fine by me. You want to commit suicide, for Christ's sake hurry up and do it so we can start looking after people who deserve to be looked after!"

"I'm sorry if I've made your life difficult," apologized Charlie, meaning it. They were clearing London but veering westward: Buckinghamshire, perhaps, maybe even farther, guessed Charlie. Aubrey Smith lived in Buckinghamshire. Whatever the irritation, it surely wouldn't have got to Director-General level!

Cooper was looking fixedly out his side window, his body partially, oddly, turned to show his back, which Charlie thought childish. Taking operational difficulties personally would explain why the man was limited to adult baby-minding. From a briefly glimpsed signpost Charlie saw that they were definitely in Buckinghamshire, although well off any major roads. He could see sufficiently through the separating glass to gauge the driver's divided concentration between the road and the dashboard-mounted GPS, from which Charlie guessed they were nearing their destination. Beside him, the back-turned case officer was showing no recognition, from which Charlie assumed that the man genuinely didn't know where they were going, which was confirmed when Cooper had to snatch for an armrest support when the driver unexpectedly turned into an unmarked driveway. The gate was set at least twenty meters back from its original supporting pillars, the centerpiece of a secondary, razor-wire-topped wall. The wire hedge was broken close to the gate head to accommodate the camera that swiveled at their approach to record the car's registration, to which the driver added by manually directing an electronic fob to a sensor that Charlie couldn't detect. The admission precautions were completed by the man lowering the driver's window to announce their presence into a door-level entry phone.

Almost directly beyond the gate, the Ford turned off the main driveway and onto a smaller but still paved road that ran between totally concealing, close-together trees and low shrubbery that unexpectedly ballooned out into a clearing in the center of which was a half-timbered building Charlie guessed originally to have been a hunting lodge. There were four cars, all anonymous Fords, regimented to the left of its heavy oak door. Charlie's driver went to its right. A dark-suited woman emerged before the car stopped. She came to Cooper's door, gesturing.

"Stay where you are," ordered the case officer, as he got out.

Charlie was uneasy. His disappearing required a reprimand but this was at a far higher level. Why? The only logical answer was that he hadn't been as professional as he'd imagined: that they'd followed him every shuffling step of the way to Jersey, knew about the bank arrangements to fund Natalia, and were about to strap him onto the rack and start twirling the bone-cracking wheel until he confessed all.

When he was told to get out, Charlie followed the woman to the lodge, but unhurriedly, hesitating at the sudden darkness beyond the heavy oak door. Predictably there was a display of antlered heads along both wood-paneled walls. The woman stood at the end of the hall, shifting impatiently. When he reached her, Charlie said: "You were too fast for me."

"I imagine most people are," she came back, thrusting open a side door for him to enter.

A quick shot or confirmation that they had been with him in Jersey? wondered Charlie, as he saw the assembled group behind a long table at the end of another paneled room lined with a wildlife massacre of glass-eyed trophies, here interspersed with the heads of a tiger and two bears. Aubrey Smith was at the center of four men, with Deputy Director Jane Ambersom to his left. The Director-General was dwarfed by the man next to him, appearing almost a foot taller, even though he was sitting, and with his jacket spread to release a bulging belly couching a bull-like chest. The other two were on Smith's right. There would, Charlie knew, be audio- and visual-recording equipment, which made him curious about the small, unmanned replay machine on a separate table.

"Where were you?" demanded Smith, without any preamble.

A clever question, Charlie acknowledged, allowing him little verbal room to maneuver, with the wrong response catching him out in a lie from the outset. "Making a point," he tried.

"Explain," demanded the Director-General. The man was stone faced, no inflection breaking the soft, measured tone. The light reflected off his rimless spectacles made the man appear sightless.

"To prove a nonsense."

Ambersom matched the frown of the unidentified man next to Smith, who remained the sole interrogator. "Explain."

There was sufficient space on the menagerie wall for his head to be mounted alongside, Charlie saw. He had to say something to get a clearer indication of why this confrontation had been escalated. "The nonsense of my being a suicide risk. If I'd wanted to kill myself I could have done so. I didn't."

Smith moved to speak but stopped at the sound of the door opening. From the quickness of the footsteps, Charlie knew it was the woman escort before she came into view from behind him. The examining panel pulled close together as she leaned forward over the table toward them. It was impossible for Charlie to hear anything of the exchange, from which Smith retreated, looking left and right as if seeking comment from those on either side. No one responded, but without any apparent invitation Ambersom said: "Nonsense is a good description of what you're saying. Now answer properly. Where have you been?"

Charlie was tempted by the fixed-face woman's intrusion, more confident of directing the questioning the way he wanted. But he still didn't have a good enough map of the minefield in which he believed himself to be. The lesser the lies the better, he determined. "Jersey. I took a trip to Jersey, ate some good food, enjoyed the sunshine."

"We've comb-searched your safe house for four hours," announced the deputy director, triumphantly. "There wasn't the slightest trace of your having been to Jersey. Or anywhere else."

They hadn't known about Jersey! The satisfaction warmed Charlie. "Of course there wasn't. I tossed it all into the Channel. The tradecraft designation is clearing your trail, remember?"

"What would you say if I told you we don't believe you?" demanded Ambersom. Her voice had the vaguest blur of a northern accent.

"I'd say you should check at the Longueville House Hotel in St. Helier: room forty-two, second floor. You can see the harbor." If they hadn't known where he'd been they could discover his reason for going there, so he wasn't giving anything away describing his room.

There was the slightest tightening of the woman's angular, makeup-spared face at Charlie's dismissal. "What would you say if I told you we still don't believe you?"

What the hell was this all about! "I'm not sure I'd know what to say."

"Tell us about this then," said Aubrey Smith, nodding to the man nearest the replay machine.

Into the silent room came the click of an answer phone connection and then a voice that Charlie instantly recognized as Natalia's. She said: "I think we need help, Charlie. Call me, please. Tell me what's happening." The line momentarily went dead before the click of a second connection. This time Natalia said: "I think they know. I'm sure we're under surveillance." The third, final segment was: "Help us, Charlie. Please help us."

The Director-General said: "We've kept on your old Vauxhall apartment, as a precaution. With the telephone still connected. We traced all three calls to separate pay phones in Moscow."

The deputy director said: "Who is she?"

The silence lasted for a very long time after Charlie finished speaking, the panel confronting him statued in apparent disbelief, none looking at the other. Before she did speak, eager to maintain her questioning dominance, Ambersom physically shook her head, like someone awakening from a coma.

"This woman is a serving officer in the FSB."

"Yes," confirmed Charlie, who'd been completely honest, omitting nothing in his explanation of Natalia's three calls, instantly aware that he would need every conceivable help from his own service and that one lie, even an inadvertent omission, would close the door against him. He didn't like to hear Natalia being referred to as "this woman."

"And before the Federal'naya Sluzhba Bezopasnosti she served in the KGB?"

"Before the Komitet Gosudarstvennoy Bezopasnosti was renamed, yes."

"You are officially, properly, married?"

"A Russian ceremony, in the Hall of Weddings."

"And there is a child?"

"I've already explained all this!"

"Your child?"

"Sasha is my child, yes."

"And you have run this woman, as an asset, for how long, six, seven years?"

"The relationship began a little over eight years ago. Natalia serves in the specialized section of the analysis division. She was appointed my official debriefer after my supposed defection, all the details of which are in the personnel archives. She has never been an asset, other than that of being my wife. And she is my wife, not 'this woman.' " He shouldn't have finished like that, showing his irritation.

"So your supposed defection becomes a genuine one? This woman turned you?"

Bitch, thought Charlie. "I am not, nor ever have been, an agent of either the Soviet Union or the Russian Federation," he replied, formally. "I never, ever, discussed with my wife any operation in which I was involved. And I repeat, neither, ever, has she. We lived together as man and wife after I was seconded to the embassy in Moscow—which is again officially in my file—but it became impossible for me. Just as she found it impossible then to follow me back to London. I obviously made contact during the most recent Moscow assignment concerning the death of a man in the grounds of the British embassy and the uncovering of an attempted FSB coup involving Stepan Lvov, the outcome of which has resulted in my having to enter the protection program. . . ." Charlie hesitated, briefly. "I had finally persuaded her to come to live with me in England with our daughter. But the retribution began, beginning with Lvov's assassination, before I could get her out. She's trapped."

The incredulity had spread to the four unidentified men. One turned and said something to the Director-General, which Charlie thought he heard as "preposterous."

"This—all of this—is beyond imagination!" dismissed the woman.

"Everything I am telling you is the God's honest truth!"

"I don't think you know the meaning of truth. Or of God."

"I need help," pleaded Charlie desperately.

"You need a miracle and there's no such thing as miracles," she said.

"I've heard the recording of the Radtsic meeting. You did well: bloody well," congratulated James Straughan.

"What about the Director?" demanded Jacobson.

"He's heard it too: says the same."

"So I've got official approval to go ahead?"

"Absolutely."

"Shouldn't that approval be official?"

"I'll send it today."

"Do you want me to come back for the planning?"

"We'll do all that here: you just give us the input when we ask for it."

"We mustn't lose sight of Radtsic's flakiness."

"We won't. It's scheduled highest priority now."

"The approval will be in the Director's name, won't it?"

"Everything will be done by the book. Don't worry."

The problem was that Jacobson did worry about fulfilling his station-chief responsibilities: he worried a lot.

5

"IT'S TOTALLY INCONCEIVABLE," INSISTED JANE AMBERSOM. "The man isn't suicidal. He's insane. Deluded."

"There were times when I thought it was so inconceivable that it couldn't possibly be made up," said Geoffrey Palmer, one of the unidentified members of the examining panel and the Foreign Office liaison to the Joint Intelligence Committee.

"Which doesn't minimize the potential disaster of the situation," argued the woman.

"I wasn't trying to minimize anything," said Palmer, who in every respect personified the career civil servant, even to the striped-trousered, black-jacketed uniform, complemented by the bowler hat and tightly furled umbrella for his daily commute from Orpington suburbia.

"Gerald?" invited the Director-General, addressing his MI6 counterpart, whose inclusion in the meeting he distrusted.

They had moved from their earlier interrogational formality to leathered armchairs and couches around a dead, carved-wood fireplace in which a man could comfortably stand without bending and in which Gerald Monsford had framed his six-foot-three-inch, bulge-bellied figure to be the focal point of the discussion. Monsford said: "From your provisional inquiries, everything he told us about Jersey checks out?"

"So far," qualified Smith, cautiously, not wanting his insecurity-spurred antipathy to be obvious.

"And it was Charlie Muffin who prevented us and the United States being sucked into the most incredibly successful Russian espionage operation I've ever encountered," said Monsford. Easily lapsing into the pretension of a Classics education he'd never actually had, Monsford added: "If he's guilty of anything it's following Ovid's belief that enemies are the best teachers."

Jane Ambersom, who'd endured that affectation as she'd endured other irritations, was amused at the startled reactions from the rest of the group at Monsford's posturing and said: "It could still be part of that Russian operation."

"How?" immediately challenged the MI6 Director, already sure he could in some way use his totally unexpected inclusion in this emergency-convened committee to extract Maxim Mikhailovich Radtsic out of Russia. He extended a hand with his forefinger close to his thumb. "Stepan Lvov, whom the CIA was convinced they had in the bag as their long-established double agent, was just this far from becoming the next president of the Russian Federation. As such, in reality a committed officer of the FSB, Lvov would have maneuvered and manipulated Washington and us down God knows how many roads to destruction: Russian intelligence would have ruled the West as well as what's left of their former empire: literally ruled the world. How could this have any connection with that?"

Jane's face blazed at the ridicule from Monsford, whom she rightly believed was the architect of her transfer to the counterintelligence service. She moved to speak but before she could Monsford went back to the Director-General: "What about other cases, before this last one? How many went the wrong way, to the other side's benefit?"

"That check began the moment Muffin's state of mind was questioned and was upgraded when he disappeared. A conclusion will take time," avoided Smith. "The preliminary assessment is that while a few weren't completely successful, none was compromised through any personal fault or failing of Charlie himself. And none of us needs reminding how he prevented the catastrophe to which you've already referred." As well as preventing my dismissal, Smith mentally added.

"On the subject of preliminary assessments, I have to give to the prime minister and the foreign secretary some indication of the potential problems we might be facing," came in Sir Archibald Bland, the cabinet secretary, who'd completed the inquiry team.

"I'm not sure we can provide that this early," apologized Smith, in reluctant admission. "Charlie Muffin will be held here, under house detention. Questioned further to learn far more about Natalia Fedova. I don't intend a knee-jerk reaction to a situation as complicated as this appears to be."

"I'm not naïve enough to believe this woman doesn't know anything about operations in which Muffin has been involved for at least the past eight years," said the deputy director, the disparagement embedded in her mind. "And as such the potential cause of huge embarrassment, if not serious, long-term harm. She should be neutralized."

"Killed, you mean?" lured Monsford, deceptively casual.

Jane Ambersom hesitated, coloring again, inherently suspicious of the man. "If it were deemed necessary. He's given us her Moscow address: we know where to find her."

"What about the child? Do we kill the child as well?" pounced Monsford, baiting her in front of the two civil servants to continue the criticism he'd engineered to achieve her transfer. "I can't imagine an eight-year-old child knowing enough to cause us difficulties, but we might as well tidy up any loose ends."

The woman's color deepened. "I don't believe we are considering this seriously enough. This is a high-alert situation that needs to be dealt with as such."

"None of us believes otherwise," said Aubrey Smith, calmly, despite his irritation at the obvious point scoring and astonished at Monsford's talking as if he'd been closely involved in the Lvov exposure. "I'd hoped to have made clear that I do not intend worsening a potential problem with a panicked reaction."

"Which eliminating a woman about whose existence we have only just learned, orphaning a child in the process, would unarguably do," endorsed Monsford.

"How, precisely, do we learn more about her?" asked Jane Ambersom, descending to mockery.

"Going into what Wordsworth described as the burthen of the mystery," Monsford awkwardly mocked back, intent upon controlling what he was increasingly deciding to be a gift situation from a God in whom he didn't believe. "The separation and independence of our two services is well established, for all the obvious reasons. I welcome, however, this opportunity for us to come together in a combined operation, to which I guarantee every contribution asked from MI6."

"This is precisely how the prime minister wants it handled," announced Sir Anthony Bland.

"It seems completely appropriate to me," quickly agreed Palmer, the functioning liaison between MI5 and MI6.

"At this early stage I don't see the reason for a combined operation," argued Aubrey Smith, recognizing how he was being railroaded, sure it confirmed his suspicion that his directorship remained in doubt.

"Perhaps I didn't make clear how I envisage such an arrangement," said Monsford. "I am offering my resources in one specific area: Moscow. I anticipate our working in the closest possible way, discussing every aspect, but equally expect you to be the controller—the Director—of a matched, one for one, team of officers."

No one else in the room appeared able to find a response.

Geoffrey Palmer was the first. "That's a very generous offer that would seem to resolve any command uncertainty: not, of course, that I would expect any."

"We are all agreed that everything is at a very early, exploratory stage," persisted Aubrey Smith, his unemotional monotone concealing the anger at so effectively being maneuvered into a cul-de-sac. "Let's look upon this operational cooperation as a step-at-a-time experiment."

"I would expect to be an active participant, too," hurriedly intruded Jane Ambersom, equally concerned at again becoming Monsford's scapegoat.

"I would expect all of us to be active participants," said the compromise-adept Sir Archibald.

Aubrey Smith, who fully acknowledged his initial survival indebtedness to Charlie Muffin, wondered how long his second chance might last. At least this time he hoped more quickly to recognize at least some of the moves against him, which he hadn't before.

For as long as he could remember, and Charlie Muffin had an elephantine memory, self-preservation had been a major preoccupation, but never so much as now, incarcerated as he was in a window-barred and double-locked room with only the glazed-eyed relatives of the other wall-mounted animals on the ground floor for sightless company. But this was the first time the preoccupation was not for his own survival. How had Natalia—and Sasha—been detected? The money trail had always been the obvious weakness although it couldn't have triggered this discovery: two of Natalia's anguished calls to his abandoned Vauxhall apartment were dated and timed before his Jersey visit. How else? He would have been the concentrated focus of the excoriating, stop-at-nothing FSB investigation after the destruction of Russia's intended puppetmaster emplacement of Stepan Lvov. What of Natalia's long ago insistence that she had wiped from KGB and succeeding FSB records as much trace as possible of their connection during his supposed defection debriefing? There was a stomach lurch of belated—too belated—realization. A search as complete and as intense as the FSB's would have encompassed every government institution. The Hall of Weddings was one such institution, in which every ceremony was bureaucratically registered, electronically as well as in a handwritten ledger.

Why was he looking backward? Charlie asked himself. Whatever the route, whatever the disclosing mistake, their relationship had been uncovered. Or had it? If it had been positively confirmed, Natalia would no longer be at liberty to telephone him as she had. Suspected at least, Charlie qualified. But sufficient for the scourging fear in which Charlie felt locked because even if she was suspected, Natalia and Sasha had to be got out of Russia.

But how? And by whom?

Judged against a lifetime's need for split-second thinking to split-second confrontations, Charlie believed he'd adequately responded to the stomach-dropping sound of Natalia's voice. But only *just* adequately. He'd answered every question about Natalia with complete and total honesty—without offering any additional information—just as he had recounted his Jersey journey, omitting only the financial reason for his making it. But the debrief had concluded without the slightest indication of what might happen to him. Far more worryingly, there had been nothing at all about Natalia and Sasha.

He had to think of a way to rescue them: a very quick, stop-at-nothing way as guaranteed as possible to get them to safety. What? he asked himself again. And again failed to find an answer.

"To quote Shakespeare, 'with as little a web as this I will ensnare': they've gone for it!" announced Gerald Monsford, triumphantly. He spoke with his back to the other two in his office in MI6's Vauxhall Cross headquarters, looking up toward the Houses of Parliament on the opposite side of the Thames.

"Even dear Jane?" queried Rebecca Street, well aware of Monsford's antipathy toward the woman whom she had replaced, although unaware of how it had been manipulated.

"She needed the assurance that she wouldn't be kept out of the loop," said Monsford, who'd appointed Rebecca not only as his deputy but as his easily persuaded mistress, which Jane had consistently refused to become, providing an additional reason for her transfer.

"What about Smith?" asked James Straughan, the director of operations.

"Palmer and Bland got in with their support first, which wrong-footed poor old Aubrey," patronized the Director. "Then I played my ace by insisting that he'd control it all, with us limited to committing our Moscow resources, which left him high and dry."

"You think he'll trust us?" asked the woman, professionally objective.

"At the moment he's totally confused by the sudden appearance of this mysterious Natalia Fedova," said Monsford, turning at last from the window. To the woman he said: "I want you to monitor everything: act as our secondary check to guarantee against mistakes."

"Nothing will go wrong," said the blond Rebecca Street, smiling. She dressed to advertise her full-breasted but otherwise slim figure. That day's promotion was a low-necked crossover black dress, the bodice pin the diamond clasp Monsford had given her as a consummation present. She'd been far more impressed by the clasp than by the over-in-seconds lovemaking she'd endured in the office's adjoining bedroom suite to gain it.

"What about our own operation?" queried Straughan.

"The entire reason for what I achieved today," declared Monsford. "This MI5 business is a bonus we're going to bleed dry, maybe even literally. Have we got an unsuspected conduit to Moscow: something the FSB will believe unquestioningly?"

Straughan considered the question. "It's not as easy as it was when there was a Soviet Union."

"I didn't imagine it would be," said Monsford, testily. "I want something to tie Charlie Muffin closer in to whatever the hell these telephone calls are all about: something connected to the Lvov business, for instance."

"There's an FSB source at the Polish embassy in Rome we've used before," said Straughan. "Not for more than a year, though."

"After all the damage Charlie did, the FSB would obviously like to find him, wouldn't they?" suggested Monsford.

"That's why he's in a protection program, isn't it?" said Rebecca, frowning.

"And because of it no longer living where he once did." Monsford smiled. "But the FSB don't know that, do they?"

"So it wouldn't expose him to any actual harm?" said Straughan.

"Of course it wouldn't," agreed Monsford.

"I'll try to set it up," undertook the operations director.

"Not *try*: *do* it," said Monsford, heavily. "It'll be an irony that Charlie Muffin's last service to British intelligence will be for us, not his own people."

"Everything's agreed," Maxim Radtsic assured his wife, his head close to hers as they went north on the Arbatsko line of Moscow's Metro service, upon which, three hours earlier, he'd kept his latest meeting with Harry Jacobson.

"When?" the woman asked, matchingly low voiced.

"Soon. They know the urgency."

"I don't like all this nonsense," Elana protested, looking around the packed commuter carriage. "It's silly, playacting like children."

"It's very necessary if we're to keep safe," insisted Radtsic.

"Why don't I go to Paris, for a holiday with Andrei, and go to London with him from there. It would be easier for you to get out alone, wouldn't it?"

She was more frightened than he, realized Radtsic, sympathetically. "It would alert them: make them suspicious."

"Andrei should be given more warning."

"It's got to be the way the British want it."

"Let's not take the Metro back to the apartment. I want to walk."

"It's a long way to walk from Kurskaya," Radtsic pointed out, identifying where they were from the route map above the seats.

"I know."

She knew she wouldn't very much longer be able to walk the streets of the city, accepted Radtsic, sadly. Would she ever properly understand what he was having to do when it was all over?

"Good-looking kid," remarked Albert Abrahams, looking down at the selection of photographs he'd taken two hours earlier outside Andrei Radtsic's Sorbonne college.

"I prefer the girl," said Jonathan Miller, MI5's station chief at the Paris embassy. "Can you imagine those legs wrapped around your neck?"

"Name's Yvette Paruch," identified Abrahams. "And I have already imagined it. Our Andrei's not just good-looking, he's a lucky bastard as well. So what do we do now?"

"London's orders are to find out everything we can without going anywhere near him. The possibility is that he's being babysat by the FSB."

"If he is, there's a risk they'll pick up on our sniffing around," warned Abrahams.

"That's why Straughan told me to be careful," reminded Miller.

"Comforting, isn't it, to get advice we wouldn't have thought of ourselves from an operations director safe and warm in London?" mocked Abrahams.

6

IT WAS TWO DAYS BEFORE CHARLIE WAS SUMMONED FOR further questioning. In that interim he was held in the barred and locked first-floor room of the hunting lodge with only the gazelle heads for company, apart from morning and afternoon exercise periods in the grounds with two male escorts who refused any conversation and during which there were intentionally staged sightings of other guards. None was visibly armed.

The second session was in the same menagerie-festooned room as before but with a smaller inquiry panel, just Smith, Jane Ambersom, and the overpoweringly large man from the initial interrogation. There was no replay machine on the side table, which had been moved away to the corner of the room.

Once again there was no preamble, although it was the woman who opened the questioning. She took photographs from a case file in front of her and said: "Who is this woman?"

Bitch, thought Charlie, at the same time recognizing the disparagement was intentional, to rile him, which he dismissed as stupid as well as clumsy. There was still the stomach jump of recognition when he took the offered photograph. It was a remarkably sharp image. Natalia was wearing the tightly belted light summer coat he remembered from their most recent Moscow reunion in the Botanical Gardens. She was looking sideways, almost over her shoulder, as if something had suddenly caught her attention. "Natalia Fedova, my wife."

"And this?"

"Our daughter, Alexandra, which shortens to Sasha," replied Charlie, looking down at the second print. The child was wearing her school uniform and hat, smiling up at someone who had been cropped from the picture. "When were these taken?"

Jane Ambersom moved to speak, but before she could Monsford replied: "The day before yesterday."

Aubrey Smith formally introduced Monsford for the first time and said: "SIS are cooperating with us."

The woman was looking tight faced between the two directors, clearly irritated at both responding to questioning.

"They're still free then?" pressed Charlie, momentarily off-balanced by MI6's involvement. It was logical, he conceded, that there would have been linked operations in the past, although he'd never actively participated in one. Charlie remembered the name. During his earlier Moscow assignment the gossip in the MI6 *rezidentura* had tagged Monsford as a reincarnation of Genghis Khan suffering a bad attack of toothache. There'd also been a rumor the man had tried to muscle in to the Lvov affair.

"Let's get some order back into this debriefing, shall we?" said Jane Ambersom. "There's a lot more answers we need to get from you."

"I have not committed any criminal offense!" Charlie said, embarking on one of the several half-formed strategies he'd considered over the preceding forty-eight hours. "Nor have I contravened the Official Secrets Act, to which I am a signatory. My being in the protection program does not require my being held under detention."

Jane Ambersom's snort of derision was too obviously forced. "Doesn't one of the most essential clauses in the Official Secrets Act cover consorting with an enemy!"

"It is an entire section, not a clause," formally corrected Charlie, both to further her irritation and for the benefit of the bureaucratic recordings. "And that question is both a distortion and a misphrasing of its wording. I have never contravened any section of any act involving, covering, or forbidding the passing of intelligence secrets or information to a foreign power or intelligence service. . . ." He gestured with the prints he still held. "I provided the specific time and date of my marriage to Natalia Fedova, which I know you will have by now confirmed from Moscow's Hall of Weddings records. I also know that in the intervening two days since I appeared before you, my operational files will have been scrutinized for the slightest indication of failure being attributed to my . . ." Charlie paused again, directly addressing the woman: "to use what appears to be a favored phrase, consorting with the enemy. No indication whatsoever of which will have been found, because none exists. I want . . . if you like, I plead for . . . help to get my wife and daughter out of a situation in which, if our relationship is positively established by the FSB, they could be physically harmed, as it was believed I would be physically harmed for Russia's failure of the Lvov affair, to prevent which I have been put under protection . . . protection, not house arrest."

Once more Jane Ambersom's face was on fire, either from her confusion or her expectation that Charlie would continue, but again Monsford spoke ahead of her. The MI6 Director, hands clasped over his expansive stomach, said: "That was a very spirited and well-argued defense of a charge not yet alleged. But do you believe that buried in all the legislation to which you've referred—the Official Secrets Act the most obvious—there isn't a legal accusation that one of our specialized lawyers could formulate against you?"

Charlie didn't think he'd left any gaping pitfalls: certainly Monsford's response was encouraging, even if the man's inclusion was unsettling and needed separate, intense examination. Don't falter, he told himself. "I'm quite sure there are several charges that could be laid. But I'm even surer that they'd be thrown out of court, although perhaps with an admonishment which I'd expect, after it was proven there has never been any breach of security."

"Haven't we wandered too far from the purpose of this meeting!" protested Jane Ambersom, finally reentering the exchanges.

"Just one thing!" said Charlie, hurriedly, pleased at the woman's exclusion and talking directly to the MI6 chief. "Were *both* those photographs taken two days ago?"

"Yes," confirmed Monsford.

"So they were both still free: not under detention?"

"Yes, both still free."

Charlie looked back at the print of Natalia, closely studying the background for the first time. "And she was outside the apartment I identified?"

"When is this session going to be formalized!" again protested Jane.

"Was there any indication of surveillance?" persisted Charlie, snatching at every opportunity.

"None," confirmed Monsford. For some must watch, while some must sleep. So runs the world away, he thought: why was it that Shakespeare had a comment for every situation? *Hamlet*, he remembered. This would have a happier ending, he was sure.

Natalia and Sasha were still safe! But how professional had the MI6 photographer been? agonized Charlie, who'd never trusted dawn to follow night. If the photographer had failed to detect Russian observation but been identified himself, he would have hastened an FSB move.

"I really do think we've answered enough of your questions," said Aubrey Smith. "Now answer more of ours."

"From the date of your wedding, which we have indeed confirmed, against the date you provided for Sasha's birth, Natalia Fedova was pregnant before you married?" established Jane Ambersom, taking up the questioning again. Her tone made it sound like an accusation.

No longer "this woman," Charlie recognized. "Yes."

"How long had the affair been going on, before the marriage?"

"About eighteen months." Everything totally honest, Charlie reminded himself. He needed their help, not their antagonism.

The woman shuffled hurriedly between several sheets of paper from her dossier before looking up. "We know the precise dates of your fake defection, of course: it was a recorded operation—"

"And a successful one, discrediting a genuine defector with whom I broke out of Wormwood Scrubs after he'd been jailed for forty years as a Soviet spy at the height of the Cold War," broke in Charlie, anxiously establishing what he considered the first of several important facts in his favor.

"I'm familiar with the records. . . ." Jane paused, to counter Charlie's defense with another point. "The *official* records, I mean. So, once more calculated against the known dates and those you have provided, your affair began about six months *after* the Russian acceptance that your defection was genuine?"

"Yes," confirmed Charlie, cautiously. He shouldn't have interjected: she was obviously building up to what she considered an undermining question.

"Tell us about those six months."

"What about them?" hedged Charlie, reluctant to answer such a generality.

"The Russians had accepted you: believed you had joined their little band of traitors. Did you ever meet, socialize, with those other defectors? With Philby or Blake, for instance?"

"No."

"Never?"

"Never."

"Are you sure?"

Charlie hesitated, seeking the trap. Unable to find it, he smiled, condescendingly shaking his head. "It's hardly likely that I would forget meeting such people, is it?"

"Unless you're lying!" she said.

Not undermining at all, if that was her best attempt. "I am not lying!"

"What job did the Russians give you, having accepted you as genuine?"

He could use this question, Charlie recognized. "I was assigned to a training school."

"What sort of training school?" There was a note of triumph in the woman's voice.

"A training school for intended KGB intelligence officers," answered Charlie, comfortably.

"Intended to operate in which countries?" The triumph was growing.

"The English-speaking West: the United Kingdom, America, Canada."

Jane Ambersom again staged her preparing pause, and when she did speak she spaced her words to heighten her supposed incredulity. "You—taught—KGB—agents—selected—to—operate—against—the—United—Kingdom?"

"No," Charlie denied, seizing his chance. "My function was to assess during one-to-one sessions—one spy was never allowed to encounter another—whether their training was sufficient for them to assimilate successfully into a Western culture without arousing suspicion. I handled a total of eight. In each case I dismissed their training as inadequate. By doing so I gained limited access but comprehensive insight into Russian espionage-training methods and systems, about which I created a manual on my return to this country. I believe that manual was later used as a textbook at *our* training academies. I also, of course, learned the identities of the eight with whom I worked, although the names were obviously not those they were assigned in the West. Over the course of the four years after my return to this country, in addition to active field assignments, I regularly examined photographs of Russians posted under diplomatic cover to the Russian embassies in London, Washington, D.C., and Ottawa. I managed to identify five, none of whom were expelled but allowed to remain, observing the principle that the spy you know is better than the one you don't. All, I believe, were fed disinformation by us and the counterespionage organizations of America and Canada." Charlie paused, dry throated, and gestured toward Jane

Ambersom's dossier. "Everything I've told you is set out in greater detail in my file, even the names of the eight Russians. You should be able to confirm it all very easily."

Jane Ambersom was puce faced yet again. Monsford actually had his hands cupped over his face to conceal his reaction to the put-down. Smith's head was lowered intently toward the floor. And Charlie burned with self-fury. The bloody woman *had* got under his skin. But what the fuck was he doing fighting her, humiliating her, like this! He couldn't afford to fight or humiliate anyone upon whom he now depended. He desperately needed each and every possible assistance to get Natalia and Sasha out of Moscow, as desperately as he needed to convince them that he'd never, ever, acted against the service to which he'd dedicated his life. And he wasn't going to achieve any of that in confronting this supercilious, mannish woman: *this woman!* echoed mockingly in his mind. Every single time he antagonized any of them he pushed further away the possibility of rescuing from God knew what the only two people of importance in his life: the *only* two people in his life.

"You were able to cultivate your relationship with Natalia Fedova as well as working at the spy school?" uncertainly resumed Jane.

"Easily," said Charlie, determined against further confrontation. "Natalia officially comes within the jurisdiction of the analysis division but her predominant function is debriefing, for which she has the Russian equivalent of a master's degree in psychology and a track record of marathon proportions. The Russians attach great importance to the psychology of their field agents, as we do. Which creates another function, that of maintaining and monitoring the continuing psychological capability of about-to-graduate intelligence officers facing, for the first time, the reality of being uprooted from the life they know and transposed into an entirely different, alien culture. That brought her frequently to the training school to which I was assigned on the outskirts of Moscow, about five miles beyond Prazskaja."

"What was the purpose of your false defection?"

He'd already covered that, although not in detail: she was running out of impetus. "In 1988 a Russian agent only ever identified by the name Edwin Sampson was jailed for forty years. He was considered one of the most damaging spies ever to be uncovered in this country but we didn't know the full extent of what he'd done, apart from the barest evidence we'd managed to get together to convict him: he never confessed or admitted anything. I was put in Wormwood Scrubs, supposedly jailed for fourteen years, also for spying. It was fixed that we'd share the same cell, in which over the course of time I'd gain his trust and get some indication of what else he'd done. It wasn't anticipated the KGB would try to free him, as they did with George Blake and which indicated the importance they attached to him. But when it emerged that they intended to do just that, it was decided I should appear to defect with him in the hope of learning what made him so important. Which I did. The idea—"

"Was that after a period of time, with the help of our people in the British embassy, you'd pretend to be disillusioned with Russia and flee back to this country," broke in Jane.

"Yes," agreed Charlie. "With the added benefit of all I'd learned at the spy school."

"With such a history no one was going to doubt your loyalty, were they?" persisted Jane.

"No one has, until now. And you're wrong."

"But there's good reason to doubt you now, suddenly presented as we are with a wife who's a serving officer in Russia's external intelligence," challenged Jane. "Is that all she is, your wife? Or could she also be your Control through whom you're supposed to liaise with Moscow after she joins you here, which you've told us has consistently been the plan?"

"What I told you is that it's consistently been my *hope* that she would join me here, but that she has always refused, held as she is by that near-mystical bond Russians have for their country," corrected Charlie, maintaining control but letting his argument come out in a rush. "If I'd been turned and married Natalia for the reason you've suggested, she would have been *ordered* to return with me in the first place, wouldn't she? And I wouldn't have told you that she was a member of the FSB. There'd be an unbreakable cover legend, giving her a background as far as possible from any connection with espionage. And would I, as a KGB-cum-FSB double, have destroyed a KGB/FSB operation eighteen years in creation to put Moscow literally in the Oval Office?"

Before Jane Ambersom could respond, the Director-General said: "There is an alternative way to judge this. You could be telling the truth. The FSB could have discovered your relationship with Natalia Fedova and be forcing her to make the approaches to trap you into going back to Russia. Where you, as the person who wrecked that eighteen-year-long operation, would face punishment it's hard to conceive, judged against the ways they've killed the people they've eliminated so far . . ."

". . . Unless they made you watch whatever they wanted to do to Natalia and the child before killing you as bestially as possible," completed Monsford.

"That's what I believe they want to do," admitted Charlie, almost inaudibly.

"You think we're going to let you go back to Russia to stop it happening, don't you?" taunted the woman.

"Irrespective of whether it's agreed I go back, they'll do whatever they want to them both," pleaded Charlie. "That can't be allowed to happen. They've got to be got out!"

"There's no way they can be," said Jane.

"All I had to do was sit and listen to Jane Ambersom stumble about like a bull in a china shop," gloated the MI6 director. "Christ, we're lucky being rid of her."

"Cow," corrected James Straughan, who always sought to lighten his encounters with someone as unpredictable as Gerald Monsford, particularly when they were alone, which they were now. "It would be a cow in a china shop, not a bull."

"Cow is certainly more apposite," agreed Monsford, who'd enjoyed his manipulation of that day's meeting as he had those that preceded it. "Charlie's on his knees, pleading for his wife and child to be rescued. Jane came close to orgasm telling him it couldn't be done."

"You broached our idea with Smith yet?"

The other man shook his head. "I need exactly the right moment. Smith believes it's his option to make and his operation to initiate, so that's how I've got to make it seem."

"Everything's virtually in place," assured Straughan, although cautiously. He knew better than to make promises that weren't guaranteed.

"No more calls from Moscow?"

"Smith hasn't mentioned any more and I'm sure he would if there'd been more. I don't think he feels very secure. What about Jacobson?"

"Anxious to get the stuff I'm assembling. The passports for Radtsic and his wife are in the diplomatic pouch tonight."

"That should reassure Radtsic."

"Something's got to, according to Jacobson. He thinks Radtsic is getting critical."

"Tell Jacobson to give Radtsic whatever assurances the man needs. I don't want the frightened old bastard collapsing on us," ordered Monsford. "What about Paris?"

"All in hand."

"I want something else," announced the Director.

"What?"

"My own recording system, here in this office. Getting Radtsic safely here is going to be the coup of our lives. I don't want any foul-ups through faulty memories, which came close with the Lvov business."

The only memory at fault with the Lvov business is yours, thought Straughan: and if there'd been a proper record you wouldn't be overflowing the chair you're sitting in. Aloud he said: "I'll organize it."

"And I want personal, manual control. We mustn't overlook the Official Secrets Act and necessary security clearances."

"No," agreed Straughan. "We shouldn't overlook that."

Charlie Muffin for the first time felt engulfed in paralyzing, impotent helplessness. He'd faced seemingly impossible, about-to-die crises before but always been able to escape, sometimes badly bruised, sometimes badly burned—often physically, too often metaphysically—always survived. Because every time it had only ever been *he* who'd had to survive, no one else to worry about or to consider. Now it wasn't only he. It was Natalia—probably bewildered, doubtless confused, with only the vaguest indication of what had happened—and innocent, vulnerable Sasha, whom he'd always pledged to care for and protect.

He wouldn't fail them, Charlie determined. He was enduring this animal-farm charade because the finance and facilities of the combined agencies were his best chance of rescuing Natalia and Sasha. None of which, from Jane Ambersom's almost sadistic dismissal earlier that day, were going to be made available to him. So it had to be just he, alone. Better, far better. He'd never liked—never trusted—other people with him or acting on his behalf: not so much from doubts of their loyalty but from doing things differently, less effectively, than he could.

Doing it by himself wasn't going to be easy, Charlie realistically acknowledged. Although he'd always insisted on working alone, there'd usually been an embassy upon which he could call for falsely named passports and air or road escape and cyberspace communications, if the ultimate shit hit the ever-spinning fan. And money: unlimited operational finance, safe openingly available whenever he needed it, which he always had, the more so since his marriage to Natalia. He'd date-staged the transfers from Jersey, so there'd still be some left there, once he'd got away from here. That wouldn't be as easy as slipping his leash the first time. But this was different. This, quite literally, was life or death: Natalia and Sasha's life or death. Nothing was going to prevent his keeping them alive: alive and eventually with him. At last.

James Straughan, who was an asexual bachelor, lived in Berkhamsted, almost sixty miles south of Charlie's Buckinghamshire interrogation lodge, with an almost totally disoriented mother whose evening meal he had just finished feeding her when his telephone rang.

"We've got a match," declared the duty officer at the Vauxhall headquarters of MI6.

"No doubt?" demanded Straughan, continuing with generalities because his was an insecure line, although the London call was being patched through a router.

"None. What do you want me to do?"

"Keep everything until I get there tomorrow." If he told Gerald Monsford tonight, the awkward bastard would probably have him immediately return to London personally to courier the stuff to the man's Cheyne Walk flat. Straughan considered cleaning, bathing, and getting his mother ready for bed a far more important duty.

Maxim Mikhailovich Radtsic patiently stood on the other side of the bed, watching Elana set aside her assortment of things, knowing from every neatly stacked item, predominantly photographs, that it was a selection she'd made and unmade several times before and hated her having to do it yet again.

"That's everything," she said triumphantly, looking up.

"No," he refused, bluntly. Watched by Elana, it had taken Radtsic two hours of fruitless searching for listening devices but he still insisted on loud radio music to defeat any monitoring installation.

"I've kept everything to the absolute minimum!" she protested, her voice wavering. "That's all our memories."

"I haven't been told yet how they're going to get us out but it'll almost certainly be by air. Luggage, even luggage going into the hold, is photographed. This amount—and these pictures—would be opened and trap us."

"I can't go with nothing!"

"You have to go with nothing. Everything is going to be new: our lives, our names, house, everything. All new. No history." It was madness talking, even softly, like this!

"I can't," she pleaded. "That'll be . . . that'll be dying."

"Staying here will be dying. Literally." This was asking too much of her.

"I don't care! I don't want to go. Won't go!"

"It wouldn't just be us. It would be Andrei, too."

"That's not fair."

"That's reality."

"Help me, Maxim! Please do something to help me!"

"I will. I promise I'll do something." What? he wondered, scrubbing the perspiration from his face with the back of his hand. Until this moment he'd never considered—had no conception—what field agents had to endure.

7

STRAUGHAN DID COMPROMISE BY LEAVING A NOTE FOR HIS mother's caregiver instead of waiting for the woman's arrival, which he normally did. He set off on the seven A.M. train and was at Vauxhall Cross by eight thirty and had personally reconfirmed the identification, determined from previous experience of Monsford's irrational impatience against any oversight reassuring himself that he topped the man's morning appointment book.

As he wasn't summoned until past eleven, Straughan knew Monsford had seen someone else before him and was doubly glad he hadn't bothered with an instant alert the night before. Playing out the melodrama to test the Director's reaction, Straughan unspeakingly placed the three enhanced infrared photographs on Monsford's desk and stood back, waiting.

"Who is he?" asked Monsford, not looking up from the prints.

"Boris Kuibyshev," identified Straughan. "Third secretary in the finance division of the Russian embassy here. These were taken last night outside Charlie Muffin's flat."

Monsford smiled up. "So my idea of leaking Charlie Muffin's address worked!"

You self-serving fuckpig, Straughan thought. He said: "Yes."

"Is he on the known list?"

Straughan shook his head. "We've had the flat under twenty-four-hour watch for the last two days, comparing every photograph against every print of the entire Russian legation and Russian trade and bank organizations. Kuibyshev wasn't flagged until now."

"So Smith's people won't have picked him up?"

"Not unless they've mounted the same watch and done the same face-by-face comparison," said Straughan. "And my team haven't seen anyone they recognize or suspect to be from across the river." He hesitated, intent upon squeezing a recorded accolade from the Director, who'd very positively activated his newly installed audio system. "This gives you unarguable proof that we're better qualified than MI5 to run things, doesn't it?"

Monsford grimaced rather than smiled. "Precisely what I wanted to achieve!"

"And there's something else: something that could be connected although there's no peg to hang it on at the moment," continued Straughan. "There was an overnight cable from David Halliday of rumors of something happening within the FSB."

"I don't trust Halliday," declared Monsford. "He was close to Muffin in Moscow during the Lvov business but didn't give us any indication to get us involved."

"He told us Charlie didn't confide in him," reminded Straughan, defensively.

"He must have known something. What's Halliday's source?"

"Cocktail-party gossip from a German embassy reception."

"Tell him to harden it up, beyond gossip. But tell Jacobson to stay away from Halliday. I don't want him involved in anything to do with Radtsic."

"And I'll maintain the watch on the flat: see if we can pick up any more new faces."

"Let's have what Shakespeare called the observed of all observers," quoted Monsford.

Straughan exaggerated his sigh. "Did Smith's people sanitize the flat?"

Monsford's face clouded at a question to which he didn't have an answer. "Why?"

"If I were controlling the Russian surveillance, I'd tell them to break in if the place continues to appear empty. By continuing to doorstep it, they must believe he's coming back."

"Good point," allowed Monsford. "I'll try to get an indication. Smith needs all the help and advice he can get."

"What do you think about Charlie Muffin?" persisted the operations director. "From the personnel and assignment files, do you think he's clean?"

Monsford's facial contortion really was a grimace this time. "I'd come down in his favor. The only thing that doesn't make sense is his marrying a woman in the FSB and before that the KGB."

"Don't the personnel assessments make a point of his not abiding by any rules?" asked Straughan, who believed he'd read everything more thoroughly than had the Director.

"That's not just breaking rules: that's the suicide wish Smith had the man examined for. He would have known he could never survive if it ever became known."

"So would she, but she still married him," argued Straughan.

"If you're making a point I'm missing it," complained Monsford.

"If he felt enough about her to go through a marriage ceremony—and she for him—he'll do anything and everything to get back to Russia to help her, whether Smith agrees or not."

Monsford frowned, disconcerted by another argument he hadn't understood. "Isn't that our whole objective?"

"I thought it was a factor worthwhile stressing to Smith."

"I've already got it flagged," lied Monsford.

"I don't want to keep Radtsic on hold. We're ready, apart from the security on a safe house."

"I'm seeing Smith at five to confront him with all the rest we've got."

"Do you want me to wait until you get back?" asked Straughan, warily. His mother's caregiver left at six.

"Yes," decided the Director. "By then I expect to hear something even more helpful from Moscow."

Awkward bastard, Straughan thought. He was sorry now that he'd asked instead of risking the wrath the following morning.

Before he'd completed his exercise-period reconnaissance of the outside security and failed on his return to his upstairs cell, as he had on his exit from it, to identify all the interior precautions, Charlie finally acknowledged that escape from his hunting-lodge prison was impossible.

Charlie slumped into a leather-creaking easy chair, head bowed to his chest again to continue the appearance of cowed acceptance, letting another half-formed idea harden. What could he do—what could he say or imply—to convince Aubrey Smith and Jane Ambersom that it was essential to *their* interests that Natalia and Sasha be brought out of Russia? And not just them. Gerald Monsford was involved, too. Why? Charlie abruptly asked himself, calling to mind his surprise at the MI6 Director's presence at his initial interrogation. Strict interpretation of the internal and external divisions between the two intelligence services would normally have decreed the Lvov affair to be that of MI6, except that it had begun with the finding in the Moscow grounds of the British embassy—internationally and diplomatically designated UK territory—of a man who had been tortured before being murdered. And even though his investigation later crossed MI6 boundaries, Aubrey Smith held off the participation demands of Gerald Monsford. So what had changed to bring Monsford in now? Could there still be an internal power problem, even though Jeffrey Smale's overthrow had failed? Or had Monsford been *invited* in by a still apprehensive Director-General in the hope of providing sideways-shifting blame for an as-yet-unknown disaster? For which his being married to a serving FSB officer would unquestionably qualify.

He'd traveled too far down rough-track side roads leading nowhere, Charlie accepted: properly understanding the reason for Monsford's presence had to remain a work in progress in a situation in which he appeared to be making very little progress. What lure could he find sufficient to convince the Director-General that getting Natalia and Sasha out was in the national interest instead of solely his? The only conceivable—and necessarily official—argument was that if left in Moscow, Natalia represented a national security problem for Britain. And he'd already double-locked the door from both sides—and bolted it top and bottom—against that contention. His entirely truthful and personal defense against Official Secrets prosecution was that they'd never exchanged the secrets of either side. To vary that now could lead to charges being proffered while at the same time further nullifying any possibility of gaining their freedom.

And then, physically blinking at its total clarity, the unarguable resolution came to him. He doubted that Natalia would cooperate by disclosing the secrets of a twenty-year-long Russian intelligence career, but Smith and Monsford wouldn't know that until she and Sasha were safe. And it didn't matter, either, that her refusal would expose his deception, making it impossible for him to remain in the service: he was already in a protection program anyway.

He could make it work! Charlie told himself. He *had* to make it work!

The sphinxlike Aubrey Smith glanced fleetingly at Monsford's offered photographs before putting them to one side and said: "Yes. Boris Kuibyshev." The Director-General took other, different prints from a side drawer and handed them in return to the other man. "This is Igor Bukharin, who's also listed in the embassy's finance section. Did you miss him?"

Monsford didn't hurry taking the easy chair to which Smith gestured, inwardly furious at the mockery. "We only began the check last night. We wouldn't have bothered if you'd told me you were already monitoring the place."

"It was such an obvious precaution I didn't think it necessary."

"You considered the possibility that they might burgle it, as well?" demanded the MI6 Director, struggling to keep up.

Smith smiled, wanly. "I've been expecting them to, ever since we identified the surveillance. It was swept clean the day we put Charlie into the protection program. There's nothing for them to find. Except the surprise I've got in place."

"What about the answering machine, with Natalia's voice on it?" Monsford retaliated.

The condescending smile remained. "From inside the flat, the receiver appears disconnected. The line's on divert, to our technical people who pick up every incoming call as well as the slightest audible sound of forced entry. They'd also hear if there were an attempted outgoing call if the Russians do go in and try to report back to their embassy Control."

Monsford hoped the fury, which was making him physically hot, wasn't registering on his face. "What's the surprise you've got waiting for them?"

The MI6 Director listened with his head bowed, more to conceal any facial redness than in concentration. When Smith finished, Monsford said: "I'd have appreciated hearing all this earlier."

"It's a contingency plan that might never be activated," reminded Smith. "Of course you would have been told in advance. If it became necessary."

At least he had more time to decide if there could be any benefit to him, Monsford realized. "It's the PM's personal decision we cooperate, so it's right I should tell you that we're getting indications from Moscow of something happening within the FSB."

Smith gave no response to the implied rebuke. "What?"

"I've ordered a specific inquiry," said Monsford, inadequately.

"You suggesting there's a connection?"

"I'm suggesting it's a possibility that shouldn't be overlooked." He needed more, much more, agonized Monsford.

"Let's not overlook it then," patronized the Director-General.

"What's your feeling about Charlie Muffin's interrogation?" asked Monsford, unsettled by the other man's superiority.

"I think they're using Natalia as bait."

It wasn't just dismissiveness, decided Monsford. The bloody man was positively excluding him. "What's Ambersom's opinion?"

"She thinks he went over a long time ago: that while our intention was for Charlie's defection to be phoney, Natalia turned him and he was sent back as a double. And now it's all gone badly wrong for them, this is a clumsy way of trying to get him safely to Moscow."

"The facts don't fit her argument," rejected Monsford.

"What's your take?"

Monsford was annoyed at continuing to be the respondent instead of the questioner. "I don't believe Charlie Muffin is a traitor. Every analysis of every assignment going back an entire year *before* the fake defection shows a lot of improvisation but not a single loyalty-questioning inconsistency."

"Right," agreed Smith.

"Against which I can't reconcile his marrying a serving officer in an opposition service—" Monsford held up his hand against interruption. "And don't give me any love-is-blind, there's-always-an-exception-to-the-rule nonsense. He's a professional—a *very* professional—operative whom I'd have welcomed with open arms crossing the river to my side."

"What do you think we should do?"

"I was waiting for you to tell me," evaded Monsford.

"Charlie Muffin *is* a complete professional," agreed Smith. "As such, he knew exactly what he was doing when he married Natalia Fedova and the consequences if it became known. He's now got to face those consequences. He'll be kept safe in the protection program and the woman will have to suffer whatever fate the Russians choose for her when they realize we're not taking their bait. I sympathize with them both, but they each knew the inevitable outcome if they got caught out."

His entire fucking alternative operation was going down the drain, thought Monsford, desperately. "We both of us know Charlie won't accept that, just as we both acknowledge how good he is. He'd abandon the protection and give you the slip, as he did a few days ago. Except this time he'll go to Russia instead."

The Director-General shook his head. "He couldn't do that without backup resources, which he doesn't have."

"You want to run the risk of his trying, which he will, and create a huge diplomatic incident?"

"You proposing we eliminate him?" There was no outrage in Smith's voice.

"I'm arguing we shouldn't close everything down as quickly as you seem to be suggesting," said Monsford. "I also believe it would be an argument that those who crack the whip in Downing Street would consider a validation."

"I don't think . . ." began Smith, but was stopped by the burp of an internal telephone. He listened for several moments before interrupting, sharply: "You know what to do. Do it!"

To Monsford's inquiring look, Smith said: "The Russians have just broken into Charlie's flat. And there's been fresh contact from Moscow. It's being voiceprinted to make sure it's Natalia Fedova."

"Isn't one thing going to complicate the other?"

"I don't see why it should," said Smith. "We'll have to see, won't we?"

He wasn't manipulating events, despaired Monsford. And he didn't know how to reverse the situation.

It was the first time they'd met, at Maxim Radtsic's insistence, in Jacobson's car. An enclosed vehicle was the easiest for an entrapment, so as a precaution Jacobson drove several times past the pickup point from every possible approach to satisfy himself there were no ambush preparations in the immediate side streets. There weren't, but Jacobson, who'd never before been involved in an extraction and was even less used to having the deputy director of Russian intelligence dependent upon him, wasn't reassured, his stomach in turmoil as, precisely on time, he made his final approach, still only minimally relieved at the sight of the Russian waiting as arranged. That relief vanished when he realized that the clumsiness with which Radtsic fumbled open the passenger door was caused by his carrying a suitcase in one hand. So instinctive was it for Jacobson to drive off that he briefly took his foot off the brake, making the car jump and almost toppling the Russian, who was only partially in, the suitcase ahead of him. It was a separate instinct for Jacobson to snatch the case farther in and haul the Russian behind it, letting the next forward lurch slam the door closed.

"What the fuck!" exploded Jacobson, finally thrusting the suitcase away from his shoulder into the rear of the vehicle. He was only vaguely aware of the clatter of loose things, his concentration tensed for the siren scream of arrest.

"Very much what the fuck!" returned the Russian, pushing himself upright.

"What's happening? . . . What's in the case . . . ?"

Radtsic recovered first. "I'm the senior FSB deputy: you actually think I would act as bait, for your seizure!"

Jacobson's fear was molding into humiliation at his overreaction. "We never talked about a case . . . about your carrying anything."

"It's not a bomb, Harry. And our listening devices are miniaturized, just like yours. The case contains all the personal things that Elana wants to take with her. But with which we'd never get past airport security."

Jacobson was glad the darkness would cover the redness flaming his face. "You should have warned me."

"Yes, I should, shouldn't I?"

"You frightened me," admitted Jacobson.

"I'm sorry." The Russian jerked his head back toward the case. "You can ship that out in the diplomatic bag, can't you?"

"I suppose . . . yes, of course we can. Will there be anything more?"

"I'd hoped there wouldn't be the need for many more meetings: that you were going to tell me the final details tonight."

"It's close. But not yet."

"Not too much longer: I can't wait too much longer. Neither can Elana."

"You won't have to," promised Jacobson, hoping he was right.

"I've told my father," announced Yvette Paruch. She was sitting naked at Andrei's dressing table, until then methodically counting aloud the brushstrokes to her waist-length, deeply black hair but looking at him in the mirror's reflection.

"You're exciting me, sitting like that." Andrei Maximovich was naked, too, still sprawled across their bed.

"I can see for myself." Yvette smiled, into the mirror. "I said I've told my father I've moved in with you."

"What did he say?"

"That he hoped I was sure. And to be careful not to become pregnant until I was."

"What did you say?"

"That I was but that I wouldn't get pregnant."

"Did you tell him I'm Russian?"

"No."

"Why not?"

"You know why not."

"So I'm not going to meet him?"

"He invited us down for the vacation."

"Do you want to go?"

"I want him to meet the man I'm in love with."

"He'll pick up my accent: know I'm not French."

"Are you frightened?"

"Having survived the Nazi occupation of Warsaw but seen both his parents killed by Russian soldiers, I think he deserves to be told in advance, not when we get there."

"One hundred!" she declared, finishing her routine, swiveling on her stool to face him. “What about you? Are you going to tell your parents?”

“Not yet.”

“Why not?”

“I don’t choose to.”

“Does that mean you don’t love me? That it’s just more convenient to fuck me if I live here instead of staying on in my own apartment?”

“That’s ridiculous and dirty and you know it!”

“Why not then! Because I’m Jewish?”

“You’re being ridiculous: intentionally making an argument. Stop it!”

“You know everything about me. I don’t know anything about you. Let’s not go down to Aix for the vacation. Take me to Moscow instead.”

“I’d rather go to Aix.”

“I’d rather go to Moscow.”

“We’ll think about it.”

“You’re not excited anymore,” she said, giggling.

“No, I’m not, am I?” he agreed.

8

CHARLIE SLEPT INTERMITTENTLY, AWARE OF THE INFRARED monitoring, and feigned sleep when he'd been awake, his concentration entirely upon how to reverse some of the impressions he'd conveyed during his original questioning in the desperate hope of gaining some personal involvement in the rescue of Natalia and Sasha. He'd stupidly confronted them, outargued the ridiculously mind-seized deputy director-general, for Christ's sake! He could probably deceive a woman as obdurate as Jane Ambersom but realistically it wouldn't be as easy with either Aubrey Smith or Gerald Monsford. And not just them. The recordings would be reexamined and soberly reanalyzed, every pause and nuance tested for the slightest suspicion-prompting, overeager ambiguity. Ambersom had been more than overeager. Desperate: as desperate as Natalia had increasingly sounded during the pleading calls that had been torturously played back to him.

Charlie wished he could listen to those recordings again. The words had registered and he'd known it was Natalia's voice and not an impersonation, but in that brief, totally startled awareness he hadn't properly *heard* them. Not the intonations or hesitations or an emphasis she might have imposed for him to gauge how exposed she and Sasha were. No, he didn't need to hear the recording, Charlie corrected himself, once more refusing the self-deception. He knew *exactly* how exposed Natalia and Sasha were, just as he knew the pressure under which she'd been put to make the calls. He couldn't—wouldn't—fail her this time. Had she failed him? Charlie frowned at the unthinking jealousy, straining for recall. Igor Karakov, he remembered: a teacher at Sasha's school. Just as quickly as the doubt came, Charlie rejected it. A friend, Natalia had said when he'd been in Moscow the last time: only a friend. She wouldn't lie.

As he had earlier, escaping from Chelsea, Charlie fought against the impatience to get up earlier than usual, to be ready. If Smith or Monsford didn't isolate his eagerness, the visually watching, voiceprinting analysts might. He actually remained in bed longer than normal but, as he had for the Jersey expedition, caught up during his showering and shaving, noting the outside rain.

"You got umbrellas?" he asked the guard, when his breakfast rolls and coffee arrived: if the debriefing was to be before noon, there wouldn't be morning exercise.

Predictably there was no response. Charlie ate half a roll he didn't want and crumbled the remainder to disguise how much he'd left and took his customary second cup of coffee, which that morning he didn't want either. He didn't try to read beyond the headlines of *The Times* that had come with his food, but did it twice to prevent the cursoriness being obvious. There was no newspaper connection with the Lvov episode, but to double check—as well as to fill time—Charlie scrolled through the Sky and BBC news channels and drew another blank. Charlie's hopes rose when there was no exercise escort accompanying the breakfast retrieval and they grew when the exercise delay extended to twenty minutes. It reached a full thirty before the two men arrived. Neither wore a waterproof.

Charlie said: "We're going to get wet."

The man in charge said: "The rain will have stopped by this afternoon," and Charlie's surprise at getting a response collided with the satisfaction of knowing there was going to be another interrogation.

He had to proceed slower than a snail with hammer-toed flat feet as painful as his own, Charlie reminded himself, entering the familiar animal-murder room.

———

The three faced him in the same order as before but with the addition today of the replay machine, from which at once Charlie knew there'd been further Moscow contact. It was important for him to hear the new recording before making his intended pitch. The delay would enable him to detect attitude changes among those sitting in judgement upon him: to detect the slightest nuance to help what he wanted to achieve. Gerald Monsford sat Buddha-like with his hands familiarly cupping his expansive stomach, as if it required support. Charlie thought Jane Ambersom's buttoned-to-the-neck Mao suit the perfect if outdated uniform for an indeterminately sexed torturer and at once stifled his wandering reflections. There had to be only one undivided concentration today and it didn't include antagonism toward the deputy director-general, of whose personal dislike he'd already had too much evidence. It was Aubrey Smith who opened the session, which momentarily surprised Charlie.

The man said: "There've been some developments."

Some developments, isolated Charlie. "What?"

"Three Russians accredited to their embassy here burgled your flat last night."

Was there something here that he could twist to his advantage? wondered Charlie, hopefully. "Were they caught?"

"They're currently in custody," said the Director-General. "They'll claim diplomatic immunity, of course. But it's a criminal offense and we're going to use it to the maximum."

"What's that mean?" pressed Charlie, curious at the unexpected leniency of the exchange.

"You're dead," announced Monsford, hurrying to appear more visibly and audibly participating than he'd so far been. "The death certificate is dated six weeks ago." He looked theatrically at his watch. "By now there'll be a named headstone on an old grave in Moss Side, Manchester—where your false identity legend has you being christened—and the church burial records will have been registered accordingly. . . ."

"That cover legend, unmarried bachelor clerk in a government pensions office, is fully in place—as you know it has been for years—and will easily satisfy the sort of media inquiries that'll follow the Russians being named," picked up Smith, seeing the other Director's intrusion as confirmation of the man's glory-seeking determination. With pointed clarification, he went on: "I've got the mystery already prepared—why should three accredited Russian diplomats burgle the no-longer-rented apartment of a very minor, now dead civil servant who has no surviving family and no known friends?"

Charlie didn't let his mild impatience at the double act cloud his recognition of danger. "I was identified—pictured on Moscow television—during the Lvov investigation."

"Not under the name in which your flat was rented and it won't be your photograph we'll leak to the media," refused Smith.

Charlie saw an opening but hesitated, deciding to wait. "Moscow—the FSB—won't accept any of it."

"Of course they won't," agreed Monsford, choosing his intervening moment. "What they will accept is that you are in a protection program in which they don't stand a chance of ever finding you and that the Vauxhall flat was nothing more than a major embarrassment trap that's cost them three agents, two of them unidentified until today. To lose that many is bad enough and what they won't know but which will terrify them is that we'll expose their failed Lvov operation. We burned them with Lvov and now we've rubbed salt into very painfully sore wounds."

And the FSB had Natalia and Sasha, balanced Charlie. The fragile opening hadn't widened, as he'd hoped. He'd wanted a lot more. There was still the unheard recording. Indicating the side table, he said: "There's been contact from Natalia, hasn't there?"

"It'll be the last, after the arrests," predicted Jane Ambersom, finally entering the discussion.

"Can I hear it?"

In the time it took the woman to activate the machine, Charlie prepared himself, determined against the slightest reaction to Natalia's voice. The initial seconds of traffic sounds were louder than before: an open street pod, not an enclosed kiosk, he guessed. When it finally came—to a stomach jump, despite Charlie's expectation—Natalia's voice was unexpectedly even, as if she'd prepared herself. "They're examining my debriefing records. I don't know how much they suspect. Remember, Charlie . . ." The cutoff was abrupt, either Natalia hurriedly putting down the receiver or having it snatched away and slammed back by someone else.

Charlie had let his head drop, not forgetting his earlier determination against reaction but cultivating it now, although undecided whether seeming to seize this late some significance from what Natalia had said would appear too obviously staged. But could he realistically hope for anything more? Jane had rejoined the two directors and all three were staring expectantly at him as Charlie looked up. The moment he did, the overly aggressive woman said: "What's the matter with you?" and despite her uncertain sexuality, Charlie would have willingly kissed her. Instead he shook his head, as if confused, continuing to string out a response.

"What's wrong?" repeated the woman.

It had to look as if the realization was starting out half formed and needed to be coaxed from him. "She's very frightened: more frightened than she ever was when we had to be careful in Moscow. But she believes they know about us. And if they do, she's realized she's caught up in the biggest espionage coup Russia has ever attempted: the total *failure* of the biggest espionage coup Russia ever attempted. They'll be convinced—any intelligence organization would—that she knew I was going to wreck it."

Jane Ambersom turned and said something inaudible to the Director-General but to which Smith shook his head, not turning to her. The man said: "Is there something important in what you've just heard?"

They weren't dismissing him out of hand! Charlie said: "What she *hopes* I've understood from what I've just heard. She's made an offer, her bargain, for her and Sasha to be got out."

Histrionically, Jane pushed herself back into her chair, snorting in customary derision. "Do you possibly imagine, in whatever dream world you're living, that you'll convince us that we've got to get your supposed wife and daughter out of Russia?"

The totally fixated deputy director could have chosen what other part of her androgynous body she wanted kissed or otherwise caressed, decided Charlie, in further gratitude. "You've established Natalia is not my *supposed* wife but my legally married wife?"

"Yes," confirmed Monsford, before either of the others.

Concentrating upon the MI6 Director, Charlie went on: "And you've also established, from studying my assignment record, that I have never sabotaged anything involving this organization during my marriage or association with Natalia?"

"Yes," agreed Monsford, again.

Continuing to address the MI6 chief, Charlie chanced the slightest of exaggerations: "And you know, from her length of service not just with the current FSB but the previous KGB that she's not just *a* but *the* senior debriefer for Russian external intelligence. You're intelligence experts, all three of you. But not even you can begin to imagine the number of defectors and spy offers and doubles and dissidents she's interrogated: the answers she could provide to the mysteries and uncertainties over the past twenty years."

"Are you trying to persuade us that's what she's offering by her reference to your debriefing records?" asked the quiet-voiced Aubrey Smith, even more softly than usual.

"I'm not trying to convince you," said Charlie. "That's what I'm *telling* you, as honestly as I've told you everything else."

"If she had all that to offer, why didn't she come with you in the first place?" clumsily challenged Jane.

I could have done a ventriloquist's act with this woman, thought Charlie. "Because until now she hasn't confronted the reality of a firing squad after undergoing interrogation that she knows would extend beyond her sort of debriefing into the KGB-perfected horror of psychiatric hospitals. While all the time knowing—because they'd remind her every day, as the most horrific part of that torture—that

Sasha would be committed to the worst of Russian state orphanages."

"The psychiatrist was right. The man's mad," declared Jane Ambersom. They'd once more moved from the formality of the interview after Charlie's departure but she was unable to sit, instead pacing up and down in front of the dead fireplace around which the easy chairs were set.

"The psychological assessment wasn't that he was mentally ill," corrected the Director-General. "It was that Charlie Muffin would recognize more quickly than anyone else the limitations of a new life in a protection program—which indicated the highest analytical intelligence that Cowley had known—as a result of which Charlie was suffering an understandable depression but which he doubted would ever become suicidal. The suicide watch was a shock warning to Charlie, not a necessary precaution."

"I don't believe there can be a single opposing argument against our getting Natalia and the child out of Moscow," declared Monsford, who'd gone through the charade of calling MI6's Vauxhall Cross building—on his cell phone from Charlie's exercise patch—before returning for the review.

"Which has to mean there's an update from your call?" sardonically questioned the fidgeting deputy director.

"There's already open speculation on *Izvestia* and in *Pravda* of retaliatory rebuttals to our arrests."

"Why should I be surprised about that?" challenged the woman.

"*Moscow News* is going further," continued Monsford, who'd added to what he considered his success in getting the address of Charlie's London flat leaked to the Russians by swallowing his antipathy to David Halliday and authorizing the suggestion being offered by Halliday to the man's contact in the English-language publication. "They're hardening the rumor into a reciprocal intelligence sensation. It's being picked up and repeated on Western wire services."

"There's not the slightest indication that what's going on in Moscow has any connection whatsoever with what we're discussing here, beyond some obviously enforced telephone contact from a woman stupid enough to trust Charlie Muffin," rejected Jane. "Our stupidly responding to it is the intended reciprocal intelligence sensation."

"If Natalia's got as much as half of what Charlie sketched out, it's a gold lode we could mine for years," judged Aubrey Smith, reflectively. "There's no obvious connection, but it would be on a par with the Lvov business. We could tie in knots not just Russian intelligence but every other service of any importance, up to and including the CIA, who've double-crossed and used us, both of us, for the past two decades."

"There can't be an argument against getting her and the child out," repeated Monsford, anxious to stoke the other man's belief.

"Except the obvious one that it's a trap, a match—maybe even more than a match—for what the Russians fell into by burgling Charlie's flat," Jane persisted.

"I'd like us to continue our cooperation by actively considering a joint rescue operation," declared Monsford, dismissing the woman's opposition.

"Why joint?" demanded Jane, instantly seeing the possibility of personal revenge. "You want her and the child, why don't you get them out by yourself."

"Willingly, despite their being the wife and daughter of one of your officers," accepted Monsford, confronting the expected question. "You couldn't, of course, expect us to share whatever she told us of all those famous defectors you didn't know were spying against this country until they gave their press conferences in Moscow."

He had no alternative but to go along with Monsford, decided Aubrey Smith, although not for the reasons the MI6 Director was advocating. He'd only too recently survived an internecine war: he wasn't going to risk walking away from this one until he knew far more than was immediately obvious. "Let's start the planning tomorrow."

"I want put on written record my total opposition to any of this," insisted Jane Ambersom.

There was an echoing silence, each man hoping the other would respond to give him a follow-up advantage. Monsford, believing himself to have the most to gain, broke first. "I'm confused. First you demand to be included in whatever we do. Now you demand your complete opposition placed on provable record. Have I missed something in what we've been discussing?"

"My matching confusion also," quickly came in Aubrey Smith, denying the SIS director whatever he'd set out to achieve.

Surprisingly, there was no renewed flush from the woman at this new confrontation. She said: "I don't see any dichotomy. You intend a reaction that risks both our organizations being exposed to international ridicule and derision. While opposing whatever you do—and wanting that opposition recognized—I believe my continued involvement as devil's advocate to be absolutely essential to maintain a balancing voice."

The immediate impression of Aubrey Smith, who was fundamentally as honest and subjective as possible in the professional position he occupied, was that his recently imposed deputy had established a necessarily important safeguard. Gerald Monsford's equally quick thought was that Jane Ambersom had put herself forward as a further—and an additional—sacrificial offering if his real objective went wrong, which even the best laid espionage plans so frequently did.

Responding first, the MI6 Director said: "You bring to mind Tennyson's line of Janus-faces looking diverse ways."

"I defer to your superior knowledge not just of classics but the art of the two-faced," Jane shot back. "Didn't Tennyson also remark that men may come and men may go but others lasting longer?"

"Has anyone got anything further to offer?" demanded Aubrey Smith, impatiently.

"I suspect Jane believes herself outnumbered," Monsford said, flushed. "Why don't we achieve a better balance by adding Rebecca to our panel."

It would give her the opportunity to oppose the whore, Jane Ambersom realized. "I think that's an excellent suggestion."

It would probably put him at a three-to-one disadvantage, but at any disaster inquest Monsford's manipulative hand would be more obvious, rationalized Smith. "If it's the decision of the prime minister for this to be a joint operation, it establishes complete equality," he appeared to concede.

"I look forward to tomorrow," said Monsford, believing himself the victor.

"So do I," said the woman, believing the same for herself.

Which was the more murderous place to be, Moscow or here in London? wondered Aubrey Smith. He'd have to be very careful that having survived once, none of his own blood was spilled, either literally or figuratively.

An hour later the London *Evening Standard* broke the story of the Russian burglary of Charlie Muffin's flat.

An essential attribute for an intelligence officer is the ability to become a wallpaper person, someone able to merge indistinguishably into any background or surrounding. Harry Jacobson practiced the art more assiduously than most, as he was practicing it now, doubly invisible deep within the shadows of a buttressed, prerevolutionary wall opposite Natalia Fedova's Moscow apartment on Pecatnikov Pereulok. The determination to perfect a chameleon camouflage developed early in his MI6 career, spurred by the fear that his noticeably cleft lip, a birth defect, would preclude his becoming a field operative, to overcome which he'd consciously adopted the appearance of a shoe-polished, department-store-suited bank clerk, complete with wire-framed spectacles and closely cropped hair. To conceal the harelip he cultivated an unclipped, walrus-style mustache that matched his hair's natural blondeness, the disguise now so accustomed that it was not until this reflective moment that the facial similarity between himself and Radtsic's heavy Stalin-like growth occurred to him. It could, decided Jacobson, be his escape from this additional surveillance assignment upon Natalia Fedova, which he resented as an extra and unnecessary burden. It was very definitely an objection to be put to James Straughan, maybe even as early as tonight.

Natalia Fedova arrived, on foot, at precisely the same time as she had the previous two evenings, wearing the same light summer coat and carrying the same briefcase, as always in her left hand with the entry key in her right. And, again as worrying as the previous two evenings, unaccompanied by the child who had until now always been with her.

London weren't going to like the absence, Jacobson decided: they weren't going to like or understand it at all.

9

THEY DIDN'T.

"We could be too late," suggested James Straughan, keeping any satisfaction from his voice at the possibility of Monsford's having miscalculated.

"It could mean a lot of other things, too," argued Rebecca Street, loyally. As usual, she was giving the Director the full benefit of a plunging décolletage.

"Being too late is the most obvious," insisted Straughan, who'd intentionally held back from announcing Sasha's apparent disappearance during the mutual-congratulation orgy between the MI6 Director and his deputy at Monsford's maneuvering Rebecca onto the planning group, savoring the moment of deflation. Although well aware she wouldn't comprehend a single word, Straughan intended telling his mother about it that evening: he had a fading hope that his nightly monologues might get through to her.

"Why didn't you tell me earlier that we hadn't seen the child for so long?" suspiciously demanded Monsford, who hadn't activated his personal recording facility.

"I didn't want to be premature. After three days I decided it should be flagged up." Sometimes, thought Straughan, he feared this devious man would send him mad.

"What else?" said Rebecca.

"I don't think we should use Jacobson to monitor Natalia's apartment," cautioned Straughan. "If the child has been taken from her, the place will be under permanent surveillance. Jacobson could be isolated."

"It's a possibility," conceded Monsford, who'd led the other two through an hour's review of Radtsic's extraction before Straughan's revelation. "I don't like the uncertainty this introduces."

"It needn't materially change what we've agreed," encouraged the woman. "We're intending a diversion with Natalia, not a genuine extraction."

"It's an uncertainty we've no way of controlling," repeated Monsford.

"How does it impact upon what we've discussed?" pressed Straughan, who'd considered Jane Ambersom a friend and wished he'd been less cowardly and confronted Monsford's apportion onto her of all his own misconceptions over Lvov. Now Straughan was enjoying Monsford's evident stress in front of a woman he wanted to impress.

"All Natalia's got to do is make another bloody telephone call: Smith's keeping Charlie's apartment line open," Monsford pointed out.

"I thought we'd decided she's reciting what the FSB tells her to say?"

"What if she somehow gets an unmonitored call out?" demanded Monsford. "Don't forget Shakespeare's warning of pernicious women."

"We'll confuse ourselves going around in hypothetical circles," risked Rebecca.

"She'd have said more if she'd been able," persisted Straughan, ignoring the warning.

"We're gaining nothing by speculating," insisted the woman. "The kid's missing and that's that. It's not our complication."

"We won't allow it to become one," said Monsford, decisive at last. "We don't tell Smith or Ambersom. Tell Jacobson to take any cable traffic referring to it off the general file."

"There's no cable traffic about Radtsic—or Muffin or Natalia's inclusion in his extraction—on the general file," scored Straughan, pleased at the small victory. "You ordered it a dedicated, Eyes Only file restricted to us three, remember? I haven't even told Jacobson why we're maintaining surveillance on Natalia Fedova."

"Of course I remember what I ordered," snapped Monsford, testily. "And don't wait another three days before briefing me on anything relevant to what we're doing."

"I'll instruct the cipher room and the duty officer to alert me at once, irrespective of time: you'll know within minutes of my knowing," assured Straughan, fantasizing himself interrupting Monsford in the final seconds of his nightly pony ride with Rebecca.

"That fucking man is insufferable!" declared the woman, minutes after Straughan left, knowing that was what Monsford wanted her to say.

"His card's marked: he's just too stupid to suspect he's going to fall upon what Shelley called the thorns of life," said Monsford, furious at the lack of respect from both Straughan and the woman.

She smiled, despite the implication that she'd overstepped the familiarity, gesturing toward the window and the sluggishly meandering Thames. "Another transfer across the river?"

"Maybe." Monsford smiled back, emptily. He feared that Straughan had a meticulously kept graveyard map of where far too many skeletons—literally and figuratively—were buried for any serious move against the man.

Aubrey Smith had never intended he and his deputy would be the first at the hunting lodge, but neither to be in the psychologically disadvantaged position of having to apologize for their lateness caused by a road-closing accident on their way. Having to do so relegated them to the secondary role in which Smith had hoped to place the MI6 duo, the initial setback furthered, despite briefing her in advance, by Jane Ambersom's below-zero frigidity at Rebecca Street's inclusion in the top executive group. The debacle was very intentionally exacerbated by the warmness of Rebecca's near-suffocating response to their apologies, assuring them the two-hour postponement had not been at all inconvenient ("the duck confit at lunch was wonderful and the 1962 burgundy exceptional") and the tour of the lodge magnificent, prompting Gerald—pointedly not Director Monsford—and her to wish they had such safe houses at their disposal.

"But these are particularly unusual circumstances, aren't they?" Rebecca concluded. For once the Chanel business suit was severely practical, although the inherent sexual frisson still sharply contrasted with its absence from the trouser-suited Jane.

"Have you spoken with Charlie?" Smith hurried on, anxious to get beyond the late-arrival discomfort.

"You're in charge . . ." Monsford continued to patronize. He gestured toward a small conference table, with a five-chair setting replacing the earlier tribunal formality. "We've waited for your seating arrangements."

Without replying, Smith put Jane beside him, nodding to the others to choose their places.

"What about Charlie Muffin?" asked the MI6 deputy.

"Not until we've talked things through," refused Smith, recovering slightly. "I want us to be absolutely clear about what we're going to do and how we're going to do it, without the slightest possibility of misunderstandings."

"It's surely all remarkably simple," Monsford bustled in, impatient to assume the other Director's authority. "We've got the photographs my people took of Natalia and Sasha. We can put prints into genuine British passports, although obviously under false, English names. In the passports there'll be Russian tourist visas: my technical division have provable Russian inks and Cyrillic type fonts for entry and exit stamps. The photographs are good enough for my technical experts again to gauge with sufficient accuracy both the height, weight, and physique of Natalia and the child, for a complete selection of English-manufactured and -labeled clothes, sufficiently worn for them not to appear obviously new. Everything will be shipped to the embassy in the diplomatic bag. My *rezidentura* there will put together a choice of Russian souvenirs a mother and her daughter would be expected to bring back to England. We make contact with Natalia and arrange a pickup—that's going to need a lot more detailed consideration, if they're under tight surveillance—to get them to the embassy, where everything I've set out will be waiting, including their confirmed reservations on a direct British Airways flight to London. . . ."

The pause was as prepared as the recitation for Rebecca to come in on cue: "Taking the urgency into account, our technicians have already started work on the passports and the clothing."

"You might like to hold on that," stopped the other woman. "We've already prepared a complete documentation selection."

Smith enjoyed the stretched silence, reluctant to snap it. "You seem to have started a little prematurely."

"As you have," challenged Monsford.

" 'You're in charge,' " quoted Smith, verbatim. "Isn't that what you said?"

"This isn't a competition." stated Rebecca, her overeffusiveness gone.

"Absolutely not," mocked Jane.

"The problem isn't one of technical resources or facilities: we can forge or manufacture whatever we need," stressed Smith, content that the balance had been restored. "The problem is physically getting under our protection—and in a way that can't diplomatically or publicly rebound—a woman and child presumably under FSB surveillance. How do you suggest we do that?"

"That's what Gerald meant about detailed consideration," said Rebecca.

"The entire purpose of this meeting," reminded Jane, as conscious as Aubrey Smith of their recovery. "What's your proposal?"

"She and the child have to come to the embassy by themselves," improvised Monsford, looking to his mistress for support.

"Once they're in the building, technically British territory . . ." tried Rebecca, loyally.

"That territorial protection would cease the moment Natalia and

Sasha took one step *outside* the embassy." Smith sighed. "But we're assuming they're under tight surveillance. How do you get a message to Natalia to go to the embassy without it being intercepted by those watching her? And—assuming that somehow you do—can you prevent their being seized long before they get into the embassy in the first place?"

"At this moment I haven't the slightest idea," conceded the SIS Director, although not as an admission of defeat. "This is a planning session, for each of us to give the most constructive input. What's your contact proposal?"

"Diversions," declared the MI5 Director-General, enigmatically. "By letting the Russians imagine we've taken their bait and that we're coming for mother and daughter. But then introduce diversion after diversion to send them around in circles until they don't know which is the genuine extraction and which isn't."

"They don't need to run around in circles," disputed Rebecca. "They've got Natalia and Sasha. They're the only people the FSB need constantly to watch."

"You're looking in the wrong direction, which is what I intend them to do," argued the soft-voiced Smith. "Of course they've got Natalia and Sasha. But Natalia and Sasha aren't who they really want, are they? They want Charlie Muffin."

"You're proposing to send him back in!" exclaimed Rebecca, in apparent surprise.

"No," denied Smith. "But they'll think it'll be Charlie Muffin and from the moment they're convinced it is, their entire concentration will be upon finding him. It's Charlie—or their belief that it's Charlie—who's going to be the diversion."

"How?" demanded Rebecca, knowing the importance of reestablishing their briefly imagined supremacy.

"Easily," said Smith, allowing the vaguest of smiles. "Natalia's calls were from ordinary public telephones—one more specifically than others—because we were expected, naturally, to trace their origin. Just as we, or rather Charlie, was expected to recognize that the calls to his flat were always at precisely the same time, giving him a pattern. But they wouldn't have been ordinary public kiosks, would they? They'll appear to be, but they'll have recording attachments, automatically triggered by an incoming international call signal, in anticipation of Charlie responding to the numbers, not that of Natalia's flat. So Charlie will respond, at the precise time which she—or rather the FSB—has established."

"What if she's not there at the appointed time?" challenged Monsford. "There hasn't been any contact from Moscow since the burglary. There wasn't any response to her calls before then. And from the Russian embassy lawyers who've already had legal access to their diplomats in custody here, they'll know the flat was empty. And we created the legend of his death, so they'll also know he's under protection."

"We've already agreed they won't accept that legend," Jane pointed out.

"Any more than they'll accept Charlie's sudden reappearance is anything more than our trying to lure them into a trap they won't be able to understand, just as they didn't understand—or anticipate—the burglary snare we set for them," said Rebecca. "But they won't risk being burned twice."

"Exactly!" agreed Jane, triumphantly. "They won't accept it and they won't understand it. But they can't afford to ignore it. And before this afternoon's over we need to come up with an even more tantalizing bait. . . ." Jane paused, caught by the presented analogy. "Our fishing line, Natalia and Sasha's safety net."

"Charlie Muffin is the integral part in this," declared Monsford, desperate to get off the constantly teetering back foot. "Isn't it time we included him in this discussion?"

Charlie Muffin had a savant's instinct for atmospheres within environments and was well into his clairvoyant interpretation by the time he shuffled, unescorted now, from the trophy-room door to the conference table already unevenly hedged by its four stiffly seated occupants.

Only the one empty chair retained its neat setting, the others at disjointed angles, separating each from its neighbors. There were coffee cups, similarly disarranged—the discarded coffeepot alone on a side table—supporting the impression of prior discussion, although there wasn't a single doodle on any of the individual memo pads before them. There was one as-yet-unknown woman closer to Gerald Monsford than to either Aubrey Smith or Jane Ambersom, similarly drawn together, both expressionless faces as stiff as their rigidly held attitudes.

Charlie went to the empty chair but didn't sit until Smith's head jerk of permission, and as he did the MI5 Director announced: "We want to get your wife and child out. It's obvious you should be included in the discussion."

"Thank you," said Charlie, who hadn't expected such immediate confirmation but pushing as much genuine sincerity into the two words as possible, finally halting the individually addressed gratitude at the unknown woman, who at once introduced herself.

Having been offered the opening, Charlie added: "At what stage is the planning?"

"It's starting here, right now," declared Smith, although looking more to Gerald Monsford than to Charlie. "Perhaps you'd sketch out the SIS ideas in broad outline."

The MI6 Director attempted to edit out Aubrey Smith's earlier point-picking but several times lost his way and instead of omitting the passport preparations actually elaborated upon them. Eventually, clearly struggling, Monsford concluded: "This isn't a proposal even in its broadest sense. It's a starting point, a basis for the sort of material they'll need when they make their break."

Charlie fought against openly showing his dismay, feeling no satisfaction at being right about the planning vacuum before his inclusion. This echelon was *too* high: obviously none of them had ever worked in the field, trained in operational practicalities, trusting nothing and no one, winning if you're lucky—or ruthless enough—dying if you're not. Carefully, initially rephrasing his words to avoid humiliating them, Charlie said: "We won't get them out disguised as British tourists wearing British clothes on British passports, no matter how good our forgeries and fake documentation. Russian entry visas are stamped and retained upon arrival, to be numerically matched with their departure counterfoils. There's no way we could introduce forged entry sections into the bureaucratic system."

"Is that your only comment?" quickly pressed Smith, guessing that it wasn't.

These posturing four weren't properly—professionally—working to evolve a rescue operation. Other, better professionals, who knew the smell of shit and what blood tasted like, should have been doing that. These figurehead bureaucrats were playacting to score off one another. But the charade was the best he could hope for at this moment: the *only* hope he had. "The embassy can be as much a prison as a haven, which links—" he cautiously began once more.

"Indivisible from the paramount problem of getting Natalia and the child under our safekeeping and away from Russian surveillance," Jane impatiently intruded, unable to hold back from the discussion any longer, seemingly unperturbed by the annoyed looks from both men.

Charlie's intention had been to continue talking about precisely that but the interruption gave him a moment to reconsider. He was, he belatedly recognized, in a far stronger and definitely more influential position than he'd realized, maybe even able to make Natalia and Sasha's escape his own, although always insinuating his suggestions to appear those of Monsford or Smith. It would all, of course, go through the pragmatic scrutiny, but the rejecting mesh sifting would be far more widely set with the proposals coming down from the gods. "Which you have obviously talked about before I joined you?"

"You were cut off before you finished what you were saying?" questioned Rebecca, in return.

After a momentary hesitation, Charlie said: "I was also going to suggest that it wasn't advisable to issue Natalia and Sasha British passports: to involve our embassy, quite apart from the problem of making contact with Natalia without FSB interception. It's what they'd expect and be most prepared for."

"The documentation we've prepared isn't British, for that obvious reason," said Aubrey Smith, ahead of the other Director. "What languages, apart from her own Russian and English, does Natalia speak?"

"German, fluently: she was assigned for a period to East Germany," replied Charlie, taking his time now, seeking his openings.

"East Germany!" picked up Rebecca, at once. "Was she there the same time as Vladimir Putin?"

Charlie came within a whisker of trying further to enhance Natalia's value by claiming she had been a contemporary of the Russian president turned premier. "I've already told you we never discussed our professional lives. But I think there's a strong possibility she was in Potsdam at the same time."

There was a moment's pause before Smith said: "Just Russian, English, and German?"

"And Polish," added Charlie. "She has some Polish, although she's not fluent."

"Well enough to communicate in Polish: not draw unnecessary attention?" pressed Smith.

"Well enough to debrief in the language," confirmed Charlie, feeling the first spurt of renewed hope. "Sasha obviously only has limited Russian."

"We've prepared Polish documentation," disclosed the MI5 Director. "There's no matching entry to exit visa regulations for rail or road crossings. Once they're across the Polish border, they're safe. Actually in the European Union."

"Yes," agreed Charlie. "Once in Poland they'd be safe."

"Which brings us back to how to reach Natalia," said Rebecca, directly addressing Aubrey Smith. "Tell us how your diversions are going to achieve that?"

"Diversions?" queried Charlie, the feeling of satisfaction growing.

"The initial phone call can be easily managed," insisted the MI5 Director-General, his entire concentration upon Charlie. "What we need from you is a way or a method—hopefully both—to make that contact with Natalia: the whole extraction stands or falls by our achieving that. And yours is the detailed knowledge upon which it depends."

Exactly as he wanted it, Charlie recognized, the final satisfaction engulfing him. Don't overplay it, came the balancing warning. "I understand."

"But can you provide it?" demanded Rebecca.

"I'm sure I can," said Charlie, maintaining the low-key reaction.

"How soon?" persisted Monsford.

"I need to think it through. I'll have enough to discuss by tomorrow."

"Sufficient for us to start moving by tomorrow?" picked up Smith.

"Definitely," promised Charlie, tightly. "Sufficient to start tomorrow."

Monsford and Rebecca sat tightly together in the rear of the car returning them to London, the soundproof glass screen fully raised between them and their driver.

Monsford said: "I didn't enjoy playing the complete idiot back there."

"You played it as it had to be played," flattered the woman. "The recordings will show Smith forcing the pace, initiating the moves that will go wrong."

"You think the woman might really have been in Potsdam with Putin?"

Rebecca shrugged. "Charlie says it's possible. Who knows?"

"If she was—as well as being as high as she's clearly been in the KGB as well as the FSB—she really would be a hell of a catch, wouldn't she?" mused the MI6 Director.

"Maxim Radtsic became the senior deputy to the KGB chairman for the last year of its existence and still has that position today," reminded Rebecca. "Getting him across, which we know we're going to do, is the higher prize."

"Getting both across would be the biggest coup of all," said Monsford. "Coming so soon after the Lvov affair, it would reduce Russian intelligence—and Putin's well-established Cold War determination—to a pile of dust."

"If we tried to do both we'd end up with one extraction getting in the way of the other and risk finishing up with neither," Rebecca warned. "Natalia and the child are our diversion to get Radtsic out. That's enough."

"I suppose you're right." Monsford sighed, as the car headed up the embankment toward Cheyne Walk. "Do you want to eat in or out?"

"It's been a long day and will probably be longer tomorrow," said Rebecca. "Let's go straight home. After that lunch, all I feel like eating is you." And that, she reflected, was an exaggeration.

Jane Ambersom flustered into the Mount Street restaurant, irritated at her second delay that day, searching anxiously around and smiling in relieved recognition at the wave from Barry Elliott, rising to meet her.

"You got my message that I'd be late?" she said, as the American reached her.

"Just as I was leaving the office: cleared my decks in the extra hour you gave me," said her FBI liaison, leading her back to their table. "Something unexpected delay you?"

Jane nodded to the offered chardonnay. "An out-of-town meeting overran."

"Anything of mutual interest?"

"Mutual to you? Or the CIA?"

"I don't understand the question?" The man frowned.

"I'm supposed to act as MI5 liaison to both. I haven't heard from the CIA."

Elliott smiled, with schoolboy shyness. "I guess they're nervous of you guys. They got their fingers badly burned the last time."

"So it's just you and I?" said Jane, risking the flirtation.

"Just you and I," confirmed the American. "And you didn't answer my question."

"Nothing that's emerged so far: no really useful chatter," avoided the woman, although carefully allowing the uncertainty.

"You don't sound very sure," quickly picked up the man, whose youthfulness was heightened by a schoolboy enthusiasm and a flop-forward forelock he constantly tried to sweep back into place, as he did at that moment.

"You are aware of all the rumors coming out of Moscow about some impending upheaval?" Jane continued to avoid.

"Nothing beyond the general traffic," said Elliott. "Your people think it's got some resonance?"

"We've got it flagged after the Lvov business," she said, nodding to the waiter that she'd have the same at Elliott, who'd studied the menu more thoroughly.

"I'm not sure what you're telling me," complained the man.

"There's nothing to tell. It could be coincidence, so soon after," refused Jane, content that she had done enough not just to plant but to water a seed she might choose to cultivate further if she suspected she was being offered up as a scapegoat for the second time.

Which was a similar although not such a self-protective thought that came to James Straughan as he replaced the telephone in his Berkhamsted bedroom, long after he'd given up hope of hearing from the night-duty officer. It wasn't the alert to which Gerald Monsford had decreed he should be awakened but it was close enough and Straughan was glad he at once called Cheyne Walk, sure from the strain evident in the MI6 Director's answering voice that he'd fulfilled his fantasy and interrupted the bastard in flagrante.

"I got everything you wanted to England!" protested Maxim Radtsic.

"You should have told me, before doing it," said Elana.

"You're shouting," warned Radtsix, looking around him. They'd parked the car and were walking slowly along the riverbank again.

"So are you!"

"Why should I have told you?"

"Because you should!" said Elana, frowning at her own childlike response. She'd known from her first case packing trial—and ensured it further by overpacking it on the trials that followed—that Radtsic would dismiss it as impractical and hoped he would reconsider their fleeing because she believed he was overreacting to coincidence. Now she'd lost every family memento.

"Why are you being like this!"

"I don't believe we have to run."

"Elana!" protested Radtsic, anguished at how it was going to be.

"I'm frightened: too frightened."

The arrangement had been for Radtsic to meet Harry Jacobson that night in Gorky Park, close to the Ferris wheel where families with their children would have provided cover. Jacobson waited, increasingly apprehensive, for an hour after their appointed time before abandoning the rendezvous. He intentionally drove in the opposite direction from the embassy, although the registration would have been traceable, the fear not subsiding until he'd zigzagged through several streets. What the hell had gone wrong now? came the mantra pumping through his head.

"Is something wrong!" demanded Andrei.

"Nothing's wrong. I just felt like calling you," replied Elana.

"I've written to Father."

"We haven't had a letter here."

"I sent it to his office."

"I'm not sure that was a good idea."

"He gave me a *poste restante* number I could use."

"Should I tell him to expect the letter?"

"It's up to you. It's nothing serious. Nothing to worry about, I mean."

"Have you made many friends?"

"A lot," said Andrei, smiling across the apartment at Yvette, curled up catlike in an enveloping chair.

"We miss you. Do you miss us?"

"Of course. But I'm kept very busy."

"When will you be able to come home?"

"I don't know. Not yet."

"I'd like more letters."

"I told you, I'm kept very busy."

"Too busy for a single page?" The correspondence was channeled through the Russian embassy in the diplomatic pouch to avoid French intelligence interception of e-mails.

"I'll write soon. I promise. Is Father there?"

"He's putting the car away. I'll tell him about the letter. And don't forget to write."

"It was my mother," said Andrei, to Yvette's inquiring look.

"I want you to teach me Russian. I like its sound."

"She wanted to know when I was going to visit. I told her not for some time: that I was going to Aix."

She smiled again. "I know my father will like you."

10

"IT WON'T WORK ANY OTHER WAY," INSISTED CHARLIE, CONFIdent he'd kept the scourging overnight doubt from his voice as he set out his rescue proposals.

"Then it's stillborn," refused Aubrey Smith, flatly. "There's absolutely no question of your becoming personally involved."

Despite its vital importance, he'd actually felt embarrassed at the previous night's close in front of an audience of Smith, Jane Ambersom, and an assortment of earphoned technicians mouthing the carefully prepared words into the unanswered Moscow public telephones from which Natalia had pleaded, *I've got your messages. I'm coming back: you know I'll come back. Don't panic. It'll all be over soon.*

"Everything needs a lot more discussion and consideration before there's talk of abandonment," quickly came in Monsford.

"Russian response?" queried Charlie, who'd already registered the return of the familiar apparatus and hoped to have learned the reason ahead of Smith's demand for his rescue ideas.

"Let me," quickly offered Rebecca Street, ahead of the other woman, briefly smiling as she went to the machine at the recollection of Monsford's impotent collapse at Straughan's previous night's telephone intrusion.

"Hurry, Charlie. I'm sure they're close," came Natalia's voice, and Charlie's stomach lurched in recognition.

"Within three hours of your call to the Moscow numbers!" declared Monsford, eagerly. "They've bitten!"

"They haven't bitten at anything," dismissed Smith. "They're going with the hand they dealt in the first place, to see if it will play out to their advantage. Which it would if Charlie actually went in. And why he isn't going. I'm prepared to hear ideas that don't personally include you, Charlie. If there aren't any, we abort."

"And lose twenty years of priceless espionage intelligence, as well as possibly even more priceless personal information about Vladimir Putin, who's going to go on running Russia for years," challenged Rebecca. "We can't discard this chance."

"I'm not dismissing it," refuted the MI5 Director. "I'm agreeing to an operation to get Natalia Fedova and her child out. But refusing Charlie's involvement beyond his inside knowledge."

"Then it *is* stillborn," risked Charlie, desperately, talking more to Monsford than to his own reluctant director. "I don't need a voiceprint to know that was again Natalia. Just as she wouldn't have needed a voiceprint to know it was me. She won't do anything, trust any part of a rescue attempt, if the contact is made in a voice other than mine. And that can't be done remotely with my being eighteen hundred miles away. Her reaction will be that it was an FSB trick, part of how they're using her. Which she'll automatically reject."

"Do you really believe, expect us to believe, that singlehandedly you could beat the entire Russian intelligence apparatus," sneered Jane Ambersom, pushing herself into the forefront.

"No, I can't defeat the *entire* Russian intelligence apparatus," Charlie replied, echoing the sneer. "But I believe I stand a better chance than a squad going in cold—a squad she'll anyway reject—just as I defeated not just Natalia herself but a group of then-KGB professionals during the phoney defection. And just as I beat a dedicated group of KGB and FSB professionals a little over four months ago to stop that Russian intelligence apparatus virtually installing itself in the Oval Office of the president of the United States of America."

"No one is questioning what you did," retreated Jane.

"Which I'm not boasting about," qualified Charlie, caught by the unexpected lessening of the woman's opposition. "Quite apart from Natalia trusting no one but me, it would take months to train an extraction team and they'd still be ill prepared because as determined as I'd obviously be to omit nothing, I'd still forget *something*. And we haven't got months. Whatever move they might have been planning against her will have been stopped now, because of my calls last night. But that hold-off won't last forever."

"I think Charlie is talking a lot of logical common sense," hustled Monsford. "I think there should be made available as much and as many backup provisions and resources as we can anticipate but that the actual extraction be headed by Charlie."

"I agree," supported Rebecca.

"What if you fail?" challenged Jane again. "What if they pick you up, which they're ready and waiting to do, and stage a good, old-fashioned show trial? What happens then?"

"Russia—certainly Moscow—isn't as controlled as it was in the days of Stalin's show trials, despite what Putin's done to turn the clock back," argued Charlie. "The ultimate humiliation would be theirs, not ours. For a show trial to work they'd need an open although orchestrated court. And some sort of apparent confession to whatever crime they falsify. What they couldn't control or prevent, when I spoke, would be my disclosing how their intelligence operation so abysmally failed and named those already known to have been assassinated by the FSB."

"Which would humiliate America as much as Russia," qualified Jane.

"Not at all," refused Charlie. "I'd tell it as a CIA success in a joint operation with us, not of the CIA being suckered as they were."

She didn't at that moment know how or why, reflected Jane, but she could have a lot more about which to talk to Barry Elliott at their next dinner. "Winning all over again, not just for the second time but publicly, is a forceful argument."

"No, it's not," resisted Smith, recognizing opinion settling against him. "They won't risk a show trial. They want you dead, like all the others in the Lvov affair they've already killed. They'd simply kill you."

"The others who've died were Russian," Charlie pointed out. "I'm English. And we've got three of their diplomats in custody."

"I don't believe you seriously imagine those diplomats equate as insurance against your being killed!" said Smith, allowing incredulity into his emotionally flat voice.

"It would give the FSB and even the Kremlin pause for thought if they learned through lawyers representing those arrested diplomats that they'd be named and linked if I died violently, even if it were staged as an accident," said Charlie.

"By then they would have moved against Natalia and Sasha," countered Smith.

"Yes," agreed Charlie, reluctantly forcing the acceptance. "By then I would have already lost them. But you'd have your publicly humiliating second coup, wouldn't you?"

"We're wasting time going around in circles," declared Monsford, impatiently. "We've got an intelligence opportunity that's potentially too promising to ignore. I accept Charlie should participate as he's proposed, to which I will add all the manpower and resources he's likely to need. . . ." Monsford hesitated, and said directly to Aubrey Smith: "Make it, in fact, an entirely SIS operation, with Charlie seconded to me, if you want no part of it and if you, Charlie, are willing to operate that way. It will overcome all the objections, won't it?"

"Perfectly," supported Rebecca, with predictable timing.

"I'll accept that," agreed Charlie. On my terms, he mentally added.

"The prime minister has ordered it to be a joint operation," reminded the other woman.

"It'll have to be approved through our government masters," said Monsford, matching the reminder. "It's still early enough to fix a meeting with Bland and Palmer today. That okay with you, Aubrey?"

"A meeting with the government group is certainly necessary," agreed the MI5 Director-General. "But to sanction a *joint* operation in the terms we've discussed this morning, not a separation of authority. Charlie will not be seconded."

"Camese!" declared Monsford.

"What?" demanded Jane, voicing the bewilderment of them all.

"Camese," repeated the M16 Director. "The mortal wife of Janus, the Greek god with two faces, able to look in opposite directions. I propose Camese be the code designation for Natalia's extraction. It's appropriate."

"So's getting to London," dismissed the MI5 Director-General.

It was Aubrey Smith's suggestion that he and Monsford share the car to London for the quickly arranged consultation with their government liaison, which protectively guaranteed the journey was in an MI5 vehicle with a security-cleared MI5 driver, who was as usual separated by the fully raised, soundproof glass screen. For the first thirty minutes they traveled through the Buckinghamshire countryside in self-reflective, self-protective silence, Smith determined upon a complete mental rehearsal, although predictably it was the impatient Monsford who eventually spoke.

"I imagine you'll want equal participation in the support group?"

"Of course," agreed Smith, content with the direction the other man had chosen.

"I suggested we accept Charlie's argument about too many cooks spoiling the broth."

"Absolutely." This really was going far better than he could have hoped, thought Smith.

"I am thinking of no more than six, three of mine, three of yours. They could also handle finance, materiel, and travel: everything that Charlie might call upon once he establishes contact with Natalia."

"Only *when* he calls upon them," balanced Smith, choosing his moment. "The timing has to be absolutely precise. The major argument against what we're proposing is the public debacle if we get things wrong by as much, or as little, as a second. We won't get approval unless we can satisfy them there is no risk of that."

"A show trial, you mean?"

"I mean totally satisfying them that success is guaranteed, with no risk of Charlie—or the government—being publicly exposed."

Monsford lapsed into further silence but when Smith didn't continue, the MI6 Director said: "You were adamantly opposed to a very specific insurance."

"As I was opposed earlier today to Charlie's participation, an objection I've since dropped."

There was another although shorter silence before Monsford said: "As you are now conceding the need for an ultimate insurance, if such a move becomes essential?"

"If such a need arose, we would have lost the advantages of bringing Natalia, with all she potentially knows, here to safety. At which stage it would be containment time."

"I agree," fenced Monsford, consciously switching the direction of the conversation onto the other man as he recognized them to be entering the north London suburbs with perhaps only fifteen minutes left in the exchange before reaching their destination.

Smith shifted on his seat, discomfited at being outmaneuvered. "We understand what we're talking about but it's not an eventuality we can openly introduce into this afternoon's discussion: the very purpose for . . ." The man hesitated, searching for the appropriate ambiguity. "For the airlock through which we have to communicate is to provide legally unchallengeable deniability in Parliament in the event of a catastrophe."

Now it was Monsford who changed position. "Surely we can sufficiently infer such a guarantee without risking any misunderstandings?"

"There are practicalities that we would need completely to clarify to avoid any misunderstandings between ourselves," insisted Smith, determined to recover the impetus. "Do you have such an asset?"

Monsford stirred again, aware how perfectly everything was slotting into place. "I have a station chief, Harry Jacobson, completely briefed upon the operation: following Eyes Only instructions, he's supervised all my preliminary preparations."

"Could he perform the ultimate insurance proposal?"

"He would need to be totally distanced from everything else. And obviously he was going to be one of my three in the combined support team. If he's assigned the insurance necessity, I'd need another officer to maintain our three-to-three balance, which creates an imbalance, my four to your three."

"I don't think we need be that pedantic," offered Smith, who hadn't imagined it was going to be so easy.

"You'd be happy with a four-to-three imbalance?" questioned Monsford, who hadn't imagined it was going to be so easy.

"We're not actually on opposing sides, are we?" Smith allowed himself. "Being on opposite sides of the Thames is simply a geographical separation."

"Of course we're not on opposing sides." Monsford sniggered, knowing he was expected to appear amused, which he was, although not at what Smith had said. "It's been easier for us to understand each other without those damn women on our coattails. Hasn't it?"

"Very much easier," agreed Smith.

It had taken close to an hour after the other four left for Charlie's euphoric mist to lift and for him to confront that his initial reaction had been more fogged than misted by his single-minded fixation upon saving Natalia and Sasha. Now, after that near-transcendental hour in the no-longer-locked-or-guarded room in what would soon no longer be his latest safe house, came the hard-assed examination. Summoning yet again that close-to-photographic recall of every incident and conversation since the numbing moment of hearing Natalia's metallic-voiced pleas, Charlie for the first time set out to create a mosaic from the pieces he could safely assume, reserving—although not positively dismissing—what he judged the more outlandish hypotheses inevitable from the sparse information available.

His starkest, most frightening awareness had to be the relentless dedication with which the FSB were hunting him, their utter determination such that they'd consciously sacrificed three undetected diplomat-concealed spies in the ridiculous burglary of his Vauxhall apartment. It had to mean . . .

Charlie's mind abruptly blocked at the first of the insufficiently considered anomalies.

How had the FSB discovered the Vauxhall flat and its telephone number, neither of which was traceable to him either from its shielded lease or its utility records? Nor was such information available through any documentation in the lawyer-supervised Jersey bank account. The remotest and already partially considered possibility—if true, a further confirmation of the Russian revenge obsession—was the FSB establishing a connection from his television exposure during the Lvov affair and his long ago faked defection. But that still wouldn't have led them to his Vauxhall flat or its telephone number. Yes it could, came the instant contradiction.

After his initial return from Moscow, Charlie had always called Natalia from an untraceably anonymous, bought-for-cash telephone card, disposable when its charge value was exhausted. But she'd very occasionally telephoned from her apartment, ignoring his repeated, sometimes even angry insistence that she always call from an unlisted public kiosk.

There was another jarring halt to Charlie's speculation. But always to charge the call collect. Under the pressure to which she had undoubtedly been subjected, reciting the words at least monitored if not actually dictated to her, it would have been far more logical—expected, even—for her to telephone from her apartment: more logical, too, for the FSB eavesdropping enforcers. So why hadn't she? Had Natalia tried to convey something beyond her obvious coercion, something she was desperate for him to recognize by using a public facility?

He might, Charlie at once accepted, be stumbling in the wrong direction, as he had when trying to lull his protective minders in preparation for his unsupervised dash to Jersey. But it was an inconsistency in their arranged understanding, and intentionally introduced inconsistency was an acknowledged danger-alerting tradecraft signal. It was something to flag up, even if at this moment it didn't contribute to his empty mosaic.

What was there that just might contribute? The FSB wasn't the only intelligence organization wanting him hanged, drawn and quartered. There'd been a substantial clear-out within the CIA after his exposure but Charlie couldn't see them making up any part of his unfilled picture. Or could he?

Irena Yakulova Novikov, first the initiating KGB and after their supposed dissolution the continuing FSB architect of the Lvov emplacement, had not so far been factored into the current context. What if, somehow, Irena Novikov was a continuing integral part of the Lvov bloodletting? In a desperate attempt to recuperate her brain child, Irena had staged her own faked defection in an ultimately failed attempt to prevent his uncovering the truth about Stepan Lvov. Now she was incarcerated somewhere in America—or perhaps a torture-permitting rendition country—undergoing the most extreme CIA interrogation to provide far more secrets about Russian intelligence.

Charlie doubted that someone as dedicated as Irena would break under American interrogation, no matter how brutal. But professionally it wasn't a risk Russia could take: they'd do everything to get her back by following their unbreakable coda of demanding diplomatic access to negotiate her return.

It was far more likely, Charlie conceded, that his London address had been disclosed to Washington by the avenging disciples stable-cleaned along with the disgraced, CIA-pocketed former deputy director of MI5, Jeffrey Smale. And in turn offered to the FSB by the disgruntled CIA.

He was looking at a brick wall, Charlie acknowledged: hypotheses stacked upon hypotheses upon a quicksand of unknowns and uncertainties. He didn't have enough about anything from which to make a half-intelligent guess, apart from the one unarguable fact of Natalia's exposure. So why was he trying? Because he didn't need the familiar foot twinge to warn him that distracted by his consuming, solely focused aim, he'd missed things that would have filled in a lot of his empty picture.

One of which surely had to be that Smith and Monsford's lack of field experience didn't by itself justify their comparatively easy agreement to his participation. The continuing foot pangs were sufficient to make him wince and with that discomfort came the further warning doubt. He'd already initiated the Moscow incursion with his hollow-voiced messages to the numbers from which Natalia had made her contact, which broke the inviolable rule that every mission, before commencement, be separately, independently vetted by experienced, field-savvy executives.

He'd had no reason for euphoria because he hadn't won anything, Charlie accepted. He was caught up in something he didn't properly understand without, at this precise moment, any hope of finding out.

About which he didn't give a fuck, as long as it got him to Moscow.

Monsford had called ahead and Rebecca Street got to the Cheyne Walk flat before the MI6 Director flustered in, the demanded glasses and celebratory champagne set out in readiness.

"You won't believe what happened!" Monsford greeted, exultantly.

"Then I won't try to guess," said the woman, who considered the man's too-quickly-stirred excitability to be immature, like the haste of his lovemaking.

"On our way to the meeting, Smith actually *asked* me to set up Charlie's assassination if there were a risk of his being seized by the Russians!"

"Did he actually use the word *assassination*?"

"Of course not!" said Monsford, irritated at the question. "It was the usual maypole dance of double-speak but it was protective assassination, pure and simple."

"What about the internal inquiry that's inevitable after Charlie's killed? Smith will deny it was ever his suggestion."

"Not when you corroborate what I'm telling you."

By her not corroborating it, Monsford's removal from the MI6 directorship would be automatic, leaving her his logical successor, calculated Rebecca. "Your last uncertainty has been resolved, hasn't it?"

"Absolutely," agreed Monsford. "What did you think of my establishing Camese as the code designation for what everyone believes to be Natalia's extraction?"

Puerile, like most of your classical allusions, thought Rebecca. She said: "Very clever."

"More than clever. Brilliant," insisted Monsford. "Janus is going to be the code for Radtsic's extraction. Everyone looking and thinking in the wrong direction!"

"Brilliant," agreed Rebecca, dutifully. Asshole, she thought.

"Have you had Andrei's letter?" asked Elana.

"It arrived today."

"What's the problem?"

"There isn't one. I'd set up a contact system with the embassy that he was finding restrictive, so I've scaled it down. Which I was going to have to do anyway."

"When are you going to tell him what's happening?"

"When everything's finalized by the British."

"When's that going to be?"

"Very soon."

"You're going to be briefed on a special, combined operation," announced Monsford. "I'm appointing you supervisor of the MI6 contingent."

"Thank you, sir," accepted Stephen Briddle. He was an intense, quick-talking man nervous of his first personal encounter with the Director.

"You'll learn all about the combined assignment at the general briefing. This conversation is strictly between the two of us and must remain that way, no one else. I've chosen you because of your special clearance, which might be called upon. I'm sure you won't let me or the service down."

"I won't, sir," assured Briddle, giving no indication of his immediate unease at the reference to special clearance.

"This meeting is precautionary. I might not need to issue the order so I won't give you any further details but I will dispatch a weapon ahead of your arrival in Moscow in the diplomatic bag."

"I understand."

"Your sole understanding at this point is that this meeting, this conversation, is totally classified."

"I do understand that."

"You are going to have a long and assured career in this service."

"Thank you, sir."

11

CHARLIE MUFFIN DISLIKED SHARED ASSIGNMENTS THAT MADE him reliant upon others whose professional ability he didn't know and therefore couldn't trust, his unease increased by the inclusion of MI6 as well as by his belated recognition at how quickly his personal involvement had been agreed to. Charlie's well-honed sensitivity to potential betrayal extended beyond the smell of a rat to being aware of them scuttling underfoot, which was the instinctive impression settling upon him.

His general discomfort began with his 8:00 A.M. arrival not at his Thames House workplace, which he'd expected, but across the river at MI6's tree- and shrub-festooned edifice, the smoked-glass car sweeping too fast through last-minute-opening steel doors into a basement garage from an unsuspected entrance a block and a half from the actual building. Charlie dismissed the security checks as far more perfunctory than they would have been at Thames House, unquestioningly following the two reimposed escorts who'd steadfastly refused conversation during the journey from Buckinghamshire. A matching electronic warning he guessed to have opened the garage doors had obviously alerted the two men waiting for him as the elevator doors opened.

"At last a face I recognize," greeted Charlie.

John Passmore was respected within the counterintelligence agency for dropping the civilian entitlement of colonel after his transfer appointment from the SAS, although he continued to wear the regimental tie, which didn't coordinate with the suit he was wearing today. He was a reserved, taciturn man who responded to Charlie with a curt, unsmiling nod and an immediate introduction to James Straughan.

"Why am I here, not across the river?" demanded Charlie, at once.

"Your own building will be under far tighter Russian surveillance than usual," said Straughan, leading the way into a directly opposite, anonymously bare office. "And Thames House doesn't have the separated entry facilities that we do."

Bollocks, thought Charlie. "You should charge for the helter-skelter approach; sell candy floss to attract the customers."

"Your proposal for getting Natalia and the girl out has been gone through in some detail," picked up Passmore, the intended briskness slightly marred by an almost-suppressed stutter. "The instructions are to give you your head but personally I think your chances of success are extremely limited."

"It's difficult for them to be otherwise, knowing as little as we do so far," defended Charlie. "It has to be governed by on-the-spot decisions according to the circumstances as they arise."

"Which operations are invariably insufficiently prepared, inadequately planned, and blow up in your face," argued the ex-soldier, feeling out with his remaining hand to the empty left sleeve of his jacket.

"It's been sanctioned?" pressed Charlie.

"With reservations beyond the obvious," confirmed Straughan.

"Which are?" queried Charlie, apprehensively.

"Shortly you'll meet your backup group," disclosed Straughan. "They're not being told of your personal relationship to Natalia or that Sasha is your child."

"It's the weakest aspect of what you'll be trying to do," criticized Passmore, before Charlie could respond. "You're team leader and because of who Natalia and Sasha are, you'll take more risks than you should. They'll know and distrust that if they're told."

"Is everything going to be independently monitored, above and beyond the people I'm about to meet?" asked Charlie, presciently. There could be gains, having so many distracting people milling about.

Passmore looked to the other operational director and Straughan momentarily hesitated. "No. But there's another reservation. There's to be no maverick bullshit from you. We accept there's a lot that's got to be worked out when you get there. But you don't initiate anything without approval. And we want your acknowledgment, right now, that you understand what I'm saying. If we get the slightest suspicion you're trying to perform as a one-man band, we abort everything and you'll lose a wife and child."

The bullshit was Straughan's, for the benefit of the inevitable protective recording, Charlie knew. "I'm not going to do anything to put Natalia and Sasha at more risk than they already are. And I've already given the undertaking about diplomatic embarrassment."

"Don't, for a moment, forget it," threatened the MI6 division chief, ending the encounter. "People are waiting for us."

Waiting or scuttling underfoot to trip him? wondered Charlie.

The briefing room was four doors away on the same level, the six men already assembled at name-carded lecture desks in front of a slightly raised stage on the wall behind which were displayed the enlarged photographs of Natalia and Sasha. At the far end of the room were visible camera-projection facilities from which everything would be filmed.

After Straughan's domination of their introductory meeting, Charlie was mildly curious at Passmore's supervising the team briefing. This was an unusually linked combination between their two services because of the importance of what had to be achieved, opened the MI5 operations director, the stutter, strangely, no longer pronounced. Each of them had been provided with a individual pack that included the maximum available information upon Natalia Fedova and her background within the FSB. Those packs were to be familiarized until their departure for their Moscow flight that afternoon but would be retrieved before they left the building. Duplicate packs were already waiting for them at the British embassy, in the residential compound of which they were all to be accommodated. The duplicate packs—particularly the photographs of Natalia and the child—were never to be taken outside the embassy. Also awaiting their collection at the embassy were Russian mobile telephones through which they would liaise with their team supervisor, Charlie Muffin. That liaison had always to be through their cell phones: they should never initiate contact by calling his cell phone, the number of which would be in their Moscow documentation, from an embassy or outside landline. Charlie would not be accommodated at the embassy but would work from hotels, between which he would move, at his decision and choosing. It was, obviously, an extraction mission, the method, timing, and manner of which could not be decided until contact had been made with Natalia Fedova. Until the moment of extraction, their function was entirely one of support, at which announcement Passmore hesitated again, identifying those among the group responsible for finance, which was to be provided internally from embassy funds, and logistics. Those logistics were to be obtained through outside, Russian sources, paid for in cash and not traceable in any way to the embassy or to Britain. Each of the Moscow packs was nominated by name and contained Russian driving licenses in their Russian cover names, together with false Russian passports and other necessary identity documents. Each had been allocated an individual code designation signaling the mission's cancellation, together with specific escape routes to be unquestioningly followed. Upon that alert they were immediately and separately to get out of the country. Under no circumstances whatsoever were they to risk identification or association among themselves and their team supervisor by attempting to contact Charlie Muffin: there had to be no evidential electronic—or any other—link whatsoever.

Throughout Passmore's presentation Charlie's attention was divided, dissecting the man's every word and phrase while at the same time comparing his initial reaction as much as was visually possible against those before him. Patrick Wilkinson was the only one of the group Charlie recognized, from a brief encounter at the British embassy in Washington, D.C., which had been Wilkinson's first MI5 overseas posting. The man showed no recognition, although throughout most of Passmore's address he was looking directly at Charlie, as were most of the others. Charlie decided they were trying to assess him from his visible responses, as he was trying to assess them. They were uniformly bland featured, an essential attention-avoiding requirement, and dressed accordingly. There were occasional frowns, one or two nose blowings, a few seat rearrangements, but no nods of acceptance or head-shaking disapproval, nor expression of surprise or uncertainty. Throughout, no one had taken a single reminder note.

"You'll have questions, in which your team leader will participate," Passmore concluded, overly formal.

At once a balding man identified by his name card as Neil Preston, another MI5 man, said: "Is this woman an embedded asset?"

Both operational directors deferred to Charlie, who hurriedly replied: "She had the potential to have been."

"I don't understand that answer," protested Preston. "She either is or she isn't."

"It's a perfectly understandable answer," refused Charlie. "She occupies a position within the FSB and before that the KGB that could provide invaluable intelligence."

A man named by his place setting as Stephen Briddle, who'd been picked out by Passmore as the operational bag man, said: "Does that mean it's uncertain whether she'll provide it?"

"The uncertainty is getting them both out, which it is imperative we do," insisted Charlie, content to use the moment. "Natalia Fedova's cooperation depends entirely upon the safety and protection of the child."

"You've indicated that I'm the finance officer," said Briddle, addressing Passmore. "It might be in my briefing pack but if it isn't, is there a budget within which I have to work?"

There were isolated sniggers among the other five at the bureaucratic demand, which increased when Passmore replied: "None. But we expect receipts,"

"Are these two detained in any way?" asked Robert Denning, a tall but stooped man whose card identified him as an MI6 officer.

"There's no indication of that," avoided Charlie. "It is something to be established when we get to Moscow."

"Does any field instruction need London confirmation?" demanded Peter Warren, disclosing his MI6 allegiance by directing the question to Straughan.

"No," replied Straughan, without hesitation. "Charlie has full operational authority. There'll need to be liaison with us here, which I don't think is covered in your Moscow packs, so I'll make you, Peter, responsible for that, particularly relaying anything that Charlie wants sent, okay?"

"I'm finding this difficult to follow," Preston continued to protest. "Has she approached us, to defect?"

"There are sufficient indications," said Charlie, acknowledging the importance of separate back-channel arrangements with his known fellow officers.

"Who's her Control in Moscow, through whom these indications have come?" asked Wilkinson, coming into the discussion.

Again the other two men on the stage looked to Charlie, who hesitated, anxious to get the answer right. "There isn't one, not in Moscow. That's what I am going there to become. I've had some prior contact."

"Sufficient to justify an operation of this size at this early stage?" frowned Preston.

They *were* professionals, Charlie judged hopefully. But then so was he. Or supposed to be. "There isn't time for lengthy ground planning, only what I can set up. Which is why there is to be the separation between us. Until the actual moment of extraction, I'm the only one at risk."

"What about that extraction?" questioned Wilkinson, whom Passmore had designated a logistics officer, along with Denning. "There's surely been advanced planning put into that?"

Straughan indicated the enlarged photographs behind him. "Already at the embassy there are Polish and English passports carrying those pictures. You and Denning have to pay locally for all transport, obviously including airline tickets. This is an in-and-out job, which is why we're manning it as we are."

"Mother and daughter," itemized Jeremy Beckindale, who completed the MI6 secondment. "What about the father?"

"There isn't one," replied Charlie, prepared before the question concluded.

"What's the likelihood of either personal or protective resistance?" persisted the most obviously doubtful Preston.

"None," insisted Charlie, as quickly as before. "They're not being kidnapped. No extraction will be contemplated if there's the slightest possibility of violent opposition."

"What guarantee is there of that being avoided?"

"Me," said Charlie, shortly. "Nothing and no one moves until I press the button."

The room became silent. Passmore said: "All through?"

Preston said: "I'd like a much better idea of what we're getting involved in."

So would I, thought Charlie.

"We saw it all on the television relay," pre-empted Monsford, as Straughan entered the Director's office suite.

"I thought it went well," offered Harry Jacobson, tentatively. As with Stephen Briddle earlier, it was Jacobson's first personal encounter with Monsford, which was unsettling in itself, and he now believed he'd made a bad mistake. The London recall, to witness the televised briefing and reinforce the physical identification of Charlie Muffin by flying back to Moscow on the same plane, had been waiting when Jacobson returned to the embassy after the failed meeting with Radtsic and on impulse Jacobson hadn't told the Director or Straughan of the Russian's nonappearance. Now it was too late and there was no guarantee Radtsic would keep the automatically prearranged catch-up meeting to be activated on his return.

"The majority of the others feel like Preston," balanced Straughan.

"I'd be disappointed if our people didn't. But they're not going to be involved, so their uncertainties don't matter." Monsford shrugged. He once more hadn't switched on his personal recording apparatus.

"What about Charlie himself?" queried Jacobson. "Hasn't he wanted more?"

"His sole interest is getting there," dismissed Straughan.

"I've read his file," said Jacobson, tapping his dossier. "He's unpredictable."

"Not this time," insisted Monsford. "His reasoning is knocked to hell by his one, single priority: getting to Moscow."

"Why don't we tell Radtsic the protective diversion that'll doubly guarantee his extraction?" unexpectedly suggested Straughan.

"Is that a good idea?" wondered Monsford, with his customary reluctance to respond to an idea without first getting the opinions of everyone else.

"It might calm Radtsic down," said Jacobson, uncomfortably. "I'm surprised every time he turns up for a meeting."

With no knowledge of the Director's earlier encounter with Stephen Briddle, the operations director wondered what Jacobson's personal feelings must be, sitting as Jacobson was sitting, discussing an assassination, a murder, that he had to commit. Straughan had always hoped never to be personally associated with a sanctioned killing, particularly one predicated upon such tenuous reasoning as this. He wished he had the courage officially to object, for which there was provision in the statutory regulations. "Natalia's under surveillance by the FSB. If we told Radtsic, he could guarantee Natalia—and therefore Charlie—being precisely where we want them to be for the distraction operation."

"It would, wouldn't it?" reflected Monsford. "Everything would be gift wrapped."

"So we'll do it?" pressed Straughan, determined against being sacrificed as Jane Ambersom had been. He'd liked the woman, refusing the sniping of others at her sexual uncertainty, and felt guilty that his own asexuality had prevented his doing more to protect her, although knowing that if she'd survived, he would have been the victim instead.

"Not in precise detail," qualified Monsford. "Tell Radtsic we're setting up a failsafe extraction: that he's got no reason to worry about anything going wrong. And tell him I'm looking forward personally to welcoming him here, in London." It was a good feeling, knowing everything was perfectly arranged, with no possibility of error.

Charlie held back in the departure lounge, waiting to let the other passengers not just board ahead of him but actually get into their seats, giving him the opportunity to study the faces of those traveling with him, which he prolonged while finding a space in the already stuffed overhead lockers for his minimally packed suit carrier before finally sitting in his personally selected aisle seat just two rows back from the business-class separation.

Only when Charlie completely settled did Jacobson properly look up from the in-flight shopping brochure. For additional concealment as well as for his assigned purpose, Jacobson had secured a window seat only three rows behind Charlie's but on the opposite side of the cabin to give him an uninterrupted view of his intended target. Which prompted the immediate reflection of how ideal it would also be to get this close when the moment came to pull the trigger of the already skipped Russian Makarov in his embassy safe. Away from the MI6 building, Jacobson's concern at having said nothing about Radtsic's failed meeting had lessened. No one in London or Moscow, apart from Radtsic, had known of the appointment, so he couldn't be caught out on that omission. Jacobson's hope was that the Russian wouldn't appear at the failsafe meeting, sparing him from the assassination order.

As the flight crew began their acrobatics of emergency flight evacuation, Charlie was mentally evaluating the potential success against the possible failure of what he had to achieve. He was encouraged by the briefing assertion of no expenditure limit. Realistically there was no way he could have got back to Jersey to retrieve what was left of the already committed money, which was why, at the final departure session with Straughan and Passmore, he'd argued up the initially proposed, personally carried working float to ten thousand pounds by quoting the irrefutable statistics that Moscow had become the most expensive city in the world. But potentially he'd need considerably more. The fine line he had to follow was obtaining sufficient additional money without arousing suspicion that he wasn't going to utilize any more bullshit backup than was minimally necessary, which anyway might be difficult after what he planned so soon to do.

Charlie halted the instinctive half turn behind him practically as it began at the expectation of there being one if not more puppet-watchers monitoring his every movement, curious if his intended actions would be accepted as proving his professional caution. Which was more than Passmore and Straughan had illustrated with their insistence that he was being allowed operational autonomy. Charlie was glad he'd managed the brief, private conversation with John Passmore before he'd left the MI6 meeting, impressed with the man's reaction.

Jacobson had been prepared for Charlie's backward look, the face-concealing in-flight magazine ready at the first indication, which turned out to be unnecessary when Charlie didn't continue, easing his seat back as the plane attained its cruising height. He would, Jacobson decided, deserve recognition, positive promotion, after this if Radtsic did turn up at the emergency rendezvous: he'd been disappointed at the Director's vagueness at the hints he'd risked, every innuendo hedged with a caveat.

Charlie put his hand to his jacket pocket, feeling the hardness of the Russian cell phone, one of the dozen air-freighted from Moscow to be technically tweaked before being returned for distribution to the backup squad upon their arrival. He'd retain it as an insurance, but always turned off as it was now, and buy himself another when he got to Moscow. What other personal adaptations did he need? He'd covered the passport changes during that brief, private meeting with Passmore, hoping Wilkinson had been properly briefed just as privately afterward. And he was carrying sufficient money for his immediate needs. Too early to think about anything more, he decided, at the copilot's announcement of the impending en route landing at Amsterdam's Schipol airport.

Charlie stood out into the aisle for his window-seated companion to get out, resuming his seat at once for other disembarking passengers behind him to follow, flicking through his own seat pocket sales magazine, his concentration entirely upon the departing line. He timed his move as the last figure disappeared from the plane, standing, stretching, and setting off unhurriedly toward the restrooms, relieved the indicator showed the farthest cubicle to be unoccupied. He started to hurry only when he reached it, partially opening the door but releasing it to continue on to the disembarkation pier, his feet at once protesting as he bustled past those ahead of him.

Still in his seat, Jacobson had craned around the business-class-curtain separation to see Charlie approach the toilet door just before his view was blocked again by a steward moving to greet arriving Dutch passengers who filled the aisle for several minutes, locating their seats and stowing their baggage. By the time they had finished, Jacobson was standing awkwardly between the seats, looking to the toilets. The occupancy indicator showed the farthest to be the only one in use. Several more minutes passed before the door opened for a woman to emerge.

At that moment, the aircraft doors thumped closed.

Hampered as they were by not knowing precisely what time of day or night they would be making the journey, Jonathan Miller stretched the reconnaissance-car journeys from Paris to Orly airport over a forty-eight-hour time frame into which he fitted six trips to establish an average, driving himself back to the city on their final run.

Albert Abrahams, hunched over his clipboard in the passenger seat, said without looking up: "Never exceeding the speed limit to ensure against traffic violations and building in an additional thirty minutes for unanticipated problems, it gives us two and a half hours during the day, two at night."

"We'll include a backup car, against engine breakdown," decided Miller.

"When's Straughan going to give us Andrei's pickup schedule? From all the guidance we're getting from London, they're expecting us to snatch the guy off the street."

"Straughan told me we'll get it all in good time."

"Including personal contact with the kid himself? He'll need to meet us, know us, in advance, won't he?"

"I've made the point. Straughan says it's all in hand."

"You been involved in an extraction before?"

"Once, ten years ago in Rome. His cover was third secretary at the Russian embassy. Turned out he was abandoning his wife for his mistress. He backed off confronting embassy diplomats at a consular-access negotiation and went back to his wife without telling us anything whatsoever of value."

"Let's hope this one goes better."

"That's all we can ever do, hope it all works out," said the MI6 station chief. "You fancy the Brassiere Lipp for lunch?"

"After two days and nights of sandwiches we deserve nothing less," agreed Abrahams. "Apart, that is, from a hell of a lot more information."

12

"WHAT!"

There was close to physical pain as well as disbelief in Gerald Monsford's voice, and Straughan hoped the Director had been engaged in a difficult athletic performance with Rebecca to cause it. "Charlie slipped Jacobson in Amsterdam. Simply walked off the plane."

"That's not possible!"

"That's what happened."

"Why didn't you patch Jacobson through to me from Moscow!"

"The Moscow embassy is secure but we don't transfer calls to your home." Straughan paused, savoring the exchange. "Your specific instructions."

"Tell me exactly what happened," demanded Monsford, the loudness lessening.

"Charlie was as unpredictable as ever," began Straughan, stringing out the pleasure although acknowledging there was an endangering hole in his own protection. "Charlie specified a seat, and Jacobson managed to get just a couple of rows behind: from there he had the perfect physical identification. Charlie stowed his suit carrier, and appeared to settle for the flight to Moscow. He didn't make a move until after the Amsterdam passengers got off and only then appeared to go to the toilet. Jacobson lost sight for just a few seconds, as new passengers got on. The toilet light stayed on. In the confusion of people getting on—and there's a separating curtain between business and economy—Jacobson missed Charlie leaving the toilet and someone else going in. . . ."

"Jacobson stayed in his fucking seat: didn't get out to walk up and down the aisle, exercising, like everyone does?"

So far, so good, judged Straughan, hopefully. "Charlie left his luggage in an overhead locker!"

"And you didn't have a backstop established in Amsterdam airport precisely to ensure that something like this didn't happen!"

"No," admitted Straughan, the paper-thin defense ready.

"Why not?"

"You and Jacobson watched and heard me warn him against doing anything like this, trying to show how clever he is," struggled the operations director. "That's all he's doing, trying to prove his streetwise independence. But he can't. He's got to get to Moscow, which means using the cover-name passport we've provided. And he's got to contact the embassy, sooner or later, to get the phoney passports for Natalia and the child. He's just getting his rocks off, like a schoolboy masturbating for the first time."

"Why didn't the cabin crew realize they were a passenger short?"

"I don't know and can't ask," said Straughan. "Charlie gambled and won."

After the briefest silence Monsford, his voice loud again, said: "You haven't finished the story!"

"I don't follow," protested Straughan, glad his own voice didn't waver.

"What did Jacobson do, when he realized he'd lost Charlie?"

"There was nothing he could do: the aircraft doors had closed," tried Straughan, weakly.

"What about the suit carrier?"

Now the silence was Straughan's, as he sought an escape. Not finding one, he said: "Raising an alarm would have compromised Jacobson's connection with Charlie."

"The suit carrier will have been found upon arrival at Moscow, which will alert the airline and the Russian authorities that the plane arrived short of a passenger," set out Monsford, his voice rising even further. "The obvious backwards check will be at Amsterdam, who'll cooperate with the Russians because they've no reason not to and with whom we can't intercede. The flight will have had a named-passenger manifest and the boarding pass will have recorded a seat number, from which the Russians will learn the cover name we allocated the stupid motherfucker. Which, additionally, will be publicly disclosed in the inevitable publicity of a disappearing passenger from a Moscow-bound flight. . . ." Monsford paused, a torturer practicing his art. "You spotted anything I've missed out so far?"

"He's attracting attention to himself, which is madness!" argued Straughan. "It makes no sense the way you're analyzing it."

"It makes each and every sense," rejected Monsford. "The FSB are expecting him to come: he's actually told them, for Christ's sake, with the telephone calls!"

"Which he's supposed to be, a distraction," broke in Straughan.

"I hadn't finished," threatened Monsford. "By creating his own diversion he's making it quite clear that he doesn't trust anything we've put in place as backup. At the moment he's not working against the Russians! He's working against us!"

As we're working against him, thought Straughan, amazed at the other man's total hypocrisy. "He can't get his wife and daughter out without us."

"And we don't have our diversion to get Radtsic and his wife out! Tell Jacobson to call me at noon our time tomorrow."

"He's got a meeting with Radtsic at noon tomorrow."

"As soon as possible afterwards," allowed Monsford. "I won't have this fall apart."

"Monsford says Charlie's telling us our planning is crap," said Aubrey Smith.

"He caught me by myself after yesterday's meeting," said Passmore. "Asked me to prepare Russian passports for Natalia and Sasha, with Russian exit visas as well as British entry documentation covering the next month. He wants them sent covertly to Wilkinson at the embassy, cutting out MI6. I briefed Wilkinson to expect the package."

"Charlie doesn't trust his own shadow."

"He tries hard not even to cast one," guessed Passmore.

"I've read your memo complaining at not being included in the early planning," said Aubrey Smith.

"Why wasn't I?"

"It's a stuck-together operation. I opposed our ever going into Moscow, until I couldn't prevent it becoming exclusively MI6, with Charlie seconded to them."

"So you agreed to it being joint?"

Smith hesitated. "I couldn't let it go to Monsford, could I?"

"I've never controlled Charlie on an operation," said Passmore, an objective rather than a responsibility-avoiding remark. "What do you expect him to do?"

Smith shrugged. "God only knows. He'll go, of course. But the cover name will be blown to the Russians from the flight information, even if it doesn't become public through the media."

"I've already checked the news wires, as well as the Amsterdam and Moscow newspapers," said Passmore. "It's not public so far."

"It's too early. There'll be something by tonight."

"So he's got another passport," accepted Passmore.

"Probably connected with the trip to Jersey," agreed Smith. "The bit he *didn't* tell us about."

"He was taken straight to the Buckinghamshire lodge the morning he reappeared after Jersey?"

"Yes." Smith frowned, questioningly.

"Was he searched?"

"As the first safe house in Chelsea was searched," confirmed Smith, understanding the question. "He didn't have a passport with him. Nor was there one in Buckinghamshire. . . ."

"And direct from Buckinghamshire he was brought here to London for the briefings and after that immediately taken to the Moscow flight. . . ."

"Yes," said Smith.

"What about luggage?"

"His suit carrier left on the plane. We brought everything up to the lodge from Chelsea."

"He's got to get back here, to England," predicted the former SAS man. "And to do that he'll have to use the cover passport, until he can make the switch to whatever else he's got. I want to issue a passport watch on the cover name."

"Extend it to Jersey," ordered Smith. "That's where he could have it."

"What do we do when we pick him up?"

"I'll decide that when we get him."

"And if we don't?"

"Then we can't do anything other than follow *his* lead."

"And the Russian passport he asked for?"

Smith hesitated. "Prepare it as Charlie wants. I don't trust Monsford either."

All Harry Jacobson's fragile reassurances had gone, compounded by the breach of tradecraft that he hadn't properly taken into account until now, when he was actually making his way to the failsafe rendezvous with Maxim Radtsic. It was an inviolable rule in defector extractions that no target meetings should ever be at the same place twice and they'd already met once before at the river-cruise terminal: Jacobson had agreed to its emergency use only because, unprofessionally, he'd never expected it to be necessary. Jacobson's most obvious fear was that he was walking blindly into an FSB entrapment, almost equaled by the apprehension that Radtsic had lost his already overstretched nerve and wouldn't turn up a second time. Which, added to his infantile airplane loss of Charlie Muffin, would inevitably mean his dismissal from the service.

Jacobson arrived almost an hour early at the Klenovy Boulevard terminal, scouring every approach as he had at the previous failed meeting place for the slightest indication of an ambush. Having failed to find one, he positioned himself at the highest possible vantage point above the pier, his concentration upon the throng of embarking and disembarking passengers, seeking close-together groups or gatherings of people who did not fit the tourist profile. And failed again to locate anything that triggered his suspicion.

Jacobson rigidly followed Radtsic's trail-clearing insistence of boarding fifteen minutes ahead of the Russian, stationing himself at the rail overlooking the gangway to ensure Radtsic wasn't followed. So tensed was Jacobson that the skin of his arms tingled at the slight pressure of his leaning against the rail and he was overly aware of people close to him, twitching away from the briefest contact.

Ten minutes until departure, Jacobson saw. Where the hell was Radtsic! He should have been here by now, visible on the pier to ensure there was no surveillance. So why wasn't he? Because he wasn't going to show, Jacobson answered himself. He'd panicked or been found out or lost his nerve, all or any of which could mean his arrest or an attack and then God knows . . .

There he was, snatched Jacobson, at the first sighting. And making no effort to merge into his tourist surroundings. The barrel-chested, swarthy Maxim Radtsic was wearing a collar and tie with his three-piece business suit, shouldering his way through the last-minute boarders, and Jacobson's relief was tempered by the thought of the other, still unresolved danger. Jacobson continued to observe the Russian's precautions, delaying an approach for fifteen minutes after departure for the Russian to complete the same check on him as he moved around the boat and even then not until Radtsic gave the signal that he was satisfied they were both clear.

Today's sign was again to discard an empty cigarette packet into the Moskva river, a gesture fitting the chain-smoking habit that had developed since the Russian's first approach.

"What the hell happened?" greeted Jacobson, as he got alongside the other man.

"There was a personal problem," said Radstic, not looking sideways. The hand holding the cigarette was shaking, creating an almost constant avalanche of ash.

"What problem?"

"Elana."

"What about her?"

"She's losing her nerve: doesn't want to come."

"Are you coming without her?"

Radtsic gave Jacobson a frowned, sideways look. "Of course not."

"What then?"

"I've persuaded her. But it's got to be soon now."

"We're setting up a diversion: want you to be involved at the very end. You can be the person who makes sure it works by concentrating attention away from you and Elana."

"How?"

"We're sending someone in, as a decoy for your people to follow," lured Jacobson. Radtsic surely had to know about the attempted FSB entrapment of Charlie Muffin, even if the man was elevated way above operational activity.

"How?" repeated the other man.

"It'll involve your service, when it happens," Jacobson hedged further.

"What's my involvement?"

"You have operational oversight, don't you?"

"Not in a planning stage. There are progress submission and reviews."

"There hasn't been anything about a potential English situation?"

Radtsic properly looked at Jacobson for the first time. "Are you trying to trick me?"

"No!" denied Jacobson, meeting the look. "I've told you it's all going to work just as you want."

"It doesn't sound right!"

"I'm not tricking you, Maxim Mikhailovich. I'm *guaranteeing* everything and more than you've asked for." Why was it all going wrong, despaired Jacobson: in less than twenty-four hours he'd been made to look an amateur by a down-at-heel dinosaur and now he was a hairsbreadth from losing the biggest catch in MI6 history!

"I need to think!"

"You need to trust me: trust that I'm telling you the truth."

"I need to think," the Russian repeated, doggedly.

"Let's meet tomorrow," urged Jacobson, anxiously. "Check your ongoing operational planning involving the British." With so much going wrong—being misunderstood—he daren't risk actually mentioning Charlie Muffin and Natalia Fedova until he talked to London and learned whether they'd found the bastard.

"Here, again at noon."

"Maxim, it should be somewhere else."

"Here," insisted the older man.

"Here," capitulated Jacobson.

"It could be a one-night stand," said Jonathan Miller, staring down at the photographs Albert Abrahams had laid out before him.

"I established the surveillance the day we got the assignment. If you look more closely, she's wearing three different outfits, leaving and entering the apartment over three different days. I ran a check at the Sorbonne. She's registered at the same address with the same telephone number as Andrei. They're on the same course."

"Perhaps this will put a finger up Straughan's ass: get him to answer all our other questions to all our other uncertainties."

"This is the one that could really fuck everything up."

"I'd never have worked that out if you hadn't told me."

13

THERE SEEMED TO BE NO PART OF CHARLIE MUFFIN'S BODY that didn't ache. His feet, of course, caused the worst agony. By the time he got back to London he was hobbling so badly that an airport driver returning from taking a disabled passenger to a flight offered Charlie a lift on his empty cart, which Charlie gratefully accepted, deciding that the privilege attracted far less attention than the way he was walking. Despite all of which, Charlie was happy. So far—a long way in opportunity, if not necessarily in miles—reversing the terms of engagement to his personal control was working.

He'd been lucky, Charlie accepted: bloody lucky. But there again, he'd made most of that luck himself. The biggest gamble had been the moment he'd fled the plane. He'd built in most of the contingency protection he could anticipate, pausing in the Amsterdam arrival hall to take the battery from the Russian phone to prevent his being traced by any tracker device installed in London but still leaving open his expectation of unknown escorts on the plane. That there hadn't been added to his suspicion of a separate agenda of which he was unaware, further supported by there having been no passport questioning upon his reentry into Heathrow triggered by watchers having alerted the aircraft crew of his disappearance. Charlie estimated that had given him at least two, maybe as much as four, hours' runaway time. He'd used some of it buying toiletries and a hold-all in which to carry them before purchasing a closing gate ticket on the last-of-the-day Dutch airline flight back to London, which he'd established to be half empty while selecting his escape seat at Heathrow three hours earlier. The hold-all provided just enough luggage for him to be accepted without question at a fifty-pound-a-night, thin-walled room in a Waterloo station hotel.

He'd still ached, although not as badly, when he woke. He no longer shuffled, just walked slowly, to get to a conveniently close internet café by nine fifteen. It took less than another thirty minutes of concentrated Google surfing to assemble a selection of holiday companies offering short Russian tours and even less to find one in Manchester eager enough to retain its newly acquired franchise—and full payment in cash, to which he agreed—to allocate him one of their three remaining vacancies on an eight-day block-visa trip to the Russian capital.

By eleven Charlie had emptied the Harrods safe deposit box of his David Merryweather passport and international driving license and used the accompanying American Express card in the same name to buy a suit, trousers, shirts, and underwear, as well as a suitcase additional to the hold-all to carry it all. From experience, he held back from risking new shoes, to which his awkward feet would have needed to adapt.

Charlie's train arrived precisely on time in Manchester, enabling him to be one of the first of the tour group independently to reach the airport. Muriel, the Russian-speaking tour guide, said she was sorry the cost dictated that it had to be a basic economy night flight. "I took a chance, accepting you as I did, but we need to maintain our booking numbers."

"What chance was that?" queried Charlie, apprehensively.

"Adding you to the block visa. We're supposed to supply the names a week before: the embassy requires master copies."

The apprehension lifted like mist in the sun, which Charlie, prepared to sacrifice his Merryweather identity, decided to be shining down upon him. "Here it is."

"Malcolm Stoat?" the girl queried. "That wasn't the name I thought you gave me on the telephone?"

"It was a very bad line. I had difficulty hearing a lot of what you said to me."

"And you've already got a visa?" she said, opening the passport.

"I didn't know anything about block visas," lied Charlie. "I thought I had to arrange my own. It does mean you're not taking any chances, doesn't it?"

"I suppose I should add your name to my list?"

"Perhaps you should."

"And I'm really sorry it's a night flight."

"I'll try to sleep," said Charlie. Which he did, dreamlessly.

By comparison, Gerald Monsford's day had been a continuous waking nightmare.

"Your future's hanging by a thread," threatened the MI6 Director, the moment his demanded connection was made to Moscow. "Because of you, the entire operation's in jeopardy. You realized that!"

If only you knew how jeopardized it really had been, thought Jacobson. "With respect, sir, you were present throughout my entire London briefing. At which it was specified that the sole purpose of my recall was thoroughly to study and memorize Charlie Muffin's appearance, nothing more. It was also specified at that briefing that every conceivable aspect of the operation was being supervised and handled by others, from whom I was separated and with whom I under no circumstance would or should have any knowledge or contact, because of the particular function I have to perform to create the diversion at the moment of Radtsic's extraction. From which I understood there were to be others of whom I had no knowledge carrying out in-flight surveillance and that there would be protective surveillance in place at the known stopover at Schipol."

The meticulously prepared defense momentarily silenced Monsford, increasing the man's fury but in turn fogging his reasoning. "You could have alerted the crew!"

Jacobson hoped he timed his answering silence to the millisecond. "I was traveling as an ordinary economy-class passenger. Why—or how—should I have been monitoring another supposedly ordinary economy-class passenger who might only have been booked to Amsterdam closely enough to spot his disappearance? Had I raised an alarm the departure would have been stopped, because security would have insisted the aircraft be searched and all hold baggage unloaded. And I, as the person who raised the alert, would have been publicly identified and even, worse, put before a televised news conference. If my diplomatic cover withstood investigation, the exposure would have been prevented by continuing with the diversion mission."

Monsford knew his continuing frustration was suffusing his face and was glad he'd taken the call entirely alone, with neither Rebecca nor Straughan as witnesses. With determination, Monsford accepted defeat. "Tell me about Radtsic."

"He's falling apart," said Jacobson, enjoying the screw-turning. "Elana changed her mind about defecting. He claims he's persuaded her to change it back again but I'm worried."

"What are you suggesting?" asked Monsford, anxiously.

Monsford couldn't handle the pressure! Jacobson suddenly realized. "I'm not *suggesting* anything. I'm simply keeping you informed of a dangerously uncertain situation."

"You must have formed some ideas?"

"I'm not sure if we're not trying to achieve too much, guaranteeing the extraction of Radtsic and his family by making a distraction out of that of Charlie Muffin and his family. . . ." Again Jacobson tried perfectly to time the pause. "Particularly as we appear to have lost Charlie Muffin."

How much he would have savored using Jacobson instead of Charlie as the about-to-die decoy, mused Monsford. "You seriously believe we could lose Radtsic?"

"I'd put that possibility as high as seventy-five percent if we don't get him out soon."

"Then we can't change course: all our preparation is irrevocably interlinked."

"We don't have Charlie Muffin *to* interlink him!" risked Jacobson.

"He's *got* to reestablish contact," declared Monsford, clinging to the earlier insistence of James Straughan. "Once he does, everything slots back into place."

"We won't know what Charlie's been doing," Jacobson pointed out. "From what Straughan told me yesterday in London there was suspicion from Charlie's interrogation, after his return from Jersey, that he'd been a long-embedded Russian sleeper. What if he *was* turned: the trip to Jersey was to meet an FSB Control to fulfill an assignment we haven't any idea about? That would slot in even more perfectly with Natalia's pleading telephone calls, so soon after Charlie's Jersey return, wouldn't it?"

"It couldn't be," groped Monsford, anguished: he'd done everything he could—and more—to promote himself as the architect of it all. "Did you tell Radtsic the use to which we were putting Charlie?"

He couldn't better have managed the exchange if he'd personally scripted and rehearsed it, thought Jacobson. "I told him there was to be a diversion, without telling him what it was to be. And I didn't mention Charlie Muffin by name."

"You get the slightest suspicion that Radtsic knows what's happening to Natalia?"

"None," replied Jacobson. "But he'd have to know if Charlie's disappearance and the sudden emergence of Natalia is part of a Russian operation?" He'd have to hold back from taking this improvisation too far: he'd completely escaped censure.

"When's your next meeting?"

Jacobson hesitated, unsure if he needed the protection of an indeterminate answer. Deciding that he didn't, he said, simply: "Tomorrow."

"Don't say anything more about a diversion," ordered Monsford. "But listen hard to everything he says, for anything that doesn't sound right."

He'd risen like a Phoenix not just unsinged but smelling of roses, Jacobson decided: sweeter than roses, even.

"What?" demanded Monsford, as the operational director came into his suite for the second time that day.

From the oddly cowed way the Director was slumped behind his desk, Straughan thought Monsford looked like a bull mastiff that had lost its nerve. "The media fanfare is in full tune. It started in Amsterdam, obviously. It was picked up in Moscow—running on the news wires—and the *Evening Standard* has jumped on it here. Their front-page headline is: 'Moscow-bound Briton in Airport Disappearance.' The story covers the whole spectrum from assassination to kidnap to spy plot, in no particular order."

"They using Charlie's cover name?" demanded Monsford, straightening slightly from his withdrawn shell.

"Of course they are," confirmed Straughan. "It's my guess that Charlie intended the publicity, which will build up when there are no answers to all the questions that are being asked. Our concern has to be that it concentrates attention on Moscow."

"Jacobson doesn't think we can run the operation as we planned, now that we've lost Charlie," said the Director.

"We can't, not until we find him," agreed Straughan, close to impatience at the statement of the obvious. Curious what the man's reaction would be, he added: "There's something else."

"What?" repeated Monsford, slumping back into his defeatist posture.

"The son, Andrei. He's living with another student, a French girl named Yvette Paruch: they're on the same course."

"What's your point?"

"Getting him here, without Yvette screaming kidnap."

"Telling him what's happening: giving him the chance to prepare himself, you mean?"

"I'd prefer that to trying an unexpected snatch."

"What if he doesn't want to come: would he regard his father as a traitor?"

"That *is* my point," said Straughan, once more close to impatience. "Too many things are going wrong. We don't want a difficulty with Andrei becoming another one."

"It can only come from Radtsic. Jacobson's seeing him tomorrow."

"Do I tell Jacobson to fix it?" pressed Straughan, determined it should be the Director's decision.

"Give me a choice of proposals," ordered Monsford.

As he wiped his mother's mouth after feeding her that night Straughan said: "He's looking for a way to avoid direct personal responsibility but I'm not going to let him. I'm not going to carry the can anymore: you mark my words," and the old lady who didn't any longer know how to mark or even say words stared unseeingly into a world in which only she lived.

14

CHARLIE'S DREAMLESS SLEEP DIDN'T LAST THE ENTIRE FLIGHT, just sufficiently for the aching finally to disappear, despite the seat limitations. He straightened, with antenna-prompted awareness, at the first change in the engine pitch, the initial priority to study the rest of the tourist group with whom he'd had no proper contact in Manchester. Charlie didn't foresee any practical use from being part of it, apart from the initial, prebooked hotel accommodation, but in the entirely unplanned, thin-iced circumstances he'd created for himself it was impossible to anticipate anything he might need.

There were sixteen other people in the party, predominantly couples apart from three teenage girls in addition to Muriel, whose surname he discovered to be Simpson and whom he guessed to be in her early twenties. She was sitting next to him when he awoke.

"You really did need to sleep, didn't you?" she greeted. She was an auburn-haired, small-featured woman who clearly believed her bust was her most attractive feature, judging from the upthrusting bra in which it was encased beneath a company-advertising T-shirt.

"I've been working flat out to get a project almost to closure," said Charlie, deciding to introduce an already determined insurance for what was soon to follow.

"What sort of project?" she asked, predictably.

"One that means a lot to me," said Charlie. "I can trust your discretion, can't I?"

"I'd hope so," said the woman, smiling at being taken into a confidence.

"You've heard of Russian oligarch billionaires settling in England?"

"Of course." The expectant smile broadened.

"I've made a particular study of Russian architecture: got this commission to build a pavilion completely in the prerevolutionary style in the grounds of his Sussex estate for one of the best-known . . . I can't, of course, tell you his name. . . ."

"Of course not," she agreed, dropping the smile to indicate her seriousness.

"If I get this right, it'll open every door. I've studied all the photographs and all the pictured art work, spent some time in St. Petersburg. I've snatched at this trip to confirm the styles that I've followed."

"I can understand the importance of that."

"I'm telling you now to warn you that I'm going to skip most of your trips."

For the first time there was a frown. "The firm's responsible for the people in this group."

"You don't have to worry about me," soothed Charlie, with open-faced sincerity.

"How are you going to get around by yourself?"

Charlie hesitated, anxious to keep the invention as unquestionable as possible. "I studied Russian at university: speak it pretty well."

The smile came back, broader than before. "Which university?"

The eagerness warned Charlie. "Was Russian your university module?"

"It's why I'm doing this job, postgraduate. I want to speak it perfectly, eventually to get a diplomatic job."

"Which university?" asked Charlie, turning her question back upon the girl.

"Manchester, obviously."

"Bristol," escaped Charlie.

On their overhead panel the fasten-seat-belt sign came on, the signal for the copilot's landing announcement.

"I hope you get what you want in Moscow," said Muriel.

"I'm determined I will," Charlie promised himself.

Charlie rehearsed for the contradictions of a night arrival, the time of the fewest incoming flights carrying the fewest number of passengers among whom to hide from the fewest number of airport immigration officers and hopefully from the constantly open-eyed CCTV, which in the case of Moscow's Sheremetyevo, while far less than the Orwellian intrusion of England, still had to be guarded against.

He scanned as much of the cabin as it was possible to see beyond his own tourist party and concluded his luck was holding with three of them—two men, one big enough to be Monsford's twin, and a woman—remaining the tallest and the heaviest. He got close behind them as they got onto the disembarkation pier and Muriel unwittingly helped by shifting back and forth, a shepherdess keeping her easily strayed flock tight together. Charlie switched his attention between the tall-statured three and one of the smallest women in the group, maneuvering her unevenly wheeled suitcase to give him the excuse to bend away from the easily spotted cameras. His most exposed moment came at the passport booth, which he guarded against as best he could by fumbling through his cabin baggage hold-all close to his face for his tourist-group documentation, aware of the watchful Muriel on the far side as he was passed through unchallenged. Charlie judged his other danger point the camera-monitored registration desk at the Rossiya Hotel on the Ulitsa Razina and again used the burly trio, the Monsford look-alike predominantly, as well as his face-obscuring hold-all.

The prebooked accommodation put Muriel in the next room to his and she paused directly in front of him, handing over the key. "I'm responsible for everyone in the party: to make sure no one breaks the rules. Don't get me into trouble, okay?"

"I've never got a girl into trouble," said Charlie, acknowledging as he spoke that it was yet another lie. Would he be able to make contact with Natalia later today, when Moscow woke up? he wondered.

"Heathrow, four hours after the departure of Charlie's Moscow flight," declared John Passmore.

"Positively confirmed?" Aubrey Smith demanded.

The MI5 operations director shook his head. "Assessed at the moment at seventy-five percent: if it's Charlie, he's bloody good. It was the last KLM flight of the day. We've got two possible CCTV shots, in each of which he's shielded, even at the passport check. Technical are doing their best to enhance and work out height and weight."

"Charlie *is* bloody good," acknowledged the MI5 Director-General. "No help from passport recognition?"

Passmore shook his head again. "If we get enough to harden up the Heathrow images I'll circulate Charlie's picture to airport-based Special Branch. It's a shotgun effort to shoot down a sparrow but it might tell us when Charlie goes out of the country again."

"If he hasn't already left," qualified Smith.

"If he's already left it'll give us a potential arrival to warn Moscow."

"I've had three buck-passing calls from Monsford, stressing that Charlie's our responsibility," disclosed Smith.

"Straughan bought me lunch," capped Passmore. "The supposedly finest Aberdeen Angus at the Reform, which unfortunately was overcooked."

Smith smiled. "And?"

"At one stage I thought he was inferring that we'd colluded: had some foreknowledge, even, of Charlie's vanishing act."

"What's your reading from that?"

"Panic, above and beyond any sensible concern," assessed Passmore. "Straughan's focus was mostly upon whether Charlie really had been turned all those years ago. I had to agree the sequence of events from Charlie's disappearance supported that doubt."

"What's the doubt I'm hearing in your voice right now?" picked out Smith.

"I don't believe this is the combined operation it's supposed to be," openly admitted Passmore.

"You suspect I'm keeping something more from you?" demanded Smith, matching the openness.

"Are you?"

"That's an insubordinate, presumptuous inference!" declared Smith, the habitual quietness of his voice reducing the intended indignation.

"And that's an avoiding answer. I lost an arm and a career because my superiors didn't tell me the whole truth," rejected Passmore, feeling across to his empty, left side. "I don't want to lose whatever career I'm trying to establish in this shadow-shifting environment, to which I still obviously haven't adjusted, through the same default. To prevent which I'd prefer to resign."

Aubrey Smith sat with his head bowed, contemplating the totally unexpected turn in the conversation. Finally looking up, he said: "I'd hoped my apology for not being completely honest was sufficient. I respect and admire your integrity and want to convince you of mine. I have kept nothing more of this operation from you. If there is a hidden aspect, I am as unaware of it as you are."

Now it was Passmore who lapsed into silence for a moment, good arm once more crossed to where his other had once been. "I'm convinced there's something else. I haven't the slightest evidence for the suspicion beyond instinct, but from some of the things Straughan said I believe there's a something being kept from us. If it is, we're being set up to be scapegoats."

"Which I won't let us be," refused Smith, emptied by what he saw as the confirmation of what he'd feared since this current episode had begun.

"How, then, do we prevent it?" wondered the operations director

"Managing independent contact with Charlie could help."

"Who could be following the same instinct by doing what he's done, as well as asking for those separate passports," suggested Passmore.

Harry Jacobson nervously lengthened his reconnaissance at the ferry terminal, the knot in the very pit of his already hollowed stomach tightening further in his despair of ever properly ensuring there wasn't a snatch squad in the ebb and flow of people he was scouring for the first glimpse of Maxim Radtsic, hoping against hope that once more the man wouldn't appear and that the operation would be aborted before it even began. It wasn't just the apprehension of becoming the victim of an FSB counterplot that convinced Jacobson the Russian's extraction was doomed. He was equally worried by the accumulated recognition that in the questionably professional planning there were far too many unforeseeable, abyss-deep pitfalls—the unexpected discovery of Andrei Radtsic's live-in girlfriend the latest—in what had been conceived more like a tin-soldiered, make-believe war game commanded by incompetents safe in their London riverside bunkers. Now the game could be over before it even began because the most undisciplined tin soldier hadn't obeyed orders, leaving him, if the analogy was continued, the first of the other tin soldiers likely to fall if it was all an FSB entrapment.

Jacobson reluctantly acknowledged that his alternative, walking away and lying that Radtsic hadn't turned up, wasn't feasible. The chances of the FSB executive director approaching another Western intelligence agency, the CIA the most likely, were too great and if the man did and there was eventual publicity, his career in MI6—already hanging by a thread, according to Monsford's most recent diatribe—would be over. But he didn't need to lie, he realized, finally identifying the Stalin look-alike barging his way through the shifting melee below.

Jacobson observed the postsailing-surveillance precautions, minimally encouraged at isolating no one showing undue interest in either of them, eventually following the Russian into a windowed observation lounge that provided a panoramic view of the red-walled, star-towered Kremlin as the ferry made its slow way parallel along the river. The view kept everyone on the fortress side, leaving the farthest section of the observation room free for Jacobson and Radtsic.

"You had time to settle everything with Elana?" opened Jacobson, choosing a gradual lead-up in the hope of limiting Radtsic's reaction to Andrei's romance.

"I think so," said the older man, although uncertainly.

"Has she really changed her mind back again: agreed to come?"

"Yes." The uncertainty was still there.

Contrary to which the nervousness wasn't as visible today, Jacobson saw, as they were constantly intent upon their surroundings: even the chain-smoking seemed less. "What about you? You happier with everything than you were?"

"I still don't understand the delay," protested the Russian. "Why can't we go right now? Tomorrow? Why can't we make it tomorrow?"

"Tell me about Andrei," avoided Jacobson, taking the obvious opening.

"Why are you bringing him into the conversation?" The Russian frowned.

"How do you think he'll react at suddenly learning what's happening?"

"I want to talk to you about that: make sure there's a proper, safe proposal."

"That's the sort of care I'm trying to convince you we're taking."

"Maybe I overreacted earlier."

They were drifting away from what needed to be talked about, Jacobson recognized. "You didn't tell me how you thought Andrei might react."

"It'll be all right, when he settles down. Understands."

The Kremlin was disappearing as the boat took the first bend in the river and people began spreading themselves more evenly around the enclosed lounge, lessening their isolation. "It's the very beginning, the moment it happens, that I want to discuss."

"What's the problem?" demanded Radtsic at once, stopping with an unlit cigarette suspended before him.

"We're making plans to get Andrei out but we've discovered he's in a relationship."

"What are you talking about? What relationship?" The cigarette remained unlighted.

"A girl, a fellow student. French."

Radtsic finally fired the cigarette, smiling slightly. "He's a full-blooded Russian."

"You knew then?"

"No. What's there to know?"

"She doesn't appear to be a casual girlfriend. They're living together."

"What!"

The Russian's surprise was genuine, gauged Jacobson. "Everything's got to be very quick, once the extraction starts: no unexpected complications. What's most important is avoiding any interference from the French authorities."

"I told you Andrei needed to be warned," reminded Radtsic.

"How often are you in contact: exchange letters or talk on the phone?"

"I'm sure all my telephones are monitored: that my mail is being intercepted. I've told you that. I also told you Andrei wouldn't accept messages through an intermediary."

"I've brought a pocket tape recorder," said Jacobson. "He knows your voice. Make a recording, telling him to trust the person who brings it to him: that he must do what that person tells him."

Radtsic shook his head, his inhalations now coming with chain-smoking regularity. "You're not listening to me! He'll think it's a trick. Or something made under duress."

"How, then, Maxim?" asked Jacobson, desperately. "Tell me how!"

"Elana," announced the Russian. "She'll have to be got out first, ahead of me, through Paris. You'll have to coordinate their extraction, together with mine here."

"Will she be allowed to travel?"

"I have the authority to approve it."

"You've told me you're being watched: that your telephone's tapped and your mail opened," argued Jacobson. "Your approving Elana's travel would trigger every alarm."

"It's me they're monitoring, not Elana. There'd be a period, a few days, before the connection was made."

Jacobson suspected that Radtsic was trying to force the pace and didn't blame the man: it actually improved the Russian's control of events, and if Elana was already out of the country it greatly reduced the chances of her suddenly changing her mind. Once in France, she'd be committed, with no way back. And so would Radtsic. "I'll put it to London: see if they'll accept it as an alternative to what they're putting in place now."

"I can put everything in motion within two days," promised the Russian, eagerly.

"Don't!" ordered Jacobson, just as urgently. "You've got to wait for London's approval. Prepare whatever preliminaries are necessary. But don't positively initiate anything, not until we meet again. And, Maxim . . ."

"What?"

"Not here. Never again here, at the terminal."

"Where, instead?"

Insurance time, Jacobson thought at once. "You've got my private number. Call tomorrow, at noon, from a public phone. I'll give you the location then."

"Will you have spoken to London by noon tomorrow?"

"About a lot of things," confirmed Jacobson.

Jane Ambersom was an intelligent woman who acknowledged her instinctive aggression to be a failing, just as she recognized its underlying psychological cause to be an ingrained resentment at her androgenic confusion. And she was further annoyed at her inability sufficiently to curb it. Her sexuality, in fact, was entirely and eagerly female, which added frustration to the resentment. She'd endured relationships at university that never went beyond a one-night stand and been hopeful of an affair when she'd first joined MI6, until, too demandingly again, she'd maneuvered her lover into a choice, which he'd made by returning to his wife. As she'd ascended the intelligence-service ladder and come under increased internal-security scrutiny, she'd subjugated sexuality for professional advancement, which she'd quite correctly doubted would have resulted from her submitting to Gerald Monsford's clumsy, experimental pawing in his conveniently constructed bedroom suite adjoining his office.

Since her transfer to MI5 and her foreign-liaison appointment, she had become extremely hopeful of Barry Elliott, even seeing in her rarely allowed fantasies a somewhat strained parallel with Charlie Muffin and Natalia Fedova. So far their encounters, although social, had remained strictly although not quite formally professional. He'd volunteered that he was neither married nor in a relationship and twice instead of restaurant encounters had suggested art-gallery meetings—the National and Tate Modern—where she'd discovered he enjoyed the same artists. It was upon his recommendation that in less than two weeks and three novels she'd become a committed Elmore Leonard fan.

Lunch that day was at Joe Allen's, which she'd initially feared she'd have to cancel because of Charlie Muffin's disappearance, until the Director-General told her there was no practical reason to remain at Thames House.

Elliott, as usual, was considerately there ahead of her, and stood to help her into her chair, with her preferred Rioja already uncorked. He didn't immediately embark upon a shared-interest discussion, which was something else that Jane preferred, but talked of a planned weekend Shakespeare festival in Stratford, having enjoyed his first visit to the rebuilt Globe Theatre in London. It wasn't until they were well into their main course that Elliott came to the official reason for the encounter and afterward Jane was quite sure she'd not overreacted to his unexpected return to their earlier discussion.

"Those transcript excerpts of Irena Novikov's debriefing have given us more problems than answers."

"I don't understand," hedged Jane.

"There's a lot of disparities between what she appears to have told you and what she's telling us. We think she's stalling. She's appearing to cooperate, which is the deal for her remaining in our protection program, but Langley suspects she's giving us the run-around. And there's a lot of access pressure from the Russian embassy in Washington."

"I've given you all I was allowed."

"We want fuller versions, to check in more detail against what she told your guy, Charlie Muffin. He spent a lot of time with her in Moscow, didn't he?"

"I don't think it was a *lot* of time," qualified Jane. "My understanding was that she persistently lied to him, trying to save the Russian operation, right up to the moment he caught her out."

"There's nothing of how he caught her out in what you've given me."

"I'll raise it," promised Jane, an idea growing in her mind.

"We'd appreciate that. Maybe I could get an idea from Langley about what she's telling them to offer in return."

"I like Stratford," risked Jane, in a complete change of direction. "Know it quite well."

Elliott looked at her across the table, half smiling. "Why don't you show me around there?"

"Why don't I?" Jane smiled back.

"You won't forget the comparison debriefings, will you?"

"Of course I won't."

15

DESPITE THE BOARD-HARD ROSSIYA BED CHARLIE MANAGED a further two hours' sleep, deciding initially to continue with the tourist-group concealment, gambling that this soon there wouldn't be an FSB connection between an inadvertent airport CCTV picture and the Malcolm Stoat name in the hotel register and the Amsterdam flight passenger list.

The broken day began with a breakfast-room getting-to-know-you gathering and a short and vaguely embarrassing promise of an experience of a lifetime from Muriel Simpson, complete with the distribution of the group's intended itinerary and an overflow of brochures, maps, and information sheets, all of which Charlie collected for later use.

Charlie's discomfort came within minutes of taking his designated place on the coach with the seat-lifting arrival beside him of the towering man behind whom he'd hopefully hidden for the earlier airport arrival.

"Wilfred Todd," introduced the man, in an echoing voice matching his size and a knuckle-crunching handshake. "Looking forward to our getting together, your being an architect and all."

"That your line of business?" probed Charlie, his stomach dipping at the possibility of his ignorance being exposed.

"My lad, John. Qualifies next June. He'll be looking for a better position then. Could be there's some openings with your firm."

Becoming the focus of an overly ambitious father was an encumbrance he didn't need but about which he could do little except, perhaps, store whatever transpired for later, as yet unknown, use. Strictly adhering to the story he'd invented for Muriel, Charlie toned down his fiction of billionaire Russian oligarchs while stressing that his was a particularly refined architectural expertise unsuited to a newly qualified entrant.

An English-speaking Russian guide took over from Muriel for the exploration of St. Basil's Cathedral in Red Square and Charlie retreated to the back of the Russian's brusquely assembled group where Muriel put herself.

"I thought what we spoke about, my slipping away, was between the two of us."

"It was. And is," replied the woman. "All I said was that you had a particular architectural interest that wouldn't interest the rest of them, to account in advance to the rest of the group for your slopping off. And I did that to protect myself, my job, and the company for which I want to go on working, okay!"

"Okay. And I'm sorry if I sounded tetchy."

"Sorry is something I hope not to be by your being on the tour," said the girl.

"I'm going now," warned Charlie, refusing a response. "I'll catch up later."

Charlie used the camouflage of other milling tourists to get off Red Square, despite the impracticality of CCTV over such a vast area, his mind sifting the unresolved uncertainties, Natalia's approach being the biggest of them all. And, startlingly, came up with the answer. Of course he knew why Natalia had made the calls to his flat in the manner and way she had: the way she'd expected him to comprehend. It gave him his all-important, just-short-of-perfect start. He hoped it would all continue that way.

Recognizing that the slightest changing breeze was psychologically important in the survival battle in which he believed himself embroiled, Aubrey Smith gained the first advantage not just by insisting the MI6 contingent cross the river to Thames House but by doing so reversed Gerald Monsford's de facto takeover. To reinforce that reversal, Smith staged the conference in a corner room of MI5's headquarters, with the fullest view of the MI6 building opposite, and warned in advance that John Passmore and Jane Ambersom would attend, knowing Monsford would match them with Rebecca Street and James Straughan. They arrived fifteen minutes early, reflecting their subordination, from which Monsford at once attempted to recover.

"Charles Muffin has very positively shown his allegiance to the Russians by what he's done. I want confirmation that this meeting is being fully recorded, for production in any future official inquiry into the cooperation between our two services."

"Of course a record is being kept," assured the MI5 Director-General, pricking the bombast. "I'll be interested to hear your proof that Muffin's allegiance *is* to Russia."

"What other interpretation is possible?" demanded the MI6 counterpart.

There were shifts of uncertainty from Rebecca Street and the MI6 operations director.

"How about something as mundane as his not trusting that he'd arrive safely in Moscow?" suggested Smith, satisfied how well Monsford's attitude suited his intentions.

"It's his wife and child whose extraction we're working to achieve: our entire, focused objective. Or at least what I believed it to be, until now," Monsford said.

"Is it?" demanded Smith, shortly.

There was a moment of silence disturbed only by more discomfited chair fidgeting before Monsford, the belligerence fading, said: "I don't understand that remark."

"And I can't expand it beyond saying that I'm curious at some . . . what . . . ? Inconsistencies, I suppose."

"The inconsistency is that of your officer with whom I mistakenly agreed to a combined operation."

"My recollection, which will be confirmed by earlier records, is that the urging came more from you than me, which is one of the inconsistencies I've mentioned."

"What are you suggesting?" demanded Monsford, the belligerence flaring.

"I'm not suggesting anything," again deflated Smith.

"I'm becoming confused at the purpose of this conference," Rebecca Street protested with strained impatience. "Are we supposed to be discussing the future of the operation in which Charlie Muffin was involved or talking in riddles?"

At Smith's gesture, John Passmore said: "It's a limited disappearance, which isn't a riddle. We've established a potential sighting of Charlie returning to Heathrow airport on a KLM flight, four hours after he got off the Moscow plane in Amsterdam: by 'potential' I mean it wasn't positive facial recognition. We're making the surmise by forensically making the comparison from weight, height, and general stature in the CCTV image. Those physical statistics and a slightly better photographic image, although again facially insufficient, matched a differently dressed man caught on CCTV entering Manchester airport late yesterday evening. Compared against the registered timing of that Manchester CCTV photograph, there was one direct Manchester flight to Moscow and three staged at Heathrow en route to other destinations, from which connecting flights from London to Moscow could have been possible—"

"What about a confirming manifest name?" broke in James Straughan.

"I'm sure you've monitored the Dutch publicity about Charlie's disappearance," replied Passmore, his voice as calm as Smith's. "We'd risk a publicity leak if we made a formal approach to an airline other than British. We didn't get our checks in place in time to flag up an alert on Charlie's legend name before the departure of the direct

Manchester flight or any of the possible transit links. We've checked the manifests that are safe for us to access. The name Malcolm Stoat doesn't appear, although there's a glitch with a block visa on which a tourist group traveled from Manchester."

"Are you reasoning that he staged the whole thing to get back to London to pick up a stashed alternative identity?" seized Straughan, professionally.

"That's the most obvious interpretation," agreed the other operations director.

"And a confirmation that he's a double agent," came in Monsford.

"Or that he didn't trust going into Moscow by our route," Smith argued back.

"Doesn't that amount to the same thing?" challenged Monsford.

"No," refused the other Director. "It could equally mean he had a facility to change the pseudonym and decided on a different route for better self-protection. Which doesn't deviate from the agreed plan that to get Natalia and Sasha out he still has at some stage to make contact with everyone and everything we've established at the embassy."

"Are you proposing we just sit back and wait for the bloody man to reappear as and when he chooses?" demanded Monsford, incredulously.

"Do you have a better suggestion?" prompted Smith.

It was Straughan, professional again, who answered. "Travel companies take block tourist bookings at hotels, as well as block group visas. It should be easy to locate the hotel in which the Manchester party are staying. Charlie might—"

"It was easy," interrupted Passmore. "It's the Rossiya, on the Ulitza Razina, and a man made a last-minute telephone booking so late that there wasn't time to copy his name onto the master log that the Manchester firm holds: that's the glitch I referred to."

"Was there any real point in stringing everything out to get to this point!" broke in Rebecca Street, her exasperation even more obvious than before.

"None whatsoever, apart from my commitment to liaise fully and openly with you," replied Smith, easily. "And we'd have got to it far sooner if our immediate discussion hadn't begun the way it did. So let's drop empty recriminations and move on. I've done nothing to fill in the blank on the tourist-group visa but I don't think we should consider it as any more than a blank we've got to fill from surveillance on the hotel."

"And if he's there, ask him what the hell he's playing at," insisted Monsford.

"We know what the hell he's playing at." Smith sighed, heavily. "And if Charlie's there it should reassure you about his loyalties: he wouldn't be there if he'd gone over to the FSB, would he?"

"It's also our thinking that we shouldn't do anything more than establishing *if* he's at the Rossiya," said Passmore. "It was always the intention that Charlie remain entirely independent, our not making contact with him or his not making contact with the embassy until the very last moment he's satisfied we can lift Natalia and the child."

"Tell us more about your thinking," encouraged Monsford, the belligerence easing once more. "Of course the Amsterdam episode doesn't rank as a diplomatic incident: it'll stay an unexplained mystery and be forgotten. But it's made headlines. Wouldn't that have been best avoided by Muffin protesting his entry arrangements at the briefing here?"

"The FSB *know* he's coming to Russia," reminded Smith, frowning at the question. "My interpretation about Amsterdam is that it's a self-devised diversion, with an accompanying message that he knows what he's confronting *by* openly returning"

"So he's issuing a challenge?" persisted Monsford.

"We were doing that by responding to the Moscow calls," Passmore pointed out.

"According to Charlie, Natalia Fedova could provide incalculable information about Russian intelligence, past and present, and much of it's up-to-date, Putin-initiated thinking," listed Monsford. "I am now wondering whether, in my determination to have access to such information, I didn't overcommit my service to a joint operation."

The movement among those around the table was different this time, more surprise than discomfort at the man's attitude swings.

"What's the point you're now making?" demanded Smith, fearing a shift in his domination.

"We're at the mercy an unpredictable officer. If he is at the Rossiya Hotel he should be confronted: told that unless he accepts superior authority everything's off."

"Which is what I proposed in Buckinghamshire," recalled Smith, believing he understood Monsford's posturing from the outset and no longer dismissing it as overriding pomposity. "We've moved on from that position now: my personal assessment is that it's a ninety percent certainty that Charlie Muffin is in Moscow. We also accepted his unpredictability in Buckinghamshire. But what he'd do if we told him the extraction was canceled is entirely predictable. He'd simply continue to try to get them out, irrespective of no longer having any embassy backup or of causing diplomatic embarrassment. There's only one way physically to eradicate that risk and that would create much greater publicity than Amsterdam, particularly as there would be the named association with Malcolm Stoat." Smith paused, taking in a much needed breath. "Are you recommending that guaranteed prevention, with all its repercussions?"

Fury had begun to flood the MI6 Director's face before Smith finished talking, coloring a look of near hatred. Monsford said: "No, I am certainly not recommending that guaranteed prevention."

"I'm relieved," remarked Smith. "Are we agreed, then, that at this stage we limit ourselves to confirming Charlie Muffin's presence, if indeed he is at the Rossiya Hotel?"

It was several moments before Monsford managed a reply and when he did it was only a throat-blocked, "Yes."

"It didn't work," judged Jane Ambersom, emerging from her silence in the directly following aftermath inquest. "Monsford overplayed the buck passing at the beginning."

"He came close to recovering at the end," qualified Aubrey Smith.

"But you got the ultimate resolution and its rejection out into the open," Passmore added, endorsing the qualification.

The woman frowned between the two men. Having seen the disconnection of the MI5 recording apparatus, she asked: "Was assassination ever considered an option?"

"I believe it might have progressed to that," allowed the Director-General.

Jane considered the reply, again looking between the two men. "You didn't expand on what you called 'inconsistencies'?"

"The possibility of assassination was one, an accusation I couldn't openly make," said Smith, showing no discomfort at the clear deception in front of Passmore, who in turn gave no reaction to the Director's unrecorded agreement during his Buckinghamshire return with Gerald Monsford.

"Am I right in inferring, then, that there are limits to our future cooperation?" asked Jane, openly again and encouraged at the prospect of more directly opposing the man responsible for ending her MI6 career.

"Everything is to be decided on an item-by-item basis," ruled the Director-General.

"Then there is a decision to be made," disclosed Jane, who took less than five minutes to recount her lunchtime conversation with Barry Elliott.

"Coincidence?" questioned Passmore, the moment she finished.

"Coincidences occur," conceded Smith. "I've never personally made a decision based upon one. What did you tell Elliott?"

"That I'd think about it."

"Drip-feed it," ordered Smith. "I want to know his each and every reaction to each and every release. I don't see how, but if there is a CIA involvement in this—which we've already, briefly, touched upon—everything changes."

"And we're not sharing Elliott's approach with MI6?" pressed the woman.

"Surely not until we're confident MI6 aren't already aware of Elliott's approach: maybe even initiated it through their contacts with Langley," said Passmore.

"Irena Yakulova Novikov was ours, whom we only handed over to the CIA because the White House was the Russian target. Everything Charlie did, including his debriefing that broke her, is still ours, unseen by Langley or Monsford," said Smith.

"I don't follow that!" protested Jane.

"I judge what Elliott said as a totally unexpected pebble thrown into an already murky pool," said Smith. "I want to see how far the ripples spread. And, Jane . . . ?"

"What?"

"I want you to stay very close to Barry Elliott."

"I will," promised the woman, the smile at her own amused satisfaction.

In his penthouse office atop the Vauxhall Cross building, Gerald Monsford settled expansively back into his chair and said: "I think I handled that exceptionally well. The onus now is entirely on MI5 and we're on provable record proposing we back off."

"Also on provable record is an unequivocal reference to assassination," pointed out Rebecca, aware that Monsford had not turned on his recording machine and irritated at losing the silver bullet to blow Monsford out of the chair in which he now lolled. She also judged his earlier performance more amateur dramatic than exceptional.

Monsford snorted a laugh. "You've missed the whole point! I said no to assassination. When Charlie Muffin, an MI5 officer, is put away with a bang, at whom will the accusing finger point!"

They both looked up as James Straughan hurried into the office from his check of the operations-room traffic to announce: "We've got a problem."

Harry Jacobson's call was patched through from the Moscow embassy's sterilized communications room to Gerald Monsford's equally security-protected office, enabling the exchange to be put on speakerphone for a simultaneous relay to Rebecca Street and James Straughan. Bizarrely for a man of his size, Monsford was once more hunched in his enclosing chair in something close to a fetal ball.

"Radtsic can't pull a switch like this, not this late!" protested Monsford. "It would mean an entirely different extraction from Paris!"

"Radtsic says if Elana talks to the boy, explains what's happening, there won't be any problem," repeated Jacobson. "If it doesn't come from her, Andrei or his girlfriend or both will scream abduction and it'll all go wrong."

"And Radtsic wants to move at once?"

"He says he could make all the necessary arrangements for Elana by tomorrow. He wants his extraction coordinated with Elana and Andrei's from Paris. If Andrei comes willingly, we could have them in London at virtually the same time."

"I personally formulated how we're getting the kid out," reminded Monsford.

"I'm telling you what Radtsic told me," retorted Jacobson. "That with Andrei agreeing, all we need to do is drive them to Orly—I didn't tell him we were using Orly—and bring them out on the passports that are ready. I did tell him the passports were ready."

Monsford looked inquiringly at the two others in the room. Straughan shrugged his shoulders. Rebecca said, softly: "We need to talk, not make any quick decisions."

Into the telephone, Monsford said: "Tell Radtsic we have to talk about it: that it's an unexpected change that we've got properly to consider, not rush into. That he's got to accept what we're saying: that it's the safety of him and his family we're thinking about."

"I already have," said Jacobson. "I'll tell him again."

"I haven't finished," warned Monsford, irritably. "We might possibly know where Charlie is."

Jacobson listened without interruption but when the Director finished said: "If he's there I go on as planned, right?"

"Wrong," corrected Monsford. "I don't want us losing the bastard again. Go separately from those Aubrey Smith is putting in place. I want our independent confirmation that we know where Charlie is: no slipups this time. I'm not sure I can any longer trust Smith to keep us fully in the loop."

"But you still want the diversion?"

"More than ever, after the way that bastard has jerked us around," insisted Monsford, vehemently. "As Shakespeare said, 'let's make us medicines of our great revenge.' "

"Mummy going to Paris to hold little Andrei's hand solves most of our difficulty but gives us another one," said Albert Abrahams.

Jonathan Miller shook his head. "We've only got to look after one extra for a few hours. It's the best we could have hoped for."

"I'd be happier with more direct contact," said Abrahams. "I'm not comfortable getting things relayed from Moscow via London."

"Neither am I," said the Paris station chief. "Straughan's promised to set a meeting up just before the extraction."

"More relayed arrangements," Abrahams pointed out.

16

FROM THE TANTRUM ANECDOTES OF HIS SADLY TOO-OFTEN-abandoned single mother, Charlie Muffin guessed he'd been born a cynic, suspicious that his bottle milk might be polonium-poisoned or his diaper pin an offensive weapon, but he'd never sneered at the apparent childlike elements of espionage tradecraft. There was nothing derisory at spy liaisons signaled by chalk marks on designated trees or walls, or particularly arranged curtains or plant pots and empty Coke cans or drainpipes or rocks. Some fakes—like others hiding miniature cameras or listening devices—made perfect dead-letter drops *because* they were so easily dismissed as childlike.

Natalia had never dismissed them, either, not from the very first, uncertain moments of their professionally insane affair. She'd actually encouraged their discussion, most specifically rendezvous locations, which, as cynically wary as ever, Charlie had at first imagined as another debriefing trap. To test which he'd chosen as a site the most historic of Moscow's botanical gardens, on Ulitsa Mira—created in 1706 by Peter the Great to cultivate medicinally beneficial plants for apothecary potions—to position his tradecraft marker, a tightly rolled copy of *Pravda* thrust as if discarded into the struts of the third bench from the main entrance. He'd returned at precisely the same time the following day to find a *Pravda* pincered in the same position but folded, not rolled. He'd responded with his rolled-up signal but concealed himself among the easily available deciduous arboretum from which he'd emerged as Natalia, not an expected then-KGB tracker, arrived to acknowledge it.

They'd kept the oldest of the city's botanical showpiece as their initial meeting place, advancing the protective tradecraft even after the physical affair had begun by adding calls between its several public, *Pravda*-discarded telephone kiosks as a double-checking confirmation that it was safe for him to continue on to her apartment.

Charlie had remembered their protective routine leaving Red Square that morning, which Natalia had expected, as she'd expected him to recognize the significance of how she'd made contact with his Vauxhall flat. Charlie didn't, though, change his already planned day, deciding the primary essential remained his continuing to be free of London, who'd now had close to thirty-six hours and the resources of both British intelligence organizations to locate him. He risked an entire hour watching the Rossiya Hotel for the slightest indication of professional observation, not entering until he was thoroughly satisfied that it wasn't, and even then limiting himself to minutes, remaining in his room just long enough minimally to pack what he could at the bottom of the hold-all but leaving sufficient belongings, including a toothbrush and shaving kit, for it to appear still occupied. He left the hold-all open to display all the tourist material accumulated that morning and pointedly told the concierge on his way out that he'd forgotten to take it with him for that day's tours.

He descended into the labyrinthine, Gothic-stationed Moscow Metro system, buying that day's *Pravda* on his way, only now slotting his Red Square realization into his itinerary. There was no cause for tradecraft evasion, enabling him to stay on the circle line to the familiar Ulitsa Mira station, unsure if the sentimentally remembered Mira hotel in which he and Natalia had become lovers would still be there. It was, although shabbier and more decayed than it had been then. It ensured, at least, that there was no questioning at his scarcely adequate luggage, which was further explained by the hooker and her work-overalled client leaving as he checked in, paying in advance, as demanded, for a four-night reservation. Charlie remained in the mirror-stained, gray-sheeted room only long enough to confirm that the dirt-rimed shower worked, although intermittently, and pocketing from the hold all he didn't expect to be there upon his return the spare David Merryweather passport, driving license, and American Express card.

It was only a short walk to the botanical gardens and Charlie made it cautiously, twice sitting on convenient benches behind the protection of his newspaper—in which there was no reference to his Amsterdam disappearance—to search for surveillance. If he was right, Natalia wouldn't have given her telephone signal if she'd suspected the gardens to be compromised, but she was working single-handedly against the full resources of the FSB. As he objectively acknowledged that his observation was strictly limited: a guaranteed ambush would be inside, where there was sufficient tree, bush, and hothouse concealment to hide an FSB army.

It wasn't until he'd scoured the other marker spots and found nothing that he needed briefly to sit and reconsider. If he'd mistaken the significance of the public-phone approach, he hadn't any idea how, unidentifiably, to trace or reach her. Acknowledging his last resort, Charlie lingered at two outside floral displays to get close to the first of the telephone boxes, which had become their second marker precaution, disconcerted that since their special use it had been converted from an enclosed, convenient-to-emplace shelter into a wall-mounted, hooded pod without useful nooks or crannies. So had the second, closest to the first tubular-roofed hothouse.

But, inexplicably, the third remained as he remembered, still graffiti-daubed and urine-stinking. And the foul floor wetness had soaked darkly upward through the three-day-old copy of *Pravda*, which, although having been partially dislodged from its under-tray support, had been folded precisely in the way he instantly recognized. Charlie refused the distracting euphoria, disentangling what remained dry to dump in a nearby bin before replacing it with his tightly rolled copy of that day's issue.

Natalia wouldn't risk a daylight visit, Charlie knew. Would she check that night? He had the afternoon and early evening to fill before finding out, and the tourist-group itinerary scheduled their return to the Rossiya at six. He checked his hotel room on his way, surprised to find the hold-all still there, and bought a pay-as-you-go Russian cell phone to replace his still-disabled London-issue before descending again into the Metro system. Charlie was in place in a panoramically windowed bar with a view of both front and side entrances by five thirty. And that day's luck stayed with him. Charlie isolated his suspect within fifteen minutes, well concealed within the covered entrance of an empty office block so dark that his initial impression was of occasional movement rather than a positive physical identification. It remained that way until the arrival and disembarkation of the tourist coach, when the shifting impression emerged for Charlie to identify as Patrick Wilkinson, the only man on his supposed support team whom he'd previously known.

And then there was another movement, closer to the front of the hotel but emerging from an equally professionally chosen concealing porch. Charlie at once dismissed the man as being another of his memorized backup group. Just as quickly Charlie discounted the obvious surveillance to be FSB, not solely because of the Western tailoring of the gray-checked suit but far more tantalizingly because of his immediate conviction that he'd somehow, somewhere, previously known—or encountered—the watching man.

But how? Where? It wasn't possible. Yes it was, came the quick contradiction, as Charlie made the positive identification. He'd isolated the man as he'd intently studied those around him on the Amsterdam flight from which he'd fled. The same suited, bespectacled person whose closely barbered neatness was marred by a bushed walrus mustache had been two rows behind but on the opposite side of the aisle.

It had been an even more successful day than Charlie could have hoped for and he was already curious at what was to follow. So, too, but independently were Aubrey Smith and Gerald Monsford, eighteen hundred miles away in London.

Both intelligence chiefs recognized the symbolism of the breakfast conference in the Foreign Office room overlooking 10 Downing Street and each made a gesture of his own by pointedly arriving separately and without prior consultation for the examination of their supposedly joint venture. Aubrey Smith entered last, although not late, behind both Geoffrey Palmer, who was to chair the session as the Foreign Office liaison to the Joint Intelligence and Security Committee, and Cabinet Secretary Sir Archibald Bland.

It was Bland, though, who quickly established the agenda. "The arrest of Russian diplomats has greatly embarrassed Moscow. Aware as we are of what else is going on, we're anxious to know how much longer—and further—you intend stretching out the situation."

"What have the Russians said?" asked the MI5 Director-General.

"They've refused anything beyond demanded diplomatic immunity and access to embassy lawyers. We've delivered two official Notes and publicly summoned the ambassador here to the Foreign Office for an explanation. Which, of course, we haven't got and didn't expect. They're offering a guilty plea, with a mitigating submission of extreme and inexcusable drunkenness. They accept without protest or threatened retaliation our declaring all three persona non grata and expelling them."

"The media will ridicule that," insisted Monsford, his own agenda prepared. "And it's naïve to imagine they won't make a tit-for-tat retaliation: they always do. With hindsight it was a mistake to stage the arrest in the first place. Had I been consulted in advance, I would have opposed it as a completely unnecessary side issue."

"I have already offered Director Monsford the opportunity to withdraw his participation," said Smith, to frowned looks between the two government officers. "That offer remains. His officers can easily be recalled from Moscow."

"If there's disagreement between you both, this discussion is even more essential," said Bland. "We accept Moscow will reciprocate. But we can't—and won't—make that reciprocation easy for them by mounting an operation about which you're uncertain. I thought we'd already made that abundantly clear. Is there a problem?"

"Not as far as I am concerned." Smith wasn't worried at Monsford's outburst.

"Director?" invited the cabinet secretary.

Monsford hesitated, off-balanced by Smith's unanticipated assertion, unsure how to reverse it. "I am surprised by the Director-General's response."

"Why?" demanded the increasingly frowning Bland.

"Yes, why?" echoed Smith.

"You will have read the newspaper furor at the mystery disappearance in Amsterdam from a Moscow-bound flight?" questioned Monsford.

"No," refused Bland. "I don't read the popular press."

"I know what you're talking about," said Palmer, more helpfully. "What about it?"

"There's no mystery: the vanishing man is Charlie Muffin," announced Monsford, who'd had Harry Jacobson's surveillance relayed by Straughan, but been prevented from speaking directly to his Moscow station head because of Jacobson's time-clashing meeting with Maxim Radtsic.

"What the . . . ?" stumbled Palmer.

"Why weren't we told?" finished Bland.

"Charlie switched his arrival, going in on a tourist flight instead of how we'd arranged," elaborated Smith, in a calm monotone. "It was, as you're aware, always the understanding that Charlie would work independently. That's what he chose to do."

"Without any approval, aware as he was of the publicity his disappearance would create, as well as blowing his false-name cover before he even got into Russia!" interrupted Monsford, emphasizing strained indignation. "It was crassly irresponsible, threatening the entire operation. And in the context of this meeting provides Moscow with a basis for retaliation as embarrassing as that they're suffering."

"It provides nothing of the sort: neither was it crassly irresponsible," rejected Aubrey Smith, contemptuously. "It was an action that, allowed to act independently, Charlie was authorized to make. We know he has arrived undetected in Moscow, as well as the hotel in which he was booked although I don't expect him to remain there."

"This is a totally unnecessary, attention-attracting charade," repeated Monsford. "I do not wish to withdraw my participation. What I do seek, at this moment, is my appointment as official, recognized supervisor of this operation, the failure to confirm which will, I believe, result in the debacle the majority of us are determined to avoid."

"In response to which, I in turn invite you to consider the available records of every shared meeting between our two services," said Smith, the flat-voiced outer calmness giving no hint of the gamble upon which he was knowingly embarking. "From those records I would suggest there are overwhelming indications of such inconsistency and prevarication on the part of my counterpart at MI6 that to agree to a single Control management would do more to guarantee than prevent a debacle. Charlie Muffin's independence was, rightly or wrongly in hindsight, agreed by us all. Your study of the records I'm offering include my belief that Muffin would disregard any cancellation and continue whatever he considered necessary to save his wife and child. Those records also contain my colleague's rejection of the one guaranteed way of removing the threat of Charlie Muffin acting alone, as I wholly reject it. If you find against me, on either continuing the extraction as a shared operation or in the only assured way of preventing my officer continuing, unsupported, then I must tender my immediate resignation."

A silence iced the room. Through the triple-glazed windows an equally silent tableau unfolded, featuring the prime minister emerging from his official residence, responding to questions after a brief statement to waiting journalists, and returning inside.

Geoffrey Palmer said: "This has turned out to be a very different discussion from what I imagined it would be."

Sir Archibald Bland said: "I think it would be advantageous for us and perhaps others to study the offered transcripts before continuing this discussion any further."

Harry Jacobson decreed their pickup should be at the obelisk commemoration to Yuri Gagarin, complete with its minuscule, actual-size orb in which the man contorted himself for the world's first manned space flight, Jacobson's alarm flaring the moment he began his ahead-of-time reconnaissance at the sight of the militia road check, two vans and at least five officers, although Jacobson's was not one of the cars pulled over. He had, though, to go slowly, which he did more than was necessary to identify the uniforms of the GIA highway police. The openly corrupt shakedown of motorists given the option of paying an on-the-spot "fine" or accepting an eventually more expensive official, invented traffic violation was not unusual, which made it perfect cover for the seizure Jacobson constantly feared. Would Maxim Radtsic be frightened for the same reason, if the Russian wasn't orchestrating the entire episode?

It was thirty minutes too early for him to find out and Jacobson let his mind return to the previous night's resented, secondary assignment at the Rossiya Hotel. It was totally unreasonable, as well as dangerously impractical, for him to juggle three balls in the air at the same time. And Jacobson hadn't been impressed with the surveillance ability of Patrick Wilkinson, whom he was sure he would have picked up even if Wilkinson hadn't been identified to him in London. But Wilkinson's lack of professionalism was MI5's problem, not his. He didn't see why the hell James Straughan had insisted he duplicate the hunt for Charlie Muffin when there were six others—three of them MI6—sitting around on their fat asses at the embassy. Or why, having insisted he make the independent check, Straughan banned a direct approach to a Rossiya receptionist with a twenty-dollar bill folded inside a friendly handshake for a ten-second look at the register. What was the point of confirming the bloody man's presence anyway? Until the actual moment the diversion had literally to be triggered, Radtsic remained his foremost priority.

Jacobson negotiated the difficult double roundabout system to prevent being automatically routed onto the ring road, to return with growing discomfort along Leninskaya. The maneuver put the highway-robbing militia on the opposite side of the multilane road, but there were uniformed, radio-equipped militia spotters on the memorial side Jacobson had isolated as Radtsic's pickup point: their presence heightened the possibility of an ambush as well as risked curiosity at the return of a car so recently passing in the opposite direction.

Radtsic was there, for once properly using what cover a tree clump offered. He needn't stop, Jacobson knew. The militia concentration was sufficient reason for him to abort and revert to another emergency contact meeting. Radtsic was actually looking at him: could see—would see—the circumstances and understand! Although the block was on the other side of the highway, the cars traveling in Jacobson's direction slowed, to gawk, forcing him to slow, too, and as Jacobson did, Radtsic moved away from his partial concealment, walking now as self-importantly as he always did. There were two motorcycles, previously obscured by militia vans but visible now: he could be chased, easily stopped, if he attracted attention by suddenly accelerating.

He didn't. Jacobson was careful to indicate his intention to move out of the slowed, otherwise occupied traffic line, paused rather than stopped at the pavement edge the moment Radtsic reached him, and at once indicated his getting back in line the moment the Russian was inside the car.

"This was an absurd place to meet!" protested Radtsic, at once.

"How the hell could I have known there'd be a GIA extortion!" Jacobson was intent on his rearview and wing mirrors, searching for pursuit.

"I didn't think you were going to stop."

"I almost didn't."

"If this had been a trap, I would have sprung it a long time ago," said Radtsic, presciently.

"Am I supposed to be reassured?" Jacobson was unsettled at the other man's awareness of his fear.

"You're supposed to believe me: believe that I'm not tricking you."

No militia vehicles were following and the traffic was picking up speed. As soon as he could Jacobson pulled onto minor roads from the inner beltway. "We're okay."

"Of course we're okay. You've told London how it's got to be done now?"

"It can't be according to your timing. They're planning the separate extraction, Elana and Andrei from Paris, you from here. But it's got to be at our signal."

"This is ridiculous," said the Russian.

"It's practical. And will be safe. The safety of you and your family is the essential, not something concocted as we go along," said Jacobson, disregarding his earlier doubts. "Direct contact has to be made with Elana and Andrei. You have to tell her that."

"I'm thinking of going to the Americans," abruptly threatened Radtsic.

Jacobson drove for several moments without responding. "I'll tell London. Stop them taking anything further in Paris that might interfere with how Washington might devise their extraction. Didn't it occur to you, though, that after the Lvov episode Washington might not be as receptive as we are?"

Now it was Radtsic who retreated into silence. Jacobson had completed the rerouting from the inner-ring road before the Russian spoke. "Why did you mention Lvov?"

"I thought it was relevant, it having occurred so recently," lied Jacobson, exasperated at what was being demanded of him. But now, suddenly, he was curious.

"I had no part in that: not the planning, I mean."

Radtsic had no need to explain or excuse himself. So why was he? Challengingly, Jacobson said: "You're the executive deputy of the FSB. You must have been part of it."

"It was a long-term strategy: you know that. Going back to KGB."

Jacobson drove automatically back onto the ring road, his entire concentration upon the other man. He was in the shit and sinking after the Amsterdam mistake, Jacobson reminded himself. And there was the outside possibility of his being wrong with the Rossiya assessment. This just conceivably might be his recovery. "You're old-time KGB, Maxim Mikhailovich. You were there when it began."

"Not part of it, though!" Radtsic once more denied. "You know when and where the Lvov thing was devised. In 1982 I was in St. Petersburg, not Cairo."

Within both British intelligence agencies the Lvov episode had already attained legendary status as the most brilliantly conceived and attempted Russian-intelligence penetration, only defeated by more than brilliant MI5 deduction. But Jacobson didn't know any details: he couldn't continue this totally unexpected conversation without almost immediately exposing his ignorance. It had to be ended with the surprise retained. "We're here to talk about Elana and her exit visa, not things that happened in the past."

"I suspected it was another test: that you were doubting me," said Radtsic.

"It wasn't. And I'm not."

"Elana's visa is arranged. Her flight's booked for noon tomorrow. Her departure will take four days, six maximum, to permeate through the system potentially to become a personal risk to me."

"You're still trying to impose your own time frame," accused Jacobson.

"Of course I am!" admitted Radtsic. "And you know why!"

"London doesn't want an ultimatum."

"I thought they already knew there had to be a strictly timed schedule."

The remark fitted the arrogance Jacobson had come to expect. Seeing the possibility of a respite, he said: "You're ready to move, the moment I give the word?"

"You know damn well I'm ready."

"So we don't need any more meetings. We can keep in touch by mobile phone, while Paris is set up."

Radtsic looked anxiously across the car. "You're not abandoning me, are you? Elana's documentation is in the system. I can't retrieve it now."

"Of course I'm not abandoning you, Maxim Mikhailovich," insisted Jacobson. "I want everything resolved as quickly as you do."

"No, you don't," contradicted Radtsic. "No one could want it resolved more quickly than I do."

"I'd hoped for more," complained Barry Elliott.

I'm certainly hoping for more, thought Jane Ambsersom, already encouraged by the easy familiarity with which the FBI man had kissed her, although only on both cheeks, when he'd picked her up from her London flat that morning. According to his estimate they'd arrive in perfect time for their already booked lunch. She said: "I warned you there hasn't been time to collate it all. I don't even know how much there is, in total."

"There will be more, though?" pressed Elliott.

Jane hoped he did other things as well as he drove the car: the signpost they were passing showed Stratford to be only twenty miles away. "I've circulated our archival and records people between whom it's apparently spread. I haven't heard back from the Director-General but I can't see why there should be any difficulty." She hesitated, her approach prepared. "I'm guessing you've approached MI6 for help, as well?"

"For what it was worth."

"What's that mean?"

"The message we got back was that Lvov wasn't their baby: that it was all down to you guys and they didn't think what little they had would contribute anything. We're switching the unofficial approach to a formal request through the CIA."

It was going her way, as she had every hope of this journey going her way, which made it essential that she weigh every word. "There are things we share and some we don't. What has our Secret Intelligence Service got to hide about a closed case in which, in their own judgment, they were only minimally involved?"

"You ask me," replied the American, rhetorically.

I just did and you didn't come up with the right answer, thought Jane. "We both understand we're being straight with each other here, aren't we?"

"I hope so."

When the fuck, then, was this guy going to prove it by doing something to guide her! Spurred by her own irritation, Jane said: "I don't think you're working professionally with me. I think Irena Yakulova Novikov is sending you guys every which way from the right direction and that having been suckered for eighteen years you're worried that it isn't over: that the Russians have a fallback that's still going to leave you swinging in the wind."

By a road-sign calculation Elliott drove for another eight miles before speaking again. "We've lost two guys, one a friend of mine who trained with me at Quantico, following up leads that emerged during what the CIA believed to be Novikov's truthful debriefing. The other was one of their own guys. Would you think that was a fallback or payback?"

"Lost how?"

"A hit-and-run in Cairo and a drowning in the Moscow river. The guy in Moscow was the one I knew at Quantico. He was his college swimming champion at Kent State."

"So it's personal as well as professional?"

Elliott shook his head. "Strictly professional."

Jane hadn't known what she might learn professionally from this excursion—even if she would learn anything—and still wasn't sure of this conversation but it was certainly something to be relayed to Aubrey Smith. "I think we've got a lot more to talk about."

"Which reminds me," said the man. "There seems to be a misunderstanding about the room reservations."

"I'm sure it won't be a problem," said Jane. I hope, she thought.

"What emerged at our last session has been fully considered, not just by us but by others," assured Geoffrey Palmer.

"It is to continue as a joint operation," announced Sir Archibald Bland.

"Which doesn't cover the absolute resolution should Charlie Muffin proceed independently," protested Monsford.

"The decision is that it continues to be jointly shared," reiterated Bland, with a hint of strained patience. "As such, the question of an absolute resolution doesn't arise."

"Getting Andrei to London is being organized by the British."

Elana remained looking down at her scarcely touched meal, oblivious of everyone in the restaurant. "It's really happening, isn't it? We really are going to defect."

"We're definitely going," said Radtsic.

"I wish we weren't."

"The adjustments won't be easy but you'll accept it, eventually. All of it."

"I don't think I will: not ever."

"Don't forget everything I've told you about the British approach."

"How will they make it? Where?"

"It'll be their move. They'll only make it when they're sure it's safe."

"What about the girl?"

"Andrei's got to understand. You've got to make him understand."

"He's a grown man, not a child."

"Talk to him as a man. And as our son."

"You're asking too much: too much of both of us."

"I'm asking you to help save our lives."

"I want to go home," said Elana. "Go home for the last time."

 17

CHARLIE'S BRIEF ELATION AT FINDING THE HOPED-FOR TALISman had frozen into ice-hard, questioning reality by the time he uncomfortably awoke in the cold, very early light of the following day, feasted upon by the more regular, multilegged inhabitants of his bed. And it wasn't because of his fruitless vigil in the botanical garden the night before. It still had to be more, much more, than a 50 percent chance that Natalia had delivered the newspaper signal, in the way only he'd recognize, to their special dead-letter drop.

But the alternative, the fear that Natalia's coercion had brutally forced from her their meeting code, remained. And if that had happened, he'd swallowed the FSB bait by going to Moscow's original herb garden. But why hadn't they sprung that trap and seized him the day before? The hope that Natalia hadn't been broken was no more than the merest wisp of straw-clutching reassurance but still something for which he could snatch out to hold.

Could he safely interpret the *Pravda* sign that it was safe to go anywhere near Natalia's Pecatnikov Pereulok apartment, outside of which Monsford's photographer had pictured her and Sasha just six days ago? Not yet. Not until he was surer the gardens were safe: that it *was* Natalia's intended indicator. Maybe not even then. It was inconceivable that Natalia's home was not under the most concentrated surveillance: the FSB would have *wanted* Natalia and Sasha to be photographed, seemingly free, to flavor their snare.

His safer course was to continue with their original, personal tradecraft. And there were other, more immediate self-protections to be established, updated now by an urgent need for medication to ease his red-hot bug bites. The stuttering shower gave some temporary relief until the trouser-chafing walk through the departing congestion of whores and their whoremongers on his way from the hotel. Charlie was abruptly halted on the pavement by the thought of checking the nearby gardens again but decided it was too soon for a visible response to his *Pravda* deposit. Instead, not abandoning the idea altogether, Charlie used a remembered kiosk conveniently close to the Ulitsa Mira Metro in preference to his pay-as-you-go mobile to dial the number he'd copied from the box in which he'd found the particularly folded newspaper, allowing it to ring unanswered for a full minute before hanging up.

He got a seat on the circle-line train, lessening his insect discomfort, which flared only when he switched for the Arbat connection, which he intentionally chose for its concealing swamp of similarly dressed Western tourists in which to sink out of detectable sight. A more fortunate, secondary benefit was a pharmacy from which Charlie bought balm and insect repellent. He dialed the unresponding botanical gardens' phone twice from different telephone kiosks as he moved through the tourist mecca, buying on his way the previous day's London *Times* and *Telegraph*, as well as a selection of that day's Russian and English-language newspapers. Charlie used them to reserve his seat in an enclosed, office workers' street buffet while he balmed his overnight wounds in its lavatory.

The *Telegraph* reported a Dutch intelligence theory that Malcolm Stoat, whom it described as a man of mystery of whom no official identification records or background existed in England, was a fleeing Russian spy kidnapped by British counterintelligence. That day's English-language *Moscow News* also printed the legend name and linked, although without explanation, the Amsterdam disappearance with what it referred to as reorganization within the FSB.

Charlie sipped his sludgelike coffee and spread soured cheese on his black bread, conscious of the Malcolm Stoat passport in his inside jacket pocket, next to that day's itinerary promising a free-time afternoon for the Manchester travel group. How free, wondered Charlie, would it remain, which was a question he needed to answer.

He risked the bar with its panoramic overview of the Rossiya, managing to get a stool and a double measure of properly distilled vodka in a shadowed area between the counter and the rear wall, calculating that his slight loss of outside view was compensated by his being hidden from at least a third of the other customers, closely studying those still visible for professionally telltale attitudes or recognizable London faces. Finding neither, Charlie switched his concentration to the hotel outside, almost at once isolating Neil Preston from the London introductory session, wincing critically at the man occupying the same porch that Patrick Wilkinson had the day before but with even less concealment. There was no one obviously watching from where he'd picked out the man with the straggled mustache.

Charlie realistically accepted the Malcolm Stoat name would have had far wider disclosure than in the two media references he'd found. The name had already been available from the aircraft passenger manifest for more than forty-eight hours now, and from his previous day's hotel observation, London had definitely discovered the location of the holiday group among which he'd hidden. But they'd had the name—and known of his vanishing act—from the outset. Moscow hadn't. Neither had it been on the block-visa documentation submitted by Manchester to the Russian embassy in London, only on the hotel registration here and at Sheremetyevo airport. Certainly not available for as long as forty-eight hours then. But he was still surprised the Rossiya wasn't swarmed by FSB, which it obviously wasn't, from Neil Preston being patiently, if amateurishly, on duty.

Noon, Charlie saw from the bar clock, as he gestured for another drink. The itinerary scheduled a twelve-forty-five return. He'd wait, he decided. He had no intention of trying to reconnect with the Manchester group but it was important he get some indication of what had happened to them. The FSB knew that he was coming, just not when and how. But they'd have made the connection from his Amsterdam disappearance. What happened—and when—to Muriel Simpson and her band of travelers would trigger the positive start of the FSB's hunt for him.

He hadn't tried the marked telephone in the botanical gardens for more than an hour, Charlie reminded himself. Now, midday, might be a good time. There was a phone on the far side of the bar but it was open fronted and the place was noisily crowded with lunchtime customers. He'd have to speak loudly, shout even, if there was a reply and probably have difficulty hearing himself. It was hardly likely Natalia would be there to pick up the receiver, anyway. His best—probably only—chance was to continue the nighttime vigils, as surreptitiously as he was professionally able.

Abruptly he saw the tourist coach.

Charlie was gesturing for a third drink, momentarily looking toward the bartender, and when he looked back to the window Charlie at once recognized the vehicle from the journey from the airport, stopped at that moment by a car emerging through the forecourt-entry gap. The coach impatiently edged forward as the car almost imperceptibly eased out, stopping altogether as it more positively obstructed the skewed coach. At the same time, the car horn blared an obvious signal for three closed, military-style vehicles to tire-scream from both directions down the suddenly emptied, sealed road to form a complete encirclement. At the same time, the scene was flooded by lights, brightly illuminating the arrival of two more slower and bigger military vehicles that disgorged helmeted, body-armored men in camouflage uniforms who at once began herding at jabbing gunpoint the bewildered, stumbling Manchester tourists, four of the women crying hysterically, from their coach into the larger vans. Briefly a white-faced Muriel Simpson appeared to stare directly into the bar at the watching Charlie.

The traffic-clearing military-convoy sirens momentarily overwhelmed the astonished uproar inside the bar, but neither conflicting noises prevented Charlie's very clearly hearing an English voice say, whisper-close to his ear: "Why aren't I surprised to find you here, Charlie?"

The MI6 Director stared up from the transcript James Straughan had protectively printed verbatim of his conversation with their Moscow station chief an hour earlier, Monsford's mouth forming the words but not able to utter them. Finally he managed: "Cairo! Radtsic very definitely identified Cairo!"

"I specifically took Jacobson over that three times. He's adamant Radtsic stipulated Cairo because the significance of Cairo didn't mean anything to him: still doesn't, because I didn't explain it."

"And Radtsic has consistently denied knowing anything but the vaguest circumstances of the Lvov case?" echoed Monsford, going back to the transcript.

"Radtsic claims he wasn't even in the KGB's Lubyanka headquarters when it began: that he was a serving officer in St. Petersburg," confirmed Straughan, irritated at the other man's repeating his point-by-point memorandum.

"It's not right," declared Monsford. "Something's definitely not right."

"Let's not overinterpret it," cautioned Rebecca Street. "According to what we know of Radtsic's history he *was* in St. Petersburg in 1982. But he *would* have been involved in the inquest after what Charlie did this year: read and heard enough to have picked up Cairo as its starting point."

"Most of what's available of Radtsic's career was provided by Radtsic himself, after he made his approach to us," reminded Straughan. "We've no independent confirmation of anything he's told us."

"So what?" dismissed the woman. "He'd still have been involved in the review of the Lvov disaster and learned before then how Cairo figured."

"Why's he told Jacobson he knows virtually nothing about it?" persisted Monsford, his mind locked on the inconsistency.

Rebecca shrugged, conscious that Monsford hadn't activated his personal recording apparatus. "He knows he's got to sing loud and clear for his supper once he gets here. Jacobson's the facilitator, not the one he's got to impress by what he knows. My guess is he let Cairo slip as a taster."

"I don't rely on guesses," rejected Monsford, stiffly.

"Fifty percent of our decisions begin largely from guesswork," Rebecca argued. "Or intuition, at least. Okay, Radtsic's provided his own legend. But we know, from our independent identification, that he *is* Maxim Mikhailovich Radtsic. And that Maxim Radtsic is *the* executive deputy of the Federal'naya Sluzhba Bezopasnosti who wants to defect to us. What the hell more do we need?"

Instead of answering, Monsford turned to the operations director, fluttering his printout. "Is this everything Jacobson had to say?"

"It's planned as a front-faced extraction," set out Straughan, determined to establish his personal safeguards. "We're providing a genuine Russian passport, with Radtsic's genuine photograph, describing him as a chemical engineer. The British entry visas are genuine, embassy issued, with all the necessary supporting documentation and accreditations for a trade visit here. It contains all the necessary Russian exit visas. He'll be accompanied by three of our people I've already sent, independently and unknown to each other, to wait in separate Moscow hotels. The Moscow departure of Radtsic's plane will be signaled to those in place at Heathrow. We'll disembark him first, holding everyone else onboard, bypass all entry formalities, and take him direct to the safe house for his reunion with his Elana and Andrei."

Monsford's frown had deepened during Straughan's presentation. "Why are you telling me what we've already planned?"

"Because I believe there needs to be reexamination and maybe replanning. Currently it's a failsafe extraction, already set up and rehearsed, except for two exceptions."

"Which are?" questioned Rebecca, aligning herself with the operations director's doubts.

"The absence of Radtsic himself from that rehearsal, which nevertheless isn't the main problem: all the man's got to do is go through an embarkation procedure. What's most likely to go wrong is the Charlie Muffin diversion."

"Your point?" demanded Monsford, angry at being confronted.

"According to Radtsic, Elana's exit visa will show up in a matter of days. When it does, Radtsic's extraction isn't any longer failsafe. It's too heavily compromised. And we don't know where the hell Charlie Muffin is, let alone have any idea how to inveigle him. We don't need the complication."

"I didn't ask for your opinion," rejected Monsford. "I asked what else Jacobson said."

"I don't think we should wait, either," intruded Rebecca, joining the objection. "We couldn't even guarantee Charlie Muffin reaching Moscow with Jacobson on the same bloody plane! We need Muffin under programmed surveillance, which we don't have."

Monsford studiously ignored the woman, focused upon Straughan. Who risked an exasperated sigh at the obduracy of the other man. "Jacobson thinks it's safer to restrict his contact with Radtsic to cell phone, until we move."

"I thought Radtsic believed all his telephones to be tapped?" challenged Rebecca.

"Single-use Russian cell phones, discarded directly after one call," elaborated Straughan. "No way it could be intercepted. Staple tradecraft."

"I'm not . . ." started Monsford but stopped at the intrusion of his security-cleared personal telephone. He said: "Yes," and listened without interruption for no more than seconds. Looking up to the other two, he said: "Moscow's staged its own theatrical production. They've arrested the entire Manchester tour group and televised themselves doing it."

"But Charlie Muffin wasn't among them?" anticipated Straughan.

"Of course he wasn't among them," snapped Monsford, peevishly.

"As he won't be around for any diversion," predicted Rebecca, shaking her head to Straughan in a prearranged signal.

Charlie didn't respond and David Halliday didn't say anything further, instead leading their way out through a side exit to avoid the still eye-squinting television strobes and continuing on foot in the opposite direction to distance themselves from the scene, picking their way through horn-protesting traffic jammed by the line of vehicles from the still-militia-sealed Rossiya Hotel.

It was Charlie who called them to a halt, demanded by permanently protesting hammer-toed feet, indicating the cinema and shop complex on Ulitsa Kirova. "There's a bar, on the first floor."

"They'll serve cat's piss."

"It'll be drinkable cat's piss. My feet hurt." Charlie's mind was way ahead of his painful, step-at-a-time ascent to the bar level. The MI6 officer had maintained an arm's-length acquaintance during the Lvov affair, tiptoeing at the very edge in the hope of personal advancement without endangering involvement, able to quote to the penny the pension he'd receive at the conclusion of a disaster-spared career. Why then, instead of slinking away, had the man risked approaching as he had? And, even more unexpected, discarded that previously avoided association by coming with him into this cigarette-smogged, body-odored shopping-mall bar into which he would not normally have allowed himself to be dragged by the wildest of wild horses?

Unwittingly connecting to Charlie's thoughts, Halliday held up the vodka that Charlie handed him and said: "It's not cat's piss. It's horse piss."

"It'll have more body," promised Charlie.

Halliday touched glasses. "Death to our enemies."

"Whomever and wherever they may be," responded Charlie, matching the other man's overly posturing toast.

"I know who they are," said Halliday, his face clearing in accepting surprise at his drink. "Gerald fucking Monsford and the rest of the conniving bastards in Vauxhall fucking Cross."

In espionage parlance, a benefit or a human source—usually embedded within an opposition—is known as an asset. And while the Russian FSB was his most obvious opposition there remained in Charlie's mind those unresolved uncertainties that still nagged from his Buckinghamshire interrogation, the FSB's knowledge of his London apartment paramount among them. Was it at all possible that while David Halliday did not totally qualify as an asset—and continuing the vodka analogy—he could be looking a gift horse in the mouth? "Sounds like you've got an in-house problem?"

"I'm out in the cold, Charlie. And being left there to freeze to death."

"You want to talk about it?" coaxed Charlie, tentatively.

"I'm offering you the same invitation."

Shit! thought Charlie. "You'll have to explain that."

"So you're part of the freeze, too!"

"Stop feeling sorry for yourself," rebuked Charlie, sure he knew enough to lead. "I'm never part of anything. I'm not at the embassy to *be* part of anything."

Halliday used the time it took to buy more drinks to consider Charlie's response. "There's a big team come in from London—a combined job, both services. I'm totally excluded. And—"

"There's nothing sinister in that: I was officially told not to include you in the Lvov business," broke in Charlie. There'd been sufficient embassy gossip for the man to infer that his distancing had, in fact, been self-motivated by Halliday's own, pension-protecting choosing and that some rapport remained between them.

"You didn't completely blank me, not like I'm being blanked now," conceded Halliday, to Charlie's satisfaction.

"You're surely not the only one?" tempted Charlie.

"That's just it," complained Halliday, petulantly. "Jacobson's pissing about, too. My own fucking station chief won't tell me what's going on! Twenty-five years' service, unblemished track record, and I'm being treated like the fucking office boy."

"Jacobson?" queried Charlie, wanting every possible nugget. . . .

"Harry Jacobson. I just told you he's MI6 station chief."

"He wasn't on station six months ago, when I was here?"

"Monsford went ape shit over the Lvov things, first at not being included from the beginning and then in his desperation not to be linked by all his efforts to be part of it when it all went wrong. I was the only one to survive. By rights I should have been appointed head of station but the bastard sent in Jacobson."

"I don't see how that means Jacobson is pissing about."

"I didn't mean Jacobson's appointment," said Halliday, exasperated. "I meant how Jacobson's treating me, closing me out from what he's doing."

Charlie gestured for more drinks without looking away from the other man. Well aware that it was not the case, he said: "Jacobson's the Control of this big team that's been sent in from London?"

"No!" said Halliday, his exasperation worsening. "It's something quite separate: just MI6 and with Monsford personally involved, which has got to mean it's big. Which I know it is because everything's classified Eyes Only, nothing on general traffic, and Jacobson—who's keeping the entire file in his personal safe—is refusing to talk about it."

"David!" Charlie smiled, touching his glass to the other man's to emphasize the I-know-what-you've-done mockery. "Are you seriously asking me to believe that having retained that unblemished record for twenty-five years, you haven't got the slightest clue what's going on!"

It took a moment for Halliday to smile in return, the exasperation slipping away. "I don't know what the big team's here for. Or what that was all about back there at the Rossiya."

Charlie paused, presented with two ways to go. Choosing to stay on track, he said: "We weren't talking about the big team or what happened outside the hotel. We were talking about your being closed out of what Jacobson's doing."

"I'm sure it's an extraction," announced Halliday.

Despite the abrupt chill and as always untroubled by his own hypocrisy, Charlie kept the mocking smile. "David! You've asked me to help you and if I'm going to do that you've got to be honest. You don't *think*. You *know*. You've got your hands on the file, haven't you?"

Halliday held his smile, too. "Not all of it. Jacobson got suspicious and changed his safe combination. And most of what I saw was encrypted."

"But you understood what you did read, didn't you, David?"

"It's a multiple extraction."

"How multiple?"

"A man and a woman. And a third, but I couldn't understand how he fitted in."

"He," seized Charlie. "The third person's male?"

"That's how it seemed. And I did get the code designation. It's Janus."

The physical chill suffusing Charlie began to freeze. "The god with two faces, able to look two ways at the same time."

"Appropriate for a defector, which it obviously is," confirmed Halliday. "Monsford's personal choice, from what I managed to see."

The code designation for Natalia's extraction had been Monsford's personal choice at the Buckinghamshire hunting lodge, remembered Charlie: remembering, too, Monsford's insistence on subject gender in the code titles along with his then-inexplicable choice of Camese, the wife of Janus. Hopefully Charlie said: "Nothing more?"

Halliday frowned. "I told you it was encrypted."

"On a scale of ten, extractions score around fifteen for potential disasters. I'm surprised you're pissed off at being excluded."

"Being kept out of one is acceptable. Being kept out of both is ominous. Now it's your turn. What the fuck's going on?"

"It's your round," reminded Charlie, offering his empty glass to gain thinking time. Throughout Halliday's diatribe Charlie had been calculating how to escape from the man, his mind shifting with each and every unexpected revelation. Now he didn't want to escape, just free himself from the Sinbad burden of having Halliday on his back.

"I'm waiting," prompted Halliday, handing Charlie his refill.

"Looks as if you and I are cast adrift in the same boat," opened Charlie. "I know a team was sent ahead of me. But I wasn't told the reason. My orders were to come in separately, stay away from the embassy, and wait to be contacted. The only thing missing was the tattoo on my forehead reading 'Fall Guy.' I jumped ship in Amsterdam and—"

"It was you!"

Charlie nodded. "I got back to England that same night and latched on to a tourist group from Manchester. . . ." He gestured vaguely back in the direction from which they'd fled and, sticking to the golden rule of telling as few lies as possible, he said: "They were the group picked up outside the Rossiya."

"That's why you were there, waiting to see what happened?"

The alarm bell rang at his oversight. "Why were you there if you're excluded?"

"I followed Preston from the embassy. He didn't pick me up."

It was simple enough to be true, conceded Charlie. But only just. "I saw Preston's surveillance."

"So would an FSB trainee, hanging about as Preston did instead of moving around. And the FSB all around the Rossiya were very definitely not trainees."

"How many did you mark?"

"Three, positively. You?"

"Four," lied Charlie, who hadn't searched beyond Preston. As well as failing to locate Halliday from his hideaway corner.

"You think you were sent here to be the fall guy?" demanded Halliday. Self-protective as always, he nervously added: "Me too, possibly?"

"Why'd you think I got off the plane in Amsterdam?"

"But then came here anyway?" challenged Halliday.

Charlie hesitated, annoyed at another slip. "I couldn't go straight back, could I? I needed to find out if I was right or not. Which was why I was watching the hotel: my trap for them."

"They're bastards!" exclaimed Halliday, his voice too loud, slurred by the vodka.

"That shouldn't surprise you, either."

"What are we going to do, Charlie?" It was more a plea than a question, the man's mind as well as his speech rusting in alcohol.

"Beat them," said Charlie, making a promise to himself.

"How!" It was still a whimpered plea.

"By you and I working together. Okay, you're being excluded but you're still on the inside, within the embassy. I'm on the outside not on their intended leash, so they can't initiate whatever they intend. We're beating them so far."

"You want another drink?"

"No. I don't think you do, either."

"What can we do?"

"You stay as you are, trying to find out what's happening inside. Get Jacobson's new safe combination. I'll stay on the outside, watching like today."

Halliday nodded, in befuddled agreement. "I need to know where you are."

"No, you don't," refused Charlie, who'd anticipated the demand. "Have you got a cell phone?"

"Of course."

"I'll call you, twice every day, ten in the morning, six at night." It had to be four hours, closer to five, since he'd tried the botanical gardens' number.

"You don't trust me."

"I'm not expecting you to trust me."

"Which I don't!" declared Halliday, with slurred belligerence.

"Why not?"

"You couldn't have just walked off the Amsterdam plane."

"Why not?"

"Jacobson was on it. The flight details to and from London were on the general file."

"Blond-haired guy, very neat and together apart from the big mustache?"

"You know him," accused Halliday, still belligerent.

"Does he have a gray-checked suit?" persisted Charlie.

"You *do* know him!"

"Not until now," said Charlie. "I remember him from the plane. And saw him yesterday, watching the hotel. But I'm not involved in whatever he's doing."

But he was going to be, Charlie knew.

"My mother's making a surprise visit."

"When?" asked Yvette.

"She's arriving tomorrow," said Andrei.

"Why with so little warning?"

"I don't know."

"Does she know about me? That we're together?"

"I told them in my last letter that I'd met you but not that you'd moved in."

"Do you want me to leave while she's here? I could, if it would be better."

"There's another bedroom. Why should you?"

"Maybe it would be better if I weren't here when she actually arrives: give you space to tell her."

"I don't understand why she didn't warn me she was coming."

"You'll be able to ask her that, too, while I'm not here."

18

CONFLICTING IMPRESSIONS AND CONFUSIONS SWIRLED through Charlie's mind like leaves in an autumn gale, constantly blown out of any order in which he tried to prioritize them, his uncertainties compounded by the distracting but essentially physical need to rid himself of David Halliday's pursuit, which the man solemnly promised not to attempt but which Charlie knew he would. That focus eventually brought Halliday into the forefront of Charlie's immediate reflection as he watched, from the concealment of a Metro station pillar, the MI6 officer carried away in the opposite direction from Charlie's botanical gardens' destination after thirty minutes of foot-aching, bite-chafing hopscotch between subway trains. Halliday's vodka-clouded chase went beyond Charlie's expectation: it was a warning, which again he scarcely needed, that he couldn't trust Halliday further than an outstretched arm if the man thought there were better personal advantages from cheating him than keeping to their agreed arrangement. Which once more neither disconcerted nor angered Charlie, who would have abandoned Halliday with even less compunction if a better opportunity had presented itself.

But at that precise moment Charlie believed Halliday to be his asset, because he was the best—the only—self-preserving asset Halliday had in return. Just as he believed that, allowing a necessary margin of exaggeration, Halliday had filled in a third of the far too empty mosaic for him to get a clearer idea of the eventual picture.

The fury that had engulfed Charlie earlier at the unavoidable inference that Natalia and Sasha were included in his clearly intended sacrifice came again and now he didn't suppress it: rather he let it burn and build, savoring the anticipation of as-yet-undecided but overwhelmingly fitting retribution. What could be sufficiently overwhelming to punish those who intentionally set out to destroy the two people central to his very existence? A question at the moment impossible to answer. But he would, Charlie determined, however long it took.

Outwardly conscious of the passing curiosity of Metro users at his standing as he was, Charlie boarded a linking train to connect to Mira station. Whom would he punish? he asked himself again, as he gratefully sat to ease his throbbing legs. They all, in some way, had to be complicit. He guessed Gerald Monsford to have been the primary instigator, too easily identifiable from his preposterous code designation. Monsford's cow-uddered milkmaid Rebecca Street would have known, too, along with their lickspittle operations director, James Straughan. What about Aubrey Smith? Charlie Muffin was too familiar with the amoral practicability of espionage—that there was absolutely no morality, successful practicability its only goal—to despair at any debt-discarding betrayal by a man whose MI5 career he'd so recently salvaged. But there was still a blip of disappointment that evaporated as quickly as it came. The man's obvious acquiescence made him as culpable and as deserving of reprisal as the others. The Janus-sexed Jane Ambersom would have looked in whatever self-serving direction the others took, and having been disabled from his army career the order-indoctrinated John Passmore would have obeyed his superiors' rules of engagement.

As he crossed to his final Ulitsa Mira connection Charlie acknowledged the background to his mosaic was still incomplete. He couldn't begin his retribution until he understood the parallel extractions. There was an unsettling similarity to what he'd imagined to be the intended rescue of Natalia and Sasha, the only difference the sex of the offspring. Except for the operational designations, came the immediate caveat. There'd be no purpose allocating two different code names to the same assignment. His earlier recognition that one was planned as a diversion from the other *had* to be the only conclusion.

Which brought Charlie's mind back to the importance of David Halliday. The MI6 man was the only source from whom he could discover more about what he now accepted to be the primary objective. And he'd already rationalized the degree of trust he could expect from a man as desperate to retain his pensioned career as Halliday.

Or was Halliday that only source? Minimally forewarned as he was, couldn't he risk contact with those waiting at the embassy? *Searching* for him from the embassy, he remembered. He'd have to endure the recriminating, explanation-demanding brouhaha from London but their responses might provide further mosaic tiles. The downside might be to confuse Halliday, who'd doubtless learn of his approach, despite his ostracism. Wiser to wait, albeit briefly.

He was, after all, no nearer linking up with Natalia. That remained *his* primary objective, he thought, as he bought a copy of *Pravda* from the station kiosk.

"A total, abject disaster," announced the flushed Sir Archibald Bland, his voice cracked from his earlier confrontation at 10 Downing Street, where his cabinet-secretary competence had unthinkably been questioned for the first time in his ten years' tenure. "Everything is to be closed down: canceled, abandoned, whatever. This is a disaster for which each of you is required to provide a full and detailed explanation, prior to your being called upon personally to account for what's happened. Neither of you will leave this room until I am given that explanation."

Gerald Monsford's squirmed reaction was heightened by the totally contrasting response from Aubrey Smith, who remained as unmoving as his voice retained its accustomed monotone. Smith said: "We've only had the opportunity of seeing the televised seizures, hearing the Russians' accusations, and reading the *Evening Standard*. What, diplomatically, has so far come from Moscow?"

The cabinet secretary made an impatient, fly-flicking gesture to Geoffrey Palmer, who said: "The indications are they intend officially charging all sixteen with spying and publicly arraign them in court, just as we arraigned their diplomats. The ambassador's preliminary assessment is that even if we try to negotiate with a release offer for their burglars, Moscow will still impose a prison term and keep us on a string for months. . . ."

"Maybe, even, including in that imprisonment the two tourists, both male, who've already suffered heart attacks," expanded Bland. Outraged, he continued: "Consider the situation you've created! Sixteen totally innocent British holidaymakers incarcerated in a Siberian gulag, for God knows how long! It's absolutely appalling."

"So where's your bloody man, Charlie Muffin or Malcolm Stoat or whatever the hell you choose to call him!" resumed the Foreign Office liaison to the Joint Intelligence Committee, directly addressing Smith.

"I don't know," admitted the MI5 Director-General. "And until I do, we can't close anything down. Nor, in my opinion, should we consider exchange negotiations involving their diplomats. They're our only bargaining lever. We shouldn't surrender it. Any more than we should be panicked by suggestions of show trials and Siberian imprisonment. They've scored an impressive PR coup and they know it. They won't risk their advantage by putting sick men in jail."

"We're not asking your opinion," rejected Bland. "We're ordering you to extricate yourselves and this government from a total, unimaginable mess. . . ." He looked around the table. "How do we find the damn man to get ourselves out of it?"

"I take it any thoughts of extracting his wife and daughter are abandoned?" ventured Jane Ambersom.

"Of course it does!" said Bland, irritably. "Do you have a constructive point?"

"One of my responsibilities is American liaison. Why don't we ask their help in locating Charlie Muffin in Moscow?"

Palmer broke the ensuing silence. "Again, what's your point?"

"The most obvious is utilizing more people in the search," offered Jane. "It would also widen the responsibility by letting an American involvement become known."

"He's still your man," challenged Rebecca Street, eager to separate MI6 from direct accountability for Charlie Muffin.

Jane smiled at the intervention. "Not if we also let it be known that Muffin is no longer in either of our services, but instead that he's gone freelance. Moscow knows Irena Novikov is in America: my American link here has told me Moscow has asked for diplomatic access to her. Moscow will also know from their swoop on the Rossiya and the observation they'll have stepped up on our embassy since Charlie's Amsterdam disappearance that he's not working from there. And from their lawyers talking to the arrested diplomats they know Charlie isn't any longer living at his Vauxhall flat. . . ."

"They'll know he had access to Natalia's calls," Rebecca said, trying again to deflate the other woman. "How could he have had that, and discovered the numbers to which to reply, without our resources?"

"Doesn't your telephone have a remote-access facility, to access calls from anywhere in the world?" mocked Jane. "Most people's have. Charlie's did. Mine has, too."

"Both the Amsterdam and Manchester flights originated from England," persisted the MI6 deputy.

"So what?" dismissed the other woman. "Freelancers can live wherever it's most convenient for them to work, can't they?"

"It's a worthwhile suggestion," accepted Bland. "We'll keep it on the table, as a contingency. What we need more immediately is a positive rebuttal to their television footage that's being globally transmitted, along with the accusations they're making."

"By now the media will have swamped Manchester, not just the travel firm but hunting every possible relative of the sixteen who've been arrested, for every photograph and anecdote," predicted Rebecca, desperate to come out ahead in the exchanges. "Every interview will insist they're not spies. The prime minister or the foreign secretary wouldn't be lying to Parliament declaring they're entirely innocent of any Russian accusation. Neither would the government, in an official protest Note to Moscow."

"What does the prime minister or the foreign secretary say if they're challenged in the House about Charlie Muffin?" asked Bland, his tone hinting interest, not rejection.

"They won't be, will they?" returned Rebecca, ready for the question. "Charlie Muffin isn't the name in the media headlines. It's Malcolm Stoat, who doesn't exist. Again there'd be no lie denying any knowledge of that name."

"The Russians have got photographs of Charlie, from his public exposure during the Lvov affair," said Monsford, emerging from his protracted silence. "So far they haven't published them. They could be waiting for just such a denial to wrong-foot us by releasing the pictures."

"He was never named, either as Charlie Muffin or Malcolm Stoat, at any of those public appearances," Smith pointed out.

"There could be another reason why they haven't released photographs," suggested Passmore, his good arm across his body.

"Associating Charlie with the failure of their Lvov operation, you mean?" too quickly anticipated Monsford.

"I don't mean that at all," dismissed Passmore. "That Lvov failed isn't publicly known, any more than that his death was a cover-up FSB assassination. What *is* publicly known is that Stepan Lvov was killed within weeks of a man being murdered in the grounds of the British embassy, with which Charlie was publicly associated."

"This is becoming convoluted," protested Monsford.

"To illustrate why we can't abandon Charlie," insisted Passmore, brusquely. "To abandon him would need our withdrawing all the support in place in Moscow, which would include, presumably, the exit passports waiting at the embassy for Natalia and the child. We've all of us acknowledged that Charlie would still try to get them out, which he wouldn't stand a chance of doing. He'd get picked up and only then be photographically identified and accused not only of spying but also of being linked—openly accused, even—with two assassinations on Russian soil."

There was a longer digesting silence before Monsford said: "They'd never be able to do that without the real truth coming out about Lvov and all the others killed in the FSB cleanup."

"Putin's put the straitjacket back on Russia," argued Passmore. "It's not as tight as it was at the height of the Cold War, but it's enough for a public exposure that'll make what they've staged so far look like an amateur rehearsal."

"We covered the possibility of his arrest and trial during the Buckinghamshire planning," remembered Monsford, triumphantly. "What's to stop Charlie exposing everything about the Lvov business in court?"

"The straitjacket," rejected Aubrey Smith, at once. "Charlie would have to be represented by a Russian lawyer and get the agreement of the judge or the tribunal to make a statement in open court. He'd be silenced before he managed to speak ten words."

"We could make sure the truth came out from here, publicly if needs be," argued Monsford.

"Which with very little editing, maybe no editing at all, could be used as confirming evidence against Charlie, not exoneration in his favor," punctured Passmore.

"Are you saying we can't do anything?" agonized Palmer.

"I'm saying we can't cut Charlie adrift, no matter how much we want to."

"And there's an obvious way that's taken us too long to reach to prevent Charlie causing any more trouble," said Smith, quietly. "And it's not what you're thinking."

"You did well, stepping in to halt the panic," Aubrey Smith congratulated his operations director as they walked across Parliament Square on their way back to the MI5 building. Turning to Jane Ambersom on his other side, he went on: "And if it hadn't been for your input we wouldn't have reached the decisions we did."

"It was Rebecca Street's idea how the hotel arrests could be honestly refuted," said Jane, only just keeping the bitterness from her voice.

"You initiated the discussion," said Smith. "And if you hadn't, the way to lift Charlie and close down the whole bloody business wouldn't have emerged."

They waited for a traffic change to cross to the abbey side. Passmore said: "Simple and obvious if Charlie does the simple and obvious thing by eventually approaching the embassy for the passports he asked me separately to provide. From his maneuvering so far I don't expect him to come through the embassy gate with his hand out, do you?"

"No," admitted the Director-General at once. "But there's somehow, somewhere, got to be a personal exchange. That's when and how we'll get him. And once we've got him, believe me he'll never be allowed to cause any more trouble, ever again."

"I wish I were as confident as you," cautioned Passmore.

"It's satisfied our government masters for the moment," Smith pointed out. "Which is all I wanted, time and space in which to think of something better."

"What about the others?" questioned the woman, ever conscious of the puppetry of her former director. "Do you trust Monsford to go on working with us now?"

"No," conceded Smith, as quickly as before. "I think he wants out. He can't say so, not after all the bullshit of seconding Charlie to MI6. But I'm sure he's got cold feet."

"What can we do to keep him onboard?"

"You tell me," said Smith, emptily.

"Which creates another uncertainty we don't need," said Passmore, matching the cynicism.

"*Do* tell me," said Smith, abruptly turning his careless cliché into a demand, stopping opposite the House of Lords to confront Jane

Ambersom. "You worked with Monsford far better than we do. How far would he go to shelter MI6 from any fallout?"

"Shelter MI6 from any fallout!" echoed the woman, contemptuously. "The only entity Gerald Monsford wants to shelter from fallout is Gerald Monsford. And there's no limit whatsoever to what or where Gerald Monsford will go to guarantee that."

"You can't mean that: not really believe that," disbelieved Passmore.

"I've never believed anything more in my entire life," said Jane.

They'd driven without speaking back to Vauxhall Cross, both Rebecca Street and James Straughan warned against any conversation by Monsford's lowering the partitioning glass between them and the driver. Both remained silent until they reached the Director's suite.

"It's time to press the button on the Janus extraction," Monsford declared as he turned from activating the recording apparatus. "Alert Jacobson and the Paris team at once. They're to liaise entirely through you, as central Control, to establish you're in personal command the entire time. Everything's on standby, ready, isn't it?"

To establish that you're in personal command the entire time, wearily recognized Straughan, "Everything's on standby but it can't be immediately activated."

"My orders were, and are, to have everything ready at a moment's notice!" accused Monsford. "Why haven't they been followed!"

If the bastard wanted a provable record he'd provide it, for every later examination to hear in crystal clarity, determined Straughan. "I've just told you everything's in place, ready. But it's got to be synchronized. A flight plan has to be filed for the private plane that's to be waiting at Orly for Elana and Andrei, whose arrival there has to be coordinated to the minute. Their departure has to be coordinated with Radtsic's flight from Moscow. If just one coordinate falls out of sequence the extraction collapses into chaotic disaster ten times worse than that we've already got."

"I didn't ask for a lecture on tradecraft!"

"I'm not lecturing on tradecraft," refuted Straughan, his nerves inwardly in turmoil. "I'm setting out the logistical practicalities. And before they've even been put in motion Elana and Andrei have to be told to be ready at a precise time for their pickup. In Moscow a ticket has to be bought for Radtsic and bookings made for his escorts on a direct commercial flight to London, with no intermediary stopovers like Amsterdam to prevent an FSB interception if there's an airport identification of Radtsic but insufficient time to stop him, which is a possibility we can't overlook. Because you've only just given me the instructions we don't yet know if there are available seats on that first convenient direct flight, the lack of which is another possibility we can't overlook. And if there aren't available seats, all the other timings have to be resynchronized. And—"

"All right!" stopped Monsford, tight voiced. "How long?"

"Twenty-four hours at the very earliest to guarantee that synchronization," promised Straughan. "Allowing for inevitable setbacks, we should get all three to London the day after tomorrow. Where a safe house is also set up, fully staffed and protected."

"You'd better start at once, to minimize those setbacks, hadn't you?"

"What about the other business?"

"There is no other business except that which we've just discussed, that and that alone. Nothing more," said Monsford

Straughan hesitated. "Jacobson might need clarification of that."

"Isn't it your remit to clarify operational details?" demanded Monsford.

"Over the last few days I've not felt that I've got your full support," said Monsford, as the door closed behind Straughan.

The recorder was still on, Rebecca thought. "I can't imagine what's given you that impression."

"Your opinion's too often contrary to mine."

"Constructively and objectively expressed, surely?" His risk was greater than hers, Rebecca decided: he wasn't going to fuck her any other way than he was already and he was finding even that difficult to manage.

"You sided with Straughan against me."

How could he be so stupid, with the apparatus running! "Only objectively, discussing whether or not to kill Charlie Muffin to create a distraction for Radtsic's defection, which just a moment ago you decided against. Which puts us all in agreement, doesn't it?"

Monsford smiled at her. "Nothing's being recorded: I didn't turn it on."

The motherfucker was setting her up if things went wrong, just as he'd set up Straughan and before that the Ambersom woman to save his own repulsively fat ass! "I don't understand the connection between that remark and what we're talking about."

"Don't you?"

"No," she insisted, her mind already ahead of her recovery.

"I want your loyalty."

"You've got that, as well as my objectivity. Which is what I have always tried to contribute. And what I want to continue contributing. On the subject of which I think it would have been wise to disclose Radtsic's extraction at today's meeting."

"Today's meeting was about MI5's mess. Bland and Palmer would have panicked and aborted the Radtsic objective if I'd announced it and we'd have lost him. As it is, we'll have Radtsic and a huge coup and those across the river will have to clear up the shit Charlie Muffin's left behind. Whose side would you rather be on?"

"The winning side," answered Rebecca, honestly. But not, she decided, that which included Gerald Monsford.

He smiled again. "That's what I wanted to hear and go on hearing. Shall we go home?"

"Not tonight," refused Rebecca. "My period's started early and I'm not at all comfortable."

"We could still eat together."

"Tomorrow. Let's have dinner tomorrow." She had more-important things to occupy her mind than boring crap about Helen of Troy and gods in loincloths fighting bulls in underground caves.

It was dark by the time Charlie got to the botanical gardens, which he approached as cautiously as always, stretching his outside checks on those entering or leaving for at least twenty minutes before finally going through the gate, lingering even further on separate benches to satisfy himself it was safe and even then feigning interest in shrubbery and trees while making his way casually to the specific telephone. The time switch had activated the interior light and before he reached it Charlie saw the hoped-for marker and had to stop himself hurrying.

Charlie had his own *Pravda* partially rolled by the time he got into the cubicle, and was leaning back to keep the door open while he completed his answering signal when the phone rang, the jarring unexpectedness startling him. For a moment he stared at it, undecided, letting it ring twice more before picking it up, keeping an unfolded page of the newspaper against the mouthpiece to muffle voice recognition when he said: *"Da?"*

"I know it's you, Charlie: I can see you," said the voice he wanted to hear.

Rebecca Street said: "I'm glad I've caught you."

"I was just leaving," said Straughan.

"It won't take long," promised the woman.

19

CHARLIE DIDN'T MOVE, HALTING THE INSTINCTIVE SWING TO look into the gardens. "The open pod by the first hothouse?" It was obvious: too obvious! He should have checked every approach, not just that from the main entrance.

"I hoped you'd come: prayed you'd come. I kept checking, hoping you'd remember."

"I told you I was coming."

"You didn't call Pecatniko!" she demanded, the alarm flaring.

"Of course I didn't call your apartment!" Fortunately, he thought, discerning her fear.

"How did you expect me to know then?"

This was verging upon the surreal, decided Charlie. "I called the numbers from which you phoned."

"Street kiosks?"

"Each of those you used: we traced them."

"I don't understand," she protested.

"I don't understand either. Are there people with you?"

There was a pause. "I'm alone. I really don't understand."

There was none of the tension that there'd been in her voice on the Vauxhall answering machine. "You can move around?"

Another pause. "So far."

Her voice was calmer, Charlie judged. "What about surveillance?"

"You taught me how to clear my trail, remember?"

Charlie felt a stir of unease: it had been little more than early relationship game playing, not proper dedicated training, although she'd undergone that at KGB academies. "Where's Sasha?"

"Summer school."

He'd forgotten the school semester dates and the additional privileges to which Sasha was entitled as the daughter of a senior state intelligence officer. "I'm at the Mira hotel."

There was something like a laugh but it was muffled. "You did remember it all, didn't you?"

"We need to talk."

"Yes."

"Leave first, now. Walk past me and through the main gate. Wait on the first bench outside, about twenty meters down on the left side of the road in the direction of the hotel. And I mean wait. I won't approach you until I'm absolutely sure you're clear."

"I told you I've guaranteed that."

"Wait."

"You've seen something: someone!" flared the demand again.

"I need to be absolutely sure. Go now."

"What if I'm not clear!"

The fear was definitely there. "I'm in room forty-six. Call it tomorrow morning: ten thirty from another street kiosk."

"I should have agreed to come before, shouldn't I? Not been so stupid, until it was too late." There was the slightest catch in Natalia's voice.

"Move now! We've been talking too long." Charlie kept the dead phone to his ear, seemingly still talking, turning at last to see Natalia go by. She did so without looking toward his kiosk, walking steadily but not hurrying. She was wearing a headscarf, which she rarely did, prompting Charlie's recollection of their discussing the use of a head covering for a change of appearance, wondering if the now-belted raincoat had a different-color reversible lining. He was concerned at a couple, the man visibly older than the woman, who appeared to follow closely behind Natalia until they settled on a bench and began fumbling each other under the imagined cover of the inadequate half-light. There was no other even vaguely suspicious pursuit and Charlie replaced the receiver, taking both newspapers with him as he moved in the opposite direction from the main entrance, against what would have been any professionally recognizable surveillance upon Natalia, separately dropping each newspaper into a different refuse bin. He studiously ignored the open pod from which Natalia had spoken but hesitated, as if seeking a direction, to study everywhere around it, relieved again at detecting nothing. He continued until he reached a bisecting junction, taking the right-hand path to a side exit from which he looped along the outside road to the main highway.

Charlie picked Natalia out long before he reached her, the raincoat already reversed, and was sure she saw him, although she gave no indication.

When he reached her she said: "I've caused a lot of trouble, haven't I?"

"Nothing I can't sort out," he said, wishing he believed it.

Natalia finally backed away from the embrace in which they'd held each other, neither speaking, each satisfied by the feel and touch of the other. She grimaced around the hotel room as they parted and said: "This isn't what I've got special memories of."

"Try to keep them as they were. Sit on the chair, not the bed. There are things that bite."

Natalia did as she was told, frowning as Charlie perched himself cautiously on the very edge of the bed. She said: "The FSB have been in turmoil ever since Lvov's killing, not just at the Lubyanka but in a lot of outstations, too. I've inferred a lot but there'll be a lot more I haven't got right. It'll help to fill in the missing parts if you go first."

Charlie started awkwardly, unprepared, needing initially to go back and elaborate until he got the chronology in order, realizing that for the very first time he was actually sharing espionage intelligence with her. At first Natalia gazed directly at him, intent on everything he said, but gradually dropped her head in what Charlie guessed to be either contemplation or disbelief or a combination of both. Charlie began imagining it would be a long explanation and was surprised how quickly he finished. For what seemed a long time, almost as long as they'd clung to each other, Natalia remained with her head bowed until he finally said: "Natalia?"

It was still several moments before she brought her face up, her hands, too, as if wanting to shield the frowned, shadowed expression that Charlie couldn't read until, uneven-voiced, she stumbled: "I got so much wrong . . . didn't understand so much. Dear God, I'm so sorry," and he realized she was genuinely, deeply, frightened.

"I said I could sort things out."

Natalia shook her head. "Not this time, Charlie. And it's me who's trapped you so because you won't be able to get away again. God only knows what they'll do to you."

"Now I need to understand," encouraged Charlie, who from the beginning had found a dichotomy between Natalia's piety and her profession, in which he'd never recognized any religion or any creed.

"I got so much wrong . . . made so many mistakes," she said again.

"I have to understand what you're talking about, Natalia. Tell me all of it."

She didn't begin at once and groped for the words when she finally started, needing twice to stop and start again. "It was the body at the embassy . . . I knew that's what you were here for the last time . . . you made that much clear when we met and then there was television. I did what I promised then, made all the plans to follow you back to England . . . realized how stupid I'd been for so long, not to have come with you when you asked me . . . sorry for that . . . sorry for so much . . . I didn't know what happened, of course. Not when you left so quickly. Didn't understand your last call, that I couldn't come after all . . . and then there was the Lvov killing and the others that followed. I guessed there had to be a connection, although I couldn't understand what it was because you were back in England when it happened. I didn't guess a connection until I was called in—"

"Called in!" interrupted Charlie, following her so far but wanting absolute clarity. "You were interrogated?"

"A formal interrogation, recorded and transcribed for me to sign."

"About us? How much about us?" She was recovering, becoming more coherent.

"About your defection. How you tricked me."

"Nothing more?"

Natalia shook her head. "Just your faked defection and my debriefing, all that time ago. I'd sanitized everything I could retrieve from those old KGB files after we got together. You knew I had, to keep us safe. I obviously had to leave some details though, in case there was a cross-reference. Which there must have been: I don't know about that. But it can only have been picked up after you left this last time. The first session didn't start out as hostile. It took your idea to change the original file to indicate you'd been passed on to another more-senior interrogator after me, which I'd done to prevent myself being held responsible for your going back to England then. I was able to say I'd doubted your defection, which was why you had been transferred up the line—"

"You said the first session wasn't hostile? Did things change?" broke in Charlie again, to keep Natalia on track.

She nodded once more. "I thought it was all over, after that first interview: that I'd satisfied them. The tone changed when I was recalled a week later. They wanted to know why I hadn't recognized you from the publicity on the embassy killing and flagged it up."

"What did you say?"

"That I simply *hadn't* recognized you from television or newspaper photographs."

"But they didn't believe you?"

"The third interrogation came after another week. I had to identify what newspapers and television I'd seen and was ordered to identify you from a collation of photographs and freeze-frames. You weren't in four sections of the collation: obviously testing me for a reaction, which I didn't give. It wasn't actually difficult. I've been on the other side, catching people out in debriefings for almost twenty years, after all."

"What did you do?"

"Replied as I knew I had to reply: stuck to my denial. I insisted there'd only been three debriefings before you were transferred, that it had all been ten years ago, and that I genuinely didn't remember or recognize you."

"You think they believe you?"

"I don't know. There've been three occasions when I thought I was under surveillance and I am not sure about my telephone: that's why I made the calls I did from public booths, as you always told me to."

"I told you I called back."

"I still don't understand that."

"Our technical people checked. The supposition was that you'd been forced to make the calls under duress. That any replies would be recorded."

"I chose the phones myself, at random. No one was with me, forcing me to do or say anything."

The feeling was one of numbness, an unreal sensation he'd never before experienced of being suspended without any control over himself. Too much surmise and supposition, he thought: situations virtually invented where nothing at all needed invention. He could so easily have come back alone, needing only false passports to be available from the embassy, and simply flown back to London with them. There'd been no need for the Amsterdam switch or the tourist diversion: no need for sixteen terrified people to be arrested. "It wasn't just you who made mistakes. I made far too many."

"But I've trapped you: trapped you and all the others you came in with."

"They'll be released, eventually."

"Eventually, not immediately," qualified Natalia. "The FSB know you're here now: those poor people will be used. And when they're released you won't be among them. Every way out is going to be locked down against you."

This far they'd been looking backward, Charlie acknowledged, hearing—but not accepting—Natalia's defeat. Now they had to look in the opposite direction. No, not yet, Charlie stopped himself at a sudden, still-backward thought. "There's something else. From what you've just told me there's no way the FSB could have learned my London telephone number?"

"No, they couldn't." Natalia frowned.

"What about my address in London?" pressed Charlie.

Natalia's frown deepened. "How could they? *I* don't know it. Why's this important?"

It would increase her nervousness if he told her of the FSB burglary. "It's something that happened in London: nothing to do with us here." He hesitated, needing to ask her about what had appeared an assignation between Natalia and Sasha's schoolteacher during his previous return. "Igor Karakov?"

"I didn't know he was going to be at Gorky Park for you to see Sasha. I told you that. Until that last time I never knew if you were ever coming back: if I was ever going to change my mind about coming to you. Igor and I were only ever friends. Never lovers. I told you my decision. It was you who told me I couldn't come. Then there were the interrogations. And now it's too late. Now it's all over."

"No it isn't!" insisted Charlie. "Nothing's all over: we're not over. I'll get you and Sasha out and we are going to be together."

"I want so much to believe you. . . ."

It had been a stupid mistake to go sideways: to give way to jealousy. "Are you still at the Lubyanka? You haven't been suspended or moved to other duties?"

In contrast to how she'd slumped earlier, Natalia fixed Charlie in a very direct stare. "This is not what we talk about: not how we've ever talked."

Charlie felt the slightest twitch of irritation, a reaction toward her so rare that he couldn't remember a previous occasion. "I'm not asking for your betrayal, I'm trying to find a way out for the three of us. If I don't find that way out, if you don't help me find it, I can't imagine what your service will do to you, just as you can't imagine what they'd do to me. The one thing I don't need to imagine—*know* for a positive, incontrovertible certainty—is what will happen to Sasha. Do you want her, from the moment of our arrests, to be put into a state orphanage until she's fifteen and then thrown out, literally onto the street, nowhere to go, no one to help or guide her except the brothel traffickers waiting outside to teach her the only way she'll be able to survive!"

Natalia began to cry, which she'd never before done in front of him, and Charlie was shocked at his own outburst, unable to believe he'd attacked her as he had. Not an attack, he tried to console himself. What had needed to be said finally to get her out of the cocoon into which she wanted to retreat rather than confront the reality of where and how they now were. "You hear what I'm saying: understand what I'm saying!"

"It would have been better if I'd understood a long time ago, wouldn't it?" She sobbed.

Because all the factors were in place, like already tested lights simply needing to be turned on, James Straughan adhered strictly to Monsford's insistence upon unbreakable security by deciding personally to flick all the switches, delegating to no one. Unlike America's CIA, MI6 does not maintain its dedicated clandestine aircraft facilities but has fee-paying call upon that under the Foreign Office budget. Availability of both aircraft and crew was reconfirmed, together with morning and evening flight plans protectively stretched over the next four consecutive days into and out of Orly from Northolt military airfield on the outskirts of London, the spread adjustable to all the other time-dictated coordinates. While Straughan remained on the secure line from the Vauxhall Cross communication center, the duty officer at the MI6 *rezidentura* at the Paris embassy relayed the intended rendezvous with Elana Radtsic to finalize the Russians' immediate readiness to move. Straughan stayed on hold for the time it took Harry

Jacobson to go from the *rezidentura* to the totally secure basement communications chamber of the Moscow embassy, his confidence growing at the smoothness with which everything was slotting into its required place.

"What's today's drama," cynically greeted the Moscow station chief.

"There isn't one," assured Straughan. "It's to be a straight extraction on the first available direct flight. Guarantee there's availability for the three escorts who'll be traveling with you. Give me the flight as soon as you can, for them to make their independent reservations."

"What about the side issues?" demanded Jacobson.

"Canceled. I thought the Director would have told you."

There was a momentary pause as the relief swept through Jacobson. "The TV channels here have been virtually cleared for nonstop repeats of the hotel seizures."

"It's been media pandemonium here, too."

"Anyone got any idea where Muffin is?"

"We don't know and don't care. And that's official."

"You okay personally: not catching any shit?"

"As okay as I'll ever be. You think you can fix a flight tomorrow? You're the trigger for everything else."

"I'll get back to you as soon as I can."

"I'll be here waiting." Straughan separately made his alert calls from the communications room to Radtsic's independent escorts and had just reentered his office when the summons came on his internal line.

"You got a moment?" asked Rebecca Street.

"I'm waiting for callbacks."

"I'll come to you."

Straughan hesitated. "It sounds important?"

"It is."

"I'll try," promised Natalia, dry-eyed again after Charlie's limited explanation. "It won't be easy."

"Don't risk anything to draw attention to yourself," insisted Charlie, urgently. "Just listen for any rumors or gossip from which I might be able to make some sense." Upon which depended David Halliday's getting something more concrete, balanced Charlie, who'd held back from telling Natalia of his earlier encounter with the man, worried that it might further unsettle her.

"There's still a lot of both at the Lubyanka. The turmoil hasn't subsided yet."

"I'm surprised some of it appears to have got into newspapers here, particularly after Putin's media clampdown."

"I suspect they're intentionally planted."

"Why?"

"I don't know. I'll try to get a steer on that, too."

"Without taking any risks," repeated Charlie.

"I heard you the first time."

"Remember what else I said. I will get all of us out, safely."

Natalia looked steadily at him for several moments. "If you say so." She looked slightly away, to the infested bed. "I can't stay. I need to be at Pecatnikov if there's anything from Sasha's summer school." She hesitated. "Or anyone else."

"I wasn't going to ask you to stay, as much as I want you to."

"I want to tell you again how—"

"Don't," stopped Charlie, positively. "Keeping one step ahead is the only thing to worry about from now on."

Which was virtually the same sentiment, expressed in virtually the same words, exchanged at that moment between Rebecca Street and James Straughan in their river-bordering building almost eighteen hundred miles away in London.

It was several minutes before Andrei Radtsic, his face drained, his head shaking in disbelief, managed brokenly to speak. "I don't understand what you're telling me."

"I still don't, not properly," admitted Elana.

"There must be something. . . ."

Now Elana shook her head. "Your father says this is the only way."

Andrei moved aimlessly around the apartment, fingering objects, picking up and putting down. He turned back, gesturing open-armed. "Everything will be over . . . finished . . . your job at the university . . . me, here, what I might have done . . . I can't take it in. . . ."

"Your father says it will all work out, eventually."

"I don't want to do it: any of it! I won't do it! You go, both of you. Leave me."

"We can't do that. You'll be seized: jailed. Used in some way to get us back to Moscow."

Andrei stood on the other side of the room, shaking his head again but not speaking.

"Tell me about the girl, Yvette."

"She's living here with me," blurted Andrei. "She stayed away, for us to talk: for me to find out why you came so unexpectedly, but she'll be back."

"We didn't know she'd moved in."

"It hasn't been long."

"Do you love her?"

"I don't know."

"Does she love you?"

"I don't know," he said again.

"We're going to be called, at this number."

"Who by?"

"The British."

"What!"

"To be told how we're being got out."

"I don't want this: any of this!"

"Neither do I, my darling. But we haven't a choice."

20

MAXIM RADTSIC'S INSISTENCE UPON RESUMING THEIR MEETings to discuss the lead-up arrangements only slightly diminished Harry Jacobson's satisfaction that the entire ill-conceived, haphazardly planned affair was soon to be over. Jacobson matched Radtsic's insistence by decreeing the Bolshoi as their venue for the very first of his personal celebrations. Jacobson was a ballet fanatic and *Swan Lake* his favorite but that night his fear of entrapment superceded his enjoyment of the performance.

Freed as he now was from the absurd assassination diversion as well as safely shepherding Radtsic to London, Jacobson was able to look past the immediate to the promotions so clearly open to him for what he'd done—and been unarguably prepared to do.

It was objectively accepted that despite the facile diplomatic charade of cover embassy titles and descriptions, Russian intelligence knew the identities of most if not all British espionage officers in Moscow, just as MI5 and MI6 knew the identities of most if not all Russian operatives in London. That was how each country was so quickly able to match the other, agent for agent, in tit-for-tat spy expulsions. And why Jacobson knew that within days, hours even, of Radtsic's defection the FSB would identify him as the MI6 Control who'd flown out on the same plane as their deputy executive chairman.

Which, following that inevitability to its only conclusion, made absolutely impossible his return to Moscow. About which, apart from the ballet, he had no regrets.

There was the slight blip in Jacobson's reasoning at the brevity of his Moscow posting until he balanced that brevity to be in his favor rather than against a fitting and deserving reward. He doubted there'd ever been, in this or any other hostile country, another MI6 station chief who, after just months, had landed a catch as big as a deputy head of intelligence. And this wasn't any other hostile country. This was *the* hostile country, the Russian Federation, led by a man so determined upon a new, even more frigid Cold War that he'd openly threatened a western-facing missile fence across central Europe after crushing the upstart former republic of Georgia as brutally as then-Czechoslovakia and Hungary had been crushed at the height of communism.

Jacobson judged Washington his most logical move, the posting for which this impending coup most qualified him. But Jacobson believed himself a true and natural European and genuinely supported its union of nations. Paris was traditionally viewed as the promotional jewel in the diplomatic crown. And of all his intelligence career ladder-scrambling Jacobson had most enjoyed his earlier tour in the French capital, although its ballet lacked the tingling magic of that approaching its intermission before him.

For which Jacobson was ready, rising as the curtain fell for the encounter ritual of checking Radtsic for unwelcome interest before the Russian assured himself that Jacobson was also clear. Which, by strict tradecraft interpretation, he wasn't, although there was no possibility of Radtsic's becoming aware of his three other intended escorts, the only purpose for whose presence was physically to identify the man whose uninterrupted flight they had to guarantee and of whose identity Jacobson himself was unaware: their Bolshoi attendance had been independently arranged by Straughan, after Jacobson's choice of meeting place.

Jacobson established himself in the shadow of a pillar close to the bar entrance after very intentionally ordering the twice-as-expensive French over Russian champagne in another early celebration of his anticipated career advancement. Radtsic bulldozed his way into the salon with his accustomed autocratic swagger, ignoring the protests of two separate groups in front of which he forced himself to be served. The swagger remained while he moved back into the now-crowded room, although away from where Jacobson watched. Tonight's safety signal, from the protection of another pillar deeper within the room, was for Radtsic to consult but quickly pocket his program, which he did more quickly than Jacobson had expected. Jacobson didn't hurry to respond, double-checking his own surroundings, irritated by Radtsic's open look of expectation before he reached the man.

"Ready at last!" greeted the Russian, sardonically.

"Everything's fixed, yes."

"When?"

"The nine A.M. British Airways flight the day after tomorrow."

"Why not tomorrow!" Radtsic instantly demanded.

Jacobson maneuvered his back to the pillar, as much to mark Radtsic for the three unknown watching escorts, who, according to Straughan, knew his identity from photographs, as for his own protective view of the chandeliered room. "This is the first completely suitable, available flight upon which you can be fully escorted."

"It's an unnecessary delay."

"It ensures your greatest security," insisted Jacobson.

"How?" persisted Radtsic.

"It's a direct flight, removing stopover interception. Our people will be onboard."

"Who?"

"I don't even know their identities. And go through Sheremetyevo more quietly."

"What are you talking about!" questioned the other man, coloring.

"The way you walk, your whole attitude, attracts attention."

Radtsic's face reddened. "I don't expect or want to be addressed like this."

"And I don't want all that's been arranged for your benefit to collapse, with your wife and son already out of the country, by your focusing attention on yourself as you've done at every meeting we've had."

He shouldn't have given way to the annoyance, Jacobson warned himself: in less than forty-eight hours he'd be rid of the arrogant bastard.

It took Radtsic several moments to compose himself. "What are the arrangements?"

"We have to meet one more time, tomorrow night. I'll tell you the place and the time by cell phone. At tomorrow's meeting I'll give you your ticket—a return, obviously, although you're not coming back—and your passport. Both are in the name of Ivan Petrovich Umnov. The passport is authentically Russian, so it can't be challenged. Neither can the exit visa from here nor the entry documentation into Britain, to which will be attached all the British accreditation for an international engineering conference genuinely being held in Birmingham. That's your cover: you're an engineer specializing in mineral-drilling machinery. I'll also give you one hundred pounds in sterling, with the currency-exchange receipts and all the Birmingham contact information, including an apparently confirmed appointment with Yuri Panin, the current deputy trade minister at the Russian embassy in London." Jacobson drank heavily from his champagne glass, needing it.

Radtsic, the color gone, said: "Your service is very efficient."

"As yours is," acknowledged Jacobson. "Is there anything we've omitted or that isn't clear to you?"

"Where is this place, Birmingham?"

"In the middle of the country."

"What about you?" asked Radtsic. "Are you accompanying me?"

"That hasn't been positively decided," lied Jacobson, self-protectively. "My job is to ensure your unhindered passage onto the plane. At Heathrow you'll be taken from the plane ahead of other passengers. You'll be taken direct to a waiting car."

"Tell me about Elana and Andrei."

"Everything is governed by your departure. That schedule has Elana and Andrei arriving in England ahead of you, because of the time difference between Russia and France. They will be waiting at the safe house already prepared."

Radtsic smiled. "I would like to tell them tonight how close everything is."

"No!" ordered Jacobson, in quiet-voiced urgency. "It'll be madness to attempt contact now!"

The resumption bell echoed throughout the salon. Radtsic said nothing but his face had colored again.

"Give me your solemn undertaking you won't try to make contact!"

"I won't make contact," said the Russian.

"Where have you been: the arrangement was six. It's almost eight!"

From the subdued noise in the background Charlie guessed David Halliday was in a bar: the underlying jazz was modern, the occasional snatched lyric in English. "Where are you?"

"The Savoy. When you didn't call I came looking for you here."

Charlie had lived at the Savoy, close to Red Square, during the embassy-killing investigation. "I'd hardly be likely to stay there, with everyone and his dog looking for me!"

"I told you this morning that I need to know where to find you!"

"And I told you the diplomatic debacle there'd be—as well as the end of your career and pension with it—if the FSB picked up our association by electronically scanning your mobile phone, which they probably do automatically to all embassy personnel. I'm calling you from a public telephone, the number of which you'll find when you access the last-number display on your phone, which I know you'll do, just as I know you tried to follow me on the Metro."

Charlie listened to the background of Ella Fitzgerald's "Summertime," which had been the bartender's favorite CD when he'd stayed there. He had to buy more Russian cell phones, he reminded himself, still refusing to trust the one issued to him in London. It was several moments before the MI6 man said: "I thought we were working together."

"We are, right now. And if we've got anything to talk about I don't want you doing so from a bar stool where you can be overheard."

"You think I'm that stupid!"

Yes, if you're already topping up the lunchtime vodka, thought Charlie. "You've got this number on your phone. Call me back on an outside line in five minutes: if I don't hear by six minutes, I'll leave this kiosk."

Charlie's phone rang in three. Halliday said: "I didn't want to keep you waiting, shit though you are."

"That's considerate of you," said Charlie, allowing the other man the weak retaliation. "Where are you now?"

"Looking at Lenin's tomb. There's no one within fifty meters of me."

"Did you get into Jacobson's safe?"

"I couldn't take the risk. He was around all afternoon. Except that he wasn't."

"That doesn't make sense."

"He spent almost two hours in the communications room. I couldn't risk going into his office, not knowing when he'd come back. When he did he time-locked the door and left early."

"What are you reading into that?"

"Something's about to happen. It's being finalized. Or already *has* been finalized."

Too sweeping an assessment? wondered Charlie. "In an ongoing situation or assignment, officers have to log their whereabouts or provide a contact procedure."

"Any contact with Jacobson has to be patched through London."

A better indicator of something imminent, judged Charlie. "How often has he done that, before today?"

"Today's the first time. And just after he left there was an internal call from the embassy travel officer. They wouldn't tell me what it was about: leave a message even."

More leaves swirled by differently blowing winds to go with those already disturbed by my meeting with Natalia, thought Charlie. "Is that all?"

"You're being judged shit of this or any other year."

"By who else, apart from you?"

"The team that was sent in."

"Actually naming me?"

"All they need to name is the Rossiya. They're sitting around in the embassy bar, complaining their being here is a waste of time now."

"Are they being recalled?" urgently demanded Charlie.

"I haven't heard about a recall but I'm being kept on the outside. I can't ask."

It was difficult to gauge the furor in London from newspapers and TV here, but cancellation of Natalia's extraction had to be a danger. Losing the manpower wasn't his concern: losing Natalia and Sasha's exit passports were. And he guessed the documentation would be sent back in the diplomatic bag if the extraction team was recalled. "It's important I know if the order comes from London."

"You haven't told me why you didn't call at six, as we arranged? In fact, you haven't told me anything: so far it's a one-way street, everything from me, nothing from you in return."

"So far," echoed Charlie, knowing he had to limit his response fractionally short of an outright threat, an explanation easily ready. "You know how *so far* extends? It extends to just short of eight hours, from the time we met. Within minutes of that meeting, both of us watching the Rossiya, I told you to stop feeling sorry for yourself, which I'm telling you again now. We're both outside whatever the hell's going on, which I also told you. Neither of us is going to survive, which I'm determined to do with or without you, sharing out who tells whom what, like children counting chocolate buttons to ensure they've all got the same. I'm the one the FSB is looking for, the fall guy, remember? And I did remember: thought back to how we met and how quickly we had to get out, so quickly I didn't check for CCTV cameras that might have picked us up together as we ran. That's why I was late calling tonight. I went back to check the possibility of you being at the same risk as me by such a photograph. Which you weren't, so that precious ass and that precious pension of yours isn't on any line. There aren't any cameras that could have caught us." Which Charlie had known from scouring the area when he'd first discovered the hotel wasn't under FSB surveillance.

"I'm sorry. And thank you."

"You going back to the embassy?"

"I wasn't planning to."

"There'll be no point in a ten o'clock call tomorrow. I'll postpone it until later."

"I'll be waiting."

So will I, thought Charlie: his problem was not knowing what he was waiting for.

Jane Ambersom was in that delicious after-sex suspension between scream-aloud exhilaration, which she'd had, and velvet-soft contentment, wanting to drift that way forever, which she couldn't but intended recapturing as often and as long as she could.

"You okay?"

"Perfect," she mumbled into Barry Elliott's shoulder, looping one leg wetly over both of his. "Everything's wonderful. I don't want it ever to end."

"Neither do I."

That had been a ridiculous thing to say: why had she let herself be lulled like that! "Let's not talk about it."

Elliott loosened the arm he'd had around her, holding her to him. "I didn't start it."

Stop! She had to stop this. "There might be something else to talk about."

"What?" he asked, no longer softly, moving farther away.

"Something big."

"How big?"

"Major."

"As big as Lvov?"

"It could be bigger."

"You'll keep me ahead of the curve, won't you?"

"You know I will," she promised, smiling into his shoulder as he pulled her back.

The discreet restaurant, close to the Pont d'Italie, was a rendezvous for illicit assignations. Its cubicle-recessed, candlelit tables did not fully compete with the wall-mirrored, chaise-longue-provided *salon particulaire* of the Belle Epoch but some had entrance curtains to pull across for assured privacy. Jonathan Miller hadn't chosen a curtained alcove for the introductory meeting with Elana and Andrei Radtsic but he had made the reservation in person, under the pseudonym Bissette, to ensure it suited their nonsexual seclusion. He and Abrahams arrived an hour early, although separately, and did not enter until both were independently satisfied there was no hostile surveillance. As an additional precaution a third MI6 officer, Paul Painter, remained in Albert Abrahams's car to maintain protective, alarm-raising observation throughout their meal.

As they were shown to their banquette, Miller said: "From how he greeted us the maître 'd's frightened we're part of a gay gathering."

"He'd probably prefer that to knowing who we really are and why we're here."

"*If* Elana and Andrei show up," qualified Miller.

They didn't. Elana arrived precisely on time but alone and as both men rose to meet her, Miller said: "I wish I hadn't said that."

The station chief ordered Chablis for Elana and as the waiter left said: "Why isn't Andrei with you?"

"He's coming later," said Elana. She was the epitome of Parisian chic in a fitted black suit that heightened the blondness of her tightly coiled chignon.

"Is there a problem?" asked Abrahams.

"He said he has a late class and would join us when it finished."

"So there is a problem?" said Abrahams, instinctively checking his watch, which read 7:35.

Elana sipped her wine, not looking directly at either man. "He doesn't want to do it. Neither do I."

"But you're here, to meet us?" said Miller.

"We don't have a choice, do we?"

"Is that what Andrei thinks?" pressed Abrahams.

"It's what I've tried to convince him. I'm not sure that I have."

"What about you?"

"I've accepted I have to run, leave everything."

"Andrei can't stay," insisted Miller, shaking his head against the waiter's approach for their order.

"I know."

"You can't have more time to persuade him. Maxim Mikhailovich's flight has been booked," urged Miller. "Everything is arranged to a schedule."

"I know that, too. That's why I'm here."

"Will you come with us without Andrei?"

"I don't want to face that choice."

"Is it the girl, Yvette?" suggested Abrahams.

Elana shrugged. "I don't know. I don't think so, although they seem very close. She's very pretty. I like her."

"If he doesn't come tonight we'll have to meet tomorrow," said Abrahams.

"I really don't think you'll have more success than me trying to persuade him," cautioned Elana.

"We'll guarantee him a place at another university in England, reading the same subject," promised Miller.

"Pretending to be someone he isn't: reborn at the age of twenty," said Elana, nodding to more wine.

"It's preferable to the alternative," risked Abrahams.

"Is it?" she demanded, pointedly.

They ordered at eight o'clock, Elana dismissively asking for a plain omelet, both men choosing steak just as disinterestedly. At Elana's hinting look at the diminishing bottle, Miller reluctantly ordered a second Chablis. Andrei arrived as their food was served, refusing to eat but gulping the offered wine. Elana and the two MI6 officers only bothered with token gestures of eating.

"We can understand your uncertainty," said Miller.

"No, you can't," rejected Andrei, sharply.

"We didn't create this situation," tried Abrahams. "We're offering your only way out of it."

"It's not the only way out!" refused Andrei, loudly, helping himself to more wine.

"The only *safe* way out," accepted Abrahams.

"Is your relationship with Yvette the problem?" risked Miller.

Andrei's head came up demandingly. "All of it's a problem."

"Yvette being one of them?" pressed Miller.

"Of course."

"All the preparations to get you out are made now," said Miller. "It's possible, when you're settled, that we could bring Yvette for a reunion. There's no reason why she couldn't come to England, is there?"

"Could you do that?" seized Andrei, the hostility lessening.

"I could suggest it, when things settle."

"What are the preparations for our leaving?" intruded Elana.

"It's to be within the next thirty-six hours," generalized Miller. "We'll meet tomorrow, for me to give you specific pickup arrangements: I'll call tomorrow to say where. It's really very simple. You'll be driven directly to an airfield where a private plane will be waiting. You will be flown to London and reunited with Maxim Mikhailovich that same evening."

"Airfield or airport?" asked Andrei.

"That hasn't been decided yet," lied Miller. "It won't, obviously, be Charles de Gaulle. There's a lot of facilities available all along the northern coast of France."

"Did you mean what you said, about Yvette?" asked Andrei.

"Of course."

"This is the only way for you all to stay together," insisted Abrahams.

"I need more time," demanded Andrei.

"You can't have more time," refused Abrahams. "It's got to be now."

"We'll be waiting for your call," said Elana.

The two men remained at their table after the Russians left, each waiting for the other to open the conversation. It was Abrahams who did. "The steak's too cold now."

"We'll order more," decided Miller. "And get Paul in from the car."

"What do you think?"

"We could have a problem. That's why I kept all the planning so vague."

"Do you think Elana would leave without him?"

"I don't know." Miller shrugged.

"London will never agree to the kid being reunited with his girlfriend!"

"Of course they won't," agreed Miller. "But if it gets the awkward sod to England, it won't matter, will it? He'll be in the bag."

As he joined them Painter said: "How'd it go?"

"Christ knows," said Abrahams. "Let's order some more food. And some decent red wine."

21

REBECCA STREET WAS ALREADY IN MONSFORD'S OFFICE when Straughan entered. Neither looked at the other. As he leaned sideways to start his recording system Monsford said: "I want to hear everything's ready: that nothing can go wrong."

The operations director waited until Monsford straightened, nodding to the unseen switch. "Everything working as it should?"

"Perfectly," frowned Monsford.

"Let's hope Radtsic's extraction does the same."

Monsford sighed. "I'm due at the Foreign Office at eleven. Diplomatically everything's going to hell. So let's get on with it, shall we?"

"Are we included in the meeting?" interrupted the woman.

Monsford shook his head. "Restricted to directors and government liaison: their decision. I'll fill you in later."

Straughan set out the operation chronologically, with Maxim Radtsic's 6:30 A.M. departure from his Moscow apartment to the FSB's Lubyanka headquarters, at which he'd remain for fifteen minutes, with an additional five allowed as failsafe, to establish his arrival. He'd assured Jacobson his leaving so quickly afterward would not be logged: according to Lubyanka procedure, he would be registered as being on the premises although absent from his desk: there'd be a staff voice mail that he was in unspecified conference. As a precaution against an unexpected summons, Radtsic would keep his pager with him. From Lubyanka he would be followed separately throughout the briefly broken journey by Jacobson and one of the three in-flight escorts. The other two would be waiting at Sheremetyevo airport to ensure Radtsic's unimpeded arrival and passage through all the embarkation formalities. Radtsic's arrival at Sheremetyevo would be the signal for the private plane's departure from Northolt and for the Paris *rezidentura* to pick up Radtsic's wife and son for Orly, where the landing and departure were factored for one hour, which again included a failsafe for unexpected delay. Straughan expected the linkup and takeoff to take no longer than thirty minutes. By that time Radtsic would be airborne and beyond interception, with just three hours' flying time from Heathrow. There, transport and cleared-in-advance arrival would already be in place. An hour earlier the plane carrying Elana and Andrei would have landed at Northolt, from where they would be taken to the prepared safe house in Hertfordshire to await Radtsic.

Straughan rose as he finished talking, glancing imperceptibly although blankly at Rebecca, to put in front of Monsford the thin file from which he'd recited the details. "Everything's there, annotated against the timings."

"Nine thirty tomorrow morning," Monsford at once challenged. "Why not today: I told you I wanted it all over as quickly as possible."

"And I made it clear we needed seat availability," reminded Straughan. "Nine thirty tomorrow was the first direct flight with four seats available."

"Is Radtsic all right about that?"

"Jacobson's concerned at Radtsic's demeanor," warned Straughan. "Jacobson says he's arrogant: walks around expecting doors to be opened for him and people to stand aside. I had all three independent escorts at the ballet last night, when Radtsic was given his escape itinerary: two of them told me this morning they hadn't needed Jacobson as their marker. Radtsic looks so much like Stalin, which gets him too many second looks when his arrogance isn't on display."

"Have Jacobson tell the stupid bugger to behave!"

"Jacobson says he already has but doesn't think Radtsic will do as he's told. . . ." Straughan paused. "It doesn't stop there. Radtsic announced he wanted to talk to Elana in Paris to tell her it was all set."

"Jesus!" exploded Monsford. "It can't fuck up over stupidity like this!"

"It won't," promised Straughan. "I'm just setting it all out, including the unpredictables."

"Is Jacobson seeing Radtsic again?"

"He's got to hand over the cover passport and tickets today."

"Tell him he's got to spell out to Radtsic the risk to which he's putting himself; putting everyone, his wife and son most of all."

"There's something else," continued Straughan. "I've made it very clear to Jacobson that Charlie Muffin's assassination, as a diversion, is aborted: that everything's canceled. We've got three of our people in Muffin's support team with nothing to support after what happened yesterday at the Rossiya. I want to utilize at least one of them to be embassy liaison between Radtsic's escorts and me, here in London. I need to know that Radtsic passed safely through Sheremetyevo to activate in their right order all the other stages of the extraction."

"No!" irritably refused Monsford. "Why have you waited until now to bring this up! You knew we'd need a pivot for the schedule to work."

"We intended using Charlie Muffin's killing as a diversion for Radtsic's extraction: Muffin was never going to leave Moscow and neither were his wife and child," said Straughan. "We always had three of our own people available to be reassigned. My understanding of yesterday's meeting and the disaster Muffin's caused is that Natalia and Sasha's extraction is never going to happen."

"Yesterday's meeting didn't cancel the Muffin extraction. Nothing's canceled until that bloody man's been brought in and the danger he's created closed down," corrected the Director, tightly. "I can't, unilaterally, transfer any of our people, who might very well be needed in that closing down. And we couldn't anyway risk such a reassignment leaking out ahead of our getting Radtsic safely here. It would disclose that all the time we were running a parallel operation, using one to guarantee the success of the other."

Straughan hesitated. "It's essential we have four on Radtsic's extraction. If I can't have one of our three, I'll have to take Jacobson off, to be my embassy link man." He paused again. "Or we could bring in David Halliday. I know you ordered against his involvement but all he's got to do is take Jacobson's call from Sheremetyevo and relay it to me here: just two phone calls. Halliday's briefing could be strictly limited, virtually telling him nothing except to pass Jacobson's call to me in London."

Now it was Monsford who hesitated, longer than the operations director. "Okay, we use Halliday. But limit the briefing as you've suggested. No name."

"There's another unpredictable," announced Straughan.

"What else!" demanded Monsford.

Straughan gave his account of the previous night's Paris encounter with Elana and Andrei in as much detail as he'd recounted Jacobson's Moscow meeting and again at the end put a written report in front of the Director.

"I can't believe this!" said Monsford, incredulously. "Doesn't the kid know what'll happen to him if he stays!"

"We're meeting with them both again today."

Monsford leaned forward over his desk. "Tell Miller to frighten the shit out of the kid. And if he still fucks about, to leave him. Tell Miller to assemble a snatch squad, to hold him long enough to get Elana airborne and then let him go. By tomorrow he'll be in a Siberian gulag with a lifetime to reflect his stupidity."

"Miller hopes Elana will persuade him."

"You just told me she's reluctant, too."

"Reluctant but accepting reality."

"You're the director of operations, the man responsible for making this work," threatened Monsford. "Don't for a moment forget that."

"I'm never given the opportunity to forget," said Straughan.

"The whole damn business has escalated out of any control," announced Geoffrey Palmer. "The Russians didn't just reject our Note. They refused to accept the ambassador, sent him packing cap in hand after ensuring their media circus was assembled to see and photograph the entire humiliation. And then kept them there to do it all over again when the ambassador responded—as he diplomatically *had* to respond—to their summons to deliver the rejected Note. They're refusing us consular access to those they've arrested, as well as the two heart attack victims, one of whose condition is reported to be giving cause for concern. I can't ever remember this degree of orchestrated diplomatic contempt."

"Incredible," sympathized Sir Archibald Bland. "Incredible and completely unsatisfactory. As well as being totally unacceptable. The cabinet decided this morning to summon the Russian ambassador in return, for an official protest Note. We're also refusing their lawyers access to their arrested diplomats here, which technically breaches the agreed consular code. We'll have eventually to concede, causing us further humiliation when we do, but we'll string it out as long as we can in the hope of getting in to see our tourist group."

"I don't think they'll blink first," cautioned Palmer.

"Neither does the cabinet," admitted Bland, the double-act confrontation clearly rehearsed. "So, tell us you've got the bloody man who's caused all this."

"We haven't yet," admitted Aubrey Smith. "And until he makes contact, which he's got to do at some stage, we don't know where to look. Which the Russians are clearly expecting us to do, to lead them to Muffin. My people are convinced there's a higher than customary degree of surveillance on the embassy and everyone going in and out."

"Are you getting the same indication?" Bland asked Monsford.

The MI6 Director shifted, more concerned at the potential danger to the Radtsic extraction than at not having heard, until that moment, about a heightened embassy observation. "Tighter than usual, certainly," he lied. "What we surely need is something more embarrassing with which to confront the Russians?"

"The purpose of this meeting is to explore practicalities, not daydreams," criticized Bland. "I don't want us even to consider anything that might blow up in our faces to compound a disaster into a total catastrophe. I want that, the government wants that, completely understood by both of you. So, do you completely understand what I've just told you?"

"I most definitely understand," replied Smith.

"I was trying to explore logic more than daydreams," Monsford defensively tried to recover, disappointed at the brusque dismissal of what he'd hoped would prepare them for Radtsic.

"It's inevitably going to dominate the House again today, as well as tomorrow morning's headlines," predicted Bland. "Are you both telling me there's absolutely nothing to add from yesterday?"

"Absolutely nothing," conceded Smith, his normally soft voice little more than a mumble. "You'll know the minute I do that we've got Muffin under wraps. Which won't provide any counterpublicity, will it?"

"If there is any news of Muffin it will obviously come from my colleague's service," said Monsford, determined to distance himself and MI6. Equally determined upon what would later be recognized as proactive thinking, he added: "And I'll alert you at once to anything else that could be relevant."

"And Palmer and Bland were a blink away from tears of gratitude at the hope of a balancing embarrassment for the Russians," boasted Monsford, ending his account of the Foreign Office encounter.

"You didn't take the hint about Radtsic any further than that?"

asked Straughan. Once more he ignored the woman as Monsford activated the recording equipment, glad he'd postponed their intended conversation after the earlier morning session.

"Only the merest wisp of hope," said Monsford, smiling: he'd omitted Bland's edict against counterbalancing the Russian maneuvering. "They'll recognize what I was talking about by this time tomorrow: that we weren't just sitting around on our hands. Aubrey Smith was practically whimpering, like an abandoned dog."

"Isn't there a risk of our being criticized for keeping it to ourselves?" suggested Rebecca.

"Palmer and Bland are sitting on their hands as well, shit scared of anything else going wrong," dismissed Monsford. "I wasn't going to risk a last-minute abandonment."

Working through Monsford's mixed metaphor was like wading through mud, thought Rebecca. "You don't sound very impressed by any of them?"

"Unlike Janus, they're only looking in one direction: over their shoulders to protect their backs." Monsford sneered, juggling his responses. "You made it clear to Jacobson he's got to rein in Radtsic?"

Straughan nodded. "I didn't just reinforce it to Jacobson. I personally spoke to Halliday. There can't be the slightest misunderstanding."

"How did Halliday take it?" asked Rebecca.

"He complained at being sidelined: not being treated as a senior operative."

"Did he now!" mocked Monsford. "What did you tell him?"

"That being a senior officer he knew the golden espionage rule that operational security dictates that agents are only told what it's individually essential for them to know for their part of an assignment."

"Did he accept that?" questioned Rebecca.

"What he accepted was that he didn't have an alternative," qualified Straughan. "What he did say was that he should have been given more responsibility."

"I definitely shouldn't have left him in Moscow after the last clear-out," said Monsford. "Bring him out the moment this is all over."

"Which brings us to a connected situation," seized Straughan. "Jacobson pointed out that he'll obviously be identified by the FSB as Radtsic's escape Control. There's no way he can return to Moscow."

Monsford shrugged, frowning. "What's the relevance of that, right now?"

"Bringing Radtsic in is going to be a hell of a coup not just for the service but for Jacobson, personally. And give the government the recovery it needs. Jacobson is staking his claim early for a fitting recognition."

Monsford sniggered, derisively. "He's doing *what*!"

"Putting himself forward to be station chief in Washington, D.C., or Paris. His preference is Paris."

Monsford sniggered again. "If we weren't as close as we are I'd consider abandoning the extraction, seriously concerned that Harry Jacobson had suffered a mental problem. I'd diagnose inflated grandeur. Harry Jacobson's future is one of the furthest thoughts from my mind and will probably stay that way for a long time to come. If he mentions it again, tell him there's absolutely no reason for him to take a French-language course or learn the words of the 'Star Spangled Banner.' "

"I'll let you tell him when he gets here," said Straughan, sighing.

"When's he handing over the passport and tickets to Radtsic?" Monsford pressed on, unaware of the other man's contempt.

"Now," replied Straughan, ready for the demand.

"We'll reconvene this afternoon," decided Monsford.

As they walked together from the Director's office, Rebecca said: "It's turning out to be a crowded day?"

"Productive, though," agreed Straughan.

The deputy director waited until they were in the outside corridor before saying: "Shall we wait until after the final meeting?"

"Probably best," Straughan agreed once more. "Could you see?"

"Yes," said Rebecca. "We're doing the right thing."

"I hope so," said the man.

"Trust me," said Rebecca.

That was his problem, acknowledged Straughan. He didn't trust her any more than he trusted Gerald Monsfod, in whom he had no trust whatsoever.

He'd been overconfident, Charlie Muffin admitted to himself. He'd swung from overcaution to overconfidence instilled by overanalyzing the overly suspicious to end up where he was now, overwhelmed by discrepancies. By far the worst had been his mistakenly imagining Natalia's fear-prompted telephone calls connected to the provable FSB burglary and staged the Amsterdam deception to evade an imagined entrapment. And by so doing provided the Russians with the propaganda field day they were utilizing to their fullest advantage. But from what Halliday told him Charlie was sure he'd correctly judged that the rescue extraction for Natalia and Sasha had all along been a sacrificial diversion for something entirely separate. Would he have compromised, destroyed even, that separate operation as he'd now so badly endangered his chances of getting Natalia and Sasha out? It would be a fitting retribution if he had, inadvertent though it would have been.

But that wasn't his major concentration. More immediate was covering his self-dug pitfalls safely. His hopes of doing that had soared after establishing contact with David Halliday and then so quickly afterward with Natalia. Both had leaked away during the near-sleepless, self-analyzing night and flattened even more with the first of his arranged contacts with Natalia.

While acknowledging it to be understandable, Charlie was still disappointed that Natalia's previous-day deflation hadn't lifted. His overnight thinking had concluded that while his mistakes made Natalia and Sasha's rescue hugely more difficult, it was possible as long as he remained undetected. Natalia, in total contrast, appeared to have sunk into acceptance of inevitable disaster. She'd dismissed the misconceptions as being his, not her, fault and heaped further remorse on herself for not having anything to offer from the Lubyanka. Trying to break her mood, Charlie actually accused her of self-defeat and self-pity and now, entering another kiosk for his second arranged call of the day, was unsure if he hadn't been too severe on her.

"Can you talk?" Charlie opened, without identifying himself when Halliday answered.

"I'm not sure, not anymore."

Charlie'e stomach dipped. "Why not?"

"I'm back on board, which I know you're not. It's different now."

If Halliday completely believed he'd been reintegrated, he'd have put down the telephone the moment he'd recognized his voice. "I believed in London that I was on board too, remember?"

"That's your problem to sort out."

"I did, by realizing in time that I was the chosen fall guy," hurried Charlie, sure he was keeping the anxiety from his voice. "Remember that, too? You really believe you're fully back in the loop? That's what you've got to be absolutely convinced of: that and something equally important. That you're absolutely safe. That's the magic word, *safety*. You got the absolute guarantee of that, David? Or aren't you suspicious that having been excluded from everything until now, you've been picked out as the sacrificial fall guy now they don't have me for the job?" Bite, you squirming bastard, Charlie thought: swallow the fucking hook!

"I can look after myself."

He *was* unsure! "That wasn't the impression I got yesterday."

"Nothing can go wrong inside an embassy."

Halliday was the point man, seized Charlie. And didn't know enough of his last Moscow assignment to identify a manipulation. "Of course nothing can go wrong inside an embassy! You know what? I wouldn't be at all surprised if that wasn't the thinking of that poor sod for whose murder I was last here. You know, the one killed in the embassy grounds?"

"It's not the same," protested Halliday, weakly.

"He certainly wasn't the same when they finished with him," pressured Charlie. "Did you hear how he was tortured? He only had one arm and they used acid to take off the fingertips of the one hand he still had, to stop his being identified. They took his eyes out, too. And his tongue. All while he was alive . . ." Charlie could hear uneven, gulped breathing from the other man. "Our being able to talk like this means you're in the *rezidentura* by yourself. Where's everyone else? Do you know how you fit into the *complete* picture?"

"It was *you* who reminded *me* how operations are compartmented!" blurted Halliday.

"Which I shouldn't have needed to tell you," coaxed Charlie, sure he had the other man well and truly on his line. "It's the first lesson, hammered home. But I never accepted it: it was such an obvious one-way ticket to the cliff edge. I kept the golden rule always in the forefront of my mind, as I was told to, and on every assignment I worked my ass off, breaking it to find out as much as I could about what I wasn't supposed to know. Which wasn't disobedience or disloyalty or any contravention of any Official Secrets Act. It was to keep myself alive in an environment in which we're also taught we're indispensable until that rule's changed for a greater indispensable need. And why I'm still alive and you're all by yourself in an empty *rezidentura* without a fucking clue what you're doing and won't be told if you ask. The only thing you can be sure about is that you don't know whether you're going to get a pat on the back or a knife stuck into it."

The breathing was heavier and more uneven, although Charlie didn't believe Halliday was actually breaking down. There was, eventually, a word that Charlie didn't catch but then it came again and Charlie heard: "Bastards."

"Why are they bastards?" Charlie asked at once, not wanting to lose the momentum he'd created.

"Keeping me out: treating me like this."

He'd made another mistake with Halliday, Charlie acknowledged, although not as great as MI6 by inducting Halliday. He didn't any longer think Halliday's constant sideways shuffle from difficulty was his pension concern. It was an abject terror of a job he'd got but never wanted once he'd discovered what it entailed and from which he'd always been running. "I'm here to help you help yourself, David. I can get you safely through this if you trust me."

"It is the extraction I thought it was."

He still had to be careful Halliday didn't spit the hook out. "Who?"

"Janus. The code name's Janes. I told you that."

More self-justification, Charlie recognized. Now the all-important question. "What's the genuine identity?"

"All I know is Janus. That's the name I've got to use calling Straughan."

"You haven't managed to get back into Jacobson's safe?"

"I can't break the combination, either into his office or the safe itself."

It had to be a major extraction for the MI6 operations director to be personally involved. "Tell me about Janus."

"It's the launch code."

"It'll be specific," demanded Charlie, professionally.

"Janus has gone."

"That's the green code, *Janus has gone*?"

"Yes."

"What's the red?"

"Janus is stopped."

"Is it today?"

There was the first hesitation. "I'm on twenty-four-hour standby."

"At the embassy?"

Another pause. "I already told you I'm working from inside."

"Who actually briefed you?

"Straughan."

Confirmation that it was a major extraction, decided Charlie, positively. "Who's your relay, here?"

"I don't know."

"What's Jacobson's function?"

"I don't know."

He'd started to row back. "They're really keeping you out, aren't they?"

"You're doing the same. You're not telling me what you're going to do."

And I don't intend to, thought Charlie, a decision half formed. "Keep out of the way, until your thing's over."

"I don't understand."

"I believe I was intended to be the disposable part in the Janus extraction."

"None of the special team is involved in Janus," challenged Halliday.

"How do you know that?"

"I asked Straughan: said I assumed they were on the same assignment. That was when I got the compartmentalization argument. He said they were nothing to do with it and that I should keep myself apart from them."

And why it had been easy persuading the paranoid Halliday that he wasn't safe, realized Charlie. "They haven't been withdrawn?"

"You think I should watch myself?" demanded Halliday, anxiously.

"I don't think you should explore dark alleys with them," goaded Charlie. "They still ostracizing you in the commissary?"

"Maybe not as much as in the beginning. I had a couple of drinks with Pat Wilkinson last night. I didn't get anything specific, certainly not what they're here for. But one of the others, Denning I think it was, said something about being pissed off hanging around, not knowing what was happening."

Getting indicators from Halliday was like pulling teeth with eyebrow tweezers, thought Charlie. "Nothing about me by name?"

"Not that I heard."

"Keep in mind what I told you: watch your back," encouraged Charlie. "Why not bring the Rossiya into the conversation, see what their reaction is?"

"Straughan told me to stay away."

"Don't you think Straughan could have gone further than telling you to recite the sort of phrases you'd use teaching a monkey to talk," ridiculed Charlie. "It feels good to know I'm safe. How do you feel?"

"Who are you really trying to help, Charlie, me or yourself?"

"You'll have your answer to that this time tomorrow," promised Charlie, which was an exaggeration because his idea still wasn't completely formulated.

"How the hell am I supposed to respond to that?" protested Halliday.

"By trying harder to break the door and safe combinations. And thinking back over this conversation to decide if you gained anything by holding back as I know you've held back." Charlie heard the other man say, "No . . . wait . . ." in the seconds before he replaced the phone.

"Why'd you keep me waiting?" demanded Rebecca Street. "We left Gerald more than an hour ago."

"I needed to guarantee the quality: enhance it if necessary," replied Straughan, easily, gesturing to the recorder on the desk between them.

"Did you have to?"

"Not at all, which I'm glad about. If the need arises to use it I don't want any technical indication of interference, not that enhancement should register. From where you were sitting, were you able to see?"

Rebecca nodded. "He turned off during the references to the assassination. And when he slagged off Palmer and Bland."

"You did well, getting a lot of that stuff on our copy," praised Straughan.

"And you did even better," returned the woman.

"You think we should go on recording our meetings with him?"

"Absolutely. I'm not going to be his scapegoat, like the Ambsersom woman before me. What odds would you give about tomorrow?"

"I don't gamble on things like this," refused Straughan, stiffly.

"When Jacobson asked him directly about handing over the passport and tickets, Radtsic was adamant he hadn't called Paris. But there's no way we can be sure. Jacobson was certainly relieved by Radtsic's new attitude: not a trace of the old arrogance."

"We've done the right thing, taking the precautions we have," insisted Rebecca, unprompted.

"And broken every rule and regulation in the book," qualified Straughan.

"With every justification, knowing the tricks Gerald's playing," persisted the woman. "I'll look after the recording, okay?"

"Okay," agreed Straughan, pushing it farther across the desk toward her. "Make sure it's well protected."

"Protection's the name of the game and I'm very good at it."

Straughan had warned his mother's caregiver he'd be late getting back to Berkhamsted, determined to guarantee the recording quality of his encounter with Rebecca Street, as well as theirs with the Director. He had broken every rule and regulation, in addition to the law itself, Straughan recognized. And was terrified. He wished there was someone in whom he could confide: someone like Jane Ambersom, who had always been so kind and understanding.

As they had been the previous night, Miller and Abrahams were waiting ahead of the Russians, this time in the bar of the George V. There were three additional MI6 officers, again under the supervision of Paul Painter, spread protectively in the expansive adjoining lobby. Painter was directly in their line of sight to give the earliest warning of unexpected, suspect arrivals.

Elana entered again precisely on time, as chic as before in a camel-hair topcoat over a heavy roll-neck white sweater. She was alone. There were no warning signals from the foyer.

"Don't be alarmed," said Elana, as she sat.

"We are," declared Miller, flatly. "Andrei can't behave like this."

"He'll be with me," promised Elana. "He resents what's

happened . . . it's going to make the situation with his father very difficult . . . but he's accepted there's no alternative."

"Are you quite sure he's coming?" demanded Abrahams, ordering the woman's wine.

"He's given me his word," said Elana.

"Is that enough?" pressed Abrahams.

Elana's head came up sharply but the rebuke was halted by the returning waiter. After he'd left she said: "It's more than enough."

"London's worried Andrei might do something unpredictable."

"He won't," insisted the woman. "What are our arrangements?"

Miller hesitated, uncertainly. "It's tomorrow. I can't give you a positive time. Everything has to be coordinated with Maxim Mikhailovlich's departure. I'll call the apartment to give you the pickup time. Both of us will take you."

"Where?"

Abrahams gestured in the direction of the Seine. "The bateau mouche ferry terminal at the far end of Avenue V. We can join the perephique from there. Don't bring any baggage. Just yourselves."

"I understand."

"Elana, I must ask you an important question," said Miller. "What will you do if Andrei backs off at the last minute?"

"I have told you he won't back off. The question doesn't apply."

"Treat it as a hypothetical question."

"No."

Charlie stalled at the very moment of commitment, confronted by the choice he'd never imagined having to make. He hadn't substantially lied to Halliday, prising from the man what little he had during their first contact that day, nor during the second when he'd learned nothing additional. Like an inferior player he'd just rearranged the pieces on a chessboard without achieving checkmate. He *had* always ignored the compartmenting edict to guarantee personal survival and when he'd discovered that survival threatened, he'd without hesitation committed every illegality short of intentional murder to stay alive. But in the process he'd never, ever, sabotaged a British assignment. Which was what he was contemplating now, the enclosed telephone just yards away in the corner of the bar. He had every justification. He didn't have the slightest doubt that the Janus-faced combination of MI5 and MI6 intended Natalia and Sasha to be included in his destruction. Why, then, was he holding back? Charlie didn't know, not fully. On that taunting corner phone he'd fifteen minutes earlier told Natalia— abruptly, Charlie's mind blocked and just as suddenly he believed he *did* know the reason for his reluctance, and it worried him because he couldn't remember the last occasion he'd been halted by self-doubt. Not about himself, he qualified. As always, about Natalia and Sasha and whether what he intended could rebound into another mistake, to go with all the others. Not just self-doubt, self-pity, Charlie recognized. Something that, encouragingly, had been markedly absent from Natalia during that earlier telephone conversation in which she'd unquestioningly told him what he wanted.

This wasn't going to be a mistake: worsen his chances of getting them to safety. This was going to be the retribution he'd always intended. Charlie rose for the second time from the bar and dialed the number Natalia had provided for the FSB-retained, communist-era neighbor-informing-upon-neighbor facility. There was an immediate automatic answer.

Through a mouthpiece muffled by his handkerchief Charlie said, first in Russian and then, hopefully, in American-accented English: "Malcolm Stoat is leaving through Sheremetyevo Airport in the next twelve hours."

22

NONE SLEPT WELL. ALL WERE UP BEFORE THEIR RESPECTIVE dawns, allowing for the time difference between Moscow and Paris and the disparity between Moscow and London. Harry Jacobson, in the last of a series of hired Toyotas used throughout in place of the identifying diplomatic registration of his embassy Ford, was outside the north Moscow apartment thirty minutes before Maxim Mikhailovich Radtsic's departure. Jacobson did not try to locate the separate, independent escorts in other vehicles parked hood to trunk in the square or its offshoot streets. David Halliday responded at once to Jacobson's cell-phone-check call to the British embassy on Smolenskaya Naberezhnaya. Not trusting the reliability of the skeletal early-morning train services, James Straughan had himself collected by an MI6 car from his Berkhamsted home, in which his mother's caregiver slept overnight. Rebecca Street stayed at Cheyne Walk to make the short journey from Monsford's apartment to Vauxhall Cross with the MI6 Director. Jonathan Miller and Albert Abrahams met for coffee and croissants at an all-night-workers' café close to the British embassy on rue d'Anjou before crossing to their *rezidentura.* Elana Radtsic was already in the kitchen, brewing black tea, when Andrei walked in. Answering her question, Andrei said he'd told Yvette he was skipping class that day to show his mother some Paris sights before her return to Moscow. There, seemingly immune now to the bed-bug attacks, Charlie Muffin lay awake but unmoving, frustrated at his isolation from a situation he knew to be happening, although without the slightest knowledge of whose extraction he hoped to have sabotaged: hoping even more that its wrecking would reverberate throughout the highest echelons of British intelligence for the utmost humiliation and career disaster for those who'd tried to destroy him, Natalia, and Sasha.

In Moscow it was raining heavily. London and Paris were overcast, with rain forecast later in the day.

Maxim Radtsic emerged precisely on time. He wore a gray trench coat, its collar turned up to a wide-brimmed, dark gray fedora he'd not worn before to meet Jacobson. The Russian carried a strap-secured briefcase in one hand and a small, weekend bag in the other. He looked neither left nor right getting into a small, unmarked Mercedes parked directly outside his apartment. Although there was no moving traffic in the street or those surrounding it, Radtsic put on his turn signal before pulling away. Jacobson allowed a gap of almost thirty meters before following. As he did so, Jacobson saw in his rearview mirror a Renault emerge from a line of parked vehicles behind but on the other side of the street. Both rigidly conformed to the speed limit.

Straughan had commandeered the mezzanine-level overview eerie normally occupied by the communications supervisor, who was that day relegated to the far side of the room and a secondary desk to which all satellite television, telephone, e-mail, and telex traffic had been transferred, with the exception of the dedicated, permanently open lines to the Moscow and Paris *rezidenturas*. Also from the overview room there was direct, two-way audio relay to the Director's suite for simultaneous exchange between Straughan and Monsford. The separately installed CCTV did not have a conference connection, preventing Straughan seeing into Monsford's office. Rebecca Street confirmed her presence there, inquiring about technical difficulties. Straughan assured her there were none: there were duplicated, already opened lines for such eventualities. He told Monsford he'd spoken to David Halliday in Moscow and that Millar and Abrahams were already at their *rezidentura*: it was still too early for their intended backup to be mobilized under Paul Painter's supervision.

"London, as ever, driving from the backseat," remarked Miller, putting his phone down.

"Without a map or sat-nav to tell them in which direction they're going," agreed Abrahams. "We'll be superfluous to requirements once we land at Northolt. I've got a girlfriend in London who's got a similarly uninhibited and free-spirited friend."

"Why not give her a call, fix it up, before everything kicks off?" suggested Miller. "We're not likely to get into London proper until early evening."

"Good idea," accepted Abrahams.

Maxim Radtsic still led when they joined the multi-lane inner beltway from the Olimpijskaka ploscad link, the cars passing with an irony no one was ever to learn within a crow's-flight mile from where the resentful Charlie Muffin still lay at the Mira hotel. By now the rain had eased and the rush-hour traffic built up, which slowed them while at the same time providing protectively intervening vehicles between Radtsic and his MI6 escorts. Jacobson's ever-hovering fear of entrapment diminished in parallel with the rain, although he refused to let his confidence stretch to a triumphant liftoff from Sheremetyevo and positive, irreversible success. What little he did allow evaporated at their approach to the CCTV-festooned Lubyanka headquarters of the Russian intelligence apparatus, the detection risk here potentially greater than at the airport. Forewarned by Radtsic of constantly patrolling plainclothes guards and perpetually staffed live television sweeps of the entire surrounding area—warnings passed on through Straughan to the separate car—the closeness of the escort was abandoned before they reached the square. Jacobson parked on a side street with a view of the side exit through which Radtsic intended to leave, on foot, abandoning the Mercedes in its reserved bay as further indication of his remaining somewhere in the building. The Renault found a space in another side road. David Halliday responded on the first ring to Jacobson's call: he'd already spoken to Straughan to establish the voice relays were operating perfectly.

At London's Vauxhall Cross, Straughan closed off his permanent

Moscow link and into his connection to the Director's suite said: "Radtsic's arrived at the Lubyanka, two minutes ahead of schedule: everything's going to plan."

"How do you know that!" demanded Monsford, at once.

Straughan didn't care if his frowned grimace was obvious on the penthouse TV. "Halliday just reported in from the embassy: Jacobson made contact from outside: he's waiting for Radtsic to come out for the airport."

"I told you Halliday was only to be used between the airport and you."

"And after I personally gave you the general outline of the extraction I left on your desk, the minute-by-minute, stage-by-stage route. Which clearly lists Lubyanka as the first to be reported to me: no geographical identification, stage one. And that's all Halliday passed on: 'Stage one completed, two minutes ahead of schedule.' It's essential I tell Paris now, to keep them in the loop. The Paris collection is also set out in your detailed dossier."

"So the Northolt departure stays on time?" queried Jonathan Miller, listening to what Straughan told him.

"That's the update I'm going to give them as soon as I've finished talking to you."

"Our backup will be in place on Avenue George V and the embankment in fifteen minutes. I've already spoken to Paul Painter. He'll give the alert if any problems arise when we're under way. We'll contact Elana and Andrei once you tell me Radtsic's airborne."

"Painter knows what to do if you get into difficulty?" queried Straughan.

"Just the sort of question I needed after I'd finally convinced myself nothing can go wrong!" complained Miller, in mock rebuke.

"So what's the answer?" persisted Straughan, humorlessly.

"If there's a problem it won't be compounded by their intervention," assured the station chief, putting his telephone down in unison with Abrahams at his opposite desk.

Abrahams said: "The girls want to meet in the Claridge's bar."

"You pay the best, you get the best," remarked Miller.

"I hope you're right." Abrahams smiled back.

Charlie Muffin's cut-off disgruntlement finally drove him out of bed and worsened when the hiccupping shower shuddered to a stop while he was still covered in soap lather. It refused to start again despite his angrily jerking at the controls. It took him ten minutes fully to splash off the soap from the sink tap, the deluge seeping wetly out into the bedroom. He should, Charlie criticized, have moved on from the Mira to a hotel with television or radio in his room, although there were no breaking-news stations matching those of London. It would be psychologically wrong to call Halliday this early, betraying an uncertainty he didn't want the man to suspect. Too early as well, and for the same reason, to attempt contact with Natalia: she wouldn't yet have left the Pecatnikov apartment, which she feared might be bugged. There might, he supposed, be a workers' café showing live television, although he doubted it would be a news program. It was worth the effort, positive physical movement instead of standing around on a damp carpet, neutured into inactivity.

Radtsic increased his time gain by a further three minutes leaving the Lubyanka headquarters through the arranged side exit. He was on foot and now carried only the weekend bag to qualify as cabin baggage on the aircraft. The collar of his raincoat was still pulled up to the wide-brimmed hat, and Jacobson's distracting, nerve-twitched imagery was of a badly cast B-movie spy. It was instantly swept away by the awkwardness with which the Russian was making his way from the square, a seemingly uncertain meander instead of following a quick, direct line. That concern was set aside when Jacobson coordinated the man's odd movements with the CCTV bank and realized Radtsic was avoiding camera observation. Once upon the outside road, Radtsic went in the opposite direction from Red Square, letting two available taxis pass before hailing the third. It took the man directly past the side road in which the escorts were parked. He let Jacobson follow first in line. Moscow's stop-start rush-hour traffic was heavier than Jacobson had estimated and they'd not only lost their time gain but fallen fifteen minutes behind schedule before reaching the airport highway. Jacobson's concern jumped again, fixed now upon another highway police shakedown that could wreck the operation. His apprehension started to subside only at the sight of landing and departing aircraft in the far distance and didn't go completely until he made out the Sheremetyevo buildings, with no obvious road blocks. Success was fingertip close now, he told himself.

"It's eight ten!"

So absolute was James Straughan's concentration that he was physically startled by Monsford's voice, irritated that it might have been visible on camera. "Yes?"

"Your staged progress puts their airport arrival at eight. What's gone wrong!"

"*Estimated* arrival," heavily qualified Straughan. "That estimate also builds in a fifteen-minute latitude for delay, for . . ." He stopped as his permanent Moscow link sounded. He listened, said: "Thank you," and as he replaced the receiver went back to the microphone. "They've arrived, with no problems."

"Let's hope it stays that way," responded Jonathan Miller to the same assurance from Straughan, four minutes later. "I've checked the traffic conditions. They're light, no roadworks or diversions to factor in."

"Don't forget, limited cell-phone chatter on the next call unless they don't show."

"I will have spoken to Elana by then: gotten a steer."

"Fingers crossed it's the right one."

"Do something for us, will you? Have a car at Northolt, to get us into London?"

"Already fixed. Enjoy your one night home."

"We plan to."

Predictably, the first café in which Charlie Muffin found a working television was showing a soccer game on a sports channel, but in the second there was a radio tuned to a Moscow news channel that Charlie judged more likely to broadcast a breaking media event. He drank his way through three cups of close-to-undrinkable coffee and forced himself to eat a second serving of black bread and sour cheese, listening to repeated accounts of government success opposing NATO's eastern expansion, its negotiating substantial price increases for natural gas exports to the European Union, and vetoing an American-sponsored resolution condemning state atrocities in the Congo.

Jacobson dumped his rental car for automatic collection, avoiding a parking delay, and entered the departure hall just five minutes after Maxim Radtsic. Jacobson noted his London-destination gate as he hurried across the concourse, already booked in online and with only a carry-on bag, unworried at not relocating the Russian, knowing the other anonymous escorts would have been ready for Radtsic's arrival. Jacobson saw the hat before the man, glad the raincoat collar was finally down, but still tensed as Radtsic approached the first passport scrutiny. Radtsic turned as he offered the MI6-created documentation. Able to see the man properly in good light, Jacobson acknowledged the practicality of the man's dress. It didn't qualify as a disguise but the hat and its sloped brim completely concealed the graying hair and much of Radtsic's upper face, substantially reducing the Stalin similarity, most important from the wall-mounted CCTV. There appeared no conversation and little comparison between Radtsic and the passport photograph. It was no more stringent at the second, dedicated ticket-and-passport examination. Jacobson went through just as smoothly and they were less than five meters apart going into the duty-free area. Radtsic hesitated at the liquor counter, turning to establish Jacobson's presence without showing any recognition, then continuing on toward the London-designated gate. Jacobson maneuvered himself to have just one intervening passenger at the final ticket-and-passport confirmation but distanced himself once they went through, again unchallenged, into the final embarkation lobby. He waited for Radtsic to enter the aircraft-connected jetway before dialing the MI6 *rezidentura*. He told Halliday: "Janus is go," disconnected without acknowledgment, and hurried after the Russian.

"Radtsic's on the plane," Straughan announced into the Director's voice link as he dialed the security-cleared Northolt airfield number. In response to the extraction code he was told the executive jet would be cleared for takeoff in thirty minutes with an estimated Orly arrival one hour, thirty minutes after that. Straughan ignored two intervention attempts from Monsford, instead dialing Miller's cell phone. To the Paris station chief he said: "Janus is go."

Miller said: "Everyone's safely with me here. We're moving."

"Transport ETA is two hours."

"Speak to you before boarding."

"I'm trying to talk to you," complained Monsford, as Straughan finished. "I don't think you've allowed sufficient time to get from Paris to Orly."

"It was to activate Paris that I ignored you," said Straughan. "Both Elana and Andrei turned up. They're on their way."

"What about their timing?"

"We've done trial runs. We're well within our margins and there are escort cars to warn of difficulties."

There was momentary silence from the floor above, before Monsford said: "I've decided to personally greet Radtsic at Heathrow."

"There is no waiting time built into the Heathrow schedule," objected Straughan. "Radtsic will be taken directly off the plane to the car taking him to Hertfordshire. His being escorted off the plane will attract attention from other passengers, the large proportion of whom will be Russian. I strongly advise against any delay, even of only minutes, at Heathrow: there's a permanent media contingent there. Your personal greeting will be better at the safe house. And more fitting, executive to executive, than in the back of a car. Camera light can penetrate smoked glass."

"I undertook to meet him personally," argued Monsford.

"Without stipulating that it would be at the airport."

"I've got time to work it out."

Which was what Charlie was trying to do in his frustrating isolation, with nothing more than instinct and guesswork from which to operate, having already acknowledged he'd made far too many mistakes relying on both. Had it been another of those mistakes to accept Halliday's story of being sidelined until the last minute? What if Halliday had instead been one of the deputed search-and-find groups at the Rossiya unable to risk losing him to summon backup to the panorama bar? Halliday had certainly tried to follow him afterward and constantly complained since at not knowing his whereabouts. But if he was part of a London search, would Halliday have disclosed the Janus operational code for the separate extraction? Yes, Charlie answered himself, if it lured him out of hiding. Again too much guesswork. There was an obvious way to test Halliday. From his independent airport inquiry, Charlie knew the first direct British Airways flight from Moscow to London had left at 9:30 that morning. Now it was 10:20.

Halliday responded on the initial ring.

"How'd it go?" asked Charlie.

"Like clockwork," replied Halliday. "And you know what Straughan told me, after I gave him the signal and asked what he wanted me to do now? He said he didn't want me to do anything—that it was all over—and put the phone down without so much as a fucking thank-you. It isn't right!"

"No," agreed Charlie, talking more to himself than the other man. "It isn't right."

" 'To the victor belong the spoils of the enemy,' " intoned Monsford from above in a voice Straughan genuinely thought the man had lowered to sound godlike. "I'm going up to Hertfordshire to meet Radtsic there."

"I think that's a better idea," Straughan replied.

"Hertfordshire was always my intention. Keep in touch if there's anything I need to hear before I get there. There can't be anything immediate, can there?"

"No," agreed Straughan. "We're in the interim period now."

The mezzanine-level communications control was the most secure of an already totally secure area within the MI6 building, its daily-changed entry combination restricted to the Director and his deputy, Straughan, and a rota of six duty officers. They did not receive the combination until arriving for their shift, which was why Straughan, in the middle of a conversation with Orly checking the aircraft arrival, was startled for the second time that day by peremptory knocking from outside. Rebecca's visible annoyance through the observation window matched the irritation of her door hammering.

"Why didn't I get today's entry code?" she demanded, as she flounced past Straughan.

"I didn't imagine it would be necessary today: you had permanent visual and audio access from upstairs," said Straughan, warning the woman with a look to the studiously oblivious duty officer on the far side of the room. "Has he gone?"

"Ten minutes ago," she said, also lowering her voice. "He thinks he'll get there in time to greet Elana and Andrei, before Radtsic. And he was pissed off at your attitude, on the voice link."

"And?" prompted Straughan, ignoring the warning.

Rebecca smiled for the first time. "He never bothered to turn on the equipment."

"Why aren't I surprised?" said Straughan, in resigned cynicism.

"Well?" prompted the woman, in return.

"Doubly backed up," assured Straughan, gesturing to the paraphernalia on his desk. "Every word's recorded and there's a tandem line to our own system."

Rebecca looked at the wall behind the regular duty officer, upon which was a five-deep battery of clocks set to the local time of every global capital. "How much longer until the French evacuation?"

"Forty-five minutes," said Straughan, without consulting the wall clock. "I was talking to Orly when you arrived. Our plane will be cleared for takeoff by the time Elana and Andrei get there. They'll get here ahead of schedule."

Now it was Rebecca who gestured to the electronic litter on Straughan's desk. "Seems as if our precautions weren't necessary after all. Everything's gone according to plan, so there won't be any buck-passing."

Straughan shook his head, doubtfully. "There'll be a lot of internal uproar, between us and our brothers across the river. And maybe a lot of internal government examination, too. I don't think we should stop doing it."

"Neither do I," agreed Rebecca.

Straughan didn't jump this time, even though the telephone's shrill was unexpected.

Rebecca said: "It'll be Gerald, from the car."

It wasn't. Straughan listened for more than a full minute before saying: "You did the right thing. It's got to be a cleanup: everything that's possible to do. I want you as my permanent liaison. This is a catastrophe."

"What is?" demanded Rebecca, when Straughan stopped although keeping the telephone in his hand.

"There was an ambush at a *peage* outside Orly. They've all been seized. Miller and Abrahams as well as Elana and Andrei."

"Russian?" groped Rebecca.

"Painter thinks it was French," said Straughan, emptily.

23

"WE HAVE TO TELL THE DIRECTOR," INSISTED STRAUGHAN.

"Not yet!" refused Rebecca. What personal benefit was there? There had to be something!

"He'll be at the safe house in less than an hour."

"All we can tell him now is that there's a difficulty. We need to know more. And get Monsford's reaction recorded." They now had a disaster of incalculable proportions and she wasn't going to be hit by a single particle of the shit Monsford would spray in every direction except his own.

"We know Radtsic's wife and son won't be there to greet him: the promise we've given him."

"What's Painter and the rest of them doing?"

"Keeping as far away as possible," guaranteed Straughan, urgently. "That was their instructions. We don't want to lose any more people. Painter's heading them back to Paris."

"Why's Painter think it's a French seizure?"

"All the vehicles were French. There were some uniforms, the sort the French use in terrorist arrests, although they didn't have any identifying insignia."

"Are we talking Service de Documentation Extérieur et de Contre Espionnage or French police?"

"I don't know." Straughan shrugged, emptily.

"What's our relationship if it is French?"

"I don't understand the question," protested the operations director.

"What's the chances of the SDECE backing off when they learn it's us?"

Straughan stared at Rebecca, not trying to disguise his astonishment. "Let me ask you a question back. What would the chances be of us backing off if we seized two French intelligence officers in a car with the wife and son of the deputy director of the FSB?"

Rebecca visibly colored. "So what do you think they'll do?"

"Take the maximum possible advantage, of course."

"They've got the wife and son: we've got the husband and father," Rebecca tried again. "What about a trade, reuniting the family for joint, completely shared access?"

Straughan again looked at Rebecca in disbelief. "Physically reunite the family where: here in the Hertfordshire house or hand Radtsic over to the French?"

Rebecca's color, which had begun to subside, flooded her face again. "It'll have been that little shit Andrei, won't it?"

"I've logged everything Jonathan Miller told me of every exchange he had with both mother and son," said Straughan. "As far as I recall, Miller never told either of them exactly *where* we were flying them from: only that it would obviously be from somewhere along the north coast. Yet the ambush was only a few miles from Orly, as if our route was known in advance. And if Andrei knowingly set out to sabotage it, wouldn't it be more likely he'd go to the Russians and their embassy, not to the French?"

"We haven't yet confirmed it was a French interception," Rebecca said.

"Whether it's Russian or French is largely academic," dismissed Straughan, philosophically. "The fact is that whichever it is has got them and two of our officers and the service is well and truly in the shit and sinking fast. And we should warn the Director. . . ." He gestured toward a computer on an adjoining table. "That's monitoring Radtsic's flight. It's on time, landing in thirty minutes."

"And it'll be another two hours after that before he gets to the safe house," said Rebecca. "Painter and the others will be back to Paris long before that, won't they?"

Straughan looked at the French chronometer on the far wall. "Probably before Radtsic's plane lands."

"Does Painter have friends in the SDECE?"

"He has contact. I don't know how friendly or not."

"We'll give it a little longer, for Painter to pull in every favor he can," decided Rebecca. "We need as much information as possible for Gerald. Get a message to Jacobson. Warn him but tell him to say nothing to Radtsic. That's Gerald's responsibility: that and informing our government liaison."

What sort of marked-card game was Rebecca Street playing? wondered Straughan. Whatever it was, it had been sensible to keep the safeguarding recording running for these exchanges, along with the rest. How much he wished again for someone like Jane Ambersom to help him decide what to do. The telephone interrupted the reflection. Straughan snatched it up, listened, and then said: "Fuck!"

"What . . . ?" started Rebecca, but stopped, trying to understand from the gabbled conversation. "Tell me!" she demanded, as Straughan slammed the phone down.

"Our plane's been seized at Orly along with everyone in it."

"You're right," agreed Rebecca. "It's a total fuck-up!"

He was properly floating, acknowledged Harry Jacobson: floating thirty-five thousand feet off the ground, on his way to justifiably well-earned rewards. Nothing could go wrong now: he'd done it! No one would ever know the fears he'd endured, the potentially calamitous mistakes and shortcuts he'd made. And now they never would. This was going to be engraved in his service record as a 100 percent, all singing, all dancing coup that could never—*would* never—be taken away from him. But he still wasn't taking chances. Twice since takeoff Maxim Radtsic had turned from his seat two rows ahead, stupidly expecting recognition, which twice he'd refused and was glad he had: Radtsic hadn't turned again but on the second occasion Jacobson overheard two Russians in the seats behind refer, laughing, to the Stalin similarities. It would be a story embellished in its telling to their families when photographs of Radtsic appeared in the inevitable publicity to follow the man's defection. There wasn't anything he'd miss about Moscow, apart obviously from its exquisite ballet. He'd thought the city dirty and its people arrogant, with any professional advancement drowned in a backwater increasingly stagnated by Putin's constantly tightened control. Until Radtsic's unbelievable, once-in-a-lifetime approach, what passed for secret information gathering was virtually the distillation of cocktail-party gossip from one espionage operative to another, flavored by the national political mindset of each teller, additionally spiced as it went around the incestuous intelligence circuit. Paris or Washington was going to be far more rewarding.

Jacobson's cell phone was switched to flight mode but he immediately felt the vibration of a mutely received text. When he got it from his pocket it read: CONTACT URGENTLY ON ARRIVAL UNKNOWN TO NOW SOLITARY COMPANION, and although he was still at thirty-five thousand feet Jacobson was no longer floating.

"It's definitely SDECE," announced Paul Painter. Despite twice using both his antiasthma inhalers the words wheezed from the man.

"Definite confirmation?" demanded Straughan, unsettled by the closeness with which Rebecca was pressed against him to hear both sides of the exchange, her shirt gaped sufficiently for him to see the pinkness of her nipples.

"Definite," said Painter.

"What else?"

"It's being dealt with at a political level."

"What does that mean?"

"I don't know."

"What about the plane? Our people at Orly?"

"The same." Painter's breathing was getting easier.

"That's bollocks."

"That's what my SDECE man is telling me."

"Has there been any formal contact with the embassy?"

"Not up to five minutes ago, when we began this conversation. What am I to tell the diplomatic ranks here? I've had to warn them there's a potential situation."

"I wish you hadn't. And don't forget this conversation is being officially recorded," warned Straughan. "You have any idea how the SDECE are going to handle it?"

"It was when I asked that question that I got the political-level answer."

"You mean that it's been taken out of the hands of the SDECE?"

"Let me tell you again." Painter sighed, fully recovered now and refusing to be pushed into speculation. "I called my man at the French service and told him I'd heard something had happened on the Orly autoroute. He said it was a security operation, as was the impounding of the plane. He told me he didn't know what was going to happen next: that it had been passed up to a political level and that everyone, the four at the toll booth and everyone with the plane, were being detained. That's it. I couldn't get any answers to how, why, or through whom the SDECE got involved. I am, of course, copying you both the complete voiceprint and hard-copy translation."

"What chance is there of it all being kept under wraps?" asked Straughan.

"Something else I can't tell you."

"What I was—" started Straughan.

"Wait a minute," stopped Painter. "There's something coming in on the news wires." There was a moment's silence. "Shit!"

"What?" demanded Straughan.

"It's an official release on Agence France-Presse. It says two Britons have been detained on suspicion of kidnapping two Russian nationals. Other Britons have been held at Orly, along with an aircraft suspected to be part of the same attempt."

Rebecca Street remained in the communications room, where there were better facilities for Straughan to participate in the conference call, peremptorily breaking across Monsford's announcement of his arrival. "You're already at the house?"

"Of course I am. Where are Elana and the boy?"

"That's why I'm calling you. It's bad."

The equipment was so finely adjusted that it was possible over Rebecca's succinct explanation to hear Monsford's increasingly labored breathing, which was scarcely less difficult than Paul Painter's, earlier. There was no immediate response when she finished. Finally Rebecca said: "Are you there? Did you hear what I've told you?"

"How . . . ? I mean, why . . . ? Kidnap's ridiculous."

"I've told you all we know," said the woman, smiling as she pushed a note across the desk to the operations director that read: "My £10 to your £5 he'll give us Shakespeare's wisdom."

"I can't stay here . . . need to get back to London. There'll be calls. . . . Downing Street. You come down here to take over . . . you and Straughan. . . ."

"I can't move from here," refused Straughan. "There's got to be a coordinator. I'm keeping the line permanently open to Paris. And I'm still waiting to speak to Jacobson."

"Bland's already telephoned twice: Aubrey Smith's been on once," picked up Rebecca, the smile widening. "You're to make contact with Bland as soon as I've located you. I need to stay here, where everything's being channeled, to field it all."

"Jacobson!" seized the man. "Where's Jacobson and Radtsic!"

"The plane's just landed: it's still taxiing," said Straughan. "I got a message through during the flight, telling Jacobson to ring me the moment he gets off."

"Jacobson's to stay with Radtsic: that was always the plan. Jacobson and the others are to bring Radtsic here. I'm leaving right now."

"What shall I tell Bland or Palmer or Smith?" asked Rebecca.

"Don't tell anyone anything!" The words came out in a near shout, which Monsford realized. More controlled, he went on: "Tell them you got me but I'm in a bad cell-phone-reception area but that I'm on my way back. I want everything up-to-date and waiting for me on my desk."

"Everything will be ready."

" 'This was an ill beginning of the night,' " quoted Monsford, at last.

"He's shitting himself," Rebecca told Straughan, when the call ended.

"With every reason," said Straughan.

"But we're ring fenced." She smiled, picking up Straughan's five-pound note as well as crumpling her wager note. "I think I should have what's recorded so far."

"I'll run it through, make sure it's all okay," said Straughan. And after making his copy, ensure he took out additional insurance, he decided.

In Moscow, Charlie Muffin was surprised at the quickness of Natalia's response until she said: "Something's broken. I can't talk now."

"Eight tonight at the restaurant we used in the beginning, behind the gardens," Charlie managed, before Natalia put the phone down. He'd have to wait for at least six hours to discover what it was, Charlie estimated. It wouldn't take him that long to complete the shopping he needed.

24

AS IT WAS, CHARLIE DIDN'T HAVE TO WAIT THAT LONG AT ALL.

He checked out of the Mira hotel, moving south to the student transient anonymity of the Moscow university district with the Komsomolskaya Metro and its pursuit-evading convenience of two major subway routes. The Galaxy Hotel was a considerable improvement upon the Mira, due chiefly to the bedroom television with a CNN channel upon which, within half an hour, he saw the breaking-news flash of the French autoroute arrests and Orly plane impoundment. Charlie sat unmoving through two repeats, the last update of which confirmed that the alleged kidnap victims were Russian and that documentation upon the two detained Britons indicated diplomatic connections.

Charlie's immediate speculation was the extent to which he could stretch what little there was to gain more from David Halliday. Not much, was the objective conclusion: scarcely anything at all, under the closest examination. His best, maybe only, hope was to lure Halliday into conjuring more ghosts from his fear-clouded mind. Charlie was encouraged by the audible uncertainty in Halliday's voice as the man grabbed up the *rezidentura* phone. To increase it, Charlie said: "Not such a clean job after all, was it, David?"

"I'm not responsible for any of it! How could I be!" gabbled Halliday.

The satisfaction moved through Charlie. "You tell me."

"I didn't have anything to do with the French end," Halliday continued to protest.

"That's how it is when things fuck up. Don't forget scapegoats and fall guys."

"Not this time," insisted the other man, in weak defiance. "They try to stitch me into this, I'm going to demand an internal inquiry to prove I can't be held responsible."

So far, so good, judged Charlie: not just good, 100 percent better than he'd expected. But it would take only one misplaced word. "How can they stitch you into it, if you didn't know about France?"

"That's the question I asked Straughan."

"What was his answer it?"

"He couldn't answer it, not properly. Said he wasn't accusing me of anything: that he just wanted to know how much Jacobson told me about Radtsic."

Who the fuck was Radtsic? Wrong question, Charlie instantly corrected himself. It was obvious who Radtsic was. And even more obvious, from Natalia's telephone reaction, was the man's occupation if not his actual rank within it until the departure of British Airways 9:30 flight that morning to London. And Halliday had lied, insisting he didn't know the defector's identity. What more was there to squeeze out of the man? "How much *did* Jacobson tell you about Radtsic?"

There was an abrupt silence. After what Charlie estimated was minutes, Halliday said: "You're part of the stitch-up, now it's all gone wrong. You just referred to Radtsic by name! Earlier you told me you didn't know who we were getting out!"

"I didn't know until you mentioned it less than five minutes ago."

"I didn't mention a name," rejected Halliday.

" 'He just wanted to know how much Jacobson told me about Radtsic,' " quoted Charlie. "That's what you said, wasn't it?"

Once more Halliday didn't reply. Charlie didn't prompt.

"I don't trust you," eventually declared the MI6 man, close to his usual petulance.

"I never asked nor expected you to trust me," reminded Charlie. "You proved that, not telling me until now that Radtsic was the extraction."

"I didn't *know* the name, not until London began the inquest," implored Halliday.

Professionally the man was a disaster, Charlie decided once more. If Halliday had ever undergone hostile interrogation he would within minutes have disclosed the identities of every agent and every secret he'd ever known, up to and including the color of his grandfather's underwear. "Tell me about Radtsic," Charlie demanded.

"All I now know is that the extraction from here worked perfectly and that he's already arrived in London. I don't know if he's been told about his wife and son."

Halliday probably didn't realize the amount of information he imparted every time he opened his mouth, for which, Charlie supposed, he should be grateful. "What is Radtsic within the FSB?"

"*The* number two."

Charlie said: "You know, don't you, that the seizure's public: been officially announced by the French."

"How could I know, chained here in the *rezidentura*! It makes it easier to understand London's panic."

Don't lose him, Charlie warned himself. "And should make it easier for you to understand the scapegoat hunt."

"I told you they can't blame me!"

"Chained to a desk in the *rezidentura*," echoed Charlie. "Where Straughan didn't even bother to tell you everything's unraveling. What chance do you think you've got to prevent your balls being turned into a necklace?"

"I'll insist on an official internal investigation if they try that!" repeated Halliday,

"Which they can refuse if they choose," dismissed Charlie. "Don't forget I was brought in as Radtsic's diversion, which I refused to be and beat them. I'm still your best chance of beating them again if they try to set you up."

"I won't forget," promised Halliday, dutifully. "And I'm sorry what I said about not trusting you."

"Don't be," refused Charlie. "Just remember who's your best guide out of this shit."

"There's so much I still don't understand," protested Halliday.

"There's still a lot I don't understand," admitted Charlie. Chief among them being how, after his anonymous Malcolm Stoat tip that should have put the FSB on the highest alert, its defecting chief deputy passed unimpeded through Sheremetyevo airport while the MI6's extraction of the man's wife and son was intercepted by French intelligence.

"I've been trying to update you, but was told you couldn't be reached," said Straughan, as Monsford settled himself at his desk.

"My phone's broken. You got everything ready for me, as I ordered," said Monsford, leaning sideways to the Record button.

"All there in front of you," indicated the operations director. "You want to read it or hear the bullet points?"

"Before you decide, there's been seven more calls between Bland, Palmer, and Smith," broke in Rebecca Street. "I told them you'd be back at four, which gives you thirty minutes to get updated. You're to call Bland the moment you arrive here."

Monsford hadn't looked at his deputy as she talked but Straughan had and picked up the head shake that told him the Director hadn't activated the apparatus. Impatiently, ignoring what Rebecca told him, Monsford said: "Give me the bullet points!"

"The French haven't named Elana or Andrei, just described them as mother and son," Straughan set out. "They've leaked a diplomatic connection for Miller and Abrahams. According to Bland there's been a French demand for an explanation. The pilot and crew have been taken to Paris. It's the lead item on every television and radio channel here and in France, as well as the *Evening Standard* here and every Paris evening newspaper. It's also included in every television and radio newscast and print media, time differences allowing, throughout the European Union, and across America and Canada."

"What about Russia?" demanded Monsford, hunched over the unread file.

"Nothing terrestrial or local-print yet: satellite will of course be available, most definitely our BBC World Service and CNN."

"Bastards!" hissed Monsford, almost incoherently. "Bastards, bastards, bastards."

At Monsford's gesture for her to deny his presence, Rebecca picked up the demanding telephone, insisted Monsford still hadn't returned, and promised the call would be returned the moment he did.

"Geoffrey Palmer," she identified. "They've been told your cell phone is unreachable."

"The circuit board's buckled," dismissed Monsford. "How did it leak to the French?"

"I haven't been able to find out yet," admitted the operations director. "Halliday denies Jacobson told him anything. It was a limited conversation with Jacobson, but he's adamant he didn't discuss anything with Halliday either. Jacobson thinks Radtsic made the phone call he'd forbidden the man to make to Elana, in Paris. That's the line he's going to take with Radtsic, when Radtsic discovers Elana and Andrei aren't at the safe house. I obviously haven't been able to talk to anyone in France, apart from Painter, but Andrei's another potential source. We know the kid didn't want to be part of it. . . ." Straughan indicated the ignored Rebecca. "We've talked about that possibility. There are several problems with it. It would have been far more likely for Andrei to have gone to his own people at the Russian embassy than to the French, wouldn't it? It would have been more natural for the girl, Yvette, to do that, if Andrei told her what was going to happen. But that falls down, too. Neither Elana nor Andrei knew precisely where we were flying from: the ambush was in place on the Orly autoroute and there was a squad already at the airport itself, simultaneously, to impound the plane."

"What about Charlie Muffin?"

Straughan frowned. "He was always the diversion. He didn't know anything."

"He's a double: tricked us all. He's gone over to the Russians!" Monsford insisted.

"Whether he has or hasn't doesn't affect this," refused Straughan, ignoring Rebecca's look. "Charlie Muffin didn't know anything about Radtsic: if he had—and has gone over—the first thing he'd surely have done was stop Radtsic's defection?"

"Charlie Muffin has to have had something to do with this!" persisted Monsford, his voice rising against their opposition.

"You're going to be asked for a lot of explanations," cautioned Rebecca."They'll need logical answers. It not logical to include Charlie Muffin in whatever's gone wrong."

"Whose side are you on!"

"That question isn't logical, either," rejected the woman. "We're confronting a disaster from which we're not going to escape with illogical accusations."

Monsford looked between the two. "Other people knew."

Rebecca broke the silence that followed. "I don't understand that remark."

"Who, outside this room, have either of you discussed Radtsic's extraction with?"

"I have discussed the Radtsic extraction with no one outside this room and every discussion I have had within this room has been recorded on your personal system specifically installed for that purpose," replied Rebecca, with stilted formality.

"Every discussion about the Radtsic extraction in which I have been involved within this room is on the same system," matched Straughan. "Every discussion I have had outside this room, either from my own office or from the communication supervisor's office, is similarly held on the equipment specifically installed for such purposes."

"I hope I can believe you," said Monsford.

"I hope you can believe me, too," said Rebecca.

"As I also hope you can believe me," said Straughan.

The jarring telephone broke this next silence and for several moments Monsfsord looked at it, once starting to look toward the woman. He finally lifted it, briefly listened, and said: "I have just this minute come into the building. I'll be with you on time."

"Do you want us to come with you?" asked Rebecca, as Monsford rose.

"No," said the man.

"You've forgotten your briefing papers," said Straughan.

"I don't need them."

Rebecca waited for several minutes after the door closed before saying: "He forgot his recording machine, too. But then he'd already done that by not turning it on."

Maxim Mikhailovich Radtsic physically rose from his chair as Jacobson talked. He remained standing, hunched forward as if worried at missing a single word, shaking his lowered head in disbelief.

"How . . . ? You told me it was all arranged . . . ? Foolproof . . ."

"That's what we've got to speak about. Sit down, Maxim Mikhailovich."

Radtsic slumped down and looking questioningly from Jacobson to the three other escorts in the room. "A drink. I need a drink. Vodka."

One of the unnamed men left the room. Radtsic pulled himself forward in his chair, making a physical effort to recover. "Tell me everything that happened."

"You've heard all I know," insisted Jacobson. "Now you've got to help us."

"What can I tell you?" demanded the Russian, reaching out for the escort-offered vodka from a tray laden with ice and the remaining bottle. "You know it all: *you're* supposed to be looking after me; after Elana and Andrei as well. That was our agreement."

"In Moscow you told me you wanted to telephone Elana: tell her it was all finalized," Jacobson spelled out, cautiously, his mind functioning on two levels. "And I—"

"Warned me against doing so," interrupted Radtsic, holding out his empty glass.

"But did you?" demanded Jacobson, hoping for a startled admission.

Instead, Radtsic stretched out unseeingly for the new drink, but with his concentration entirely upon Jacobson. "Of course I didn't!" he said, his voice no longer uncertain. "What you told me made obvious sense. The risk was too great."

Unspeaking, Jacobson in turn held his concentration on the man, trying to prevent his mental focus going sideways to the nagging concern at his personal expectations.

"You don't believe me!" accused Radtsic when Jacobson didn't speak, his normal peremptory tone completely restored. "I did everything as you wanted: never allowed the slightest risk, not taking any chances. You're the one, you and your people, who fucked up . . . who've got to sort it out . . . make it work as you assured me you would."

"I told you Andrei didn't want to come," Jacobson reminded, flatly. Why had the arrogant bastard so clearly identified him on the automatic recording system!

"And I told you however reluctant Andrei was, after hearing his mother explain, he'd cross with her. Andrei isn't the cause of this: none of it."

Another personal identification, Jacobson recognized. "That's not the impression of the people who made contact with Elana and Andrei in Paris."

"The impression of the people who made contact in Paris!" sneeringly echoed the Russian, holding his glass sideways for more vodka without bothering to look at the man serving it. "Are you talking about those people who allowed themselves to be captured with my wife and son and ruined their escape!"

"Your escape's not ruined!" refused Jacobson, desperately.

Radtsic, his face clearing, came farther forward in his chair, ignoring the man with the third drink. "At last, some sense! When are they arriving?"

"I didn't say they're coming," squirmed Jacobson. "We're trying to sort it out and to sort it out we need to know how and why they were intercepted."

"Answer your own questions!" loudly insisted Radtsic. "Find out and sort it out! It's the French: your allies, your European partners who are holding them! Tell Paris to release them and bring them here, to me."

"That's what we're trying to do: why we're talking like this."

"I was promised I'd be personally meeting your director. Where is he?"

"Working on what we're all trying to achieve, a way of resolving this."

"I want to see your director, which you told me was his personal wish. I want him and everyone else, all of you, to understand something. My being here, my coming here, was entirely dependent upon Elana and Andrei being here with me. I will not stay, cooperate in any way whatsoever, unless we are together."

"I will tell them what you've said."

"Speak to your director and tell him what I'm telling you. Undertakings were given and agreed. You are not keeping your part in those undertakings."

"I will speak to my director," promised Jacobson. Everything had gone, vanished. Straughan had been right: it was a total, unmitigated disaster.

Gerald Monsford tried to match the blankness of the expressionless men confronting him around the table, his uncertainty worsened by one of them being Aubrey Smith, in whom, despite the facial emptiness, Monsford believed he saw triumph.

"Throughout the formulation of a joint operation approved at the highest level of government to extract an officer of the FSB, the absolute and clearly understood imperative was that there should be no diplomatic risk. Contrary to every order and instruction, you independently organized a parallel extraction of another FSB official, without any consultation or reference to us, your direct liaison to that highest level," said Sir Archibald Bland, pedantically setting out the accusation, made that much more ominous by the calm, measured delivery.

"Yes, I did," immediately admitted Monsford, at once encouraged by the frowned break in Smith's composure.

"Why?" demanded Geoffrey Palmer.

"Precisely because the extraction of Natalia and her daughter *was* a joint operation," declared Monsford, embarking upon what he'd concluded his best and least challengeable rebuttal. "That our two organizations were brought together was, according to my recollection, acknowledged to be an extremely rare and unusual decision. There's been no precedent during my tenure as Director of MI6, nor, as far as I'm aware, during that of at least two of my predecessors. MI6 and MI5 are in every normal circumstance entirely separate and autonomous. It was my decision that the extraction of Maxim Mikhailovich Radtsic, the FSB's executive deputy, was completely within the customary autonomy of my organization and did not conflict or impinge in any way with that of the woman and her child. To have conjoined the two would have created confusion and endangered both, the first of which has been destroyed anyway by the antics of the MI5 operative Charlie Muffin. . . ."

"You were categorically ordered against anything that could potentially exacerbate the difficulties already existing between us and the Russian Federation," persisted Palmer. "Orders you just as categorically ignored. What you—"

"Indeed I was," interrupted Monsford, his earlier uncertainty diminishing. "Close examination of the transcript of the meeting at which those orders were given will show my intimating the possibility of our nullifying Moscow's actions by confronting the Russian Federation with a far greater embarrassment, which it's my contention we've achieved by facilitating the defection of Maxim Mikhailovich Radtsic."

"At the cost of at least six of your operatives, an executive jet, and Radtsic's wife and son, who to my understanding are accusing us of attempted kidnap," qualified Aubrey Smith. "It's inconceivable you expect us to accept you've put us ahead in any tit-for-tat exchange, which was something else absolutely forbidden."

"Nonsense," rejected Monsford, welcoming the challenge. "We've still got their diplomats to exchange for the Manchester travel group, a swap Moscow will fall over themselves to agree when we make Radtsic's defection public. And following that announcement, our having established Radtsic's presence in England, it will be little more than a formality negotiating the French release of my officers, along with that of Elana and Andrei to continue their journey here."

"The indications so far are that it will be anything but a simple formality," contradicted Palmer. "The French are furious at our mounting an intelligence operation on their soil without prior consultation and agreement with their Service de Documentation Extérieure et de Contre Espionnage."

"Of course they're furious," dismissed Monsford, almost contemptuous in his now totally restored confidence. "We'd be just as furious if they did something similar here. There'll be a lot of backroom sniping and threats of broken understandings, which don't matter a damn. What matters is that we've got Radtsic, who's been at the pinnacle of Russian intelligence and espionage activities for almost three decades. Wrecking Russia's Lvov operation was a coup without much practical benefit to us. Getting Radtsic in the bag is the espionage prize of the century."

"As you've presented it, and if the French difficulty with the wife and son can be resolved, it would appear to be so," conceded Bland.

"Then all that's necessary," seized Monsford, "are some discreet diplomatic negotiations with Paris—along, perhaps, with an equally discreet apology to the SDECE, which I am quite ready personally to make—for this to be recognized exactly as I've described it."

Having destroyed his cell phone, Monsford had to use a pay kiosk within the Foreign Office to reach Rebecca. "'Dogs, easily won to fawn on any man,' " he quoted the moment Rebecca lifted her receiver. "Which is what I made them do, eat out of my hand, like the well-trained pets they are. Book Scott's for dinner: we're going to celebrate."

"Shall I tell Straughan you don't want him to wait here?"

"I don't want Straughan much more for anything. Tell him what you like."

Which is what Rebecca did, verbally repeating to the operations director Monsford's every word. In London it was 5:15 P.M., in Paris it was 7:15 P.M.; and in Moscow it was 8:15 P.M. when Charlie rose at Natalia's entry to the restaurant.

25

"I'M SORRY I'M LATE."

"We didn't set a time." Natalia hadn't come straight from the Lubyanka, Charlie knew. Her hair was perfectly in place and the black dress didn't look as if it had been worn throughout a busy day. What little makeup she wore appeared fresh, too.

Natalia hesitated, studying the table, placing it within the restaurant. "Sitting here isn't a coincidence, is it?"

"I wondered if you'd remember."

Natalia gave a brief smile. "I remember this table from our first-ever time here and I haven't forgotten, either, that beneath Charlie the hard man there's Charlie the romantic. . . ." The smile went. "And you'll never know how much I wish things weren't as they are now."

What the hell did that mean? "Why don't we order before we talk?"

"You order for me?" she said, uninterestedly.

Charlie chose fish for her in preference to the boar he'd decided upon while he'd waited and the already selected Georgian wine, unsettled by her mood. "Now let's talk."

"How much do you know?"

"Just what I've picked up from television, that a Russian mother and her son are being held in France. The diplomatic reference to the two Englishmen is a clear enough espionage identification even without the impounded plane." Charlie intentionally limited his reply to avoid Natalia's suspecting he had a secondary source.

Natalia sipped her wine to cover the hesitation Charlie recognized not just to be her positive, no-going-back moment of commitment but the point at which she knowingly crossed their self-erected barrier against their betraying either country's intelligence. The hesitation continued even when she began talking, naming Radtsic and his wife and son but not knowing how the French seizure had come about. Charlie didn't interrupt, not wanting to lose something more important for a less essential clarification. Only in the last few moments did she bring her head up, the guilt obvious. "I hated doing that. I . . . I despise myself."

The arrival of their meal allowed Charlie a brief reflection. "All our professional lives we've kept our oath, adjusted our morality for institutions whose only morality is the expediency of the moment. You're not betraying anything or anyone. It's time for *our* expediency. Not just yours and mine. Sasha's, too, which is maybe even more important."

Natalia was looking away again, picking at her fish as he was at his meal, neither properly eating. Abruptly she said: "That's my problem. Is it best for Sasha to be taken from everything and everyone she knows to what might as well be the moon, where she'll get a new name and be told to forget her own, never ever to mention it to anyone: learn a new language and accept a near stranger as her father. That's what it's going to be, isn't it? A suspended life—not really a life at all—in a protection program, not able to tell her why we can't trust anyone, be proper friends with anyone, terrified at an accent or an intonation that could be Russian and mean they've found us."

He couldn't lie to her, not after his own so recently fossilized existence. "I came out of a program to get you both. It was everything you've described it to be. It's the beginning, the adjustment, that will be bad. But we can adjust: Sasha's young enough to adjust. We could become happy, eventually."

"Where?"

"Anywhere you choose. And aren't we overlooking *why* I came here: why you made the calls?"

"There's more to tell you. Nothing's complete, as nothing's ever complete in what we do: how we work encapsulated in an incomprehensible whole," groped Natalia. "There's total uproar at Lubyanka, more open talk than I've ever known, more combined action than I've ever experienced. But it doesn't seem like uproar: panic. It *isn't* encapsulated. People are talking, discussing things, speculating, which they've never done. . . ." She put down her fork to raise an apologetic hand. "I know I'm not making sense. I'm trying to explain it as the words come to me."

Was there another fear adding to that of a protection program? "How's it affecting you personally?"

Natalia abandoned her meal altogether, nervously revolving the gold band she carefully avoided wearing on her wedding finger. "I've been seconded to an inquiry committee, six of us from the analysis division of the First Chief Directorate, which never changed its functions or designation from the old KGB—"

"You've been personally selected!" seized Charlie, aware of the significance.

"Me, personally," confirmed Natalia, with another brief half smile.

"To inquire into what?"

"Maxim Mikhailovich Radtsic," she announced, simply. "Our brief is to go back into everything—every operation, every contact, every department, every officer both here and abroad in either the KGB or the FSB—with whom Radtsic had dealings since the day he enrolled in the KGB. The FSB reasoning is that he wasn't alone but part of a long-established cell from which he's trying to distract attention for the rest to go on working against us."

Us, immediately registered Charlie, believing he was beginning to understand. "You're no longer under the slightest suspicion. Only a person beyond reproach would be considered and only then after the strictest vetting. Which you underwent and clearly passed even before Radtsic defected."

"I know."

Charlie didn't hurry, not to reflect but to examine their conversation and pick up any inconsistency to avoid the wrong interpretation.

Unable to find it, he said: "You're safe. You and Sasha are safe. You don't need to run after all."

"No."

Charlie searched for the appropriate words, which didn't come. "You're giving me your decision, aren't you?"

"That's a stupid, self-pitying remark!" Natalia flared, too loudly.

"I'll be able to get out all right," Charlie exaggerated, shaking his head to the waiter's inquiring approach.

"That's even more stupid. I didn't say I didn't want us to come."

"Then what are you telling me?" demanded Charlie, exasperated.

"I'm trying to say, but saying it badly, that I love you. That I've confronted all the mistakes I've made and that I *do* want to get out with Sasha, despite both you and I knowing how difficult that's going to be—"

"What then!" broke in Charlie, the exasperation growing.

"You're the only person who could have made it work, got us out. After the mistakes I made happen it would still have been a miracle if you'd managed it. . . ." Natalia stopped, her voice catching and needing to recover. "After Radtsic, it'll be totally impossible. We'd never get past all the new checks and surveillance, every passport scrutinized for forgery, eye iris and fingerprint verification, CCTV doubled. We'd be picked up and lose each other and both of us would lose Sasha. We've got to lose each other, give up the fantasy of my getting out with Sasha, to ensure we keep Sasha safe."

Charlie held back from an immediate reply, conscious of the hovering waiter, ordered coffee, with brandy for himself. The waiter gone, Charlie leaned forward urgently and said: "I *can* do it: we can do it. The added restrictions are too late. I'll do what they don't anticipate."

"I'm frightened, Charlie: too frightened."

"I expect you to be frightened, but more than frightened I expect you, want you, to be professional. Concentrate on being professional, more than upon who Sasha is and who I am. Put as far back in your mind as you can that this is personal."

"I'm not sure I can."

Charlie wasn't sure she could, either. She was a professional intelligence officer but not trained or inculcated with the field tradecraft as he was. He had to get her past her mental barrier. "Work with me, plan with me. If, at the end, you think the risk of failing is greater than that of succeeding we'll abort and try something else and something else after that, until you're satisfied."

Natalia hunched noncommittal shoulders. "I'm not totally satisfied yet that my committee appointment guarantees that I'm safe."

"Why not?"

"I told you mine isn't the only group. God knows what'll be thrown up by them all. I still don't know if I got rid of all the questionable links between us."

"Their absolute, unswerving focus will be upon the background of Maxim Mikhailovich Radtsic. Your right to be part of the investigation is already decided."

"I'd like to think you're right," said Natalia, uncertainly.

"I am right," insisted Charlie, dismissing his own uncertainties. "How many more encapsulated committees are there?"

"At least six."

"Why so many?" queried Charlie, eager to move Natalia on from her introspection.

"To discover the cell, if there is a cell, as quickly as possible: Radtsic's been part of the Russian intelligence apparatus for almost thirty years. It would take almost as long again for just one group to go through his entire archive."

"That's what's going to be made available, Radtsic's entire archive?"

"That's the gossip. I've never known it to happen before, certainly not involving someone of such seniority," said Natalia. "But then, I don't know of a defection of someone at such a senior level. And being spread between so many separate groups it'll be impossible to get an overview of all that he's done."

Still an incalculable treasure trove, gauged Charlie. How many more nuggets remained to be sieved? "The inference is obvious from the French identification of Britons but has it been definitely confirmed that Radtsic is in England?"

"We haven't been officially told."

"What of the wife and son? What's going to happen to them?"

Natalia's shoulders rose and fell again. "I don't know. Nor do I have a way of finding out. Our brief is to look back, not forward. The kidnap claim is obviously an attempted evasion if they're repatriated here."

He still hadn't resolved his nagging uncertainty, realized Charlie. "Is that anonymous reporting system going to remain at Moscow airports?"

Natalia frowned. "Why *did* you ask me about anonymous disclosure?"

"It was classic Stasi tradecraft, taught to them by the KGB. I was exploring all the possible barriers we might face, not knowing then about Radtsic," replied Charlie, easily. "Has it been retained, with all the other additions?"

There was another shoulder movement. "It's been in place for a long time. Why discard it now, of all times?" Her frown remained. "It's obviously British intelligence with the wife and son. Didn't you really know Radtsic was going to England?"

"I really didn't know," said Charlie.

"The committee convenes tomorrow. I'll still have my cell phone with me but I won't be able to take calls as freely as I could in my own office: probably won't keep it on when we're in session. I won't know how we're going to work until after tomorrow."

"I'm introducing another precaution," announced Charlie, lifting from beside the table a bag she hadn't seen. "Details of your cell phone will be on record at Lubyanka, easily scanned. I'm giving you six new phones, all charge-card operated, so there's no billing address. I didn't buy more than one from any shop, choosing new names and addresses at random. Nothing's traceable to you. Or me. Use one a day, discarding it when you leave Lubyanka at night but taking out the SIM card and battery before you do."

"Do you think it's necessary," Natalia accepted, doubtfully.

"I do," said Charlie, glad she'd moved on. "I'll call at noon. If your phone's off I'll call at seven and if it's still off every hour on the hour, after that. If you keep it on mute and still don't reply I'll know you're with people, disconnect, and try again later."

"I understand."

"Understand something more," stressed Charlie. "You're not under suspicion, but don't take the slightest chance. In the conditions you've described, internal security will be paranoid. Don't contact me. I'll call you, always from a different phone. And I'm no longer at the Mira."

"What's your new hotel like?"

"A great improvement. I've got the bed all to myself."

"You needn't be all by yourself, at least not for an hour or so."

"Thank you both for coming back now. I didn't want this to extend overnight," said Aubrey Smith, coming to the end of his account of the Foreign Office encounter. "I want you to sleep on what I've told you and have ideas ready first thing tomorrow."

"You caught me before I'd got home," said Passmore.

"I've put my plans back," said Jane Ambersom, relieved she'd reached Barry Elliott still at the American embassy. "I told you the sort of man Monsford is, didn't I?"

"He's been using the Charlie Muffin business all along," acknowledged Smith.

"Where did Charlie's extraction fit in?" questioned Passmore.

"I don't precisely know and won't guess," admitted the Director-General. "The only thing I am sure about is that he didn't have anything to do with Monsford's maneuvers. It's essential, now, that we find Charlie. Monsford's trying to load the blame onto Charlie for everything that's gone wrong with Radtsic."

"If Charlie wasn't involved, he was ahead of us all, suspecting it wasn't a straight operation," Jane pointed out.

"We won't know that until we get hold of him but it looks that way. I just wish he'd break cover."

"The last orders to those waiting for him to do just that were to use force if necessary," reminded Passmore. "I think we should scale that down."

"Agreed," said Smith, at once. "Everything has to be reevaluated."

"I'm surprised Monsford wasn't challenged more strongly," said Passmore. "His story still doesn't explain his total disregard of what he was specifically ordered *not* to do. He's built an embarrassing diplomatic foothill into a bloody great mountain."

"Bland and Palmer are desperate for any way out and if Monsford's scenario works, they've got it," judged Smith. "I didn't have anything to oppose him. But there's a very fine line we've got to stay behind. Whatever we do to distance ourselves, we don't screw up Radtsic's defection. We do anything and everything to help get the wife and son here. Which means supporting Monsford, who's right, Radtsic *is* the prize of the century."

"You've just rounded a circle we can't break," complained Passmore.

"That's why tonight, starting right now, is important," insisted Smith. "So far we've caught all the shit, some of it deserved. I'll acknowledge the mistakes in what Charlie's done. But none of those for which we're not responsible. If Elana and Andrei are allowed to continue on, Monsford will be the golden boy who took a huge risk that worked. We'll be the incompetents who got everything wrong and don't deserve to be here any longer. That's the circle we've got to make into a square with enough sharp edges to snag Monsford and we've got a little over twelve hours to do it."

Passmore turned sideways to Jane. "You know how the wheels go around over there."

When all the brakes were taken off, which she now believed they were, she thought. She was encouraged minutes later when the number she rang from her office was answered and all the more so by the conversation that followed. As usual, Barry Elliott was waiting ahead of her when Jane entered the grill room at the Connought hotel an hour after that.

"I'd like to think you were held up by something involving a certain mother and son I'd guess right now are somewhere close to the Eiffel Tower," he greeted.

"Things are happening even nearer than that," said Jane.

Charlie's reaction had been surprise before excitement at Natalia's suggestion and probably because of it their lovemaking hadn't been as good as it usually was. The real satisfaction had come afterward, entwined and tightly holding each other, neither one needing sex or to talk or even to think, just to be there and have the touch and the feel and the comfort of each other.

It was only after Natalia left, carrying her disposable telephones, that Charlie let his thinking run, although at the beginning unfocused, and his once-more-tentative mosaic turned upside down into yet another heap. Natalia was objectively right about the repercussive effects that Radtsic's defection would have upon his getting her and Sasha safely away, but putting more locks on a stable door from which its horse had bolted was predictable. Unlocking them quickly afterward wasn't, which just might give him the sufficient advantage of surprise. But there was a long way to go and a lot more to evaluate before they got that far, the major imponderable of which was whether Natalia would be strong enough at that final, nerve-snapping moment of crossing from one existence to another. And because it would remain imponderable it was going to hang over them, undermining their confidence until that precise moment. Which required he do as much as was conceivably possible to instill additional confidence within Natalia. He hoped he'd begun well, insisting the committee appointment was incontrovertible proof that her loyalty was now unquestioned. How was he going to maintain that necessary momentum? The most obvious way was by no longer remaining unconnected and out of touch on the periphery.

It was time to contact the embassy.

26

IN THE COLD DAWN AFTER OVERNIGHT REFLECTION CHARLIE acknowledged the reaction to his reemergence would be so unpredictable that he needed not just Janus but a virtual army of two-way-facing protectors to watch his back. And all he had was David Halliday, who unquestionably qualified as two-faced but for that reason was very definitely not a protective friend. Halliday did, however, sound more in control when he answered Charlie's arranged contact. There'd been no overnight traffic from London, Halliday said, but from online surfing of the news wires he'd established the French seizures had achieved widespread international coverage. There was no named identification but increasing speculation that the alleged kidnap had been part of a major but now-foiled espionage operation. There was further speculation that an explanation was being demanded by the French government from London, from which there had so far been no response. Neither had there been any public reaction from the Kremlin.

"I've got it all ready, every regulation and agreement there is for an internal inquiry if they come at me," declared Halliday.

"Good for you," encouraged Charlie. "What's happening with my support team?"

"Probably nothing more than professional curiosity," said Halliday. "But I've already had two separate visits from your guys, asking me what's going on."

The first glint of light, gauged Charlie. "What did you tell them?"

"That I didn't know: I told you I'd been ordered against sharing with them."

Could he trick Halliday unsuspectingly into the answer he wanted? wondered Charlie. "Not even now it's all over with Radtsic safely away? They're your guys, not officially mine."

"Briddle was my second unexpected visitor. The first was your man, Wilkinson. He was waiting when I got here this morning."

Why would two men supposedly working together make separate approaches? The most obvious answer, confirming Charlie's double-cross suspicion, was that they *weren't* working together. He said: "They appear worried, anything like that?"

"Difficult to say," hedged Halliday. "Probably wondering if it might be something more interesting than sitting around on their asses."

Had London made Wilkinson supervisor of the MI5 backup team during the time he'd been out of contact? Charlie said: "What else is happening at the embassy?"

"A lot, indicated by its total, ostracizing silence," said Halliday. "As always, when something goes wrong at our end, we cease to exist, remember?"

Charlie decided he probably didn't need Halliday to tell him anything more, but it was important to retain the man as a potential source, which required avoiding frightening the man away. "I'm thinking of making a move."

"Doing what?" demanded Halliday, instantly alarmed.

"At the moment it's you I'm considering," lied Charlie. "It was wise of you to stick to London's edict with Wilkinson. Keep doing that, if you hear anything involving me. I don't want your being linked to me: no hint we might have been in contact."

"Neither do I!" said Halliday, sincerity obvious in his voice for the first time.

"Just listen to everything," urged Charlie.

"You'll tell me what's going on, though, won't you?"

"That's our deal, isn't it: mutual self-protection?"

Wilkinson's cell phone was answered on its fourth ring without any identifying acknowledgment, and from the total silence beyond and the response delay Charlie guessed Wilkinson had quieted those around him. Charlie said: "You know who this is, Patrick. Don't let the others waste their time trying to isolate where I am. It's a public kiosk. You've probably discovered our technicians fitted trackers into the ones issued to us in London."

"It's good to hear from you at last." Wilkinson's voice sounded more computer generated than human.

Despite the pointlessness they'd still attempt to locate him, Charlie knew. "The reason for your being here hasn't changed but I'm only working with you, Warren, and Preston. Tell London that. Tell them also that the four of us were part of a setup, me most of all. I want you to make sure that gets through to the Director-General."

"I need—"

"The need is for the two of us to meet."

"That's what I want."

It was going to be foot aching and tiresome, Charlie accepted, but there was no other way. "Are you familiar with the Moscow Metro system?"

"No."

"It has a circle line, just like London. Here it's called Kol'cevaja. Ride it, tomorrow, between ten and noon."

"What else?"

"Just that."

"Where will we meet?"

"Where—and when—I decide," said Charlie.

"I don't follow what you're saying. . . ."

"The scanners haven't picked up where I'm speaking from, have they?"

"I don't follow that, either."

"Everyone around you have been scanning ever since we started talking, trying to locate me, haven't they?"

"We're not all together."

"What you've got to understand is that none of you will be able to find me now and none of you will be able to pick me up tomorrow, irrespective of how closely they stay with you. I'm telling you—and I want you to tell the Director-General this as well—that we were decoys and that I know Monsford's operation has gone bad."

"You expect me to go around and around in circles, until you decide to make contact?" demanded Wilkinson.

"That's precisely what I expect. I also expect all of the others to go around and around with you, although pretending *not* to be with you. I'll find you but neither you nor anyone with you will be able to locate me. I'll only approach you when I'm completely satisfied you're alone."

"What about the reason for our being here."

"It's still active but without MI6. Make that very clear to London, And tell the Director-General that the other extraction has hugely increased the value of ours."

"Thanks for meeting me," said Jane Ambersom.

"What meeting?" said James Straughan, pointedly. He hadn't realized how much he'd missed being able to talk to her.

She smiled. "There isn't one. You know you can trust me as I know I can trust you."

"We committed ourselves when you called last night and by my being here," said Straughan. She'd concealed her car among a line of other anonymous vehicles close to the Oval underground station at which she'd been waiting for him, fifteen minutes earlier.

"Smith told me all that happened at the Foreign Office yesterday."

"Told only you?"

"Passmore was with me."

"I'm not sure whether what I was told is the truth."

"It probably was not."

Straughan didn't answer as spontaneously as Jane had hoped, staring directly ahead at the empty cars. At last he said: "More than probably not."

It was a chance she had to take, Jane decided. "Monsford set us up, didn't he, with Charlie and his family?"

"He intended to sabotage it."

"Is he still trying?"

"I don't know. It's a repeat of what happened to you, Monsford protecting himself."

"Is Charlie in physical danger?"

Straughan didn't reply.

"James?"

"He should be careful."

Jane felt nothing, neither surprise nor anger. "Aubrey Smith thinks Monsford could still get away with it, bringing us down in the process."

Straughan frowned across the car. "The French have so far refused to see anyone from the Paris embassy, not until we respond to their demand for an explanation. They're seeing the Russian *chef du protocol,* though. Radtsic's refusing cooperation until we get Elana and the boy here. Jacobson's having an emergency meeting with Monsford right now. Monsford told Rebecca there's no reason for either her or me to be there with him: that's how I was able to get away." He looked instinctively at his watch. "I can't be much longer."

"Where are you supposed to be?"

"With a dementia specialist: discussing getting my mother into care."

"You think Monsford's making his escape arrangement?" risked Jane, openly.

"We *know* he's making his escape arrangement," said Straughan.

"*We?*" isolated Jane, instantly.

"Rebecca is determined she won't go the same way you did."

"You going to tell her about this?"

"No."

"So she's making her own escape arrangements."

"She imagines she is."

"What about you?"

"I have but it's difficult."

"We committed ourselves the moment you got into this car," reminded Jane.

Straughan smiled. "Haven't lost your touch, have you?"

"I lost it the last time. I'm not going to let the motherfucker beat me again. What's your difficulty?"

"He's had his own sound system installed in the office. But he's using it selectively."

Jane answered his earlier smile. "So you've installed yours?"

"After we discovered what he was doing. He's always very careful to avoid anything incriminating."

"How much have you got?"

"All of it."

"Including how Charlie was to be used?"

"All of it," repeated Straughan. "The difficulty is how to avoid suicidal self-destruction getting it to those who'll sit in judgment. It contravenes every internal security regulation as well as the entire Official Secrets Act."

"I agree you couldn't personally make it available," said Jane, the excitement stirring through her.

"You couldn't, either," insisted the man. "You'd be even more culpable after all that Charlie did. And what Monsford did to you."

"There could be a way: maybe even more than one."

"It's better you don't tell me," Straughan said, hurriedly.

He was backing off, Jane recognized. "Would you make all you've got available to me?"

Straughan hesitated. "I didn't imagine I'd find a problem answering that."

"I didn't believe Monsford was capable of sacrificing me."

"If it hadn't been you it would have been me: he gave himself two choices. By accepting the sideways transfer you saved me."

"I know," said Jane, tensed.

"So it's payback time?"

Right on the button, Jane thought. She said: "I'd appreciate that."

"A source investigation could only lead to me."

"It's not inevitable," argued the woman. "I'm assuming Rebecca's escape is her own copy?"

"It's the original: mine's the copy."

"Could yours be forensically proven to be a copy?"

"No."

"Then there's a way to prevent your ever being discovered."

"I made a mistake, coming here like this. I wish I hadn't," declared Straughan.

"We haven't met, remember?"

"I should get back."

"Are you seriously considering putting your mother into care?"

"I'll do everything I can not to."

"Then you've got to save yourself, as Rebecca is determined to save herself."

"Shit!"

"Rebecca's double protection is that she got her recordings from you and did her duty bringing them to Bland or Palmer not just to expose Monsford but to protect the service from your ever making it public," bullied Jane, devoid of hypocrisy. "And that would put you before a security-closed court who'd jail you for a very long time. You wouldn't be able to go on caring for your mother from a prison cell, would you, James? Without a job you wouldn't even be able to get her anything but the minimum of care."

"We work and live in a sewer, don't we?"

"We do. Your poor mother doesn't. I'm offering the way to keep her out of it."

"I've got to get back."

"We can beat Monsford. You know we can."

"I need to think."

"Do that, James. Go and think long and hard when you're caring for her tonight."

Gerald Monsford didn't like the continuing impression of so much thin ice creaking dangerously underfoot. Maxim Mikhailovich Radtsic remained the job-for-life prize upon whom, if the pendulum swung the wrong way, his very survival depended. And with whom, therefore, it was imperative the man's wife and son were reunited. He'd done the right thing sending Jacobson ahead of him back to the Hertfordshire safe house but so far, his own time-to-think journey there almost completed, Monsford hadn't come close to a guaranteed way of bringing that about. At least getting postponed that day's Foreign Office session gave time for a resolve to emerge elsewhere, but he wasn't encouraged by Sir Archibald Bland's warning during their rescheduling that France's current presidency of the energy-dependent European Union held it hostage to Moscow's blackmail to cut off its natural-gas supplies.

There was, too, the until-now-relegated alert from Paris of Andrei's reluctance to defect in the first place, from which the suspicion naturally followed that the boy was responsible for the French interception. Even if he wasn't, Andrei might change his uncertain mind after the first failed attempt. To each and all of which had to be added Jacobson's insistence at their meeting earlier that morning that Radtsic's cooperation hinged entirely upon their being together in exile.

As his car bypassed Letchworth, Monsford saw through the separating glass that the driver was triggering the automatic signal of their approach and took his own security-cleared telephone from its rear-seat armrest for an update of what he was approaching.

"He's not physically unwell," reported Jacobson. "He's taken his morning exercise but told me he's not going out this afternoon. The only thing he's said otherwise is to ask when Elana and Andrei are getting here. When I told him that wasn't yet known, he demanded the time of your arrival."

"What's he done in between?"

"Stayed in his room with a bottle of vodka, watching television. We're monitoring him on CCTV. He's flicking between news channels, obviously searching for announcements: as far as I know there haven't been any updates from France. The vodka bottle's half empty and he's already chosen a bottle of burgundy for lunch."

"We should be with you in less than thirty minutes."

"Should I tell him that?"

"No."

"Anything?" Monsford asked when Straughan answered his next call.

"The Novosti news agency is saying our ambassador is again being summoned to the Russian Foreign Ministry, without giving a time or date," relayed the operations director. "Associated Press is reporting under a Washington dateline but without accreditation that there is an impending Russian political development connected with the French arrests. There's a Press Association sidebar that the Russian and French ambassadors have been summoned to our Foreign Office for clarification. Agence France-Presse are saying our embassy in Paris have delivered a second Note seeking access to our detained nationals."

"Anything direct from the Foreign Office?"

"Nothing routed to me. Rebecca's heard nothing, either."

"Call me at once if there's anything, anything at all."

"You told me that before you left," reminded Straughan.

"Now I'm telling you again. Tell Rebecca the same."

Jacobson was waiting at the door for Monsford. "He's still in his room: probably seen you arrive. I've set things up in the drawing room."

Monsford shrugged, discomfited at not having control over the automatic audio and film equipment throughout the house. "I'm to be interrupted if there's any contact. And you were wrong about no news updates. There've been several."

"I told you I wasn't checking the coverage," reminded Jacobson. "Do you want me to sit in with you?"

"Why should I: he's got good English, hasn't he?"

"I'm the person Radtsic knows: is most familiar with. I thought it might help."

"I'll see him alone." It would still be recorded.

"Will you eat with him?"

"Let's get on with it, for Christ's sake!" demanded Monsford, impatiently.

The drawing room was at the back of the house, overlooking an expansive, terrace-stepped grassland sporadically hedged between stands of well-established, tightly cultivated trees. At the very bottom of the terrace was a swimming pool that ran its entire width, and far beyond that, over the tops of still more trees, there was the hazed outline of Letchworth. In the interior of the room, over couches and enveloping easy chairs were pleated and tasseled loose covering chintzes, an inner circle grouped casually around a fireplace fronting a low but large table upon which a vacuum coffeepot and cups were already set. Filling the dead fireplace was a huge flower display of what Monsford guessed to be from the outside garden.

Forewarned by the sound of its opening, Monsford, hand outstretched in readiness, was directly behind the door when Maxim Radtsic started to enter. The Russian abruptly halted, visibly pulling both arms back in refusal. "In Russia it is not done to shake hands on a threshold. It signifies it will be the only meeting." He intruded a pause. "Perhaps it is indeed an omen."

Monsford backed away, changing the offered hand into an indication toward the flower-dominated space and its encompassing couches and chair. "I'm sure it isn't."

Radtsic followed the gesture but didn't sit. "What time are my wife and son arriving?"

"Please sit," encouraged Monsford, doing so himself, glad the door was closing behind Jacobson, although always conscious of the cameras. "There's coffee."

Radtsic perched himself awkwardly on the very edge of an easy chair. "I do not want coffee. I want vodka. And a reply to my question."

Monsford pressed a summons bell bordering the fireplace. "It is through no mistake or fault of ours that this problem has arisen. I'm aware you've been told in the greatest possible detail all we've been able to discover. From that you know your wife and son were being escorted by my officers to an aircraft waiting to bring them safely here."

"They're not *safely* here, are they!" rejected Radtsic, irritably. "They're very unsafely in France, where they will have been fully identified."

The eavesdropping Jacobson entered already carrying a tray upon which were a full, freezer-frosted vodka bottle, an ice bucket, and two glasses. He almost filled both, adding more when Radtsic shook his head against ice. At Monsford's refusing head shake, Radtsic said: "You're not prepared to drink with me!"

"Like you, I did not want ice," Monsford tried to recover, hot at the awareness of his second filmed mistake. Monsford raised his unwanted glass and said: "Here's to your new life, here in the West."

"Only a new life if it's with my family," corrected the other man, "About whom you still have not properly answered my question."

Having until now seen the facial resemblance only from photographs, Monsford was struck by Radtsic's similarity to Stalin. "They are still in France, where they have accused my officers of kidnap, escalating what could have been negotiated away as a misunderstanding into a criminal matter."

"Are you accusing them of being responsible for what's happened!" flared Radtsic, outraged.

"Of course I'm not," denied Monsford, his disappointment at the antagonism slightly eased by the first wisp of the so-far-eluded idea. "I was, though, worried when my officer in Paris told me that Andrei initially refused to come."

"You *are* accusing them!"

"What I am doing, Maxim Mikhailovich, is being subjective. We do not yet know how the French interception was instigated. Which shouldn't, though, be our immediate focus. That has to be getting them released and safely here." Monsford was surprised at what little effect the already consumed vodka had upon the Russian, watching him refill his glass.

Radtsic frowned. "That's what I'm waiting for you to tell me, how and when they're getting here!"

"They're not, not today," declared Monsford, positively. "Our problem is the kidnap allegation. And the association of my officers in that allegation. Because of that the British government are being refused access: any contact whatsoever . . ."

"What the hell's your point!" demanded Radtsic, seizing the intentionally allowed pause.

"You, the husband and father," said Monsford, simply, the concept complete in his mind. "There can be no legal prevention against your being allowed contact. Nor does your being here contravene French law. I've obviously held back from publicly announcing your being here, *because* of what's happened to Elana and Andrei. Now I want to announce it, publicize it. And at the same time connect you by a visual TV conference link not just to Elana and Andrei but simultaneously to French officials. If you can persuade Elana or Andrei to withdraw the allegation they'll have to be released, to continue here to join you."

For several moments Radtsic remained unspeaking, all truculence gone. "Is it technically possible?"

"Yes," insisted Monsford. "I can have technicians here in hours, setting it up, as well as French-speaking lawyers to argue the law on your behalf."

Once more Radtsic considered the idea, topping up what little could be added to Monsford's scarcely touched glass and refilling his, which he held out to Monsford. "I have not behaved as I should. I apologize."

"It is totally understandable," accepted Monsford, as their glasses touched. "I drink to your reunion."

Shakespeare had been right, as he always was, thought Monsford:

sweet are the uses of adversity. And from where better could the sentiment come than *As You Like It,* which he did like, very much indeed.

"You are sure?" insisted Aubrey Smith.

"Absolutely positive," said Jane Ambersom.

"And you can get hold of it?"

"Yes," she risked.

"There's still the self-incriminating problem," accepted Smith.

"I think there's a way around that," said Jane.

"Does it tie in with what Wilkinson's relayed from Moscow about Charlie's refusal to work with MI6?" asked John Passmore, joining the review.

"I haven't the slightest idea what Charlie's uncovered," said Smith. "But Jane's story seems to support what Charlie's demanding." He smiled, humorlessly. "I can hardly wait for Palmer and Bland's reaction."

"From what little we think we know, Charlie and our three aren't just confronting the Russians to get Natalia and Sasha out. They're opposed by Monsford and three of his people already in Moscow and completely briefed on the intended extraction," cautioned Passmore.

"Go back to Straughan," the Director-General told Jane. "Promise him every protection, whatever he wants, to get whatever he's got. Tell him I'll meet him personally if it'll help."

"He's terrified," warned Jane.

"So am I," said Smith.

27

BY THE TIME HE ENTERED THE FOREIGN OFFICE EVERY UNCERtainty was perfectly resolved in Gerald Monsford's mind, the creaking ice hardened into a solid conviction that he was unassailable. Even Straughan's message during the return from Hertfordshire of Charlie Muffin's reappearance hadn't unsettled him. The man and his family were no longer of any practical use, easily discarded encumbrances.

Monsford intentionally avoided Vauxhall Cross to arrive early but wasn't concerned, either, at finding Aubrey Smith ahead of him, alone with Geoffrey Palmer. "Congratulations upon the return of your prodigal son," he greeted the blank-faced MI5 Director-General.

"I hope you've equally good news of your errant mother and offspring," Smith mocked back, as Sir Archibald Bland came into the room to complete their quorum.

"Is the long-awaited emergence of Charlie Muffin good news?" questioned Monsford, setting the stage for his intended lead.

"That'll have to be judged on the outcome of both extractions," suggested Smith.

"And we're here to examine the more immediate difficulties of Maxim Radtsic," halted Bland, impatiently. "Which is dominating the cabinet, who want it concluded in the shortest time possible with absolutely no further problems. I'm authorized to tell you both that you are losing the confidence of this government effectively to continue in the positions you currently hold."

For the briefest moment Geoffrey Palmer appeared as shocked as the two directors. It was the confidently prepared Gerald Monsford who recovered first. "Then it's clearly important that on behalf of MI6 I restore that confidence."

"That's precisely what we expect you to do," said Palmer, his stiffness the only indication of his anger at not being warned in advance of the cabinet secretary's threat.

The drive back from Hertfordshire had allowed Monsford not only to formulate his proposals but mentally to rehearse their presentation, which he did flawlessly. "It will overwhelm all the Charlie Muffin embarrassment," Monsford concluded, delivering his patronizing coup de grâce to Aubrey Smith, "We can warn Russia through back channels that any retaliation will be met with public exposé of their Lvov disaster." Unable to stop himself, Monsford went on: "Which is, perhaps, some mitigation against the directorship changes you've indicated towards my MI5 colleague."

"That's an extremely convincing proposal, supported by an equally convincing argument," cautiously acknowledged Bland, looking to the Intelligence Committee liaison for agreement.

"Providing the kidnap allegations *are* withdrawn," qualified Palmer, equally cautious.

"My proposals also make it impossible for Moscow to impose any coercion upon France," insisted Monsford. "They'll be neutered."

"I am grateful to my MI6 colleague for his concern at my professional future," said Smith, anxious to match Monsford's condescension. "I also want to make it clear that I am not playing devil's advocate. But getting the accusation of kidnap withdrawn isn't the only hurdle. There's mollifying bruised French pride at MI6 mounting an espionage-linked operation on its sovereign soil. There's the danger of detained MI6 officers having made incriminating admissions, too. And we don't know what's passed between Moscow and Paris. There is absolutely nothing to suggest that this will produce any of the speculated success."

"None of my officers will have admitted anything, so I won't bother addressing that canard," dismissed Monsford, contemptuously, "Nowhere in my proposals have I discounted or minimized our difficulties. What I *have* done, to confront them, is bring to this country the highest-ranking Russian intelligence executive ever to defect and already have his agreement personally to persuade his family to deny they are kidnap victims, removing any criminal justification for France to detain them. France's precious pride can go to hell. Moscow's, too. We hold the better hand for whatever poker game they choose to play. We can't lose."

None of the others spoke, each of the three waiting for one of the others to comment or commit first. Monsford, too, lapsed into quiet, self-satisfied reflection, amused at how persuasively he'd utilized so much of Charlie Muffin's arguments to justify his personal involvement at their original Buckinghamshire discussions. He'd started out properly confident, Monsford admitted to himself, but he'd never imagined gaining such an overwhelming victory. Even the condescension he'd directed at Aubrey Smith, a finger snap, unprepared decision, had worked. He was the rule maker, the motivator: the others, Aubrey Smith their leading supplicant, had obediently to follow.

It was Sir Archibald Bland, the permanent civil servant whose influence spanned all political and diplomatic divides, who at last broke but tried too hard for cynicism. "Some diplomats might sometimes be mistaken for gangsters but very few aspire to such gunpoint blackmail."

"I've put forward practical, workable proposals," insisted Monsford, impatient at last with too many confused metaphors. "I'm looking forward to hearing alternatives."

"I believe we've taken this discussion as far as we can and from which there might well be a place for the suggested diplomatic involvement," said Palmer.

"But isn't there something further?" questioned Monsford, reluctant to quit while he was so far ahead. "What about the resurrection of Charlie Muffin?"

"I'm curious at your describing Charlie's reappearance as a resurrection?" quickly seized Aubrey Smith. "Do you have a reason for imagining he might have been dead?"

Monsford's balloon didn't burst but the air began to seep from the overinflated euphoria. "It was an inappropriate remark," he forced himself to admit. "But I'm sure all of us are curious about what he's been doing."

"Charlie's surfaced," Smith told the other two. "I've heard very little, apart from discovering he's refusing to operate with MI6, which makes me as curious as I'm sure it does all of you."

"With which I'm more than happy to accept," Monsford hurried in. "I'm no longer willing to risk either my officers or my service on such an irresponsible operative. I would even suggest the extraction of Charlie Muffin and his family is abandoned and all our officers withdrawn before anything else goes wrong."

"We talked . . ." began Smith but Palmer talked over him.

"Are you telling us the confounded man's still refusing specific instructions?"

"No!" denied Smith emphatically, unsure how far he could manipulate Monsford with Jane Ambersom's limited information. "There are indications that he's discovered a situation making it unsafe—maybe even physically dangerous—for him to be associated with the MI6 secondment."

"I demand an explanation of that remark!" exploded Monsford, exaggerating the outrage, the fragile confidence wavering.

"Which I'm as anxious to give as you are to hear," said Smith, enjoying the quick reversal. "But as we're discussing your operatives I was hoping you might have some input."

"I haven't the slightest idea what you're talking about," blustered the MI6 Director.

"In which case there'll need to be the most rigorous inquiry, which I assure all of you it will get," undertook Smith. "Perhaps we could get some early indication the three seconded, no-longer-acceptable MI6 officers will be recalled."

"Or perhaps they should remain to prevent further disasters," argued Monsford, panicked half thoughts refusing properly to cohere.

"You've changed your mind remarkably quickly," challenged Smith, hoping the two government grandees were assessing Monsford as he was. "You began hardly able to wait to disassociate your service from mine: now you're demanding they remain."

"That was before your accusations started!" Monsford threw back, awkwardly.

Turning that awkwardness back upon the other man, Smith said: "What accusations! I haven't accused anyone of anything. I merely speculated in the widest possible manner on a reason for Charlie's curious message. And I would, in passing, strongly argue against abandoning Charlie's mission. I believed we'd accepted Charlie will try to get his wife and child out, with or without our support."

"Precisely the potential danger I'm warning against and why my men must stay," blurted Monsford, to the frowned confusion of both Bland and Palmer.

Bland said: "This is spiraling into absurdity. We'll adjourn but by tomorrow I want this sorted out, to be discussed and resolved constructively. I opened this session warning of lost government confidence. Little of what I've heard today has changed the sentiment. I think . . ." The man stopped at a summoning buzz from outside the room.

Palmer pressed the door-release button and accepted the message slip from a Foreign Office messenger. Looking up, Palmer said: "It's just been announced in Moscow that one of the two heart-attack victims from the tourist group has died."

After its productive start, Charlie's day went downhill. He'd spent a frustrating forenoon failing to reach Natalia and too much of the early afternoon unable to reconnect with David Halliday to learn of a reaction to his approaching Patrick Wilkinson.

Long before the clumsy Russian entry into his Vauxhall flat, Charlie acknowledged the onion-skin overlap of espionage and burglary, the cardinal credo of both being always to establish a guaranteed exit before contemplating an entry, which required the utmost preparation for the following day's Metro merry-go-round with Wilkinson, which he hoped would be as successful as his London evasion of his original safe-house guardians. Smolenskaya was the station closest to the Moskva-bordering British embassy and the logical place for Wilkinson to set off. To guard against his expectation of Wilkinson's not being alone, Charlie spent a full thirty minutes refamiliarizing himself with the station layout and hideaway surveillance spots. He twice rode his chosen route and following that refamiliarization disembarked at each of the linked intersections to memorize their individual geography. At four randomly chosen stops Charlie interrupted his protective survey to return to ground level for still unsuccessful telephone attempts. It took Charlie three hours to complete his personal mapping and isolate the best-suited stations. Charlie finished at Smolenskaya with the last of the continuous tests he'd risked during the journey testing the recharged British-adapted Russian mobile that was to feature heavily the following day, knowing the replacement Russian pay-as-you-go devices wouldn't operate at the depths of the Moscow underground system. He moved as deeply into the station as possible, impressed as he had been every previous time that the phone's indicator showed a full battery. As soon as he'd proved its effectiveness Charlie once more removed the battery to defeat the suspected tracker application.

It was past six before Natalia eventually answered and from the obvious terseness Charlie knew at once she was not alone. He named the time and restaurant, in the university district, quickly enough for her to dismiss the call as misdialed as she disconnected. Charlie tried from the same kiosk and twice more from others during his next reconnaissance before accepting that Halliday's refusal was deliberate, which was irritating although predictable. Charlie wondered how difficult it would be to restore their situation. It depended, he supposed, on London's response to his reappearance and insisted separation from MI6. To get an indication of that he'd have to wait until he met

Wilkinson: *if* he managed to meet Wilkinson, came the realistic qualification.

There had been, as always, a professional practicality in Charlie's booking dinner that night at the Wild Egret. It had been a favorite of both at the beginning of their marriage, conveniently close to their prerevolutionary-mansion apartment, the nostalgia of which he hoped she'd appreciate as much as she had his earlier choice. He enjoyed the nostalgic significance, too, but equally important was its nearness to the multientranced warren of Kurskaya Metro station, from which he planned to leave the Wilkinson carousel. He studied that as intently as he had Smolenskaya, going in and out of all three entrances, marking every concealment and vantage point and back once more aboveground rediscovered the tributary streets to the treble-lane highways and connecting ring road. Gratefully approaching the end of his professional preparations, Charlie sought out a half-remembered landmark that he found closer to the Wild Egret than he'd recalled, slipping easily into the alcove's completely dark interior. It had once contained a horse-watering trough, now removed but still with a wide ledge remaining for Charlie to perch on to relieve the foot-burning discomfort after so much walking, refusing even to contemplate how much worse it would be the following day. Charlie picked out Natalia when she was still more than a hundred meters away, approaching from the direction of the Kurskaya station, and was at once caught by the caution she was showing, discreetly checking her trail twice before reaching a cross-street intersection where she hesitated longer to ensure she was not under parallel road surveillance. He couldn't detect any either but waited a full five minutes to make absolutely sure Natalia was alone before he left the alcove to follow.

She was being seated as he entered. She smiled up as he joined her and said: "So you were checking I didn't have unwanted company?"

"The alcove where the trough used to be: you were very good."

"I was trying to impress you."

"You knew I'd be watching?"

"As I expected you'd choose this restaurant."

"Let's hope it lives up to the memories."

They took their time ordering, Charlie insisting upon celebration beluga.

"Was my call a problem?" asked Charlie.

Natalia shook her head. "We'd finished but I was still in the building, with people around. I had it on mute, so no one heard it."

"You dumped the phone?"

"After removing the SIM card and the battery," said Natalia, smiling at the insistence. "And I didn't dispose of them in the same bins."

Charlie smiled back at the gentle rebuke. "So how was your first day?"

Natalia sipped her wine, considering her reply. "Not what I expected: not that I knew exactly *what* to expect. There are six of us. I'm the only woman. I don't know any of the others: three have been drafted in from St. Petersburg. There's no chairperson. We each work on a document batch." She paused. "Does your service operate by naming, with time, date, and location of each encounter, every potentially useful outside contact?"

Did she want a matching contribution with what she was disclosing or was it just a point of comparison? Charlie waited for them to be served before saying: "It's universal, isn't it?"

Natalia nodded. "That's how we have to work. When we come to any outside name with whom Radtsic's ever had unsupervised contact, particularly British, we've got to flag it as well as verbally announcing it around the table for further recognition if the name appears in someone else's separated document batch."

"How thick is each individual batch?"

"About a third of a meter."

"Have you a better idea of how many other groups there are, apart from yours?"

"Approximately a dozen, as far as I can establish. But there's an equal number, starting tomorrow, to refine the initial results. The lunchtime rumor was that at that stage the flagged names will transfer to computer analysis and comparison."

"Is that all you have to flag up, Western—particularly British—identities?"

Natalia shook her head. "Repetitive destinations and locations, again concentrated on the West. Vacation spots, stuff like that."

"The checking and cross-checking will take months," estimated Charlie.

"I know."

"How much cross-referencing did your particular group assemble today?"

"Twelve at the end of the day."

Natalia was talking on the turned spy's psychological profile, Charlie recognized: once the initial dyke breaches, the tidal wave of disclosures follows. "The analysis won't take months. It'll take years, even computerized."

"How long it'll take isn't the point," said Natalia. "It's the documentation itself."

"What about it?" Charlie frowned.

"It's all duplicated, no originals, although from its font and typeface it was created on a typewriter, not a computer."

"Just your duplicates or everybody's?" queried Charlie.

"Everybody's. Do you understand my point?"

"Elana and Andrei Radtsic were detained less than forty-eight hours ago," calculated Charlie. "Allowing a generous twelve for the connection to be established between Paris and Moscow, that gives thirty-six hours for the Kremlin to discover Radtsic had gone. What's your estimate of Radtsic's combined KGB and FSB service?"

"Nearly thirty years," responded Natalia, at once.

"We've no way of knowing if *everything* has been duplicated," cautioned Charlie.

"All the other examining groups are handling copies," said Natalia.

"Then you're right," finally agreed Charlie. "It's impossible for them to have photocopied a thirty-year archive in just thirty-six hours,"

"So what's going on?" asked Natalia.

"I don't know," replied Charlie. "It's not our problem. When's Sasha back?"

"The day after tomorrow."

"Thursday," identified Charlie. "Are you working weekends?"

"Of course."

"I'll have everything before then. We'll go for Sunday."

After several moments, Natalia said: "How?"

"The safest way. I haven't yet chosen which."

"Sasha will know it's not a holiday: that it's still term time."

"Don't say anything to her until Saturday. And only then that it's a surprise and that the school has agreed. And don't let her see any of her friends, after you've told her."

"You'll be with us, won't you? I won't be going alone?"

Charlie was unsettled by her complete reliance. "That's the idea, isn't it: that at last we'll all be together?"

"I hope so: hope so very much."

Charlie wished there weren't so much uncertainty in her voice. "This is probably the last full time we'll have together."

Natalia checked her watch. "I could come back to the hotel for two hours."

"I'd hoped you could."

"I want you with me when we go, Charlie: I want to know you're somewhere close," she suddenly blurted. "I don't want it to be just Sasha and me."

"From Sunday you're never going to be by yourselves, not ever again."

It was just after nine when they left the restaurant. In London it was still only six thirty and everyone was still working.

"There's got to have been a leak." Monsford was striding up and down in front of the panoramic river view, more angry than nervous. From beside the man's desk, Rebecca Street had already indicated the sound apparatus was inactive.

"How can there have been a leak?" demanded James Straughan. "Jacobson and Charlie have never met and Jacobson categorically denies he said anything to Halliday, who wasn't ever involved until the last minute, upon your orders, which were also that Halliday worked blind."

"It's not difficult to work out," calmed Rebecca. "We're misleading ourselves. Charlie Muffin can't have had any reason for getting off the Amsterdam plane, apart from distrusting his own shadow. Now he's got a reason, after the publicity over the seizure of Elana and Andrei. Charlie's a consummate professional who's learned and practiced ten times more than anyone ever learns at training school. He'll have worked out that we're involved with the two Russian nationals in France at the same time as we're supposed to be part of the extraction of his wife and child."

"Elana and Andrei haven't been identified and there's been no publicity that Radtsic's already here!" rejected Monsford, slumping back into his chair.

"People like Charlie Muffin, who trusts no one, can multiply two plus two into the national debt!" argued Rebecca. "What little is publicly known is more than enough to spook Charlie Muffin from coming within a million miles of any of our people."

Monsford shook his head in refusal, turning to Straughan. "What's Briddle say?"

"Just that MI5 have retreated into their *rezidentura,* slamming the door behind them."

"I beat Aubrey Smith into a frazzle in the beginning but he recovered almost completely with the fucking cooperation refusal," said Monsford, in a rare admission.

"What do we do about our three in Moscow?" asked Straughan.

"They stay!" insisted the MI6 Director, at once. "Now Muffin's crawled from beneath the stone he's been under, I want to be his shadow: every time he farts, I want to hear it. I'm not having the Radtsic coup taken away from me by Charlie Muffin."

"I've nominally appointed Briddle our field supervisor," said Straughan. "Do you have any specific instructions?"

Monsford hesitated, head bent. It certainly wasn't better to face slings and arrows, he decided: the only way was to take up arms against the sea of trouble. Looking up, he said: "Tell him to call me at ten prompt tomorrow, his time. I'll take the call personally."

"It sounds as if you won?" suggested Jane Ambersom.

"We won't have won until Monsford's removed, which I'm determined to make happen before I'm fired," said Aubrey Smith.

"Do you think it was a serious threat?" queried John Passmore.

"Totally serious," confirmed the MI5 Director-General. "And if I go I'll go down in flame, which means it's imperative you get whatever Straughan has."

"He's not taking my calls either on his landline or his cell phone," said Jane.

"Keep trying," said Smith.

"Are the MI6 backup being withdrawn?" asked Passmore. "Wilkinson doesn't think it's going to be easy operating separately out of the same building."

"I want to speak to Charlie direct," demanded Smith. "Have Wilkinson tell him that. Tell him also to warn Charlie to watch his back. Talking to Jane, Straughan didn't rule out physical violence."

"It's unthinkable that Monsford would contemplate anything physical against a British intelligence officer," insisted Passmore.

"No, it's not," said Jane, even more insistently. "That's exactly what he'll be thinking if it means saving himself."

28

CHARLIE WORKED ON THE ASSUMPTION THAT PATRICK Wilkinson, either knowingly or otherwise, would not be alone on the circle line, which he'd most likely join from the station closest to the British embassy. It was also possible they'd imagine he'd get on at Smolenskaya, too, and assemble an ambush there long before his ten A.M. departure, using Wilkinson as their on-time bait. Their obvious concentration would be around the entrance, to avoid which he started his approach from Kurskaya at the height of Moscow's eight o'clock rush hour, sandwiching himself into the second-to-last carriage, which he'd established from his previous day's footslogging disgorged its passengers into the instant concealment of a vaulted support column and an angled wall. From its cover he allowed himself a protective sweep for a recognizable face, with the train still at the platform for instant escape, before edging himself back into the human flow that took him to his already chosen observation spot, a set of metal service stairs leading up to a mezzanine range of Control offices twenty meters beyond the towering escalator banks to the circle line's snack, media, and tobacco kiosks. The overshadowing darkness of the service stairwell gave Charlie unbroken observation of arriving and disembarking commuters as well as an uninterrupted view of the other most likely hideaways from which others trained in his craft would wait in readiness for him to appear. And if they chose his hideaway to be theirs, he had a second girdered stairwell farther along the concourse beneath which he could merge unseen. There was even a conveniently low horizontal stress bar separating two of the upright girders against which he propped himself to take his full weight off his troublesome feet.

It was eight fifty before Charlie made the first recognition, relieved it was Neil Preston, a fellow MI5 officer. The fair-haired, overweight man was close to the top of the farthest downward escalator, tightly clutching the hand support to prevent himself being forced down the stairs by the crush behind, anxiously scanning the crowded platform below from his diminishing elevation. Preston hesitated at platform level, pulling himself out of the current of people. Briefly, for no more than seconds, Preston appeared to look directly at Charlie, who tensed, ready to retreat. But then the man looked away and moved in the opposite direction and positioned his back to another of the major support pillars. From the inside pocket of his unbuttoned raincoat Preston took an unidentifiable newspaper already cleverly folded smaller than its tabloid size for commuter-crowded reading, which he gave the impression of doing without obscuring his platform view.

Robert Denning appeared at the top of the escalator exactly four minutes later but pulled himself into a small recess at its top to stare down at the human sea below. Charlie knew he was totally concealed from above from the tall, balding MI6 officer, who also wore a raincoat, although unlike Preston tightly buttoned and belted. Charlie was also sure that from his vantage point Denning wouldn't be able to locate Preston, whom he'd presumably followed. Denning's head moved from side to side as he scanned the platform, straining forward at the arrival and departure of trains. After at least ten minutes Denning took from his pocket what Charlie at once recognized to be one of the special Vauxhall-issued Russian cell phones. It was a brief conversation, after which Denning turned back against the crowd, disappearing toward street level.

Charlie kept his concentration on the upper level, at the same time keeping Preston in sight. Preston, in turn, maintained his constant vigil from behind his newspaper screen. Preston had obviously been followed by Denning, whose telephone alert had most likely been to Briddle or Beckindale, but not both: he'd appeared to dial only once and the conversation hadn't been long enough to involve more than one person. Why hadn't Denning come down to platform level? To avoid his descent being visible to Preston, Charlie guessed. He hoped it indicated that London had accepted his message to exclude M16.

Nine forty-five, Charlie saw, from the platform clock. Where was Wilkinson? If Wilkinson was going to keep to the timetable, the man should have been here by now. But only if he was joining the merry-go-round from Smolenskaya, Charlie qualified. It would have been wiser, more professional, for Wilkinson to evade pursuit by boarding at a different station, using Preston and Warren to lay false trails. But they hadn't, came another qualification. Preston had led Denning to the underground system and Denning had doubtless alerted the other M16 men. So even if Warren and Wilkinson were using different stations, the intended encounter was compromised.

Which it definitely was, Charlie accepted, as Patrick Wilkinson appeared at the top of the escalator. By now the rush hour had thinned and as he descended Wilkinson expectantly swept the platform below, seeking Preston, whose head jerk of recognition was even more obvious. Preston left his pillar as Wilkinson reached the platform and for a moment Charlie thought the two were actually going to link up. They didn't, but Preston stopped close enough for both to enter the same carriage. Charlie's distraction from the escalator was only seconds but when he looked back Denning was halfway down, using a group of uniformed soldiers for cover, and as the man reached the bottom, Beckindale got on at the top and descended with even less concealment behind a fur-hatted, fur-coated woman. Neither Wilkinson nor Preston looked behind him to check his trail.

Charlie replaced the battery in his adapted cell phone before Beckindale got to the bottom, his attention wholly upon the two MI6 officers hurrying to board the second and third carriage of the incoming train behind that of Wilkinson and Preston. With the carriage doors still open, Charlie texted Denning: WOMAN IN FUR HAT AND COAT, TWO SEATS IN FRONT, IS FSB, and saw Denning's grab at his pocket as he went back to the mobile phone. Charlie texted Wilkinson: GET RID OF PRESTON. STAY WHERE YOU ARE. DENNING AND BECKINDALE IN CARRIAGES BEHIND. The train pulling away from the station prevented Charlie's catching the second reaction.

Charlie waited ten minutes to guard against Warren or Briddle arriving late before using the underpass to the opposite platform for counterclockwise trains, knowing from his previous day's reconnaissance that he would be at Paveletsky long before Wilkinson's train, the numbered designation of which was 986. It hadn't started well, Charlie acknowledged, objectively.

"You know where he is!" interrupted Gerald Monsford, hunched forward over the telephone in his empty office.

"I said there's positive movement," refused Briddle. "Wilkinson's told me they've been ordered to break from us. I'm guessing there's a link-up with Charlie—"

"When!" broke in Monsford again.

Briddle sighed, audibly. "After the Wilkinson confrontation we started monitoring. This morning Denning followed Preston to Smolenskakaya Metro. Preston established observation. Just short of an hour later, Beckindale followed Wilkinson to the same station. Wilkinson and Preston got on the same train, but not together. Our guys are with them, although not together, on the same train as the other two—"

"It's a meeting!"

"Please let me finish!" protested Briddle, whose only professional contact with the Director had been during his private assassination briefing. "Before their train pulled out, Denning got a text from Charlie, telling him that a woman in front of him was FSB." Briddle stopped expectantly, but for the first time Monsford didn't break in. "Denning got off at the next station. The woman didn't follow."

"She wouldn't have been alone: there would have been a switch," said the M16 Director, filling in the exchange while he composed his intended story to the other man.

"Or it was a trick to screw our surveillance," suggested Briddle. "Whatever, it means that Charlie was watching everything: my guess is that he was on the train."

"Is Beckindale searching for him?"

"Of course he is. But he can only risk the carriages behind his own. If he goes forward he'll be seen by Wilkinson or Preston. I've told him to do his best to get some view into Wilkinson's carriage, to establish if Charlie's there. If the meeting's there, he's to follow Charlie when he gets off."

"You haven't forgotten our private meeting, have you?" said Monsford, everything clear in his mind.

"Of course not."

"What have you been told by Straughan?"

"Little more than that the French business is our operation."

"It's the wife and son of Maxim Radtsic, the executive deputy of the FSB."

"Jesus!" exclaimed Briddle.

"And we've got Radtsic, safely here in England. I'm working to extract the family here, too: expect to initiate it today. That's background information, for you to understand the echelon at which we're working: the three of you won't have any active involvement in that. Your undivided concentration is to be on Charlie Muffin, whose message to Denning definitely wasn't a trick: the trick was all that crap about his having to get his wife and daughter out of Russia. Radtsic's confirmed Charlie Muffin is a double, but M15 won't accept it: that's why they've ordered their people to block you out. And I'm giving you the same order. There's to be no further liaison with MI5. I want them watched until Charlie Muffin is located. But you are not to tell Denning or Beckindale *why* I want him found."

"Work against our own people!" questioned Briddle, uneasily.

"Charlie Muffin isn't our people: Radtsic insists he was turned years ago in the old KGB days and that he's been responsible for the deaths of at least eight loyal officers, four of them ours."

"If he's gone over he's here, safe," said Briddle. "If he's got away, why's he apparently got into contact with Wilkinson and the others?"

"Three and eight make eleven," said Monsford. "And if he identifies you three, that eleven could come up to fourteen. I'm not going to let him have that final count as his swan song."

Briddle lapsed into silence and this time Monsford didn't prompt, content to wait. Eventually Briddle said: "There's no way the three of us can detain him, get him out of the country, even if the others lead us to him."

"I know," said Monsford, shortly.

"What do you want us to do?"

"*You* to do," qualified Monsford. "We established at our private session that you hold the clearance authority, in extreme circumstances. Which I judge these to be."

"Are you authorizing me with the direct and specific order?"

"Yes. There will be no paper trail. That direct order, under a classified seal, will be logged with your personnel file. Which you know, from your clearance categorization."

"What do I tell Denning and Beckindale?"

"Nothing. Use them as trackers, nothing more," insisted Monsford. "And the restriction I'm imposing also includes the operations director and the deputy director. Is that properly understood?"

"Yes," said Briddle. "I understand."

Two preceding trains gave Charlie the time to reposition himself for the Paveletsky arrival of service 986, but its decreasing speed was still too fast to satisfy Charlie that the unwanted three hadn't remained unobtrusively on the train. None was in the same carriage as Wilkinson, who'd acquired a newspaper prop but was ignoring it, only once risking a quick sideways glance out toward the platform before turning back to look fixedly ahead. Nor, now the train was stationary, were any of those he sought in the carriages directly in front or behind.

From every rehearsal the day before Charlie had been sure this initial precaution would have worked but still refused the twinge of frustration that it hadn't. By using his suspected tracker telephone MI6 would know he was in Moscow's Metro system, despite his having once more removed the battery. Disappointed as he was by the so-far-evidenced lack of professionalism, it should become obvious from his next text transmission how he was monitoring them. There was little if anything they could do to trace his exact location, but further to confuse them—and possibly cause the disembarkation of those still possibly riding the carousel—Charlie waited until the train moved off before reinserting the battery to text Wilkinson: STAY ONBOARD AFTER DOBRYNINSKAYA. GET OFF KOMSOMOLSKAYA. WAIT. Dobryninskaya was the next station along the line, into which the train should be pulling as Wilkinson read the message. Charlie used the 3a, Filevskaya subline, changed at the midring hub, and arrived at Komsomolskaya within twenty minutes. It was one of the stations he'd personally surveyed the day before to choose his observation hide. Charlie was glad his feet weren't so far aching as badly as he'd feared.

"He didn't tell you anything?" demanded James Straughan.

Rebecca Street shook her head. "Nothing about the Moscow call. Just that he was getting a decision on the Radtsic linkup and that he expected to go directly from the Foreign Office to Hertfordshire. What did he say to Briddle?"

"I don't know."

"Why don't you know!" demanded the woman.

"He had Briddle's call patched directly through from the communications room to his extension. There's no way I could attach a tie-line: both circuits are alarmed."

"Didn't you ask Briddle?"

"Briddle told me it was officially restricted to himself and the Director: that the exclusion applied to you and me."

"He can't do that!" protested the woman. "That undermines the position and authority of both of us!"

"Monsford's done it, cut us completely out."

"We've got enough," declared Rebecca.

"Cut out, we don't know what he's saying, putting in our names, or making us appear responsible," warned Straughan. "We can't afford to overlook how much of what he did to get into the Lvov affair was dumped onto Jane Ambersom the moment it all went wrong."

"She didn't have what we've got."

"He does know everything the three of us have discussed up to now, even if he's been selectively recording it all," reminded Straughan, unconvinced.

"You keep running around in fear circles, you're going to disappear up your own ass," derided Rebecca.

"It would be safer there than where I believe myself to be now," said Straughan, self-pityingly.

On this occasion Gerald Monsford got to the Foreign Office ahead of the other three, his quick irritation at being relegated to an anteroom to wait for the government liaison compounded by Aubrey Smith's arriving next. The M15 Director-General nodded curtly but didn't speak. Monsford didn't bother with any response. Sir Archibald Bland and Palmer were fifteen minutes late. Neither one apologized or explained their delay. As they sat, Bland said: "The French have agreed to a visual conference exchange between Radtsic and his family but they're insisting upon conditions, as we are. . . ." He looked directly at Monsford. "How much time will you need to set it up?"

"No time at all," responded the MI6 Director. "My security-cleared engineers are already in Hertfordshire, waiting. Being a permanent safe house, all the technology is already there, too. They'll only want the French technical information to make the two-way communication connection."

"Did you prepare it all ahead of the diplomatic agreement?" queried Palmer.

"I thought I'd made it clear that I'm working proactively. It didn't require a great deal of preparation."

"How involved are the Russians?" questioned Aubrey Smith.

"One of the French insistences is that Russia has full access, through their Paris embassy," said Bland.

"You mean a simultaneous, live tie-in to everything that's said?" pressed Smith.

"Yes," confirmed the cabinet secretary.

"Radtsic's in a safe house," Smith pointed out. "Isn't there an obvious danger of the Russians technically pinpointing his whereabouts to mount a recovery operation?"

"I've anticipated that possibility with my technicians." Monsford smiled: he'd hoped for an intervention he could mock. "It will be a satellite transmission which, for the recipient, begins and ends at the satellite. But as an added safeguard against the Russians' having the scientific capability to overcome that cutout, the connection will not be direct from Hertfordshire. It will be routed through a booster station just outside Ashford, in Kent. That cutout totally precludes anything being traced back to where Radtsic is."

"Admirable forethought," congratulated Bland. "We're interpreting Russian constraints in some of the French conditions. Their major insistence is that there should be no pressure or threatening accusations: that it is all conducted unemotionally."

"What about pressure or threats that the Russian diplomats will have already made upon Elana and the boy?" asked Smith, professionalism overcoming his personal antipathy toward the M16 Director.

"There's no way we can discover the extent of that, nor counter it," said Palmer. "We're actually surprised, astonished almost, that they've agreed at all."

"Weren't our strengths made clear?" demanded Monsford, belligerently.

"I have no knowledge of the actual negotiations," avoided Palmer, unconvincingly.

"Radtsic's strong-minded, to the point of arrogance: I've already told you that, several times," said Monsford. "I'll spell it out again but there can't be any guarantee."

"Spell out something even more clearly," urged Bland. "The moment it degenerates into a shouting match the French will disconnect from their end and it'll all be over."

"The Russians are orchestrating it," judged Smith, quickly. "Their simultaneous access enables them to make a complete transcript. It's a preposterous insistence that it won't be emotional. They'll let the exchange between the family continue for as long as serves their purpose but at some stage, whether or not Radtsic loses control, they'll cut the link and have a recording they can edit to whatever benefit they choose. . . ."

"That's a wild hypothesis prompted by nothing more than the despair of a counterespionage service that's proved itself incapable of performing its function or controlling its officers," accused Monsford.

Aubrey Smith ignored the outburst as well as the man, continuing to address the cabinet secretary. "The entire encounter will obviously be in Russian, won't it?"

"With simultaneous English and French translation," confirmed Bland.

"In what other language would a conversation be conducted between a Russian family?" demanded the M16 Director.

Once more Smith ignored the other director. "It will somehow be manipulated into a Russian propaganda coup, most definitely within the country itself: my guess is that it'll be turned into apparent proof that we've kidnapped Radtsic and are holding him here against his will."

"So what, if it's only for internal consumption!" demanded Monsford.

"What spin do you imagine the French will put upon it?" asked Smith, speaking at last to his counterpart. "Certainly not that they're under Russian duress. And their version—remember, they hold the European presidency—will get a strong play throughout the Union. . . ." He went back to the other two men. "And our problem has been counteracting Russian publicity and public perception, hasn't it?"

"Has everyone forgotten my suggestion how to counteract that?" dismissed Monsford.

Aubrey Smith waited, hopefully.

"Aren't there several points there?" questioned Bland, in cautious agreement.

"No," rejected Smith, satisfied. "We can't anticipate the publicity this will generate until it's happened. So we'll be following their lead, with each and every rebuttal we attempt: appearing that we have to defend ourselves."

"What, then, are you suggesting?" demanded Palmer.

"That the conference connection is established, that Maxim Radtsic is warned as strongly as possible of the potential traps, and that we all pray that he manages to persuade his wife and son to continue on here," said Smith, establishing his reservations. "If, that is, the kidnap allegations are withdrawn and the French agree to release them into our protection and not Moscow's. If we get them here we achieve the defection. If we don't, it'll be unmitigated professional disasters."

"I'm sure we all of us defer to your knowledge of professional disasters," said Monsford.

"Your favorite, Shakespeare, had a view of professional disasters, didn't he?" said Smith. "Something along the lines of how he was wearied by them: the first murderer in *Macbeth*, I seem to remember."

The 986 circle line service hissed into Komsomolskaya more slowly than it had at Paveletsky, which Charlie assumed to be dictated by platform length, making it easier to identify Beckindale and Warren in their respective carriages. Both were standing, as if to get off, but which Charlie guessed made it easier for them to scour the arrival platform, taking it as confirmation of their surveillance realization. Wilkinson snatched to answer Charlie's call as the train squealed to a final halt. Charlie said: "Appear to be getting off the train but don't," and disconnected, watching Warren and Beckindale move separately in their respective carriages toward the opening doors for a closer platform search.

Warren must have had his cell phone in his hand, from the awkwardness with which he answered it getting off the train. Charlie said: "Beckindale's with you. Lose him. I'm at the top of the escalator. I'll make the contact."

Warren's reaction was better than Charlie had expected. There was no startled backward look. Warren continued purposefully on as Beckindale got off, appearing surprised at the sight of the other man ahead of him. Beckindale hesitated, uncertainly looking between Warren and the train, edging just close enough to see Wilkinson getting up from his seat. Beckindale remained momentarily undecided before hurrying after Warren. Charlie moved, too, having to thrust his outstretched arms between the closing doors for them to reopen to admit him.

He was taking a hell of a chance, Charlie accepted, with no idea if any of the others remained on the train. It would be safer to stay where he was, next to the door, at least until he cleared the next station.

29

THERE WERE AUDIBLE VOICES, SPEAKING FRENCH, BUT NO picture. The screen flickered, distorted images breaking up, then settled to show Elana and Andrei side by side behind a table, which was how Radtsic was positioned in Hertfordshire by M16 technicians. They'd also covered the entire wall behind him with beige, nonreflective fabric, as the French had also done in Paris, in the same color. The microphones on both tables virtually matched, as well. The water carafes were similar, each oddly set with four accompanying tumblers. Monsford was behind the camera, with earphoned technicians and engineers, hands cupping earphones to his head to hear the simultaneous translation.

"I can . . ." began Radtsic, uneven voiced, at a gesture from a technician off camera.

Radtsic stopped, clearing his throat, and started again. "I can see you."

"We can see you, too," said Elana. She was wearing a vivid red dress, with a diamond brooch pinned close to her left shoulder. Her hair was immaculately coiffured. Her voice was even, showing none of her husband's uncertainty.

"How are you?" asked Radtsic.

"All right."

"Andrei?"

"All right." Andrei shrugged as he spoke. He was wearing an open-neck shirt beneath a sweater, which appeared too big for him. His hair was tousled, uncombed, and he constantly fidgeted, both hands first on the table, then in his lap, quickly back to the table again. Unlike his mother, instead of looking into the camera he seemed to be seeking people behind it.

Radtsic cleared his throat again. Stiltedly, enunciating each word as if reading from a script, he said: "Are you being well treated?"

"Very well," assured Elana, for the first time glancing behind the camera.

"I am in England."

"Yes." Almost hurriedly she said: "We know."

"I want you both here in England with me. We're going to live here. You were mistaken, about being kidnapped. They were friends, helping you. You must tell people that: make it clear to people there, so they understand."

The French transmission began to break up and Monsford came too close to the technician operating the English equipment, jogging him. Abruptly the screen cleared.

"I—" started Elana but Andrei talked over her.

"No!" he declared, loudly. "I'm not coming . . . not agreeing. You're betraying us . . . traitor . . . you're a traitor."

Radtsic visibly clenched his hands, outstretched on the table, and Monsford tensed forward again, anticipating the outburst against which he'd warned the Russian, but Radtsic's voice was controlled, although still stilted. "I am not a traitor. . . . I want you here, with me and your mother."

"I want to come . . . will come," Elana managed before Andrei overwhelmed her, shouting now.

"I don't want to come . . . don't want to be with you . . . see you . . . dead, that's what I think . . . you're dead to me."

"Please," pleaded Radtsic, still controlled although his hands were bunched into fists. "Please, Andrei. Don't break up the family. I need you here, with me. You can't stay there . . . stay anywhere except here with me. You know that—"

"I will come . . . want to come," Elana repeated.

"Go with him!" yelled Andrei, turning to his mother. "Go with the traitor. I don't want to be with you, either of you, not anymore. . . ." He began to struggle up, physically to separate himself from her.

"Stay where you are!" roared Radtsic, all restraint gone, red faced with fury. "You *will* come here . . . do as you're told . . ." But the link was cut long before he'd finished.

"I warned you what would happen," said Monsford, stopping just short of the exasperation that might have antagonized the Russian into worse anger. They'd moved from the room in which the conference link had been established, into a glassed conservatory overlooking the grounds. Radtsic had refused vodka, demanding scotch.

"Disobeying me . . . actually disobeying me, his father!" struggled Radtsic, disbelievingly, oblivious anyway to what Monsford was saying. "He must come. They won't let him stay in France. He'll be taken back . . . punished."

"We're trying to reconnect," said Monsford, emptily, desperately trying to think ahead. "It was the surprise, of actually seeing you, knowing that you're already here, after what's happened in France. He'll come round when he adjusts to the reality. . . ."

"He called me a traitor . . . denigrated me . . ." remembered Radtsic, overwhelmed in disbelief. "I must speak to him: make him understand."

"I told you we're trying to reconnect. There are discussions in France: diplomatic channels opened. Don't forget Elana is coming to be with you. It's all going to work out."

Radtsic shook his head, comprehending what Monsford was saying. "I must speak to Andrei. Make things clear. He'll come when he understands. . . . It's taking a long time to reconnect to Paris . . . why can't we go back to where the camera is, to be ready?"

Harry Jacobson appeared at the door, gesturing there was a telephone call.

"Wait here," Monsford told the Russian. "I don't want you coming near the television setup. I need to make sure it's safe for you."

When Monsford reached him Jacobson said: “Geoffrey Palmer wants you personally. And France is refusing to reestablish the link.”

“Tell them to keep trying,”

“I already have.”

“We’ve seen the replay,” announced Palmer, when Monsford identified himself. “What happened?”

“You saw what happened,” said Monsford, irritably. “Who else watched it?”

“All three of us. Why didn’t you tell Radtsic to hold his temper: to stay calm.”

“I did,” snapped Monsford, the irritation more at knowing Aubrey Smith had seen the transmission than at Palmer’s facile questions. “What is the embassy saying in Paris?”

“They’re still trying to reach someone who’ll talk to them.”

“Elana said she wants to come.”

“I told you we saw it,” said Palmer. “We also saw Andrei refuse and call his father a traitor. What’s his reaction been?”

“He wants to talk to Andrei. He thinks he can persuade him to change his mind if he can speak to him.”

“I’m not. Neither are the others. And even though they haven’t made direct contact, the embassy don’t think it’s a technical breakdown. They’re sure the French—which means the Russians—carried out their threat when Radtsic started shouting.”

“It’s too early to judge,” insisted Monsford, anxious to escape from the Foreign Office mandarin.

“The judgment being made here in London is that the whole episode has been a complete disaster,” said Palmer.

And I know the bastard who’s promoting that verdict, Monsford thought. “I’ve got to get back to Radtsic.”

“What you’ve got to do is sort this mess out,” said Palmer, putting down the phone ahead of the other man.

He'd have to take the risk, Charlie accepted, as the train came into Kurskaya. No one against whom he was tensed appeared during the six-minute journey between stations, which left two suspect MI6 officers unaccounted for as well as Neil Preston, who, from their standard of tradecraft so far, could still lead the MI6 hunters back to him after cell-phone contact with Wilkinson. If, that is, they were still somewhere on the train. Or waiting at one of the intervening stops farther along the line, ready to board.

It seemed a relatively slow entry, giving Charlie a platform sweep, and he didn't see a hostile face among the waiting passengers. But he was more vulnerable on a train than on a platform with a choice of exits and escape tunnels. The train came to its final halt as Charlie made his decision, abruptly pushing against passengers preparing to get off, ready to run with them if he saw unwelcome faces. Which, from Wilkinson's instant recognition as he reached the man's carriage, Charlie suspected his to be. Charlie scarcely paused or bent as he passed, saying, "Follow me, now!"

Charlie didn't hesitate on the platform, either, striding on now agonized feet to the linking tunnel to the Metro services' third, Arbat-designated line, hunched against an identifying challenge, which didn't come. Charlie pulled to the rear of the platform, satisfied at last with Wilkinson's following arrival. The man didn't repeat his earlier recognition but came to the same platform section, close to the wall. Charlie's concentration was beyond the man, seeking pursuit, relieved at seeing only strangers. He moved toward the first incoming train, bringing Wilkinson with him, but hung back for the man to board first, relieved again that Wilkinson chose a separate, two-person side bench sufficiently isolated from other passengers.

"I'm never going to take another metro," greeted Wilkinson, as Charlie slumped beside him.

"Nor am I," said Charlie, gratefully stretching out his overworked feet. He'd got away with it but the Metro merry-go-round had proved more difficult than he'd imagined and the sucked-in street-level pollution was worse than he'd remember, even during his earlier reconnaissance. "I'm relying on guesswork. Start from my plane disappearance."

What in Charlie's opinion Wilkinson lacked in tradecraft he more than compensated for in succinct recall and Charlie didn't interrupt, abandoning his intended train change at the central hub, continuing on instead to the Arbat, where it was quicker anyway to transfer to the south-to-north Sokol'niceskaja route. It still took another ten minutes for Wilkinson to finish. "Smith believes you're in genuine, physical danger. He ordered me to tell Briddle there's no longer any partnership: that all cooperation is over. Smith's trying to get Monsford's people withdrawn, but there's no sign of it happening."

"You let them follow you today. That was stupid," openly accused Charlie.

"I was sure I'd slipped Beckindale."

"Denning was with Preston, too. Why bring Preston with you, believing MI6 want me eliminated. Why weren't Preston and Warren decoys, drawing them away!"

"Smith's orders are that we provide maximum protection."

"On today's showing I'm safer on my own."

"It was a mistake and I'm sorry."

Charlie shrugged, dismissively. "Radtsic's definitely in London, right?"

"Yes."

"And Elana and the boy are held in France?"

"As of yesterday. I haven't heard anything new today."

"Why is Smith so convinced Monsford's planning a move against me? Where's Monsford's gain doing this?"

Wilkinson matched Charlie's earlier shrug. "Smith doesn't know, not yet. He might have learned more since we last spoke. But isn't it about time you told me what the hell you've been doing."

He had to be careful, Charlie knew. Natalia's extraction value was hugely increased by her secondment to the Lvov investigation but that value would be quadrupled by keeping her in place and using him as a conduit. "Before we get to the details there's something important to pass on to London. Which means your getting some background. We misinterpreted Natalia's calls to London: she was interrogated after the Lvov affair. I was identified during it, which threw up something that happened a long time ago: she debriefed me, after I worked a phoney defection. That's what brought her under suspicion after Lvov. But she's been cleared. And now she's been appointed to one of at least eight separate damage-limitation teams to investigate Radtsic's complete background to discover who turned him."

"She's got access to Radtsic's records?" demanded Wilkinson, incredulously.

Enough, decided Charlie. Now he had to ensure against a London insistence that Natalia remain in place. "She and a lot more, to prevent any one person getting a comprehensive overview: that's why it's being split between so many different initial analysts. Anything they find is to be passed on to other groups for further examination. Her secondment is strictly limited: I don't how short."

"It's still an incredible opportunity," gauged Wilkinson.

"A gold mine," expanded Charlie, pleased at the reaction. "That's what you have to tell London, for them to realize how much more important it's become to get her out."

"But not before she's got everything she can: not until she has to leave her group."

"Of course not," agreed Charlie, satisfied.

The train had passed the circle-line intersection without any MI6 presence but Charlie maintained his usual caution, jerking up without warning at Dmitrovskaya, knowing there was a conveniently close although neglected postage-stamp park in which he could end their meeting as well as observe his pursuit precaution.

"There's not a lot more to discuss at this stage," he resumed, choosing a bench that kept the Metro's single entrance and exit in sight. "I met with Passmore after the general session at Vauxhall Cross."

"I know. The Russian passports were shipped separately, direct to me."

"Unknown to the three from MI6?"

"Yes."

"You're sure?"

"Positive."

"Those are the ones I want. As well as twenty-five thousand pounds, all in U.S. dollars."

"What about tickets?"

"The twenty-five thousand is traveling expense."

"Traveling about which you're not going to give me any details?"

"No. But I want you to be overheard by the others discussing the Polish exit."

"We're not to be involved at all, are we?"

"No."

"That's ridiculous," protested Wilkinson. "You're not just an FSB target: I've just told you Smith's convinced our own side might even want to kill you. You spell out how much more important Natalia has become: why it's imperative she gets to England. And cap the whole fucking thing telling me you're going to do it all by yourself."

"I'm still free because I know how to stay that way. And I performed the Amsterdam vanishing trick because Monsford's involvement stank from the beginning and now we know why."

"No, we don't," rejected Wilkinson. "We don't know why you're at risk from Monsford. I accept we fucked up this morning. You've got every reason to be pissed off. But you'll fail, trying to run the extraction entirely alone. And you know it!"

And Aubrey Smith wouldn't allow it either, Charlie accepted. And could forbid the passport handover. "I don't intend running the extraction alone: of course that's impossible. You'll all be part of it at the very end. It's the logistics I'm compartmenting, just as the FSB are compartmenting their Lvov investigation. You've got MI6 in permanent pursuit: I haven't. I can move about, make the plans. You can't."

"Aubrey Smith still won't sanction it," warned Wilkinson.

"He wouldn't have liked people from whom he believes I'm in physical danger being led to me this morning," said Charlie.

"How will I get the passports and money to you, if London approves?"

"I'll call you, personally, at the *rezidentura*."

"I might not get a quick response from London, with so much going on elsewhere."

"Nine o'clock tomorrow morning, as it's striking," said Charlie. "And I know you'll try to follow me when we split up and my feet hurt too much to fuck about losing you, so I'll come with you back to the Metro to know where you are. . . ." He took the London-issued cell phone from his pocket. "Did you pick up the tracker signal?"

"After your first call," admitted Wilkinson.

"Why didn't you tell me?" asked Charlie, glad he'd followed his instinct.

"Our orders are to look after you, now we've linked up," reminded Wilkinson. "You don't have to worry about cell-phone trackers anymore."

There'd been an element of luck, Stephen Briddle congratulated himself as he saw the two get up from the park bench, but he'd worked most of it out himself after learning from Denning and Beckindale's calls that Wilkinson wasn't moving from the circle line's 986 service, positioning them on clockwise platforms to confirm it and already onboard, waiting, when Charlie finally joined it two stations later. He'd managed to keep up with all the line switches, allowing them the longest possible lead. Because of that intentional distancing and the ski-lift height of the escalators, Briddle had still been inside the Dmitrouskaya station when Charlie and Wilkinson found their park bench. The Metro provided complete concealment throughout their encounter and as they came toward him, Briddle recognized he couldn't be in a better place not just to continue his surveillance but even to stage Monsford's demanded fatal accident, aware despite his newness to Moscow that there were at least 150 suicides a year on the underground system and that one extra statistic would not arouse any official suspicion.

Briddle was invisibly within the shadows of the platform food stall by the time the two men rode the escalator down for the simultaneous arrival of a train to board and Wilkinson didn't pause. Neither did Briddle, joining a noisy group of departing food-stall customers to sit two carriages behind his quarry. Briddle had an unbroken view of the outside platform, which was where, as the train lurched into motion, he saw Charlie not on the train, as he'd imagined, but still standing there. And although there was no obvious recognition, Briddle knew Charlie had seen him, too.

An expectant, serious Jane Ambersom was waiting in the anteroom to Smith's suite with an equally grave-faced John Passmore when the Director-General flurried in from the Foreign Office, gesturing them to follow him.

"You could call it a Solomon resolution, I suppose," announced Aubrey Smith. "Elana and Andrei withdrew their kidnap claims and the French are releasing Elana into the custody of our Paris embassy, along with all our people. Andrei's refused to go with them. He was released into Russian protection. Monsford's hailing it as a victory."

"Monsford can't have heard yet," said Jane.

"Heard what?" Smith frowned.

"Why I haven't been able to reach Straughan," said the woman. "Security didn't immediately react when he didn't arrive at Vauxhall Cross this morning: he was sometimes delayed because of his mother. Her caregiver found them but Straughan's protective cover legend caused a delay in Vauxhall being told. The mother could have been dead since last night, overdosed. Straughan's death is apparently more recent, delayed probably because of what he did after killing her. I don't know precisely what was found: we probably never will. There were some letters, I believe. I've no idea what else."

"Could they have been killed?"

"If Monsford wanted them to be," judged Passmore. "The mother's dementia left her catatonic. She would have swallowed whatever she was given without knowing who gave it to her. MI6 will have taken over everything by now. There won't be a public inquest or any pathology details released. James Straughan and his sad mother will simply have ceased ever to have existed."

"How did we find out?" asked Smith.

"Straughan had listed my private number to be contacted in an emergency. It was the police who called me, when the caregiver gave it to them."

"He'll have made some arrangement for you to get whatever he had."

"We can only hope," said Jane. "I was just leaving for Berkhamsted when Rebecca called, saying there'd been a mistake: that she was taking over."

"Damn!" exclaimed Smith.

"Maybe it'll protect Charlie," suggested Passmore.

"Maybe," said the other man. "What's come from Moscow?"

"Nothing yet from Wilkinson, but we know from the others Charlie was using the Moscow Metro," said Passmore. "Somehow he found out Preston and Warren were support for Wilkinson. He made cellphone contact, warning that Denning and Beckindale were following. Warren thinks they decoyed them off, but he's not sure."

"If Charlie used our phone the tracker would have been activated."

"It was," confirmed Passmore. "Both here and in Moscow. MI6 would have got his location."

"And we haven't heard from Wilkinson," repeated Passmore.

"When the hell am I going to get ahead of this, start calling the shots instead of trailing behind in somebody else's dirt?" demanded Smith, unusually venting his anger.

Charlie Muffin was thinking something similar as he replaced the kiosk telephone after being told by Natalia that it was impossible to meet that night. His call before that, to David Halliday, hadn't been answered, either. And there'd been more luck than tradecraft expertise in his evading Stephan Briddle, one of possibly three men he'd been warned were trying to kill him.

30

THEY'D KISSED BUT PERFUNCTORILY, ACQUAINTANCES rather than husband and wife, and afterward remained standing although not together, Radtsic staying close to where he'd greeted Elana just inside the door, Elana, still wearing the vivid red dress, wandering aimlessly around the conservatory like a disappointed prospective buyer.

"This isn't how it was supposed to be," said Radtsic, breaking the awkwardness.

"It was my duty to come but I didn't want to," said the woman. She stopped close to a corner of the windowed room, frowning up at a roof joint. "They'll be listening to everything, I suppose?"

"And filming," confirmed Radtsic. "What's happened to Andrei?"

"There were always three Russians in the room. After Andrei's outburst they asked him to go with them, so they could protect him. They asked me, too. I refused. The French officials there asked Andrei if he wanted to go with them. He said yes, at once, and left with them. They would have been your people, wouldn't they: FSB?"

"Yes," Radtsic confirmed again. "What did Andrei say to you before he went?"

"Just repeated that he never wanted to see or hear from us again. That we were dead to him, both of us."

"He's my son: supposed to respect me and do what I tell him!" It was a plea, not an angry demand.

"He's a man: a young one but still a man," corrected Elana, finally slumping into a overpadded, solitary positioned easy chair making it impossible for Radtsic to sit close to her. "He doesn't respect you anymore, Maxim Mikhailovich. He hates and despises you. And now me, for coming here to you."

"Do you hate and despise me?"

"I'm not sure, not yet," admitted Elana, with brutal honesty. "I do know I don't want to be part of any of this. But I know even more than I've ever known anything in my life that I never wanted to lose my son, which is what you've made happen."

"You don't understand what—"

"Don't you dare tell me that I don't understand!" stopped Elana, giving way to shouted anger. "I understand every fucking thing you've made me do and with which I went along because I am your wife! And while I don't know yet if I despise and hate you, I *do* know that I despise and hate myself for doing it, for allowing it to happen. . . ."

Radtsic began to move toward her but Elana started up, moving away from him. "I don't want you near me. What will happen to Andrei?"

"I don't know."

"Don't lie to me!" she erupted into almost screaming frustration. "He'll be punished for what we've done, won't he? Become a nonperson at the age of nineteen. How do you feel about that, Maxim Mikhailovich? You proud about destroying your only son?"

"Stop it, Elana!" demanded Radtsic, matching her anger. "You know why I had to do this. How everything would have worked if Andrei had done what he was told instead of babbling about kidnap, giving the French the legal excuse to hold you—"

"He didn't say we'd been kidnapped!" halted Elana.

"You?" questioned Radtsic, uncertainty lessening his anger. "But you knew . . . ?"

"I didn't say it either. Neither of us said we'd been kidnapped."

"Stop wandering about!" ordered Radtsic, loudly. "I need to know what happened: *how* it happened . . . if there's a way of getting him back."

Elana hesitated, seemingly unsure, but went back to the overstuffed armchair. "I can't answer your question: don't have any answers."

"Tell me from the beginning, from the time you arrived in Paris."

Elana frowned in recollection. "I did everything you told me. I went to Andrei's apartment direct from the airport. Yvette wasn't there. Andrei and I ate dinner at a café quite close. Everyone knew him: I was very proud at how popular he was. I didn't meet Yvette until the second night. I like her. That first night he kept asking why I'd come so unexpectedly, almost without warning. I decided against telling him outright: I wasn't sure how he'd react. I told him my coming was part of a surprise: that together we were going London to meet you and that you had something very important to tell him."

"You didn't say anything, hint even at a defection?"

"I've just told you I didn't," said Elana, irritably. "He seemed so happy, so confident. Even a hint would have been a mistake. I wanted to get Andrei here first." She smiled, wanly. "I was the one guilty of kidnap. I expected him to be more excited at my arriving and of our coming on here. I thought it might have been to do with Yvette: not wanting to leave her, I mean."

"But he agreed to come?" said Radtsic.

Elana nodded. "But without much enthusiasm."

"How did you explain being escorted, by English people?"

"He only ever met two English people, Jonathan Miller and his partner, whom I only ever knew as Albert. Remember, Andrei never knew precisely what you did: the position you held. Just that it was something important and very high in the government. I told him you were in London with a Russian delegation for an internal conference and that you'd arranged for us to get to London on a plane taking some people from the British embassy. I told Miller and his partner, so they wouldn't make any mistakes on our way to the airport. Andrei didn't like either of them. He was rude when he met them."

"You think he suspected who they were?"

Elana shook her head. "Although he didn't know exactly what

you did, he did know how powerful you are." She hesitated. "How powerful you *were.* And he was used to your going away, without any explanation."

"He didn't questioning it?"

"After the awkward restaurant meeting with the British he said he couldn't understand why we couldn't travel on a normal flight."

"What did you say?"

"That it was how you wanted it. He never challenges you, does he?"

"Not until now," corrected Radtsic.

Elana looked up to the conservatory corner she'd examined earlier. "I don't like being listened to."

"I'm going to have to cooperate to get Andrei back. I don't understand how you came to be intercepted or how—or why—the kidnap claim came to be made."

Elana stared at her husband for several minutes. At last she said: "Maxim Mikhailovich, you're not making sense! You were always going to have to cooperate, tell them everything for us to be accepted: protected as we'll have to be protected for the rest of our lives. And we can never get Andrei back. He's gone: we've lost him forever."

"I won't lose him. I'll do a deal."

"What deal? With whom? You ran away from Russia because you were going to be purged: what do you imagine would happen to you if you changed your mind now and we went back? You've got nothing with which to negotiate with the British. To keep us safe you've got to tell them everything. Andrei won't come. Stop fantasizing, accept reality. And that reality is that you've made a terrible mistake and wrecked the family."

"What if Andrei accepts reality and recognizes he's made a terrible mistake: changes his mind?"

"What do you imagine the reaction would be to his going up to the commandant of whatever Siberian gulag he'll be sent to and saying he doesn't like it there and wants to come to England after all!" derided Elana.

"He won't be sent to a Siberian gulag: things aren't like they were, in the old days. There's law and Andrei hasn't broken any law."

There was another long silence before Elana said: "If there's law that's got to be followed, how could you have been purged? You didn't break any law."

"What I've done, all my life, isn't governed by any law," said Radtsic, in subdued reflection. "There has been a terrible mistake. But I didn't make it: wouldn't have made it because I knew everything, devised it all, and could still have prevented it being turned into the disaster it became if I'd been brought in when I should have been. But I wasn't. Others with ambition intervened. But there's no proof, no paper trail, of their intervention: that was the first, internal purge I didn't suspect. Which left me the architect who didn't react quickly enough. I should have left the service honorably, an internally recognized and acknowledged legend. Instead I leave it not just as a failure and a traitor but as a failure and a traitor to you and to Andrei. . . ." Radtsic stopped, brought out of his reverie by the awareness of Elana silently weeping, hands cupped to her face to hold back any sound. "I'll make it better: try to stop you hating and despising me."

Elana stayed with her hands covering her face, still weeping.

"My deputy director is handling the situation," declared Monsford. "I've no specific details, other than the indications that Straughan killed his mother before killing himself. Nothing will ever become public: a complete blackout has been imposed."

"What security implications are there?" demanded Sir Archibald Bland.

Monsford's eyes flickered toward Aubrey Smith. "Absolutely none."

"What about letters, an explanation?" intruded Smith, savoring the other director's discomfort.

"I haven't had the chance to talk to my deputy," said Monsford, his voice uneven. "I'll provide all the details as soon as I have them myself."

"Which brings us back to the original point of this gathering," said Aubrey Smith, turning away from the now-dead screen on which they'd watched the encounter between Radtsic and his wife. "What happened after she recovered?"

"They walked outside in the grounds," said Gerald Monsford, inwardly squirming at being questioned by the other director. "Neither wanted to eat when they got back to the house. Elana insisted upon sleeping in a separate room."

"What did they talk about walking in the grounds?" Smith continued to press.

"Surely you don't imagine—" started Geoffrey Palmer.

"Nothing that added to what they'd talked about inside," hurried in Monsford, eager to save Palmer's embarrassment. "They hardly spoke, as far as we could detect."

"So they were heads down?" persisted Smith.

"Could someone help us here?" demanded Palmer, irritably.

"They were filmed throughout their walk," explained the MI6 Director. "The cameras have special enhancing lenses enabling what's said out of microphone range to be recorded and then lip-read."

"Lip-reading that can be defeated by a person walking with their head lowered, avoiding the camera," added Smith. Directly addressing his counterpart, Smith said: "You didn't answer my question?"

"Yes," confirmed Monsford, tightly.

"So we don't have recordings of everything they said to each other?"

"No," Monsford was forced to admit.

"What's your point?" protested Sir Archibald Bland.

"What's your assessment of the confrontation inside the house, where we did hear every word?" demanded Smith, answering a question with a question.

Bland hesitated, unaccustomed to the reversal. "Very emotional, which was understandable considering every circumstance: Radtsic defecting after being at the top of his profession for so long, being reunited with his wife after what she's been through, neither knowing if they would ever be together again, all of it topped by their being reviled by a son who's abandoned them."

"And I'm intrigued by whatever it is Radtsic was talking about at the very end," added Palmer.

"All of which you were supposed to be," warned Smith.

"What the hell are you suggesting!" demanded Monsford.

Again Smith confronted question with question: "Do you normally allow encounters like that to be completely unsupervised?"

"I don't have a precedent," Monsford quickly came back. "Neither my service nor yours has had someone from such an echelon of Russian intelligence cross over to us. Nor, after managing such a defection, succeeding in getting released from at least nominal Russian detention a wife with whom to be reunited."

"Indeed, neither of us has," agreed Smith, smiling in return. "You've very definitely established the precedent. But how did that unsupervised reunion come about? Did you offer it? Or did Radtsic insist upon meeting his wife alone?"

Monsford hesitated. "He didn't insist: he asked. And it was hardly an unsupervised encounter. We've just watched and listened to everything that took place."

"With no debriefing intermediary to direct or guide it," Smith pointed out.

"In the intrusive absence of whom, caught up in their emotion, we've already got a lead to something Radtsic expected to be the culmination of a thirty-year intelligence career but instead, because of an internal power struggle . . ." Monsford stopped, his mouth physically distorting to avoid the intended singular boast, "we've got the coup."

"Let's not keep credit from where credit is due," enthused Smith, layering the condescension. "The coup is yours and yours alone. Which was how it was initiated and carried out, without the participation of anyone else. Just you, alone."

"We're becoming increasingly irritated at this perpetual antipathy," declared Bland. "As well as becoming increasingly concerned that it's endangering the matter at hand. True, we've got our coup. But externally it's greatly mitigated by a number of unresolved issues. We want—as others more important want—this constant bickering to stop for the concentration to instead be upon tidying up those issues."

"I reiterate that to resolve those issues I am offering every assistance asked of me and my service to help the Director-General, whose officer created them," said Monsford.

"That offer would best be achieved by the immediate withdrawing from Moscow the three MI6 officers seconded to the original extraction for which I am responsible but for whom there is no further need," responded Aubrey Smith, at once. "MI6 has succeeded with their extraction and achieved its coup, but upon which there would appear to be a need for much more work."

The only sound in the room for several minutes was that of differing seat and chair shifting prompted by differing reasons. The first-to-speak concentration settled upon Bland, the nominal chairman, who avoided the conflict with a matador's deftness by inviting Monsford's contribution.

"Unfortunate and public embarrassments aside, I am not aware of any changes in circumstance—in which, of course, I do not include the reemergence of Charlie Muffin—justifying the Director-General's astonishing demand."

"Are there any changes of circumstances?" Palmer asked Aubrey Smith.

"I believe there are considerable changes, none of which I intend discussing here," said the MI5 Director-General. "I shall, of course, discuss them in full and complete detail when the extraction of Natalia Fedova becomes a wholly independent MI5 matter."

"Not only is it outrageous to impugn my service, as I believe the Director-General is doing, it is arrogant for him to imagine that the separation of our two services is for him to decide," said Monsford.

"It is for the Director to make whatever interpretation he chooses," dismissed Smith. "In making your decision, which I was in no way taking from you, it's important I make totally clear that I am not prepared to continue the extraction of Natalia Fedova in partnership with MI6."

"And I must make it equally clear, as I have already done, that I am prepared completely to take over the extraction as an MI6 operation," declared Monsford.

"You took it over the edge," accused Jane Ambersom, objectively. "You didn't have a fallback if the ruling had gone against you."

"I'd have done what I know Monsford's going to do, ignore it," said Aubrey Smith, unoffended at her directness. "The whole intention was to get Monsford and MI6 *officially* out of our operation. Which is what I'm determined to do: get Monsford out, not just from this extraction but out of Vauxhall Cross. He's the paranoid megalomaniac to MI6 that J. Edgar Hoover was to the FBI. Monsford's dangerous: out of control."

"After today he'll be even more determined to destroy you," cautioned the woman. "And now he's excluded we've no way of second-guessing what he'll do."

"We know what Monsford's going to do: or try to do," repeated the MI5 Director. "What we've got to do is wrap up Moscow, get everyone safely back here." He turned to Passmore. "So when's that going to be?"

"As of fifteen minutes ago Charlie hadn't contacted Wilkinson," said the operations director. "I've authorized the money Charlie wants, as well as the Russian passports for Natalia and the child. As soon as we've finished, I'll add the decision officially to cut MI6 adrift and tell Wilkinson to make that clear to Monsford's people—"

"Do that," broke in Smith. "Once Wilkinson's completed the

handover, he and the other two are out, too. Their only function from now on is to take Monsford's people all over Moscow on wild goose chases. Wilkinson is to tell Charlie we're sending in independent backup. Who'll head the new group?"

"Ian Flood," responded Passmore, without hesitation. "He's one of four on standby, all with valid visas,"

"Charlie likes the Savoy, near Red Square," remembered Smith. "That's where he lived during the Lvov investigation. Flood's to book in there and Charlie's to be told that's where his contact is. But don't tell Wilkinson the hotel name. I don't want any more mistakes. Charlie will identify it by being told it's his favorite." Smith looked between the other two. "What else do we need to do?"

"Once Charlie's got his travel money and the passports there's no reason why he can't move at once," picked up Passmore. "I can get our second team in today, with Flood going in first. All we'd need from Charlie is routes and arrival day."

"I wasn't exaggerating Monsford's paranoia," said Smith. "I also believe he's capable of paranoid orders, dressed up with whatever justification. Tell Flood's team, upon my authority, to confront like with like if necessary."

"You're surely not imagining a gunfight at the O.K. Corral?" asked Passmore.

"Those are the orders, in my name," said Smith.

"I've got an idea," announced Jane. "First I need to know if anything was said this morning about Straughan?"

Smith shook his head. "It was mentioned. Monsford denied knowing any details, apart from it not being a security problem and that Rebecca was handling it."

"Ducking and weaving again," Jane recognized. "How'd it be if there was an alert that MI6 has been penetrated, particularly after the suicide of its operations director? A security purge might even find Rebecca Street's copy of what Straughan made."

"I think it might cause Monsford a very big problem." Smith smiled.

"Not if the internal search is controlled by Monsford," Passmore pointed out.

"It can't be," insisted Jane. "The regulations are that it would have to be independent of currently serving officers."

Gerald Monsford's purple-faced fury, accompanied by seemingly uncontrollable facial twitching, was greater than Rebecca had witnessed before, although the irrational pacing was familiar. For a long time after his stormed entry it was impossible for the man to speak comprehensibly: even attempted words burst out incomplete or slurred.

"Bastards . . . fucking bastards . . . imagine!" Then came what appeared another indecipherable splutter. "Sided with him, with Smith . . . against me! Me . . . gave them their fucking coup. All Smith's fault . . . all the mistakes. Incredible. Unbelievable . . ."

Rebecca remained silent, letting the diatribe burn itself out, beginning to interpret and still listening but giving over most of her concentration to review all that she'd personally done or put into practice since James Straughan's suicide. She'd left nothing undone or unchecked, nothing that Monsford could pick up and challenge: she was sure she hadn't. Apart, of course, from the involvement of Jane Ambersom, which was causing the unease to churn through her. She was convinced Straughan had kept his own copy of the incriminating material. There was still a chance, a lot of chances, of its being uncovered and it was to her that each and every discovery had to be handed, unopened, unheard, or unread. But she'd wanted to recover it by now: needed to know she had the protection of the only one in existence.

Rebecca's concentration refocused at Monsford's sighed collapse behind the expansive desk, ignoring the folder in readiness before him. Risking a renewed eruption, she said: "We need to redefine a few things. Are you going to handle Moscow or shall I do what needs to be done there?"

"Leave it!" snapped Monsford. "I'm handling Moscow personally. What the fuck's happened with Straughan? How did Smith know?"

She had to get it out of the way, Rebecca knew. "Jane Ambersom's name and number was on a call-in-emergency list at Straughan's house."

This time Monsford was rendered completely speechless, and there was a change when he did recover, quiet-voiced fear instead of irrational fury. "They were friends . . . sometimes ate together in the canteen. What's he left with her: told her!"

"Nothing," insisted Rebecca, hoping her precautions proved her right. "We were also on the list, obviously. According to the police, I was contacted within fifteen minutes of Ambersom. I called her, told her it was an overhang from her time here, and that I was taking over. Which I did. It's all contained, under our control."

"I don't like it: didn't like him."

"Trust me. It's all contained."

"Tell me how," demanded Monsford, his voice still hushed.

"There was no other family, apart from him and his mother," set out Rebecca. "The Home Office has confirmed to the local chief constable my instructions for no public inquest. I personally supervised the total clearance of the Berkhamsted house: everything movable has already been brought here, to be reexamined. There's a second, deep-search team taking the house apart: after they've done that they'll excavate the garden. We're separately going through all the local banks to locate what deposits he had." She gestured toward the studiously ignored folder. "That contains what's immediately relevant: his suicide note, all the medication he used to kill his mother and himself—samples have been taken of all of them to confirm our autopsy that's being conducted now that what killed him came from those sources and every piece of documentation of his and his mother's existence—"

"What's the suicide note say?" Monsford interrupted.

"It's there for you to read yourself," persisted the woman. "Nothing that's a problem. He considers his work has been undermined by the strain of constantly caring for his mother, he's made mistakes, none of which he lists."

"The bastard wanted to bring me down," insisted Monsford.

So do I, thought Rebecca.

31

IT USUALLY CAME AT THE LIVE-OR-DIE PART OF AN ASSIGNment, without warning and irrespective of place or time. Charlie Muffin didn't think of it as fear, although that's what it was: instead, as he always did, he considered it the essential senses-sharpening adrenaline boost to react faster and think quicker. And win. But this time the fear was different: more hair-triggered, the keep-ahead intensity stronger.

Charlie knew why. Winning, emerging the victor, had never been enough by itself. To win totally meant surviving, which he'd always done, disregarding the cost to friend or foe alike. But not this time. This time he had far more—everything—to win by getting Natalia and Sasha safely out of Russia but far more still—everything—to lose if he failed. Which made the predictable adrenaline-spurred fear the wrong sort, the dangerously overcompensating, overreactive sort of fear that risked skewing his subjectivity to cause the forbidden, inconceivable failure. The possibility of which, from the moment of his Amsterdam sidestep, had been compounded almost daily by inconsistencies and uncertainties. Which, subjectively again, was par for the course of professional espionage but from which he'd hoped to be spared in this particular instance.

It was twelve ten, later than he'd intended, when Charlie literally pushed his way into the tourist-packed Arbat, sure he was alone but after the Metro debacle of the day before with no confidence in Patrick Wilkinson's ability to detect surveillance. Charlie let himself be carried, unresisting, along the stall-cluttered thoroughfare, seeking the remembered centrally placed, brick-built emporium, disappointed from the outside at the limited escape options if Wilkinson once more guided MI6 pursuit to him. After two further top-to-bottom street reconnoiters Charlie failed to locate a better alternative.

Charlie correctly guessed Wilkinson would arrive at the Arbat Metro, despite the man's vow never again to use the underground system. Wilkinson emerged, manila package tightly clutched beneath his right arm, precisely ten minutes ahead of their appointed time. Charlie remained in the station-bordering café, his *Pravda* spread before him but concentrating upon recognizable faces, needing a second vodka to justify his staying where he was during the forty-five minutes it took Wilkinson to get through the tourist crush in both directions. He let Wilkinson get twenty meters ahead on the man's third promenade before following. He caught up at the emporium and said: "To your left, with the green-painted shutters," sure the man would visibly jump, which he did.

Wilkinson moved without turning. Charlie went with him, but didn't enter, lingering at the outside displays to satisfy himself the man was alone. Wilkinson was in the back of the incense-perfumed arcade, examining icon reproductions, when Charlie finally entered. It took a full meandering five minutes for Charlie to reach him.

Charlie reached out for Wilkinson's package, slipping it between the pages of his newspaper before turning to keep the main door in view. "What did London say?"

"You've got new backup," announced Wilkinson, copying Charlie's icon interest. "No connection to the embassy, no connection with us. Your contact is an Ian Flood. He's at your favorite hotel: you're supposed to understand that. We're to decoy the others."

"Try to get it right this time," said Charlie, unforgiving.

"I'm glad to be out of it," blurted Wilkinson. "All three of us are."

"So am I," said Charlie. "Did you also tell London MI6 did more than just *try* to get to me: that Briddle was with you and through you was with me right up to Dmitrouskaya? From where he obviously watched us in the park and afterwards rode the train with you: the train upon which he imagined I'd be, a sitting target."

"How do you know that?" said Wilkinson, disbelievingly.

"Because watching you leave I saw him in the carriage behind you."

"I . . . I mean I should . . ." stumbled the man.

"Don't bother," stopped Charlie. "Is there anything more to tell me?"

"MI6 have been officially taken off, their guys withdrawn."

"Have they gone?"

"We only got the cable this morning, just before all three of us left the embassy to give us—me—time to lose surveillance. But I told him last night I knew about London's order: that they were out of it."

"What did he say?"

"To go fuck myself: that he took his orders from London. That's why the three of us are staying as decoys."

Another uncertainty in the lucky dip tub, thought Charlie.

In an afterthought Gerald Monsford stopped to buy roses for Elana. The fumble-fingered florist took almost half an hour to gift wrap them, complete with red ribbon to match the flowers, and he was practically an hour late getting to the Hertfordshire safe house. Radtsic was alone in the conservatory.

"I'm late because I stopped to get these for Elana," said Monsford, offering the bouquet as if for approval. "Where is she?" He already knew from his arrival meeting with Harry Jacobson.

"Resting," said the Russian, ignoring the flowers. He was in the chair Elana had chosen the day before, preventing Monsford's sitting close to him.

"Perhaps she'll join us later for me to give them to her?"

"She doesn't want to see you: be part of anything."

"I'm sorry about that," said Monsford, putting the flowers on a side table.

"You already knew," accused Radtsic, looking up to the ceiling joist Elana had identified.

Monsford instinctively followed the look and wished he hadn't, uncomfortable that it would have been filmed. "It'll get better."

"Not without Andrei," refused the man.

"You've got to be realistic, Maxim Mikhailovitch," cautioned Monsford. "We're trying, you know we're trying, but it's going to take a lot of time."

"Then it'll have to take a lot of time," said Radtsic, flatly. "Our deal was that we'd all be together, a complete family. There's no deal if we're not a complete family."

Not anticipating its weight, Monsford had to struggle to get another chair opposite the Russian and knew the film would show his overweight awkwardness. "What happened in France wasn't our fault. We don't yet know how or why it happened. We'll find a way to get Andrei back. But our deal can't be put on hold indefinitely."

"I can't accept anything without Andrei being here. Neither can Elana."

"Andrei *will* be here! But during the time it'll take we've got to start work. There are people you're going to meet: people you'll regard as friends as you work together."

"I know what debriefing is," snapped Radtsic, in a small spark of his old arrogance. "Just as I know what you want and which you'll get. But that's got to be met with what I want. And that's not empty words and talk of indeterminate time. It's got to be a balanced exchange: what I have to tell you equated against getting Andrei back."

"That's not a balanced exchange," protested Monsford, tensed against his anger at the other man's belief that he had a bargaining position. "It's tilted entirely in your favor."

"Which creates the incentive to get Andrei here."

The bastard was playing with him, cat to mouse, realized Monsford, hating his own analogy and hating even more that others would witness Radtsic's derision. "I won't be coming down every day. Tomorrow I'll introduce you to the people you'll be dealing with all the time. And to a liaison officer, a woman, to ensure Elana's got all she wants."

"The only thing Elana wants is Andrei, like me," repeated Radtsic. "I hope that tomorrow you'll have something to tell us about that."

"The confounded man's refusing to cooperate," complained Bland.

"It's early days, as Monsford said," reminded Palmer. "It'll settle down when Radtsic realizes he hasn't any real option."

"Why did Monsford tell him we can get the boy back?" Bland demanded. "We don't stand a chance of doing that."

"It would have made Radtsic even more difficult if he hadn't," said Palmer.

"Every day I tell myself it can't get any worse and every day it does get worse," bemoaned the other man. "I'm fearing the time when we're no longer able to shift all the responsibility on these two bloody directors and start getting it apportioned onto us."

"I don't want that to happen," said Palmer, unsettled.

"I'm not going to *allow* it to happen," determined the cabinet secretary. "Mine isn't going to be the head that rolls."

"Nor mine," said Palmer, even more determinedly.

It took Charlie a long time to move between individual booking outlets to make, one from each, paid and confirmed reservations on separately available flights on his intended, hedge-hopping escape route the following day. And then to duplicate the entire process from different booking facilities to ensure there were two situation-dictated alternatives for himself, Natalia, and Sasha. In addition, improvising upon their changed roles as decoys against both his M16 pursuers and the FSB, who by now would have identified their presence from embassy surveillance, Charlie confirmed booking on LOT Polish Airlines to Warsaw, with a direct transfer connection to London from Moscow's Domodedovo Airport—from which none of his other escape flights was departing—for Patrick Wilkinson, Neil Preston, and Peter Warren. Throughout the second ticket buying Charlie also booked tickets for his new protection squad, for only one of whom he had a name. At the end he had only three thousand pounds left from the twenty-five thousand earlier provided by Wilkinson in the Arbat.

The delay made Charlie much later getting to Moscow's permanent state circus for his premeeting security check, restricted anyway by the Saturday-afternoon throng of arriving and departing audiences. Natalia responded at once to his precisely timed call, as she had to be told their rendezvous, and said she was twenty minutes away. Charlie bought admission tickets before becoming a crowd person among the outside refreshment and souvenir kiosks. The area was slightly higher than the main approach and from its elevation Charlie picked out Natalia when she was still some way away. She showed no recognition at seeing him, halting at a souvenir seller five booths away. As he reached her, she said: "It's definitely tomorrow?"

"We need to go through it," confirmed Charlie, disappointed at her nervousness. "I've got tickets for the circus. We'll be less obvious inside."

"No," she refused. "Let's walk: maybe find somewhere to sit."

Charlie took her firmly by the arm, leading her back against the incoming crowd. "You have to get what I'm going to tell you totally clear in your mind. Your actual extraction depends on your getting this right."

"I'm frightened I'll make a silly mistake and—"

"You won't make stupid mistakes," stopped Charlie, as they reached the main road. "If you do what I tell you, you *can't* make a mistake. All you've got to do is take Sasha to the airport, go through the normal formalities, make one change en route, and you'll be safely in England by this time tomorrow."

"You're saying me, me and Sasha. Where are you going to be?"

"With you, all the way. With others to protect you both."

"There's a bench." She pointed. "I want to sit, to concentrate."

Charlie was concerned at the indecision he'd never seen in Natalia when they'd lived together at greater risk of discovery. "These are new Russian passports. They've got all the necessary exit and entry visas and documentation. Everything is valid. You and Sasha are booked on Finnair flight 362, leaving at noon from Vnukovo Airport to Helsinki. There's a transfer connection within two hours on Finnair flight 028 to London. I won't acknowledge you: keep as far away as possible. Sasha won't remember me. There'll be three other people on the plane you won't know: I'll only know one. We'll be taken off before other passengers at Heathrow."

"Stop!" demanded Natalia, urgently. "You'll definitely be on the same plane? I want you to be with us. I don't want to be alone, not knowing what to do."

This was far more difficult than he'd anticipated: as close as he was to her, he could feel her nervousness vibrating along the bench. "I will always be with you but as far back as I can be: the last, probably, to board the plane. The others you don't know will be onboard, too. I have to tell London we're on our way. The moment you enter the embarkation lounge I'll trigger that alert. . . ." He had to stop her physical shaking, Charlie decided. "What's the first principle of entering an operational situation?"

Natalia frowned sideways. "Don't play tradecraft games, Charlie!"

"I'm not playing a tradecraft game!" he insisted. "Answer the question!"

The twitching spread to Natalia's face at Charlie's tone. "Guarantee an exit: why do you want me to acknowledge that?"

"There's a second complete set of tickets, doubly to guarantee our exit," said Charlie, tapping the bulky manila folder on his lap. "I've booked the three of us, as well as our escorts, on a direct MEA flight to Nicosia, also from Vnukovo. I'll only have minutes from my London call to catch the Helsinki flight. If I miss it you'll still have three other escorts and an assured, protected arrival in London. I'll simply call London again, tell them what's happened but that you're still on the Finnair flight. If, when we're all at Vnukovo, there's something I don't like, all of us will abandon the Finnair route, although staying booked on it, and switch to Cyprus. But Cyprus is only an exit insurance. But remember, once you've started to board, don't turn back. That's the unbreakable rule: don't turn back, keep going."

"Why can't one of the escorts alert London, use the Cyprus plane if it's necessary?" asked Natalia.

Her shaking had subsided and Charlie was reassured by the professional question. "I personally want to guarantee you're onboard, safe.

"I feel confident every moment I'm with you but so frightened, so incapable, the minute I'm not," Natalia said, feeling out for his hand.

"Twenty-four hours from now we'll be exaggerating our stories about it all, laughing."

"I don't think I will be."

"But you're going to go through with it," encouraged Charlie. "Not let Sasha down."

"I won't let you or Sasha down. You know that."

Finally handing her the package, Charlie said: "Everything you want is there. We'll talk a lot on the throwaway phone, on your way to Vnukovo airport."

"Yes," she said, looking down at the package before closing her handbag.

"What have you told Sasha?"

"Nothing. I didn't want her talking at school. I'll tell her tonight. She'll be excited."

"Are you?"

"I will be, this time tomorrow. Excited and happy for the rest of my life."

"You can't be serious!"

"I couldn't be more serious," said Jane Ambersom. She was glad she'd waited until after their lovemaking, anticipating his reaction to the story prepared between her and Aubrey Smith. Barry Elliott had pulled away and was now sitting directly opposite on their crumpled sheets, naked but with all intimacy gone.

"Why the hell haven't you told them!"

"You can't begin to understand Monsford's outright animosity."

"But they've got to be warned! It's . . . it's what you said, absurd: absurd not to."

"I'm telling you. They'd dismiss it as disinformation if it came from us."

"You think it's this guy Straughan: that it's why he killed himself?"

"He must have known something: suspected something. There's got to be a damn good reason for the operations director of M16 to kill his own mother and then himself."

"This new?" demanded Elliott, head suspiciously to one side. "Or is this something that Irena Novikov told Charlie about the Lvov penetration?"

They hadn't anticipated the question. Improvising, Jane said: "There could be indications."

"You going to give them to me: an actual printout of the debriefing?"

Shit, thought Jane. "There isn't a debriefing paper. It was conversation between them when they were still in Moscow: before Charlie had any reason to suspect her."

"He didn't file a proper, official report?" pressed Elliott, head still to one side.

"I wasn't at M15 during the Lvov affair," escaped Jane, "I'm picking up secondhand, telling you what I've been told. Certainly there's nothing officially logged."

"But you know both camps. What's the problem between you?"

"Monsford," said Jane shortly. "The bastard who framed me for his mistakes."

"You're surely not suggesting . . . ?" stumbled Elliott, incredulous.

"I'm telling you what we suspect from what I'm told of the Lvov investigation. I can't tell you anything more."

Elliott looked down, appearing surprised at his nakedness. "I'm cold and think I should get back under the covers."

"I think so too," invited Jane.

Within fifteen minutes of their being together Charlie was reassured, a feeling he'd rarely experienced since the very beginning of the attempt to get Natalia and Sasha out of Moscow. Ian Flood appeared a totally controlled, self-confident man who allowed himself to think before speaking, which wasn't slowness but sensible consideration, not interrupting as Charlie outlined in detail the following day's extraction. Charlie was enjoying, too, being back in his familiar corner stool at the Savoy bar, brief though the visit had to be. The FSB had discovered his preference for the hotel during the Lvov investigation: Mikhail Guzov, the involved FSB colonel, had personally confronted him as he'd sat on the same stool. At this time of the evening the bar was filling with the professional girls, two of whom Charlie recognized from before, but the bartender had changed.

"There are photographs of Natalia and Sasha with the tickets: you'll have to add the names I don't know to the two left open," concluded Charlie. He hadn't demanded the other names and Flood hadn't offered them.

"Aren't you following in tandem from Pecatnikov to ensure they get to the airport?" questioned Flood, polishing his spectacles for the second time since they'd made contact. It wasn't a mannerism, Charlie knew, but an added, head-lowered precaution against their conversation being overhead despite their carefully established separation from anyone close.

Charlie shook his head. "Natalia doesn't think she's under observation but I don't want to take the risk: the FSB know what I look like. I'll keep beyond airport CCTV until you enter and for Natalia to see me."

"I'll have one of the others in a separate car from Pecatnikov," decided Flood. "I'll put the other one inside the terminal. Is that how you want it?"

Charlie nodded. "Make sure everyone understands there's to be no interference if I'm challenged: the only essential is to get Natalia and Sasha out."

"What have you told Natalia about that?"

"Nothing. I've said I might miss the flight alerting London."

"You think there could be CCTV recognition?"

"It's no secret that I'm here," said Charlie. "I've got to ensure against the possibility. That's why I want you to keep me permanently in view inside the terminal, until the last minute. If I'm not satisfied I'm clear after checking in for Helsinki I'll switch to the Cyprus flight."

"Why bother?" questioned Flood. "You're the weak link. The essential is getting Natalia and the child out. Why can't I and my team extract them, leaving you to make your escape later?"

"She's as tight as a spring, about to snap," judged Charlie. "If she doesn't physically see me, she'll abandon. The major FSB and CCTV concentration will be at Sheremetyevo, not Vnukovo. And I've laid a false trail to Warsaw from another airport. I'm making myself visible to Natalia and you, no one else."

"It's your call," acknowledged Flood, doubtfully. "Okay, we don't intervene if you're challenged. What if she sees it? Do we try to make her get on the plane?"

"If you can, without turning it into a second incident," said Charlie. "If I am intercepted I'll try to concentrate the attention as a distraction for you."

"You must consider this a hell of an important extraction," said Flood, head bent for the third time, covering the preceding two by holding his spectacles up to the light as if there were a blemish he couldn't clean off.

The man wouldn't have been told of the personal relationship, Charlie realized. "If it weren't important, it wouldn't have been initiated. You come with any guidance from the Director-General?"

"There's an internal war between us and MI6," said Flood. "He knows we were used as dummies to get Radtsic out. But Smith's convinced, without knowing why, that there's also an order out for you to be eliminated."

"I've already been warned."

"Smith wants you warned again: wants you to believe it," said Flood. "And why I was also told getting you out was as essential as extracting Natalia and the girl. My orders are to follow your instructions, without question. But whatever those instructions are, that you've got to be brought out too."

"Which gives you a problem," said Charlie.

"Which gives us both a problem," agreed Flood. "You got a God you can trust that it'll all go to plan?"

"No," said Charlie.

"That's another problem," said Flood. "Neither have I."

It was inevitable that he should think about Charlie Muffin as he approached the Savoy Hotel, supposed David Halliday: it was where he and Charlie had spent a lot of time during Charlie's previous assignment and because of which it had become a favorite watering hole of his. It was, reflected Halliday, about the only benefit he'd gained from his association with the man. It had been a mistake not to have held back the day the FSB picked up the Rossiya tourist party. And made an even bigger mistake imagining an advantage in cooperating with Charlie instead of maintaining the monitor that others in the MI6 *rezidentura* had been ordered to keep to locate the man. But he'd got away with it, Halliday reassured himself: broken the contact until finally Charlie had stopped trying to reach him. He wasn't being ostracized as much after his inclusion in the last stage of the Radtsic extraction and wasn't being blamed for the French fiasco. Now he reverted to the trusted practice of avoiding each and every difficulty.

It was initially only a fleeting image, as Halliday pushed through the hotel entrance, looking instinctively to his left, into the bar, but he was sure it was Charlie getting off his accustomed bar stool, another man beside him. The door leading from the lobby to the baroque dining room was heavily engraved but there were sufficient gaps in the etching for Halliday, hurriedly concealed on its far side, to confirm the sighting and to see Charlie pass something to the other man before turning to leave.

Halliday left, too, after five minutes, crossing the square to the Metropole, relieved the shaking had gone when he lifted the brandy snifter for the first recovering sip. It was, he decided, his chance to be completely rehabilitated: of not being kept out any longer.

32

HE'D GOT EVERYTHING WRONG, ACKNOWLEDGED DAVID HALLIDAY: done it all by the book, except perhaps insisting he speak personally to the Director, but instead of getting the congratulations and gratitude he deserved for finding Charlie Muffin he'd been berated by Gerald Monsford for not following the man and relegated to being duty driver for Stephan Briddle and Robert Denning outside the Savoy Hotel at three o'clock in the fucking morning! Briddle was openly mocking him and Denning was an unapologetic farter who'd already stunk the car up.

"You know what they say about life?" reminded Briddle, to whom Halliday had complained of the Director's tirade. "It isn't ever fair."

"You come across Flood before? asked Denning, from the rear gas chamber.

"No," said Halliday, who'd gone with Briddle into the hotel because his Russian was better with a fifty-dollar bribe to the night porter to identity the replacement MI5 officer.

"You absolutely sure Flood's still in his room: didn't leave separately after Charlie?" pressed Denning.

"I already told you he ate dinner in the restaurant, has a wake-up call booked for five thirty, and a Hertz car's being delivered at seven," said Halliday, irritably.

"I really would like to know what's in that package you saw Charlie pass over," came in Briddle.

"It's passport-and-ticket size," snapped Halliday. "They're moving."

"And it's happening early," said Briddle, reflectively. "There's two direct London flights from Sheremetyetevo before eleven and three transfer connections by one P.M."

"It'll be direct," predicted Denning. "Transfers risk interception wherever they stop."

"*If* it's Sheremetyetevo," cautioned Briddle. "Charlie Muffin's a sneaky fucker."

Would it have been better if he'd stayed with Charlie? wondered Halliday. Hardly, except for being spared Monsford's wrath and this ignominy. Certainly not professionally. Was there any point in staying in the service, apart from the final pension entitlement? He didn't stand a chance of promotion. Even if Monsford was replaced, he was the sort of vindictive bastard who'd poison all the personnel files. And why should he be replaced, after the Radtsic coup? The man's directorship was set in stone.

"Here's Beckindale with breakfast!" announced Denning, as the second anonymous rental car came down the street. He farted as he spoke, and Halliday knew he wouldn't be able to eat anything Beckindale had bought.

Charlie finally abandoned the idea of sleep at five and was showered and dressed by five thirty. Charlie wished he could have started out with Natalia, be with them all the way from Pecatnikov, as unrealistic and unprofessional as that would have been. He was confident of Flood: didn't doubt the man's professionalism. Natalia had recognized the risk of Sasha's doing or saying something unexpected and would guard against it. Six fifteen, Charlie saw, checking his watch. Too early to call even though she'd already be awake: probably hadn't slept at all, as he hadn't. He'd give her a little longer.

Peter Warren was the last decoy to arrive in the embassy cafeteria, at six thirty. As he joined the other two, coffee spilling as he maneuvered his self-service tray onto the cluttered table. "You sure it's necessary for us to be up this early?"

"I wouldn't have set the time if I hadn't been sure," said Patrick Wilkinson, tetchily. "Or booked the six o'clock wake-up call for them to find on the internal personnel computer, which I discovered they were monitoring."

"You hear any movement?" Neil Preston asked Warren, whose compound apartment was on the same floor as Briddle's and Denning's.

Warren shook his head, heaping scrambled eggs and sausage onto his fork. "Quiet as a grave when I passed both doors. I stopped to listen outside both."

"Let's decide who's going to go where," demanded Wilkinson. "I'll ride the Metro: call Charlie's phone for the tracker to be picked up. They'll think that significant, after the last time."

"What about my doing a river cruise?" suggested Warren. "If I get one to follow me on a steamer he'll be out of action for two or three hours."

"I'll go to the Metropole and con my way onto a tourist coach: there's always spare seats and guides with their hands out for beer money. I'll pick out the following car after a few blocks."

"We'll all keep in touch on cell phones to add to the tracker confusion," declared Wilkinson. "It'll convince them something's happening."

"But where the fuck are they?" demanded Warren, looking toward the entrance.

"You've spilled egg down your tie," said Preston.

"Here's the rental car," identified Halliday. The coffee had been disgusting and he hadn't bothered to drink it. He felt physically sick.

"I guess the Hertz sticker gave you the clue," Briddle continued to mock.

"You think Jeremy will have realized it?" questioned Denning, jerking his head toward the side street in which Beckindale was parked.

"Stay where you are!" ordered Briddle, hurriedly. "Flood and the other MI5 replacements will have photographs of us all."

"I was going to phone." Denning sighed.

"Let me see the photographs of Natalia and the kid again," said Halliday and wished he hadn't when it was the odorous Denning who offered them.

"Hello!" exclaimed Briddle, bringing Halliday's concentration up from the prints at the arrival of another Hertz car.

"And that's Flood," identified Halliday, as the man emerged from the hotel with the delivery driver of the first vehicle and continued on toward the second car. Together the two MI5 men went back into the Savoy.

"Jeremy says he's already clocked both of them," reported Denning, the cell phone to his ear. "Any change from simply following them?"

"He's to stick to the second car, leaving Flood to us," ordered Briddle. "And to make sure he's not seen to be following."

"Jeremy says thanks for the lesson and to go fuck yourself," relayed Denning.

Gerald Monsford had slept overnight, and alone, in the studio-apartment extension to his office suite and in which he'd established Rebecca Street as his gratefully rewarding mistress a month after securing her as his deputy. He wished now that she had stayed that night, even though he didn't completely trust her any longer. Right not to have trusted Straughan, either: dangerous, deceptive motherfucker. Wished he didn't have to rely on Rebecca for the Straughan business. Didn't have to, Monsford decided. As soon as he sorted Radtsic out he'd take Straughan off her hands: important he personally ensured Straughan hadn't left anything dangerous behind. He had to concentrate on Moscow for the moment. Not that there was anything to do at this predawn moment. Except wait. His insistence upon total one-to-one control with Briddle to guard against a later, evidence-providing intermediary meant he couldn't risk Russian scanner interception of cell-phone communication with the man now outside the hotel at which new MI5 support had been discovered. Halliday's name threatened an outburst of pointless anger. Why the fuck hadn't the man followed Charlie Muffin to wherever he'd been hiding? Right now Briddle could have been there carrying out the disposal that so easily could have been accepted as an FSB assassination. The fallout from which, compounded by all the preceding publicity, would have brought about Aubrey Smith's dismissal not just as MI5 Director-General but as a threatening professional adversary. Now there was too much uncertainty, particularly involving the plausible denial of any personal involvement: what Shakespeare had so rightly described as right perfection wrongfully disgraced.

The summons on his personal line broke into Monsford's reflection, making him physically jump, despite his expectation of Briddle's call. "Director Monsford?"

It wasn't Briddle's voice: one he didn't recognize. "Who is this?"

"Matthew Timpson."

"Who?"

"Matthew Timpson, head of internal security. When I didn't find you at home I checked in-house registration and discovered you were already here, which is fortunate. I'm already in the building. I need to see you immediately, of course. It's a matter of urgency."

"What's a matter of urgency?"

"The reason I need to see you immediately."

"It's not convenient," refused Monsford. "Arrange a meeting through my appointments secretary in two or three days."

"I insist it's now, sir: immediately, as I've said."

"*You* must insist! I'm the Director!"

"Which is why it must be now. I shall be with you in five minutes, with my support staff."

"You will . . ." began Monsford, outraged, but the line was already dead.

It was, in fact, three minutes. With Timpson were a woman and two men. Timpson was a round-faced, rotund, balding man in a bank manager black, three-piece suit complete with chain-linked fob watch in the waistcoat pocket. The other two men were dressed identically, except for the pocket watch. The woman was in black, too.

"What the hell is this?" demanded Monsford.

"I'm confident of your complete cooperation." Timpson smiled. "We have information, the reliability and source of which is unquestionable, that there's been a hostile penetration. . . ." The man indicated those behind him. "This is my advanced group: team leaders. My full investigatory staff will be here by midmorning. The first essential will be to install independent listening and monitoring facilities upon all incoming and outgoing electronic lines. It's a comparatively simple procedure: I expect that to be largely established by midafternoon. We require complete and total access to all files, recordings—electronic, audio, written, or printed—initially for the preceding and current year. It may, of course, be necessary to extend that over a longer period. Our inquiries will, inevitably, go beyond the building to encompass the homes of officers and employees . . ." There was another quick smile, "including, of course, your own. . . ." The security head reached behind, for documents held in readiness by the woman. "Here's our necessary documented authority."

"No!" objected Monsford, loudly. His mind blanked, refusing orderly words, and all he could again manage was "No." It was a physical strain to recover, to pull himself up to confront them. "Why haven't I been told? Properly informed . . . I mean . . ."

"You are being informed now, sir."

"What's the reliable source?"

"I can't disclose that at this stage," refused Timpson. "Our investigation has to be total, from the very top to the absolute bottom, until proper safeguards are established."

"You can't suspect me!" insisted Monsford, new outrage hovering.

"You could be compromised," Timpson pointed out, calmly. He indicated those behind him. "Initially, until those safeguards are in place, you'll have one of my senior officers with you at all times, as will your deputy and division directors."

"This is absurd: ridiculous!" persisted Monsford. "I can't have . . . won't allow . . . people wandering about the building, looking wherever they choose. Have you forgotten where we are?"

"People will not wander unsupervised around the building, looking wherever they choose," corrected Timpson. "I and those with me have the same level of security clearance as yourself and your deputy."

"It's the Straughan business . . ." started Monsford but was stopped by the ringing of his personal phone. Briddle, from Moscow! he thought at once, staring down at the receiver, which blinked its red light as well as rang.

"Shouldn't you answer that?" suggested Timpson.

Monsford did so tentatively, said: "Yes?" and held the receiver tightly to his ear so that only he could hear.

"Glad I caught you before you left," said Harry Jacobson. "Radtsic doesn't want to see you or those you were bringing down until you've got something about Andrei."

"Here we go!" announced Briddle, as Flood and the other man emerged from the Savoy. To Halliday he said: "Your job is to make sure he doesn't see us behind him."

"Go fuck yourself," echoed Halliday. To Denning, who'd pulled forward to look through the windshield, he said: "Get back. You're in the way of my rearview mirror."

Halliday waited until the second Hertz car turned in line behind Flood and allowed two vehicles to intervene before following. Beckindale came directly behind.

As Flood took a left turn Briddle twisted to the rear of their vehicle and said to Denning: "You following the route on the map?"

Denning broke wind but didn't reply. Halliday said: "East, maybe. The beltway would be better for Sheremetyevo."

"They've got pickups to make, haven't they?" said Briddle.

"You all right?" asked Charlie.

"Yes," said Natalia, tightly.

"Sasha?"

"She's excited. She was awake early."

"What have you told her?"

"That it's a surprise holiday."

"You didn't tell her I'd be with you, did you?" questioned Charlie, the possibility of Sasha's recognizing him in his mind.

"Of course not. Where are you? I can hear traffic."

"On the street," said Charlie, "looking for a taxi." There was a grunt. "I've just flagged one down. I'll be outside the terminal but not obvious."

"I'm leaving in fifteen minutes."

"I love you. It's all going to go as I told you it would."

"I'll look for you."

Beckindale overtook the others but pulled directly in front, leaving the barrier of the four other vehicles that had built up between them and the MI5 men.

From the rear, Denning said: "Pecatnikov is three streets away."

"They're picking up Natalia and the child," decided Briddle, his voice catching. He coughed, to clear the nervousness, one hand over the other, glad there was no tremor. The Makarov suddenly felt heavy in its holster, hard against his ribs.

"Charlie could be with them," suggested Denning.

"Call Beckindale: warn him to be careful," ordered Briddle. "Charlie won't take the slightest chance." Would it be possible here, outside Natalia's apartment? If Charlie tried to resist it would provide the excuse but he'd planned to do it close, the Makarov hidden as much as possible and not with the others as witnesses. Nor in front of Natalia and certainly not Sasha. There'd be panic, hysteria: the child could get in the way, get hurt. Killed even. He didn't want to shoot a child: wouldn't shoot a child.

The log had switched from night to day registration by the time they got to the gate house and there was further delay going back to the security office inside the embassy to retrieve it to discover all three MI6 officers were recorded leaving the legation at 2:00 A.M., with the MI6 resident, David Halliday. All three were in Halliday's embassy car. None of the names was listed on any of that morning's flights, direct or transfer connections, from Sheremetyevo to London.

"And they wouldn't have needed to leave at two A.M. to catch a plane," said Warren.

"So where have they gone?" demanded Preston, rhetorically.

"I think I should tell London," said Wilkinson.

"What's there to tell them?" said Warren.

"We're in enough shit already, according to what you've told us," agreed Preston. "You really think it's a good idea for London to know we've lost everyone we're supposed to be leading all over Moscow?"

"I think it's better than waiting until London hear it some other way," said Wilkinson. "We were supposed to mislead them: we couldn't physically stop them, could we?"

"You've got a point," conceded Preston.

"I think we should tell London," capitulated Warren.

"It's definitely Pecatnikov," declared Halliday. "It's the next turning and Flood's indicating."

"I agree," said Denning.

Briddle could feel the tremor now, not just in his hand but trembling through his arms, and he had to press his left leg hard against the floor to stop it pumping.

"Beckindale's signaling," said Halliday, unnecessarily.

"Stay back," ordered Briddle. "Let's not screw everything getting too close."

"What are we supposed to do, if they're all together?" complained Halliday.

"Leave it all to me," said Briddle. "That goes for you, too, Jeremy. I make the approach alone. You stay back, guard against my being intercepted."

"We should have gone through all this earlier," said Denning.

"I'll approach alone," insisted Briddle. "But not here." Even if Charlie was with them, he couldn't shoot here. They'd have to halt way back from Natalia's apartment to avoid being seen. Charlie would be warned by their driving up fast.

Beckindale had stopped just after the turn into the road, at least one hundred meters from Natalia's known address.

"Stop here," ordered Briddle, waving Halliday in about ten meters farther on. To Denning he said: "Tell Jeremy to keep out of the way: to leave me alone."

"There's a taxi pulling up outside," said Halliday, straining through binoculars. "And there's Natalia: must have been waiting just inside. Just Natalia and the girl. No sign of Charlie."

"You all right?" Denning asked Briddle, from behind. "You're shaking."

"They haven't any idea!" exclaimed Aubrey Smith, passing the printed message slip to Jane Ambersom, whom he'd summoned after Passmore's alert.

"None. Nor any chance of finding out," said Passmore, to whom Wilkinson had confessed.

"And we haven't heard from Flood?"

"It's all being done away from the embassy, away from secure lines," reminded the operations director. "It's all at Charlie's lead. That's the arrangement."

"There's no way Monsford's people could have found out," said Jane.

"It's got to be some kind of MI6 move," said Passmore.

"Our only link to Charlie is through Flood," said Smith.

"We don't have secure communication," insisted Passmore.

"Route it through one of our European relays," decided Smith. "We've got to warn Charlie."

"Tell me where." Sasha giggled.

"It's a surprise," insisted Natalia.

"Hot or cold?"

"Sometimes hot, sometimes cold."

"You're holding my hand too tightly," protested the girl. "Mountains or flat?"

"Small mountains."

"But we can swim: you packed my costume."

"I hope we can swim. Do lots of things."

"I wish you'd tell me where we're going," Sasha complained.

Natalia started forward at the sound of the mobile telephone. "We're on our way."

"I'm already at the terminal, waiting," said Charlie.

"About thirty minutes."

"No problems?"

"No."

"I told you there wouldn't be."

"Who was that?" demanded the child.

"Someone from the airline, wanting to know we were on our way."

"Vnukovo," declared Halliday. "This is the road to Vnukovo."

"Can they get to London from Vnukovo?"

"Direct and via a lot of other links," confirmed Halliday.

"How far is the airport?"

"Maybe two miles."

"We've got to be careful," said Briddle. "Charlie might already be there, waiting. Drop us off at the approach to the terminal, before you park the car."

Behind them, Denning broke wind.

Halliday said: "I won't drive back with you. I'll catch an airport bus."

Charlie saw them before their taxi stopped, sure Natalia wouldn't be able to locate him on the farthest side of the booth from which the baggage handlers and traffic supervisors operated. Natalia got out first, at once searching, and Charlie stepped out, saw from her facial reaction that she'd seen him, and withdrew. He had the briefest sight of Sasha before the booth blocked his view of their entering the building. Charlie hoped the unknown escort had picked them up inside. He'd failed to isolate any professional indicators earlier, getting his boarding pass from the prebooked electronic dispenser, and been reassured because it proved the expertise of whoever Flood had put there ahead of their arrival.

Charlie's replaced contact emerged from the passage connecting to the parking and rental-car return, moving surely but unhurriedly, and slowed at the main entrance when Charlie stepped out for the second identification, pushing a previously withdrawn luggage trolley back into its line. Flood understood at once, offering Charlie the release coin to avoid the procedure with those already locked and said: "Briddle and the others can't be found."

"You think they've picked you up?"

"Possibly. At least one car stayed all the way from Pecatnikov."

"You take over," Charlie ordered, taking the man with him as they entered the terminal. "You give London the arrival details, make sure Natalia and Sasha get there. If there's a challenge, I'll distract."

"London's orders—"

"Get Natalia and Sasha out!" stopped Charlie, splitting away from the other man. How could it be blown! There'd been no link to the embassy: no way the extraction could be compromised. Natalia had physically to see him to know nothing was wrong. The terminal was far more crowded than it had been earlier, making it difficult to isolate anyone. Earlier! echoed in his mind, like a warning bell. He had a boarding pass, a ticket record, in his pocket identifying the flight they'd be on. Charlie transferred the boarding pass from his jacket to his trouser pocket, keeping his hand on it. He had to get rid of it at the first hint of trouble.

Charlie saw her. Natalia was at the edge although not positively part of the line of people straggled into the departure area. Imperceptibly her face relaxed as she saw Charlie. She turned at once, properly joining the line to move forward. Charlie couldn't see Flood. The red boarding message was flashing on the departures board.

He'd fall back to the Cyprus flight, Charlie decided, discarding the Finnair boarding pass in a rubbish bin on his way to the MEA desk, this time ignoring the automatic boarding machine, knowing Flood and the other escorts would realize what he was doing as he got into the MEA check-in line, his back to the main hall.

David Halliday saw Charlie as he entered after parking the rental car. He saw Briddle, too, and then Denning and Beckindale by a wall. Briddle was walking strangely, both arms across himself as if he was in pain. Halliday continued on, his concentration upon the oddly hunched Stephan Briddle. And because of that concentration glimpsed the gun. It was the briefest sight, an open-and-closed gap in Briddle's jacket from the contorted way the man was holding himself, but Halliday knew it was a gun, a Makarov, and then he saw it more properly as Briddle took it from beneath his jacket and without any conscious thought Halliday yelled: "Charlie!"

Who didn't hear. Briddle did, though, jerking toward the sound, still bringing the gun out, and Halliday shouted again and this time

Charlie did hear, turning back into the hall to see Briddle and Halliday, one in front of the other.

The shot sounded very loud, a reverberating echo, and very quickly there was another and the screaming began and people ran and Charlie ran, too, blindly, pushing against other running people crashing into him. There seemed a lot of shooting now, echo after echo, and in the first seconds Charlie thought the numbness was somebody running into him harder than before but then there was more numbness and he knew he was falling although he didn't want to fall, he wanted to keep running. It didn't hurt when he hit the ground, but he knew it should have done. Charlie's last, conscious thought was that the lights had been turned off, which he couldn't understand.

33

CHARLIE'S FIRST AWARENESS WAS OF SOUND, NOT VOICES, and he hoped his eyes hadn't flickered: weren't flickering, now he was consciously keeping them closed. There was some pain, probably where he'd fallen, but not a lot: mostly he still felt numbed and didn't know why. Didn't understand much at all, although he could remember what had happened: Briddle with a gun in his hand, Halliday behind, arms outstretched as he ran forward, the shots—a lot of shots, impossible to count because of the echoing reverberations, falling—falling, although he hadn't wanted to fall, not able to save himself because he was so numb. He could distinguish voices now; Russian, but he couldn't properly determine the words. It was as if they were talking softly, whispering even: couldn't understand why they were doing that, either. He tried to tense his body but not visibly move, to discover if he was restrained, but the numbness wouldn't let him. Please don't let me be paralyzed. Why should he be paralyzed?

"Why don't you open your eyes?" came a voice, loud now, which strangely Charlie believed he recognized.

Charlie did but couldn't focus: several people, some in uniforms, a small room, a bed. He was in a hospital. His vision cleared, intermittently. Mikhail Guzov, the FSB colonel he'd outwitted and beaten to expose the Lvov plot, was at the end of the bed, smiling down at him.

"We're going to be together for a long time, you and I," said Guzov. "Let's start properly, shall we? How shall I call you? Malcolm Stoat, as you were listed on the Amsterdam plane? David Merryweather, as you were booked on the Finnair and MEA flights? Or Charlie Muffin?"

"Why don't . . ." started Charlie but stopped, his voice cracking. He cleared it. "Why don't you take your pick?"

"Charlie, I think. That's what the two we've got in custody call you."

Sasha didn't know his name, snatched Charlie. Natalia and Sasha had got away! It had to be Briddle and Halliday. "Charlie's fine."

"You're right, you are fine," agreed the Russian. "The bullet, a bullet from your own side we think, went straight through your lower shoulder, didn't even hit a bone. You were knocked unconscious from the impact shock: that's still affecting you now, according to the doctors. But they say you'll be up and about in a week, able to tell me all I want to know."

Now wasn't the moment to argue: finding out about Natalia and Sasha was the only thing that mattered. "What about the others?"

"Not so fine. The two colleagues coming for you, Briddle and Halliday according to the identification they were carrying, are both dead. So's a Russian militia officer: another one's badly wounded. So is an Arab who was in the line behind you."

Who were the two colleagues who'd been arrested? "I'm surprised those you've got are talking so readily. What did you do to them?"

"Nothing." Guzov smiled. "It's amazing how fear affects some people. What about you, Charlie. Are you going to tell me so readily all I want to know?"

"I don't know anything there is to tell you."

"I do, Charlie. I've got a very long list."

"What happened? The truth: you must tell me the truth, not lie."

"There was an incident, a mistake. Caused by our own people," said Aubrey Smith.

"What sort of incident?" persisted Natalia.

The Director-General hesitated.

"The truth," she demanded.

"Some shooting."

"Was Charlie shot?"

"Yes."

Now it was Natalia who hesitated, lips tightly together. "Is he dead?"

"We don't think so."

"I know a lot about Stepan Lvov. It's not right, what you think you know. You'll make mistakes; are already making mistakes."

"We want you to tell us about that, Natalia: to tell us all you know."

Natalia shook her head. "Get Charlie out. I'll tell you nothing until you get Charlie out. Then you'll get everything. Save everything. But Charlie's got to be saved first."